# FILM ADAPTATION AND THE REAL

## PSYCHOANALYTIC HORIZONS

Psychoanalysis is unique in being at once a theory and a therapy, a method of critical thinking and a form of clinical practice. Now in its second century, this fusion of science and humanism derived from Freud has outlived all predictions of its demise. **Psychoanalytic Horizons** evokes the idea of a convergence between realms as well as the outer limits of a vision. Books in the series test disciplinary boundaries and will appeal to scholars and therapists who are passionate not only about the theory of literature, culture, media, and philosophy but also, above all, about the real life of ideas in the world.

**Series Editors**
Hilary Neroni, Esther Rashkin, and Peter L. Rudnytsky

**Former Series Editor:**
Mari Ruti (2018–2023)

**Advisory Board**
Salman Akhtar, Doris Brothers, Aleksandar Dimitrijevic, Lewis Kirshner, Humphrey Morris, Dany Nobus, Lois Oppenheim, Peter Redman, Laura Salisbury, Alenka Zupančič

A list of volumes in the series appears at the end of this book.

# FILM ADAPTATION AND THE REAL

*Subjectivity and Cinematic Mediation*

**Hee-seung Irene Lee**

BLOOMSBURY ACADEMIC
NEW YORK • LONDON • OXFORD • NEW DELHI • SYDNEY

BLOOMSBURY ACADEMIC
Bloomsbury Publishing Inc, 1359 Broadway, New York, NY 10018, USA
Bloomsbury Publishing Plc, 50 Bedford Square, London, WC1B 3DP, UK
Bloomsbury Publishing Ireland, 29 Earlsfort Terrace, Dublin 2, D02 AY28, Ireland

BLOOMSBURY, BLOOMSBURY ACADEMIC and the Diana logo are trademarks of
Bloomsbury Publishing Plc

First published in the United States of America 2025

Copyright © Hee-seung Irene Lee, 2026

For legal purposes the Acknowledgments on pp. ix–xi constitute an extension of this copyright page.

Cover design by Daniel Benneworth-GrayCover Gray
Cover image: UnsplashCover Unsplash

This work is published open access subject to a Creative Commons Attribution-NonCommercial-NoDerivatives 4.0 International licence (CC BY-NC-ND 4.0, https://creativecommons.org/licenses/by-nc-nd/4.0/). You may re-use, distribute, and reproduce this work in any medium for non-commercial purposes, provided you give attribution to the copyright holder and the publisher and provide a link to the Creative Commons licence.

Bloomsbury Publishing Inc does not have any control over, or responsibility for, any third-party websites referred to or in this book. All internet addresses given in this book were correct at the time of going to press. The author and publisher regret any inconvenience caused if addresses have changed or sites have ceased to exist, but can accept no responsibility for any such changes.

Library of Congress Cataloging-in-Publication Data
Names: Lee, Hee-seung Irene author
Title: Film adaptation and the real : subjectivity and cinematic mediation / Hee-seung Irene Lee.
Description: New York : Bloomsbury Academic, 2026. |
Series: Psychoanalytic horizons | Includes bibliographical references and index.
Identifiers: LCCN 2025005937 | ISBN 9798765138380 hardback | ISBN 9798765138373 paperback | ISBN 9798765138397 epub | ISBN 9798765138403 pdf
Subjects: LCSH: Film adaptations–History and criticism | Motion pictures–Psychological aspects | Reality in motion pictures | LCGFT: Film criticism
Classification: LCC PN1997.85 .L33 2026 | DDC 791.43/6–dc23/eng/20250502
LC record available at https://lccn.loc.gov/2025005937

| ISBN: | HB: | 979-8-7651-3838-0 |
|---|---|---|
| | PB: | 979-8-7651-3837-3 |
| | ePDF: | 979-8-7651-3840-3 |
| | eBook: | 979-8-7651-3839-7 |

Series: Psychoanalytic Horizons

Typeset by Integra Software Services Pvt. Ltd.
Printed and bound in the United States of America

For product safety related questions contact productsafety@bloomsbury.com.

To find out more about our authors and books visit www.bloomsbury.com and sign up for our newsletters.

*For John and Alexandra*

# CONTENTS

| | |
|---|---|
| Acknowledgments | ix |
| | |
| INTRODUCTION: SCREEN ADAPTATION, A SYMPTOM OF CULTURE | 1 |
| | |
| Chapter 1 | |
| THE REAL OF A TEXT AND THE TASK OF THE ADAPTER | 17 |
| Lost in Adaptation | 17 |
| The Task of the Adapter | 20 |
| From the Debris of the Tower of Babel | 23 |
| The Real of a Text | 29 |
| | |
| Chapter 2 | |
| THE OEDIPUS COMPLEX IN FILM ADAPTATIONS OF SHAKESPEARE'S *HAMLET* | 37 |
| The Ghost of the Dead Author | 37 |
| Super-ego versus Super Ego | 40 |
| Reading *Hamlet* through the Oedipus Complex | 49 |
| The Man Who Has Lost the Way of His Desire | 55 |
| Desire in Film Adaptations of *Hamlet* | 61 |
| Laurence Olivier's *Hamlet*: The Oedipal Drama of Shadows | 64 |
| Franco Zeffirelli's *Hamlet*: A Close-Up on the Oedipus Complex | 74 |
| Kenneth Branagh's *Hamlet*: The Dream of a Complete *Hamlet* | 82 |
| The Play's the Thing | 90 |
| | |
| Chapter 3 | |
| THE RESISTANCE TO THE ORIGINALS IN HITCHCOCK'S ADAPTATIONS | 93 |
| Texts of Doubt: Uncanny, Unpleasure, Anxiety, and the Mother | 93 |
| The Uncanny at Home | 97 |
| Unpleasure and Anxiety | 105 |
| The Mother and the Gaze | 113 |
| The Function of the Negative | 117 |
| Hitchcock's *Rebecca* without Rebecca | 121 |
| Adaptation in Reverse: *The Birds* | 135 |

Chapter 4
THE THING (*DAS DING*) THAT SPEAKS OF ITSELF IN STANLEY
KUBRICK'S *THE SHINING*   145
Re-presentation of *das Ding*   145
The Play of *the Thing*   148
The *objet petit a* in the Shadow of *das Ding*   154
The Maze That Is a Monster   166

Chapter 5
TRAVERSING THE PHANTASY IN SPIKE JONZE'S *ADAPTATION*   179
An Allegory of *Adaptation*   179
The Original Phantasy and Its Adaptations   181
Adaptation *in vitro*   195
The Traversal of the Phantasy   212

CONCLUSION: ADAPTATION, THE METAPHOR FOR
SUBJECTIVITY   217

Bibliography   224
Index   233

# ACKNOWLEDGMENTS

As I complete this book, I find myself surrounded by a proliferation of artificial intelligence tools, such as ChatGPT, DeepL, Speechify, Soundful, and DeepBrain. These technologies have revolutionized how texts are adapted, translated, and reimagined, facilitating processes that once demanded painstaking effort. This new environment invites us to reconsider the dynamics of creative labor, adaptation, and authorship, particularly in contexts where texts cross cultural, linguistic, and media boundaries with unprecedented ease. Had such tools been available earlier, I wonder how they might have reshaped my approach to adaptation—a process rooted as much in negotiating with others and transforming the self as in translating originals.

For me, the task of adaptation has been deeply tied to linguistic and cultural displacement. As an immigrant from the East working within the linguistic domain of the West, adaptation is not merely a thematic concern but a lived reality. Every text, voice, or thought I encounter must pass through the mediating filter of English, a language that is both a tool and a challenge. Drawing on Lacan's dictum that the unconscious is structured like a language, my unconscious remains shaped by Korean, even as the theoretical frameworks and texts I engage with are articulated in other linguistic systems—Freud in German, Lacan in French, and their translations into English. Access to meaning is always mediated, making adaptation not only a continuous endeavor but also an inherently unfinished one.

This dynamic has been central to shaping the analyses in this book. The study of screen adaptation through the lens of psychoanalysis has required navigating multiple webs of language, including the interplay of English literary texts, French psychoanalytic theories, German philosophical concepts, and the visual language of cinema. These intersections reveal that adaptation is far more than the transfer of content from one medium or language to another; it is a reconfiguration of meaning within a new system, a process that produces a new subject. This transformative power of adaptation lies not only in its ability to bridge differences but also in its capacity to generate something entirely new and distinct from what exists.

Writing a book on adaptation while adjusting to a new environment presents unique challenges. Like the adapter described throughout this book, I often found myself caught between countless texts and disciplines, with no singular "original" to return to and no definitive "adaptation" to achieve. Adaptation, then, became a series of deliberate detours, encounters with impasses, and creative negotiations. Without the collaboration and support of various individuals acknowledged here, this project would have remained far more fragmented than it is now, and the "I"—as the speaking voice of this book, intrinsically a palimpsest overwritten by the misunderstood discourses of the masters and the maladapted speech of an émigré or exile—could not have emerged. Not as an author but as a failed adapter, I find myself able to confront failures and incompletions in the following pages, where inadequacies, I sincerely hope, are reimagined as generative moments.

I owe the book's completion to many people whose guidance, encouragement, and support have been indispensable throughout this personal and transformative process. What began as a doctoral thesis has grown into this book thanks to their invaluable contributions. The following acknowledgments can only begin to express my deep gratitude for the time, insight, and energy so generously given by so many.

At the heart of this journey, Professor Misha Kavka offered nurturing supervision—the kind that every doctoral candidate hopes to experience. Her timely questions, thought-provoking suggestions, and unwavering encouragement provided the ideal conditions for this project to flourish. Her belief in my potential, despite the challenges of writing in a second language, both during and beyond my PhD, has left an indelible mark on this book. I am equally grateful to Professor Laurence Simmons, whose introduction to the intricate world of Lacanian theory and inspiring guidance laid the groundwork for my research and shaped its passion.

The Film, Television, and Media Studies Department (now Media and Screen Studies) at the University of Auckland offered a welcoming home, allowing me—a mature immigrant student—the opportunity to pursue studies through to a PhD. The department's warmth and inclusiveness were instrumental to my academic development. The University of Auckland's generous Doctoral Scholarship supported the early stage of this work as a thesis. During this time, I formed a cherished friendship with Dr. Cherie Lacey, who has been traveling together for many years to grow my thinking and passion. Professor Allan Cameron and Dr. Jenny Stümer contributed moments of both inspiration and joy through our conversations over coffee, lunch, and drinks. My colleagues in the New Zealand Forum of the International of the Forums of the Lacanian Field, especially Dr. Chantal Degril, deepened my engagement with psychoanalysis and its theoretical richness. Similarly, the mentors and teachers at the Australian Centre for Psychoanalysis offered invaluable guidance through their academic and clinical seminars, while Dr. Leonardo S. Rodriguez stood out as an inspiring role model, exemplifying extraordinary commitment and scholarly rigor.

Since 2015, I have been privileged to be part of the School of Cultures, Languages, and Linguistics at the University of Auckland. Its vibrant intellectual and collegial community has been instrumental in bringing this book to fruition. I am particularly grateful to the School for the research development fund, which supported the final stages of editing, and to the Faculty of Arts for their generous grant that made the book's open access possible. I am incredibly fortunate to be surrounded by many invaluable colleagues in the faculty, including Sunhee Koo, Rina Kim, Ellen Nakamura, Rumi Sakamoto, Nicole Perry, and Bernadette Luciano, to name just a few. I owe a deep debt to the late Professor Mari Ruti, who selected my thesis for the Psychoanalytic Horizons series at Bloomsbury and patiently guided its transformation into this book. Following Mari's passing, Professor Hilary Neroni and Editor Amy Martin provided thoughtful guidance and editorial care, ensuring the book's completion. I am also thankful to the anonymous reviewers and Professor Justin Clemens, whose invaluable feedback strengthened this work and inspired me to see it through to publication.

To my family and friends in both Korea and New Zealand, words cannot fully convey my gratitude for their love, patience, and support throughout this task of adaptation between two worlds, two languages, and two homes across the ocean. My late father shaped my destiny by choosing a name most fitting for the title of doctor, and my mother's selfless care and continued belief in me have been a continual source of strength. My brother's quiet yet steadfast encouragement and humor have been deeply comforting. Above all, my husband, John, has accompanied me through this process with his enduring love. When we embarked on a new life in New Zealand with little preparation, our journey was often challenging but ultimately rewarding, thanks to his devoted support of my curiosity and desire to learn. To my daughter, Alexandra, I offer endless thanks for her patience and generosity in sharing her mum with this project since its inception. Watching her grow from a baby with a heart-melting smile into a beautiful and kind young lady has been the greatest joy of my sleepless, caffeine-fueled years spent developing and writing this book.

Finally, while this book has benefited greatly from the insights and help of many, all errors and shortcomings remain entirely my own.

# INTRODUCTION: SCREEN ADAPTATION, A SYMPTOM OF CULTURE

Adaptation is omnipresent in the modern media landscape. Moreover, as numerous adaptation studies scholars have observed, it continually extends its reach into every branch of mass media as soon as a new trend or technology emerges. Linda Hutcheon captures the prevalence of adaptation in her assertion that "Adaptations are everywhere today: on the television and movie screen, on the musical and dramatic stage, on the Internet, in novels and comic books, in your nearest theme park and video arcade."[1] Her account acknowledges not only the pervasiveness of adaptation but also its organic flexibility, which threatens to annihilate the presumed boundaries between different texts, genres, and media. Existing texts evolve into new texts through either self-conscious or unwitting practices of pastiche, appropriation, reference, transference, transformation, and transmediation. Furthermore, the rapid development of digital technologies and the emergence of new cross-media formations render adaptation a trans-territorial phenomenon, through which production processes and outputs are distributed globally. Indeed, the incessant and unbounded mobility of stories across media, texts, and contexts has emerged as a defining characteristic of contemporary culture. This characteristic warrants an interpretation and, hence, a theory of adaptation from a psychoanalytic perspective.

Structuralist and narratological studies of adaptation initially investigated the transposition of stories from page to screen; since the 1950s, however, the field has now expanded to encompass a wider range of dialogical and intertextual transactions. The continuing popularity and ubiquity of adaptation have prompted the field of adaptation studies to extend its formal parameters and redefine adaptation within the contexts of media culture, the burgeoning volume and variety of adaptations, and the theoretical scaffolding of other disciplines. However, two key facts that underpinned adaptation studies during

---

1. Linda Hutcheon, *A Theory of Adaptation* (New York: Routledge, 2006), 2.

its formative period should be acknowledged: first, many pioneering studies of adaptation focused on cinematic adaptations of literary works, and second, they uniformly condemned criticism that framed film adaptations as subsidiary and forever inferior to their literary *predecessors*.

Pioneers of adaptation studies, to varying degrees, had to deal with the notion of fidelity, which is a contentious notion that regards faithfulness to a source text as the yardstick by which the aesthetic value of a given adaptation should be judged. At odds with the evolutionary nuance of the term "adaptation," the deeply ingrained negative stance of fidelity discourse discouragingly frames screen adaptation as the unsatisfactory *copying* of literary originals. Against fidelity as a dominant critical measure in evaluating films based on canonical literary works, seminal research on the topic of screen adaptation strove to create a new, unbiased forum for discussion, following the example of George Bluestone's 1957 *Novels into Film*. Adaptation studies now accommodates diverse interests in response to the growing variety of adaptations as media practice, but it has also advocated the need to establish "a discipline of its own right"[2] and has built up a lively locus of multidirectional discussions on adaptation, thanks to both individual and collective efforts on the part of a range of scholars, including Deborah Cartmell, Timothy Corrigan, Kamilla Elliott, Linda Hutcheon, Brian McFarlane, Thomas Leitch, James Naremore, Alessandra Raengo, Robert Stam, and Imelda Whelehan.[3]

In my opinion, the maturation of adaptation studies alongside the field's strong orientation toward disciplinary pluralism has opened up more room for a farther-reaching interdisciplinary project. This book hereby adopts a psychoanalytical perspective on human subjectivity to elucidate the figure of the adapter, who is trapped at the juncture between the original story and a new story that is to come or between the past and a future that has yet to unfold. The chapters that follow examine the subjective position of the adapter, a position that might

---

2. Deborah Cartmell, Timothy Corrigan and Imelda Whelehan, "Introduction to Adaptation," *Adaptation* 1, no. 1 (2008): 4.

3. Kamilla Elliott's contribution to *The Oxford Handbook of Adaptation Studies* offers a critical overview of adaptation scholarship and its taxing process of theorization: see Kamilla Elliott, "Adaptation Theory and Adaptation Scholarship," in *The Oxford Handbook of Adaptation Studies*, ed. Thomas Leitch (Oxford: Oxford University Press, 2017), 680–98.

arguably epitomize the ontological condition of modern subjects who are born into the rich, ever-evolving fabric of cultural legacies and who attempt to carve out their places and identities by adapting themselves to the world while simultaneously creatively adapting the given environments to their wishes.

Who is the adapter, and what stakes are involved in understanding the nature and functions of this particular subject-position? Although studies of adaptation rarely engage with such conceptual (rather than biographical) questions, major scholarly research on screen adaptation has already raised the issue. Indeed, the very tenor of the debates surrounding fidelity proves my point: adaptation studies approaches fidelity as the haunting essence of precursor literary texts that are transmediated to the visual medium. From this perspective, fidelity not only predetermines critics' and audiences' perceptions and evaluations of film adaptations but also overpowers the imaginations of screenwriters and directors. For this reason, it is difficult to wholly banish the enduring concern that stories may become "lost in translation" or the commensurate urge to faithfully re-present the "truth or spirit" of a given source text. In Cartmell and Whelehan's *Screen Adaptation: Impure Cinema*, for example, fidelity is described as an exasperating phantom that defies exorcism. As the authors remonstrate:

> Fidelity is tiresome as a critical strategy not least because it is an inexact science deployed to compare often something as inchoate as the 'spirit' of the thing; but *the desire for it or the dread of it* haunts many a film spectator's imagination and the intent lurks behind many a screenwriter's claim to get to the heart of the source text.[4]

The above account implies that the persistent presence of fidelity has something to do with the subjective and psychological rather than the objective and textual: fidelity *haunts* adapters, critics, and audiences alike.

Among those scholars who have examined adaptation as a significant cultural practice, Robert Stam greatly contributed to publish a three-volume series devoted to film adaptation of literature. This ambitious and influential series, led by Stam as the editor of two anthologies and a single author of a monograph, develops and extensively broadens the

---

4. Deborah Cartmell and Imelda Whelehan, *Screen Adaptation: Impure Cinema* (New York: Palgrave Macmillan, 2010), 20. (My italics.)

conceptual frame of screen adaptation, examining the multifarious theories, histories, practices, and methodologies of adaptation. In his introduction to the series' first anthology *Literature and Film: A Guide to the Theory and Practice of Film Adaptation*, Stam proposes a new expansion of the notion of fidelity by elaborating on the experience of *loss*, something that all readers inevitably encounter when transcoding a text into one's own imagination. The proposal thus implies that such loss is more psychic than textual in nature. His evanescent yet revitalizing interest in this psychic loss appears to presage a more direct engagement with psychoanalytic theory.[5] The sense of loss is inevitable, given that the adaptation process materializes and reinstates a subject's encounter with "someone else's phantasy."[6] In other words, a text is inevitably intertwined with both the creator's and the reader's imaginations. Here, it is possible to detect a degree of overlap between the interstitial dimensions of *inter-textuality* and *inter-subjectivity*, which, my book suggests, refers to a psychic encounter between the author and the adapter, whose position fluctuates between that of reader, writer, director, viewer, and critic.

Most compellingly, in explaining the subjective, psychic experience of "the gaps between very different media and materials of expression," Stam remarks that these gaps should be regarded not merely as an irreversible loss but also as an inevitable condition of redistributing "creative energy" across the intertextual network of different media and

---

5. Aside from the cited text by Robert Stam, several studies acknowledge the presence of psychological factors in the undercurrent of screen adaptation, although most such comments remain auxiliary. See David L. Kranz and Nancy C. Mellerski, Introduction to *In/Fidelity: Essays on Film Adaptation*, ed. David L. Kranz and Nancy C. Mellerski (Newcastle: Cambridge Scholars Publishing, 2008), 1–11; Shannon Donaldson-McHugh and Don Moore, "Spectres of Psycho: Freud, Fear, and Film Adaptation," in *From Camera Lens to Critical Lens: A Collection of Best Essays on Film Adaptation*, ed. Rebecca Housel (Newcastle: Cambridge Scholars Press, 2006), 98–108; and Rachel Carroll, "Introduction: Textual Infidelities," in *Adaptation in Contemporary Culture: Textual Infidelities*, ed. Rachel Carroll (New York and London: Continuum, 2009), 1–7.

6. Robert Stam, "Introduction: The Theory and Practice of Adaptation," in *Literature and Film: A Guide to the Theory and Practice of Film Adaptation*, ed. Robert Stam and Alessandra Raengo (Malden, MA: Blackwell, 2005), 15.

texts.[7] In his use of the phrase "creative energy," the idea of a libidinal manifestation within the intertextual transmediation of adaptation emerges as particularly distinctive. Stam discovers in the vigor and ubiquity of adaptation "its anthropophagic hunger to devour and digest and change antecedent arts."[8] In response to this cue, the discussion that follows aims to closely examine the complex psychic dynamics that are at play within the adaptation process: therein, we shall find an adapter who is haunted by the urge toward fidelity and encounters with the alluring authorial voice yet who is nonetheless fueled by their own creative impulses. Ultimately, my book aims to confirm the libidinal force of an adapter whose "hunger to devour and digest and change antecedent arts" perpetuates adaptation as a fundamental feature of culture.

Put otherwise, my interest henceforth fundamentally lies with the subject-position of the adapter, who seeks to transmit messages through this practice that is so characteristic of culture. Indeed, if adaptation is an expression of a certain libidinal energy—whether Stam's "anthropophagic hunger" or the desire for perceptual verisimilitude that Kevin Cohen terms "cinematic desire"[9]—it cannot be regarded merely as a textual transmediation that initiates autonomously. Rather, adaptation is better understood as a *symptomatic* formation motivated by the psychic functions of human subjects, exemplified herein by the figure of the adapter whose singular subjective position switches between that of reader, writer, director, viewer, and even super-egotistical critic of one's own adaptation. Moreover, insofar as adaptation signals a psychic function beneath its textual surface, the act of adaptation highlights the need for interpretation, just as symptoms in the psychoanalytic sense do.

However, symptoms are never easily deciphered given that such messages, which carry psychic undercurrents or the repressed materials of the unconscious, are never straightforward: human subjects invariably say one thing while meaning another. In *adapting* Freud's theory, Jacques Lacan redefined the relationship between symptoms and the repressed material that finds an outlet in symptoms by effecting

7. Ibid., 46.
8. Ibid., 23.
9. Keith Cohen, *Film and Fiction: The Dynamics of Exchange* (New Haven, CT, and London: Yale University Press, 1979), 50.

a deconstructive investigation of how such symptoms are formed. That is, although Lacan agreed that symptoms reveal the mechanisms of the unconscious, he was suspicious of the formulaic and symmetrical connection between the symptom and that which the symptom discloses, believing that such an interpretation risks underestimating the complexity of the message.

Lacan's teaching gradually relocates the symptom and its significatory function from the Freudian vertical topology, which places the conscious on the surface, the preconscious in the middle, and the unconscious at the bottom, to a structure comprising three coexisting psychic registers—the symbolic, the imaginary, and the real. Within this structure, a message—to the subject—can never be reduced to the correspondence between signifier and signified; rather, it must be defined in fluid terms because the subject is permanently entangled in an ongoing interrelationship between the three registers. In this light, the symptom provides a site of incessant conflict and compromise between the repressed and its symptomatic manifestation. Simply put, each message must undergo a complex process of transformation or adaptation, a process that entails the breakdown of the hierarchical relationship between a prior, underlying, and thus original meaning and its surface representation (or symptom). Herein, one might discern a connection between the concept of the symptom in the Lacanian adaptation of the Freudian lexicon and that of adaptation as it is placed within the webbed intertextual relationship between a source text and its adaptation(s).

Although this line of thought in adaptation studies influences the following chapters, my focus will nonetheless remain on the position and function of the subject of the unconscious within this intertextual nexus. In other words, this book approaches adaptation as a symptom derived from the subject-position of the adapter, whose psychic complexity incessantly complicates the linear transmission of any message from page to screen.

However, although an adaptation may undeniably add a new dimension to its source text and thereby exert a retrospective influence on an anterior text, it is also necessary to maintain a critical distance from the reductive application of the Darwinian view of the term "adaptation." The Darwinian use of the term often advocates for the evolutionary value of adaptations, valorizing their ability to modernize and improve original texts' narratological potential. While this interpretation seems unnecessarily reductive, an alternative—and arguably more proper—Darwinian conceptualization of adaptation might usefully be applied to expand and advance the notion of adaptation as a more profound symptom of culture. In relation to biological examples from Darwin's investigation, Julie Sanders argues that "adaptation proves in these examples to be a far from neutral, indeed highly active mode of being, far removed from the unimaginative act of imitation, copying, or repetition."[10]

To me, Sanders appears to capture one of the most unresearched dimensions of adaptation in using the term a "mode of being." While I shall revisit this idea repeatedly in the discussion that follows with reference to several different terms, I wish to remark here that adaptation is, above all, the *fundamental mode of being* of culture. In this vein, adaptation arguably also explains the mode of being of the speaking subject, who is born into the sphere of culture and is subject to its codes. Moreover, the fundamentality of adaptation becomes apparent by virtue of the fact that adaptation remains ongoing. It is foundational to the ontology of the human subject, who is destined to the unavoidable task of adaptation whether adaptation is seen as a biological and genetic process or a cultural and psychic process. To my mind, this ontology of the human subject manifests explicitly in the cultural loop of the incessant practice of adaptation, as will be examined herein from a psychoanalytic perspective.

At the end of *Adaptation and Appropriation*, Sanders highlights the trajectory of a *detour* embedded in the presumably "forward" motion of adaptation owing to the compounded temporality of desire in play, quoting Jacques Derrida: "Perhaps the desire to write is the desire to launch things that come back to you as much as possible in as many forms as possible."[11] This insight, which adapts Derrida to the study of adaptation, is meaningful for my investigation in two ways: first, with regard to the significance of desire as a driving force in narrative re-tellings. The chapters that follow are primarily interested in the centrality

---

10. Julie Sanders, *Adaptation and Appropriation* (London: Routledge, 2006), 24.

11. Ibid., 160. (The original quotation is from Jacques Derrida, *The Ear of the Other: Otobiography, Transference, Translation: Texts and Discussions with Jacques Derrida*, ed. Christie V. McDonald and trans. Peggy Kamuf (Lincoln: University of Nebraska Press, 1985), 157–8.)

of the desire that lies beneath the phenomenological dimensions of adaptation. As Sanders suggests, adaptation is neither a neutral nor an accidental phenomenon; rather, it is a symptom that belies underlying cause—desire according to Derrida's insight. From a psychoanalytic perspective, my study aims to interrogate the desire for adaptation as it relates particularly to the incessant and ubiquitous presence of adaptation as a symptom of culture. Indeed, the omnipresence of adaptation suggests that the urge to create neither precedes nor outshines the desire for adaptation, given that the detour or return of a message through adaptation is doomed at the very moment of the detour's creation.

Hence, my study's second objective relates to the circular trajectory of adaptation, whereby the desire to adapt a literary text for the screen ultimately returns the adapter to the scene of writing the original text in his or her pursuit of a truth or spirit of the original. That is, I insist on the significance of the fantasized scene of writing the original to be adapted. It is because this moment of the birth of the original by the hand of the author functions as a source of admiration, repression, and anxiety for screen adapters as well as the primary locus to which their desire tends to return. Without exception, reading the original text is the first step in each screen adaptation process. Paradoxically enough, the film adaptation trajectory begins by recalling the scene of writing the original and asking, "What did the author mean by that?"—as any reader might do. This question, I argue, ties the imagination of screenwriters to the scene of writing that begot the original texts that they are seeking to adapt for the screen, whether consciously or unconsciously. However, owing to the complexity and fluidity that characterize the relationship between a message and its meaning, this question cannot easily be answered; neither can the anxiety surrounding it be easily resolved, and the scene of writing must forever haunt the scene of adaptation. Therefore, this book's overall structure is designed to make a detour back to the scene of writing after having looped through various scenes of adaptation.

The first chapter opens with an analysis of the mythical scene that transfixes the speaking subject's destiny within the inevitable task of adaptation. In effecting a close reading of two interconnected works by Walter Benjamin and Jacques Derrida, the chapter attempts to comprehend the biblical myth of the tower of Babel in which *translation*—a foundational tenet of adaptation—becomes a task that both manifests as a curse and offers the speaking being an opportunity to engage with the world. From there, the discussion shifts to the field of psychoanalysis. The introduction of psychoanalysis in this opening chapter serves as the theoretical basis for the later investigation of the desire for adaptation. In particular, the Lacanian theory of the real, which grounds the impossibility inscribed in any signification, is used to clarify our understanding of the psychic mechanism that perpetuates the circular movement—or *detour*, to use Derrida's terminology—of adaptation to the extent that the entanglement between desire and its dissatisfaction transforms the desire for adaptation into an obligation or demand, as is foreshadowed by both Benjamin's and Derrida's use of the term "task."

This first chapter lays the groundwork for four subsequent case studies, which attempt to analyze specific symptoms that are caused by different variants of the interrelation between an original text and its film adaptation(s). Although all four case studies orbit the concept of adaptation, each adopts a unique approach and deploys a different set of psychoanalytic concepts to identify the psychic dynamics that propel the ongoing practice of adaptation. Consequently, the weight and length assigned to each chapter vary in response to the volume of theoretical history and psychoanalytic knowledge required to facilitate the discussion of the individual cases. The first two case studies are supported by extensive psychoanalytic lexicons, which also offer theoretical foundations for the final two chapters. By contrast, the last two case studies focus more on their film examples with the intention of interrogating less conventional facets of adaptation once the two previous cases have dealt with the more commonplace *symptoms* that emerge from the relationship between an original and its film adaptations.

Before introducing each case study in greater detail, it is worth briefly considering the book's use of a limited number of film adaptations as example. In *Enjoy Your Symptom!*, Slavoj Žižek justifies his frequent (and often criticized) use of examples as follows: from his materialist perspective, "there is always more in the example than in what it exemplifies, i.e. an example always threatens to undermine what it is supposed to exemplify since it gives body to what the exemplified notion itself represses, is unable to cope with."[12] This view, he explains, stands in opposition to the Platonic-idealist approach, which always

---

12. Slavoj Žižek, *Enjoy Your Symptom! Jacques Lacan in Hollywood and Out* (New York and London: Routledge, 2008), xi.

demands "a multitude of examples—since no single example is fully fitting," because the idea that they exemplify remains eternally greater than the sum of those examples.[13] Following Žižek's example, this book's structure confirms that the exemplary film adaptations that its case studies examine are more (rather than less) than the chapters' analytic exegesis of them can offer because these exemplary film adaptations of literary works not only initiate, inspire, and demand the corresponding psychoanalytic interpretation but also embody that which such interpretative attempts miss out, ignore, and repress, just as a symptom is not only a message that reveals repressed materials but also a gesture against any exhaustive interpretation.

In addition, some readers might be puzzled by the four case studies' occasional attempt to search for the traces of the unconscious from each film director's approach to the practice of adapting literary originals. As Todd McGowan clarifies, "Even if the film provides insight into the psyche of the director, this has no inherent interest for anyone else."[14] I am completely in the same opinion that cinema, unlike an individual subject's dream, cannot be regarded as the manifestation of the director's unconscious and a psychoanalytic study of film is not to be reduced to "a window into the psyche of its creator."[15] Psychoanalytic film study is firmly founded upon the role of cinema to speak to the psychical structure of the subject because it is a dream connecting not only filmmakers, staff, and spectators but also, for this book's interest, authors of literary originals and their readers. Instead of using a psychoanalytic reading of film adaptations as an observation of individual film directors, this book takes a different path to a psychoanalytic case study of film in the following chapters. Surely, the significance of case studies is not new to the field of psychoanalysis at all: since Freud, case studies have been "important vehicles of psychoanalytic knowledge."[16] Freud's case studies illustrate *how he thought with patients or the objects of clinical observations* in

13. Ibid.
14. Todd McGowan, *Psychoanalytic Film Theory and the Rules of the Game* (New York: Bloomsbury, 2015), 2.
15. Ibid.
16. Carl. E. Pletsch, "Freud's Case Studies and the Locus of Psychoanalytic Knowledge," *DYNAMIS: Acta Hispanica ad Medicinae Scientiarumque Historiam Illustrandam* 2 (1982): 265.

search of the universal knowledge of human subjectivity and psyche. The book's aim is similar: it seeks to understand a facet of the psyche which repeatedly returns individuals to the task of an adapter by means of the detailed observation of each director's own encounter with a particular, and even peculiar, manifestation of the unconscious in the process of adapting a literary original to the screen.

The chronological arrangement of the following four case studies traces the historical development of adaptation as a media practice, highlighting the evolving relationship between literature and cinema. From the birth of cinema as a storytelling medium, filmmakers turned to literary texts, viewing film as a natural extension of written stories. Early examples include Georges Méliès's *A Trip to the Moon* (1902), inspired by Jules Verne's novels, and Edwin S. Porter's *Uncle Tom's Cabin* (1903). Directors like Laurence Olivier, Franco Zeffirelli, and Kenneth Branagh, all of whom had theatrical backgrounds, famously adapted Shakespeare's *Hamlet*, displaying the profound influence of the canonical original on cinematic adaptations. However, as cinema developed into a self-standing popular medium, filmmakers like Alfred Hitchcock began to consciously distance their work from the constraints of fidelity to source material, instead embracing the visual and cinematic arts as storytelling tools in their own right. While Hitchcock's adaptations, such as *Rebecca* (1940) and *The Birds* (1963), were still seeking literary inspiration, his focus was on cinematic technique and narrative control, often downplaying the literary source's importance. This trend of asserting cinema's autonomy continued with later directors like Stanley Kubrick, who further distanced themselves from traditional literary narratives, favoring uniquely cinematic forms of expression—an attitude and approach that became consolidated thanks to movements such as the French New Wave. Kubrick's *The Shining* (1980) was less about fidelity to the source text and more focused on exploring the cinematic medium's potential to encounter and evoke the real of a text, if borrowing from Lacanian theory. By the new millennium, commercial cinema embraced postmodern storytelling, treating film adaptations as part of an intertextual web of references and influences. This approach decentered the traditional, hierarchical relationship between source text and adaptation, highlighting a fluid, multilayered interaction with various texts and contexts. Spike Jonze's *Adaptation* (2002) exemplifies this shift, blurring the boundaries between Susan Orlean's original book and its film adaptation, while also dissolving distinctions between author, adapter, and character in a self-reflexive exploration of the creative process. Furthermore, it is important to clarify that my use of Freudian and Lacanian concepts—such as the Oedipus complex, the phallus, the Name-of-the-Father, paternal metaphor, and the Mother—is made with full awareness of their multiple interpretations, including feminist critiques. While these terms are often viewed as reinforcing patriarchal structures within the human psyche, prominent feminist scholars have reexamined their critical potential. Juliet Mitchell, in her influential book *Psychoanalysis and Feminism* (1974), argued that "psychoanalysis is not a recommendation *for* a patriarchal society, but an analysis *of* one."[17] She emphasizes that Freud's theories expose the mechanisms of patriarchy, making psychoanalysis a valuable tool for critiquing, rather than endorsing, patriarchal ideologies. Similarly, Deborah Luepnitz contends that Lacanian psychoanalysis does not naturalize the family structure or mandate a traditional family centered on a male father figure. Instead, Lacan's references to the paternal metaphor and the Name-of-the-Father are "not gender-specific," and his use of the Oedipus complex hinges on "a more fundamental case of mistaken identity" at the core of subjectivity formation.[18] Thus, in this book, these terms are used positionally, rather than biologically or in a gendered sense, in the psychoanalytic investigation of film adaptation as a cultural symptom, while avoiding a reductive endorsement of patriarchal structures that predetermine the functions and desires of adapters. What follows aims to explore how the human psyche is manifested and captured in narratives—whether in myths, poetry, novels, plays, or films—that are in a continual process of adaptation, reflecting the ongoing transformation of both culture and subjectivity.

The first case study begins with a paradigmatic case of screen adaptation, which instantiates the Oedipus complex experienced by cinematic sons in relation to their great literary fathers. This chapter on filmic adaptations of *Hamlet* investigates the psychic configuration that determines a film adaptation's respectful attitude toward its original.

17. Juliet Mitchell, *Psychoanalysis and Feminism: A Radical Reassessment of Freudian Psychoanalysis* (Middlesex: Penguin Books, 1974), xiii. (Original emphasis.)

18. Deborah Luepnitz, "Beyond the Phallus: Lacan and Feminism," in *The Cambridge Companion to Lacan*, ed. Jean-Michel Rabaté (Cambridge: Cambridge University Press, 2003), 226 and 223.

Various screen adaptations of Shakespeare's *Hamlet* under the shadow of the Father's ghost appear to epitomize the pervasive relationship between a canonical literary original and its film adaptations. In particular, I examine the awe-struck attitudes of *Hamlet* filmmakers through one of the most fundamental psychic configurations of the speaking subject—Freud's Oedipus complex. In unpacking related theoretical concepts and interdisciplinary notions, the chapter closely examines three film adaptations of Shakespeare's *Hamlet*—Laurence Olivier's *Hamlet* (1948), Franco Zeffirelli's *Hamlet* (1990), and Kenneth Branagh's *Shakespeare's Hamlet* (1996)—to determine the most conventional rapport between anterior and posterior texts. I also interrogate the relationship between different film adaptations of the same material by analyzing these three *Hamlet* films, which manifest an extension of the Oedipal relationship between the first and the latter adaptations.

In contrast to the respectful attitude toward the original text that the *Hamlet* films canonize, the second case study investigates a more adversarial relationship to paternal authority. My chapter on Hitchcock's screen adaptations focuses on the director's resistance to and defiance of the very notion of a source text. Hitchcock was notorious for the control he exerted over the entire filmmaking process and actively denied any significant connection between his films and the literary sources that he adapted for the screen, despite the fact that his filmography of fifty-three films includes forty-four adaptations of literary works. This chapter investigates what such resistance might reveal about the hidden message in Hitchcock's disrespect for and negation of originals. I employ the concept of anxiety with regard to the subject's abhorrence of the Mother, as the overpowering Other in the Lacanian sense, in reading Hitchcock's *Rebecca* (1941) and *The Birds* (1963). These two films are intriguingly based on a novel and a short story, respectively, both of which were written by the contemporary female author Daphne du Maurier. I contend that Hitchcock's vehement denial of the influence of these originals reveals the deep-seated anxiety inherent in confrontations with the alluring shadow of the Mother, in which Lacan reads an insatiable and devouring authority that appears in the guise of the first love object. In a Kristevan sense, the abhorred Mother is represented as the uncanny object, which masks and marks the lack or lacuna at the center of the symbolic domain of the Father. The chapter reads Hitchcock's repressed anxiety through the lens of his cinematic representation of this uncanny object—the Mother—and suggests that this persistent anxiety is the unconscious force that ironically fixed his six decades of filmmaking to the locus of adaptation.

My third case study moves from the dialectical tension between the Oedipal Father and the uncanny Mother in an attempt to seek out a psychic locus that escapes and transcends these two conflicting forces. After scrutinizing the apparent and identifiable presence of these two types of super-egotistical pressures from literary originals, the chapter on Stanley Kubrick's *The Shining* (1980), an adaptation of Stephen King's 1977 novel of the same title, detects a clandestine trace of a more unfathomable dimension of the unconscious. Herein, I am interested in what happens when the Lacanian real—which never surfaces through the deciphering or interpretation of symptoms—appears in the process or outcome of adaptation. The chapter approaches this enigmatic kernel of the human psyche by examining one of the most mysterious concepts in Lacan—*das Ding* (the Thing). For Lacan, *das Ding* points to that which is inaccessible through the subject's imaginary and symbolic registers yet speaks the Truth of the human subject. Interestingly, Kubrick's adaptation of King's conventional horror novel overlaps with Lacan's path to *das Ding*: Kubrick adopted an exceptionally extended approach to this adaptation, in which he carefully peeled the imaginary and linguistic masks away from the nexus of the novel's horror, as though he desired to discover what remains when adaptation is performed as a meticulous process of deprivation. Kubrick's adaptation leads spectators to an uncanny maze and causes them to experience the nameless and shapeless horror that emerges when one confronts the non-being at the heart of one's being or no-thing in the midst of things. The Lacanian concept *das Ding* will serve as the Ariadne's thread in exploring the labyrinthine void at the core of Kubrick's adaptation.

The final analytic chapter offers a close reading of Spike Jonze's *Adaptation* (2002), which is an allegory about adaptation rather than an adaptation itself. The story concerns the on-screen persona of the real adapter Charlie Kaufman, who pens the film's script as loosely based on Susan Orlean's popular nonfiction book *The Orchid Thief*. *Adaptation* is an exemplary film that shows how adaptation can be treated in postmodern terms; it self-reflexively delineates the manifestations and operations of desire, drive, anxiety, and obsession in the course of writing a screen adaptation. This chapter overtly returns the discussion to the scene of writing, in which the adapter seeks to encounter the "original or authentic" meaning so that he can begin his writing from that point. As the film's recurring metaphor, writing epitomizes what Freud and Lacan termed as the original or fundamental fantasy with its irreducible gravity. Kaufman's struggle with severe writer's block illustrates how this self-conscious and neurotic film about adaptation becomes pathologically transfixed by the fundamental fantasy embodied in the scene of writing the original. As long as the adapter is caught up in his futile obsession with "what the author of the original really meant," the film's narrative, like a dream, is barely coherent and features a dazzling array of fragmented scenes from that overlap one another.

The analysis in this chapter focuses on how the film, through the figure of the onscreen adapter, not only dwells on but also recreates the original fantasy—the scene of writing *the original*—and demonstrates how its disorienting narrative structure successfully deconstructs the seemingly linear logic of adaptation from past to present. I argue that the film's circular narrative and lack of closure instantiate the act of "traversing the fundamental fantasy," which Freud and Lacan both understand to be the end of analysis. That is, Kaufman, as both the protagonist and screenwriter/adapter of *Adaptation*, ultimately traverses and encounters the nothingness of the enigmatic scene of writing the original that haunts him. The fantasy tied to the scene of writing an original text is merely a veil that conceals the adapter's inability to access the scene in which the Author (here, the capitalization of "author" invokes Lacan's use of the Other) created the original meaning. The implication of the film's conclusion is that, by traversing such a disabling fantasy, Kaufmann ironically *become*s a writer—an author of his own original—and realizes that an adaptation of an original is ultimately no different from writing one's own story.

With this last chapter, the book's arc returns to the fundamental fantasy that is deeply buried in the process of adaptation; it suggests that adaptation is driven by the desire to fill the gap that is created by the subject's inability to access the scene of its own birth. Jonze's film spells out this, first, in the opening scene where Kaufman asks himself, "I've been on this planet for 40 years and I'm no closer to understanding a single thing: why am I here, how'd I get here?" The following narrative entangles his attempt to answer this question with the task of adaptation as it mixes the scene of the original text's composition and that of Kaufman's adaptation. To a human being, the unfathomable and ungraspable moment of birth is comparable to the Truth or true meaning that is concealed in the original text which is sought after by the adapter. The original's inaccessible true meaning is admiringly revered, disdainfully rejected, contemplatively unveiled, or endlessly fantasized about, as my four case studies demonstrate.

Seen in this light, adaptation is a doomed process that resembles the subject's pursuit of the scene of its own birth—and hence the reason for its existence—by diligently fabricating fantasies that seek to grasp the inaccessible core of its being. Owing to the innate impossibility of this pursuit, it is occasionally transformed into a pathological symptom, which may cause the subject to become trapped in an endless loop of lethal repetition.

However, like the clinical practice of psychoanalysis, adaptation also incorporates the possibility of breaking free from the loop by constructing a new and less painful link to the forbidden scene of one's own birth. Lacan conceptualizes this radical moment of replacement or substitution with reference to the notion of metaphor. In the book's conclusion, I explore this nexus of human subjectivity supported by the Lacanian concept of metaphor. In so doing, the book's conclusion seeks to finally probe the deepest layer of adaptation, in which subjectivity and textuality are no longer distinct. At this point, adaptation becomes a new name or metaphor for the subject that is a being in the process of becoming and thus adapting.

# 1

# THE REAL OF A TEXT AND THE TASK OF THE ADAPTER

> Desire is a relation of being to lack. The lack is the lack of being properly speaking. It isn't the lack of this or that, but lack of being whereby the being exists.
>
> —Jacques Lacan, *Seminar II*

## *Lost in Adaptation*

The judgmental view of screen adaptation "not as good as the book" is often expressed in a variety of terms referring to this media practice such as simplification, ruin, mutation, betrayal, dilution, trivialization, dumbing down, commercialization, and popularization of literary originals. These demeaning tags on screen adaptation based on literary originals, to different degrees, imply the sense of loss that is shared and commented on not only by audiences and critics but also by filmmakers, who adapt literary texts for the screen. This experience of loss, which emerges as a common denominator in most negative reviews, is often justified by assuming a lack that is considered to be inflicted by the course of adaptation itself. In other words, most complaints about the "missing part"—whether this means actual elements of the original narrative or a measure of depth and complexity—presuppose something that must have been lost in adaptation and whose loss has provoked the disappointment and dissatisfaction that many experience. Therefore, my aim here is to speculate on what has been lost in adaptation and on the irreparable lack that thereby characterizes posterior texts, at least as the arguments go.

Various works of cultural studies have attempted to locate the cause of the sense of loss in the gap between the two different media—literature and cinema. As outlined in the introduction, fidelity criticism is one such attempt, specifically one that is characterized by its hierarchical configuration of the two media in the sense that it perceives the loss as an outcome of film's inferiority.¹ Although adaptation studies does not discriminate against film adaptation as such, it does admit the existence of an irreducible fissure that separates literary representation from cinematic representation. Such a view posits that screen adaptation can be conceived as a practice of *translation*, which denotes a "horizontal migration" from the register of literary language to that of filmic language. Timothy Corrigan points out that, in this sense, adaptation "implies a translation between 'languages' that will always be only approximate."² Robert Stam also suggests that translation is one possible trope that may be invoked to make sense of adaptation: "The trope of adaptation as translation suggests a principled effort of intersemiotic transposition, with the inevitable losses and gains typical of any translation."³ Adaptation's alignment with translation or "intersemiotic transposition" proposes a renewed perspective of something *lost in adaptation* not as revealing a particular flaw of screen adaptation as cultural practice but rather as gesturing toward a fundamental dimension of the symbolic system called language.

Where once it registered that what is lost in adaptation is an inevitable result of inter-media translation, adaptation studies can now address its inexplicable persistence more directly by comparing the source's semiotic components with its adaptation. However, this chapter does not aim to detect *what* is missing in the process of intersemiotic transposition; rather, the discussion utilizes the inevitable *sense* of loss as a locus of the book's interrogation of the psychic underpinnings of adaptation. To put differently, the chapter attempts to suggest that adaptation is a task that is mobilized by that which is registered as being lost during the adaptation process everyone had to go through in order

---

1. Robert Stam speculates on the origins of the pervasive allegation of the superiority of literature to film in his introduction to *Literature and Film: A Guide to the Theory and Practice of Film Adaptation*. In particular, he notes that the prejudice derives from "deeply rooted and often *unconscious* assumptions about the relations between the two arts." In "Introduction: The Theory and Practice of Adaptation," 4. (My italics.)

2. Timothy Corrigan, "Literature on Screen, a History: In the Gap," in *The Cambridge Companion to Literature on Screen*, ed. Deborah Cartmell and Imelda Whelehan (Cambridge: Cambridge University Press, 2007), 31.

3. Robert Stam, "Beyond Fidelity: The Dialogics of Adaptation," in *Film Adaptation*, ed. James Naremore (New Brunswick, NJ: Rutgers University Press, 2000), 62.

to translate somatic needs and drives to a human language. In fact, the stubborn presence of loss is pivotal to understanding the psychic dimension of adaptation, which has hitherto remained unexplored in adaptation studies. As a theoretical framework, a psychoanalytic approach allows my study to relocate the sense of loss from the textual level of screen adaptation to the psychic level at which adapters begin to engage with the fundamental lack at the core of human subjectivity. In this sense, the Jacques Lacan epigraph that begins this chapter lends insight by suggesting that—although lack appears to frame the experience of screen adaptation as a kind of deprivation—the *presence* of the lack can uncover the powerful driving force that is desire. In attempting to understand the psychoanalytic correlation between loss, lack, and desire, this chapter investigates the intricate meaning of the common phrase "lost in translation."

Based on the abovementioned correspondence between adaptation and translation, I would first like to examine the specific primordial desire that operates at the heart of adaptation by taking the discussion to the meanings of translation in relation to the embedded sense of loss. In particular, the first part of the chapter examines the relationship between the speaking subject and the loss invoked in adaptation with reference to the notion of "the task of the translator," as pioneered by Walter Benjamin and Jacques Derrida. Both Walter Benjamin's "The Task of the Translator" and Jacques Derrida's "Des Tours de Babel" ("The Tower of Babel") discuss the urgency that is manifest in the speaking subject's insatiable desire for translation. They highlight the fundamentality of our desire for a *complete* translation (or adaptation for the book's interest) by accentuating a sense of obligation in the subject's confrontation with the practice of translation. The innate impossibility of completing this mission, which Benjamin and Derrida highlight, prompts a discussion of Lacan's concept of the real, which points to the unrepresentable dimensions of our psyche. Through the Lacanian concept of the real, I attempt to associate the feeling of "lost in adaptation" with the primordial sense of loss inscribed in the unconscious of every speaking subject. Interestingly, closer examination of the elaboration of the real reveals that Lacan attributes this immanent sense of loss to the origin of human desire, as the opening quotation proposes. In other words, the chapter suggests that what appears to be lost in adaptation reflects the paradoxical nature of the persistent desire for adaptation given that this desire is generated from the loss and deprivation that are characteristic of both semiotic and psychic *reality* into which a speaking subject is born. Indeed, this lack-in-adaptation never deters us from our desire to retell the same story over and over again; on the contrary, it keeps the desire for adaptation on track and ensures its persistence.

## The Task of the Adapter

In his influential essay "The Task of the Translator," Benjamin considers translation to be a fundamental mode of being of any text.[4] He maintains that to "comprehend translation as mode one must go back to the original, for that contains the law governing the translation: its translatability."[5] This phrase, however, does not endorse the original's priority over its translation, on the basis of which fidelity criticism retains every translation or adaptation under the authoritative command of the original text. Rather, Benjamin's argument highlights the role that posterior texts play in understanding any anterior text to be translated. He asserts the existence of certain works of art whose value and life spans should be appreciated through "a vital connection" between the original and its forthcoming translations or adaptations.[6] Benjamin thus defines the term "translation" as a central and inclusive metaphor that represents the text's ontological mode in relation to succeeding texts that translate or, for the purpose of our discussion here, adapt the original. In doing so, Benjamin lays the groundwork for understanding translation not as a fringe of the cultural sphere but as a significant gateway to understanding the primal relationship between human subject as a translator or adapter and text. In short, Benjamin

---

4. In a recent version of the same English translation by Harry Zohn in *Walter Benjamin: Selected Writings Volume 1*, ed. Marcus Bullock and Michael W. Jennings (Cambridge, MA: Harvard University Press, 1996), the word "mode" is replaced by the word "form." Yet, although the word "form" may be able to indicate a mode in which a thing exists, it also has an implication of a complete structure. Hence, "mode," I believe, can convey a closer sense of what Benjamin meant by translation—that is, an indecisive and temporary status of a text in the long line of history—throughout the whole article.

5. Walter Benjamin, "The Task of the Translator," trans. Harry Zohn, in *Theories of Translation: An Anthology of Essays from Dryden to Derrida*, ed. Rainer Schulte and John Biguenet (Chicago, IL, and London: The University of Chicago Press, 1992), 72.

6. Ibid., 73.

seeks to answer the central question that also lies at the core of this book—why are we "saying *the same thing* repeatedly"?[7]

Benjamin supports his concept of translation as the perpetually transitional mode of a text by aligning it with the Hegelian notion of history as a constant dialectic progress. The Hegelian framework allows Benjamin to employ a series of metaphors to position the text's history as an organic entity whose life eventually arrives at its *afterlife* through translation. This prompts us to ask what Benjamin means by the afterlife of a text. In accordance with the general understanding of afterlife as a life after an end or death, a text's afterlife comes about only after the text has ended. Benjamin's work interprets this death from a Judeo-Christian perspective. On the one hand, it signals the death of the original text as the extermination of direct access to its "meaning"; on the other hand, the death prompts the departure of the original for a perpetual rebirth "governed by a special high purposiveness," which is enabled through its translation or adaptation.[8] Most importantly, Benjamin stresses the role of the subject by suggesting that the passage from death to rebirth is a task for the subject—in the position of a translator or adapter—who must come to terms with terminating the text's core in its original form and the process of transposing it into another. Moreover, Benjamin regards this task as inevitable, given that it is through such transposition that the innate purpose inscribed in the original text ultimately manifests.

What, then, is the nature of this task inscribed in the act of translation? In Benjamin's words, "translation ... serves ultimately the purpose of expressing the innermost relationship of languages."[9] To my mind, it is this "innermost relationship of languages" that permits the linking of Benjamin, Derrida, and Lacan, all of whom probe the speaking subject's inability to access the core of the symbolic system. Benjamin uses the phrase *pure language* to indicate the primordial level of signification and communication that characterizes the nexus of the complementary relationship between individual languages. In other words, that which Benjamin refers to as pure language is the ineffable and inaccessible center around which each language forms a complementary relation to another. Using poetic metaphors, he demonstrates that languages, as used practically by human subjects, are "fragments of a vessel that are to

7. Ibid., 71.
8. Ibid., 255.
9. Ibid.

be glued together [and] must match one another in the smallest details, although they need not be like one another."[10] Undoubtedly, this vessel is what he regards as pure language, which precedes or transcends the irreparable disjunction between the signified and the signifier in every semiotic system. For Benjamin, pure language is "the language in which it expresses itself, as its own kind of *intention*."[11] In this sense, Benjamin's concept of pure language is one of a language that includes no gap between the signified and the signifier—a language that relegates all other languages to a relationship with itself that is "the law governing the translation."[12] Despite Benjamin's aspirational tone, we may discern a note of impossibility and inaccessibility in his conceptualization of pure language and the task of reaching for it. Indeed, this ungraspable level of pure language creates a hole—a vacuum—at the center of the speaking subject's linguistic reality. Benjamin's insight appears to foreshadow that which Lacan implies by the real, to which I shall soon return.

Benjamin also interrogates the relationship between pure language and the task of the human subject who is constantly cast as a translator or adapter. Either consciously or unconsciously, the speaking subject experiences reality as a coded matrix in a perpetual process of linguistic or symbolic construction and transposition. However, the innate impossibility to reach pure language within this structure creates an irreducible sense of discontent and, simultaneously, an unquenchable desire for that which is impossible to achieve. In his attempt to bind this structural impossibility and the ontological condition of human subjectivity as fundamentally limited but permanently yearning for completion, Benjamin illuminates the translator's task as being provoked by "the great motif of integrating many tongues into one true language" and as entailing the "ripening [of] the seed of pure language in a translation."[13] The translator or adapter must thus confront the unavoidable task of ripening the buried seed of pure language, or the authentic meaning of an original, by transforming the text into another language, form, or medium. The desire for translation and adaptation is transfixed by nothing other than the imperfection of every symbolic creation, which invariably leaves something yet to be translated or

10. Ibid., 260.
11. Ibid.
12. Benjamin, "The Task of the Translator," 72.
13. *Walter Benjamin*, 259.

adapted. To return to the problematic sense of loss with which this chapter opened, it is clear that the sense of loss or lack for which screen adaptations are often criticized is always already inscribed in the literary texts that undergo adaptation. Moreover, the fundamental lack evoked in the course of adaptation explains not only the persistent sense of deprivation but also the incessant longing for a perfect adaptation, which Benjamin would term the revival of pure language. Below, we shall see how Derrida, in his interpretation of Benjamin's work, clarifies the way in which this longing becomes a debt that imposes an ineluctable obligation on the subject.

## *From the Debris of the Tower of Babel*

When considered through the lens of literary history, Benjamin's concept of pure language echoes the craving for one perfect language that many poets have dreamed of. In a chapter entitled "Languages in Paradise" in *Serendipities: Language & Lunacy*, Umberto Eco delineates Dante's lifelong search for the language in which Dante believed Adam to have conversed with God in the Garden of Eden. Eco explores how Dante's quest for this perfect language in paradise is embroidered throughout our culture in religion and myth. In Eco's words, Dante is seeking "the perfect *forma locutionis* whose principles permitted the creation of languages capable of reflecting the true essence of things, languages, in other words, in which the *modi essendi* of things were identical with the *modi significandi*."[14] The great poet made every attempt to reenact the language of paradise with the aim of transcending the inevitable gap between the signified (the *modi essendi*) and the signifier (the *modi significandi*). This not only echoes the desire that binds the speaking subject to the lacuna or lack that is discovered in the field of textual transformation; Eco also acknowledges that what drove Dante's journey was nothing less than a sense of sacred duty and, more compellingly, a sacred duty haunted by mythical inscription. Here, I shall examine how Derrida contemplates this relationship between the speaking subject and translation as a task, which emerges through the biblical myth of Babel. Derrida reconsiders Benjamin's text with reference to the collapse of the tower of Babel in Genesis, which not only dramatizes the scene

14. Umberto Eco, "Languages in Paradise," in *Serendipities: Language & Lunacy*, trans. William Weaver (London: Weidenfeld & Nicolson, 1999), 40.

of a traumatic confusion of languages but also materializes the loss through the image of the collapsed tower. Herein, the tower of Babel is read as a mythological symbol that fuels the demand for its restoration through the act of translation and, more discursively, adaptation.

Derrida regards the story of Babel as a foundation myth that reveals the primordial essence at the heart of culture. According to the biblical parable, men enjoyed prosperity after the Deluge which had swept everything on the surface of the earth except Noah's Ark. The survivors, a united human race speaking a single language, ventured east, discovering a plain in Shinar. There, they built a city and began to construct a tower that would reach to the sky and make men equal to God. In a rage, God confused their language so that they could not concoct their plan of usurpation, which would have been possible only if they spoke one tongue. The tower's construction had to be discontinued because people were unable to communicate with one another, and the unfinished tower of Babel became the symbol of the one language that is forever lost. Since then, men have been obliged to translate one another's languages to facilitate communication.

At the beginning of his essay "The Tower of Babel," Derrida writes:

> Telling at least of the inadequation of one tongue to another, of one place in the encyclopaedia to another, of language to itself and to meaning, and so forth, it also tells of the need for figuration, for myth, for tropes, for twists and turns, for translation inadequate to compensate for that which multiplicity denies us. In this sense, [the myth of the Babel tower] would be the myth of the origin of myth, the metaphor of metaphor, the narrative of narrative, the translation of translation, and so on.[15]

Responding to Benjamin's "The Task of the Translator," Derrida posits a link between pre-Babelian language and Benjamin's pure language insofar as both belong to "a kingdom which is at once promised and forbidden where the languages will be reconciled and fulfilled."[16] Most significantly, Derrida seeks to demonstrate how the alluring promise

---

15. Jacques Derrida, "Des Tours de Babel," in *Difference in Translation*, ed. and trans. Joseph F. Graham (Ithaca, NY, and London: Cornell University Press, 1985), 165.

16. Ibid., 191.

of pure language "fascinates and orients the work of the translator."[17] Moreover, the allegory of Babel allows Derrida to bring the Benjaminian *task* into the presence of God. For Derrida, the name of God is a transcendent word that stands in for the incontestable command ruling men's symbolic reality, to which the speaking being is subject. It is worth noting that, in *adapting* Benjamin's essay into his own words, Derrida leads the text in a more psychoanalytical direction. In particular, I wish to speculate on the implicit links between Derrida's reading and fundamental Lacanian concepts, including the Other, desire and its forbidden satisfaction, and the real.

First, Derrida expands the translator's limited reference to every speaking subject in relation to God, who "destines them to translation [and] subjects them to the law of a translation both necessary and impossible."[18] Indeed, owing to the fact that Benjamin's "The Task of the Translator" was written as a preface to his own German translation of Baudelaire's *Tableaux parisiens*, the term "translator" as it is used in Benjamin's essay may easily be interpreted as referring to a professional who is assigned to translate or adapt a given text into another language or mode. In other words, the Benjaminian notion of the translator's task is imbued with professionalism and even elitism in the sense that it presupposes expertise in handling languages other than one's mother tongue and even seems to connote the sacred duty of a chosen few. Adopting a philosophical tone, however, Derrida traces a parallel between the translator and the speaking subject, thereby transforming translation into an ontological task for every human subject who becomes a translator or adapter under this law. He notes that from the traumatic moment of the tower of Babel's destruction, "translation becomes law, duty and debt, but the debt one can no longer discharge."[19] Herein, the translator's task must be understood as the mission undertaken by all subjects who are destined to participate in the ceaseless process of transmission and transformation of messages so that they might live in society.

In this sense, one could argue that Derrida's "adaptation" *grows* the word "task" (*Aufgabe*) that was seeded in Benjamin's essay. Derrida translates the German word *Aufgabe* as "the mission to which one is destined (always by the other), the commitment, the duty, the debt, the

17. Ibid.
18. Ibid., 174.
19. Ibid.

responsibility."[20] In reading the word *task* through the allegory of Babel, Derrida suggests that, from birth, a human being is bound by fate to the obligation to translate another's language as well as that of having one's own language translated by others. This doomed destiny manifests itself in the field of translation and, more broadly, that of adaptation in its most intensive form. However, Derrida seeks to imbue the notion of task with a positive inflection: he proposes that, although translation comes to the speaking subject as an inescapable punishment or debt, this debt is transferred to an *heir* who can ripen the seed in translation. From this perspective, the translator's task possesses the potential "to render what was first *given*" in his or her own terms.[21] In this manner, Derrida claims that although the translator is "an indebted subject, obliged by a duty," they are "already in the position of heir, entered as survivor in a genealogy, as survivor or agent of sur-vival."[22] It thus becomes possible to identify another intriguing and significant implication that Derrida brings to his encompassing notion of translation or adaptation—namely, that Derrida interprets the translator as the "survivor or agent of sur-vival" and translation as the "sur-vival" of texts.

Contrary to Derrida's positive nuance, in his response to the same essay by Benjamin, Paul de Man argues that "*Aufgabe*, task, can also mean the one who has to give up."[23] From the word that Derrida translates as "survival," de Man invokes a pessimistic verdict that dooms the translator to failure from the outset: "the translator has to give up in relation to the task of refinding what was there in the original."[24] In a condemnatory tone, de Man maintains that all symbolic activities that aim to restore what they were given "kill the original, by discovering that the original was already dead."[25] De Man's pessimism may not be misplaced if we recall the fact that insofar as translation or adaptation is haunted by what was lost with the tower of Babel's collapse, all attempts to adapt an original must remain predetermined failures. However, his wholly pessimistic frame includes no scope for explaining the desire

20. Ibid., 175.
21. Ibid., 178.
22. Ibid., 179.
23. Paul de Man, "Conclusion: Walter Benjamin's 'The Task of the Translator,'" in *The Resistance to Theory* (Minneapolis: University of Minnesota Press, 1986), 80.
24. Ibid.
25. Ibid., 84.

intertwined with the sense of doomed obligation. Unlike de Man's reading of the task as a predestined failure, Derrida's view grasps the paradox embedded in the survival of the *Aufgabe* without thereby seeking the possibility of contentment, satisfaction, or fulfillment in a naively optimistic note. This reveals a psychoanalytical insight on Derrida's part, as he understands the paradox of human desire. Indeed, the inextricable coexistence of death and sur-vival is captured in the Lacanian concept of *jouissance*, which Lacan invokes to explain "the paradoxical satisfaction that the subject derives from his symptom."[26] Insofar as adaptation is the universal symptom of a speaking being, de Man's death and Derrida's sur-vival represent two aspects of the same reality—that is, the reality that determines the subject's place and its task as an adapter under the prohibition of the universal language as allegorized by the collapse of the tower of Babel.

If Derrida's intention is to answer the question of "what drives the subject toward the endless loop of translation or adaptation?," it is worth investigating how he perceives the function of an original text. For Derrida, an original text exists neither as an object to be translated nor as a vehicle for the author's *true* intention to be transmitted by a receiver of its message. Rather, it substitutes for a psychic site of command and law to which the speaking subject must subscribe: the original "requires, mandates, demands or commands in establishing the law."[27] More significantly, the subject's prior presence is unnecessary, given that the original's demand for its adaption—its death and rebirth in the line of history in Benjamin's sense—is already present. Derrida posits that "the original requires translation even if no translator is there, fit to respond to this injunction which is at the same time demand and desire in the very structure of the original."[28] To paraphrase, the authority of the original lays down the law of textual transformation prior to the subject's emergence as an adapter in carrying out the task. This highlights a remarkable similarity to the function of the Other in the realm of the symbolic, which represents the locus of the Law in the human psyche as defined by Lacan.

To understand what Lacan meant by the Other, we must first examine the symbolic, one of the three psychic registers—the symbolic,

---

26. Dylan Evans, *An Introductory Dictionary of Lacanian Psychoanalysis* (London and New York: Routledge, 1996), 92.

27. Derrida "Des Tours de Babel," 181.

28. Ibid., 182.

the imaginary, and the real—in Lacan's theory of the subject of the unconscious. For Lacan, the symbolic is characterized by its linguistic organization, according to which the subject is destined to move from one signifier to another in search of the Truth, as though commanded by the incontestable authority that is symbolized as the Other. Under the command of the Other, whose desire is wholly incomprehensible to the subject, the sense of duty merges with the construction of the subject's desire. Hence, I would claim that Derrida's adaptation of Benjamine inserts a psychoanalytic framework when casting the original text as a reminder of God's prohibition of the universal language and the demand for translation.

As noted above, the highlight of Derrida's psychoanalytic tenor is manifested in his articulation of the original text as a symbol of "this injunction which is at the same time demand and desire."[29] In this rendition of the original text, the tasks of translation and adaptation do not punitively force the subject to trudge along an utterly hopeless path but rather fuel them with an ardent wish and irresistible desire. At the end of this path of desire, I argue, there waits the real (*sensu* Lacan), which lures the subject. The real is none other than a different name for Benjamin's pure language and Derrida's pre-Babelian language: it connotes that which we have lost access to yet constantly wish for. Along the endless chain of signifiers, the subject, from the corner of its eye, may glimpse the real as a lacuna or gap between two signifiers—or, in our case, between two texts. The occasional glimpse of the lacuna can explain, for the purpose of the current discussion, the psychic experience of something that is untranslatable yet, like a Siren, persistently calls out for translation and adaptation. Overall, Derrida delineates the ways in which the subject experiences the demand for translation in its encounter with an original text as a command and how it is interlaced with the constitution of desire for translation. This valuable insight opens up the study of adaptation onto a terrain where psychoanalytic concepts, such as desire and the unconscious, play key roles in contemplating the ubiquity and the *survival* of this media practice.

Benjamin and Derrida clearly construe the field of textual transformation, including translation and adaptation, as a site that articulates the truth of the speaking subject's symbolic reality at its most primordial—or mythical—level. In one sense, both essays on translation

---

29. Ibid.

form an exemplary original/translation (or adaptation) pair that continuously opens up new meanings in their perpetual conversation. Moreover, the dialectical shift from Benjamin to Derrida ushers our discussion toward a more psychoanalytical dimension by illustrating that adaptation is not merely a matter of the textual relationship between an original and its remakes but profoundly interlaced with individual subjects—including authors, readers, adapters, and filmmakers as well as audiences—who find themselves experiencing an inexplicable sense of obligation while simultaneously provoked by intense desire. The penetrating insight that both philosophers share appears to suggest that screen adaptation is not solely an outcome of recent technological developments in modern mass media. Rather, a closer look at screen adaptation might return us to the constitutive myth—that is, the story of the tower of Babel—that is to unfold through its infinite adaptations. The field of screen adaptation, therefore, might offer an opportunity to contribute to the long-standing philosophical speculation surrounding human subjectivity, which, in Lacan's words, demands a detailed study of "men's relation to the letter"—a relationship that calls history itself into question.[30]

## The Real of a Text

Above, I introduced a simplified definition of the real in Lacan's configuration of the unconscious. Here, I wish to accentuate the sense of impossibility which Lacan's elaboration of the real strives to embrace. Although conceptualized on significantly different disciplinary grounds, Benjamin's designation of the translator's task and Derrida's deconstruction of the myth of Babel converge with Lacan's conceptualization of the real at the point of acknowledging what is left indecipherable and untranslatable in the subject's relationship to a text. It is interesting to note how Robert Stam reifies the metaphysical nexus shared by the three thinkers and initiates speculation on this nontextual factor in adaptation studies discourse: "The author, Proust taught us, is not necessarily a purposeful, self-present individual, but rather 'un autre moi.' Authors are sometimes not even aware of their own deepest

---

30. Jacques Lacan, "The Youth of Gide, or the Letter and Desire," in *Écrits: The First Complete Edition in English*, trans. Bruce Fink (New York and London: W. W. Norton & Company, 2006), 624. (Original emphasis.)

intentions."[31] Stam's recognition of the unstable and decentered subject in place of the author supports my shift in focus from the gap between texts or media to the gap within the subject as an assumed agent of creation, interpretation, and adaptation of a text. This shift depends on a discussion of the void or gap that Lacan terms the "real," by which he means "a point which cannot be grasped in the phenomenon, the point where the relation of the subject to the symbolic surfaces."[32] In borrowing Freud's expression, I propose that this dimension of impossibility constitutes the *navel* of adaptation.

From a Lacanian perspective, adaptation is not a cultural phenomenon that is distinct from the ontological condition of human subjects. Lacan supports this view by noting that "the living being is an adapted being."[33] Elsewhere, he declares that the subject can be defined only in transitional terms.[34] Bruce Fink provides a relevant exegesis of Lacan's definition of the subject in *The Lacanian Subject: Between Language and Jouissance*. Here, Stam's question about the authorial intention quoted above is conceptualized as the universal question of human subjectivity: according to Fink, "the speaker ... is not entirely in agreement with what he or she is saying."[35] Indeed, the irreversible split emerges like a mythical scar left behind by the collapse of the tower of Babel and is manifested at the moment when a speaking subject "while saying one thing, insinuates another."[36] In this light, every message is already translated and adapted even before it is enunciated and written down as an original text that calls for adaptation. If so, however, we may ask what the point is of interrogating this vanishing point of human discourse—namely, the Lacanian real—in a study of screen adaptation?

In addressing the above question, it will be useful to define the concept of the real—by which Lacan means "what is ungraspable"—as it relates

---

31. Stam, "Beyond Fidelity: The Dialogics of Adaptation," 57.

32. Jacques Lacan, *The Seminar of Jacques Lacan, Book II: The Ego in Freud's Theory and in the Techniques of Psychoanalysis 1954–1955*, ed. Jacques-Alain Miller and trans. Sylvana Tomaselli (New York and London: W. W. Norton & Company, 1991), 105.

33. Ibid., 106.

34. Jacques Lacan, *Seminar XIV: The Logic of Phantasy*, trans. Cormac Gallagher, 6. (Retrieved from www.lacaninireland.com.)

35. Bruce Fink, *The Lacanian Subject: Between Language and Jouissance* (Princeton, NJ: Princeton University Press, 1995), 45.

36. Ibid.

to the other two psychic dimensions—the symbolic and the imaginary. First, Lacan's conception of the real must be differentiated from that which we call reality. In his elaboration of the three psychic orders at play, that which the subject perceives as reality does not refer to a neutrally objective environment of their being. Reality is a construction of the symbolic on the screen provided by the imaginary. In other words, reality is none other than a sphere or bubble of the imaginary surrounding a speaking subject whose unconscious is constituted and sustained by the linguistic structure, as is captured by Lacan's famous aphorism—*the unconscious is structured like a language*. A closer look reveals that the components of a subject's reality are represented by an endless string of signifiers, akin to the matrix composed of infinite rows of letters in the Wachowskis' *Matrix* trilogy: the matrix, as the films' metaphor for the gloom reality of modern subjects, is the imaginary surface of a kaleidoscope built by a purely symbolic organization.

With reference to the above illustration of the symbolic scaffolding and imaginary surface of the subject's reality, it is possible to define the real as that which is encountered at the very limit of these two registers. In his 1960 seminar series, Lacan elucidated the position of the real, in one sense, in its relation to the imaginary by saying that "man ... is interesting for the hollow the image leaves empty."[37] Later, he returns to the point with a more elaborate, truly Lacanian concept of *objet petit a*, which refers to "a nonspecularizable remainder, a void that resides at the frontier between the imaginary and the real."[38] In the other sense, the real is associated with the innate limitation of the symbolic function, which invariably leaves something that has yet to be signified. The real is beyond representation and resists symbolization, and yet the paradoxical bond between the subject and the real as sheer impossibility is captured by Lacan when he notes that the real is "the central defect around which the dialectic of the advent of the subject to his own being in the relation to the Other turns."[39] In this light, Lacan

37. Jacques Lacan, *The Seminar of Jacques Lacan, Book VII: The Ethics of Psychoanalysis 1959–1960*, ed. Jacques-Alain Miller and trans. Dennis Porter (New York and London: W. W. Norton & Company, 1992), 196.

38. Lorenzo Chiesa, *Subjectivity and Otherness: A Philosophical Reading of Lacan* (Cambridge, MA: MIT Press, 2007), 106.

39. Jacques Lacan, *The Seminar of Jacques Lacan, Book XI: The Four Fundamental Concepts of Psychoanalysis*, ed. Jacques-Alain Miller and trans. Alan Sheridan (New York and London: W. W. Norton & Company, 1981), 205.

teaches us that the subject can encounter the real as a lacuna in the imaginary as well as a limitation in the symbolic. Paradoxically, owing to this built-in impossibility at the nexus of the human psyche, which Lacan terms the "real," a speaking subject is bound to repeated attempts to grasp it by means of the net of both imaginary and literary signifiers.

The above sketch of the real in the Lacanian field may to some extent already insinuate the ways in which the real is essential to understanding and identifying that which is (felt to be) lost in adaptation; that is, the real conceptualizes the vanishing mediator between the original text, which was written in letters, and its film adaptation, which is realized in images. The real is experienced only as negativity because it emerges as a lacuna at the juncture between the letter and the image. In this sense, this lacuna or gap manifests acutely in the course of adaptation because adaptation is an act of crossing over between the two dimensions, and hence the transposition is destined to disclose the fatal disjuncture in the middle. Insofar as the real is perceived as the irreparable loss created by the split between the symbolic constitution of a speaking subject and the imaginary arena of the ego, no attempt to transfer a story from page to screen can avoid evoking a sense of loss and, consequently, some degree of discontent owing to the exposure of the underlying lack. Put differently, the real conceivably limits the subject's "full" access to the symbolic and imaginary dimensions of not only the original text but also its film adaptations as long as the real is present as the structural lapse in human subjectivity in relation to both letter and image. Insofar as the present study interrogates what appears to be lost in adaptation with reference to the designation of the intrinsic lack in human psyche, the psychoanalytic conception of the real, whether manifest or implied, will remain at the nexus of the following chapters.

Above, I have attempted to identify the relative (not definitive) position of the real in terms of its relationship to the other two dimensions of the human psyche with reference to Lacan's theory of the three registers. The next step is to examine how the real manifests itself. First and foremost, Lacan pinpoints that the manifestation of the real is glimpsed by "that which always comes back to the same place."[40] If we recollect that the real points to the gap between the letter and the image, repeated attempts at adaptation trace a peculiar route in returning the subject to the site of "impediment, failure, split" between an original text and a film adaptation—a split that it is impossible to

---

40. Ibid., 42.

close.⁴¹ In other words, it is interesting to note that the task of realizing the meaning implied in an original on screen is never cut short by the dead end in which the subject encounters the impasse between the symbolic and the imaginary that is common to every screen adaptation. Rather, as Lacan describes, "this discovery becomes a rediscovery and, furthermore, it is ready to steal away again and, thus, establishing the dimension of loss."⁴² Indeed, as Lacan points out, the biblical scene of Babel is rediscovered in the pursuit of what appears to have been lost in screen adaptations, inasmuch as the myth of Babel already related the rediscovery or reinscription of the divine one-ness that had long since been lost.

That dimension of loss organized by the *repetition* of discovery is what Lacan terms the "real." In this sense, the real in the text—where "the *modi essendi* of things were identical with the *modi significandi*"— designates the primordial and mythical dimension of what appears to become lost "again" in translation and adaptation.⁴³ This loss, which is embedded in a text and perpetuates a journey of adaptation, is, I wish to highlight, what this chapter has sought in Benjamin's pure language, whose irreparability is acknowledged by Derrida and which transformed every speaking subject simultaneously into a debtor and an heir. Therefore, the psychoanalytic concept of repetition explains how the adapter's task is permanently tied to the real of the text, where every speaking subject makes the unwanted yet unavoidable discovery of what had to be lost even before their inception as a subject.

Benjamin, Derrida, and Lacan all confirm the gravity of this loss, which far exceeds desire and to which Derrida directs our attention when he construes the original text as the seat of the Law for adaptation. Indubitably, what drew Freud and Lacan to the dimension of the loss was its gravity, which appeared to tie their patients' symptoms to sites of unbearable trauma that was literally beyond words. Freud and Lacan confronted this enigmatic nexus, presented in its sheer negativity or absence, in their praxis, which hauls the subject to the innate gap in human discourse.

Indeed, it is not merely desire that they all encountered in search of their explanation of the impasse in human discourse. Likewise, in this book's attempt to seek the secret driving force of adaptation, the real as

41. Ibid., 25.
42. Ibid.
43. Umberto Eco (1999), 40. (My emphasis.)

a concept transcends the conventional perspective that regards desire as a primal cause of human discourse and reaches out to the philosophical notion of *cause*. Herein, cause refers to something that exists prior to and beyond desire, a desire often taken as an immediate motivation of the subject's act. With reference to Kant's essay *An Attempt to Introduce the Concept of Negative Quantities into Philosophy*, Lacan explains that it is the dimension of the loss, or the gap in Kant's term, that "the function of cause has always presented to any conceptual apprehension."[44] What Lacan intends to set forth here by means of the conceptual elaboration of the real as a gateway to the ultimate cause of any human act is none other than the very name given to this cause in psychoanalysis—the unconscious. Therefore, by encountering the real as such, it is possible for psychoanalysis to approach the impasse of authentic human reality—in a negative, not positive, sense—termed the unconscious. The word "approach" must be read as literally as possible, because it never connotes "comprehend" or "understand." While taking care not to make the unconscious an object of conceptualization, Lacan's intention is to mark the gravity and centrality of the dimension of the loss through the conception of the real. This becomes clearer when he compares the real with the navel of the unconscious—that is, "to designate [the subjects'] unknown centre—which is simply, like the same anatomical navel that represents it, *that gap* of which I have already spoken."[45]

The lengthy theoretical discussion above is intended not only to emphasize the gravity of the original text's real as a magnetic force behind the repetitive loop of adaptation; it is also intended as a foundation for the ultimate psychoanalytic concept—the unconscious—which lies at the nexus of the chapters that follow. Here, I wish to clarify that the four case studies after this chapter aim to approach the unconscious as a primary cause operating in the field of film adaptation from a psychoanalytic stance. Hence, the study may diverge from the more traditional frame of textual analysis, which views the signified as the cause that produces its signifier, instead aiming to uncover a hidden connection where the signifier is the cause and the signified the effect. These case studies seek to identify the moment of discontinuity, split, and detachment between a text and its intended meaning, an original and its film adaptation, or the spoken and written words of an adapter and their desire, because the unconscious can be glimpsed

---

44. Lacan, *Seminar XI*, 21.
45. Ibid., 23.

only when "something stumbles" in the seamlessly coherent reality that appears to function by virtue of the smooth operation of the symbolic and the imaginary registers.[46]

I wish to close the chapter with a quotation from Bruce Fink that reiterates from a psychoanalytical perspective what Benjamin attempted to articulate in his use of the term pure language and what Derrida sought to evoke through the image of the collapsed tower of Babel. Fink writes:

> It is the non-representational nature of the real that brings on repetition, requiring the subject to return to that place of the lost object, the lost satisfaction. Every other satisfaction pales in comparison with the one that was lost, and the subject repetitively returns to the site of that absence in the hope of obtaining the real Thing, and yet forever missing it.[47]

As such, the subject is thus subject to the task of an adapter, who experiences an overwhelming compulsion to translate the lost Truth written in the Benjaminian pure language to access that which, as Derrida sees, long remained forbidden. However, we must remember that it is not bitter despair but rather incomparable satisfaction—if we recall Lacan's concept of *jouissance*—that propels the subject through the infinite loop of adaptation.

46. Ibid., 25.
47. Bruce Fink, "The Real Cause of Repetition," in *Reading Seminar XI: Lacan's Four Fundamental Concepts of Psychoanalysis*, ed. Richard Feldstein, Bruce Fink and Maire Jaanus (Albany, NY: State University of New York Press, 1995), 228.

# 2

## THE OEDIPUS COMPLEX IN FILM ADAPTATIONS OF SHAKESPEARE'S *HAMLET*

> We see, then, that the differentiation of the super-ego from the ego is no matter of chance: it represents the most important characteristic of the development both of the individual and of the species: indeed, by giving permanent expression to the influence of the parents it perpetuates the existence of the factors to which it owes its origin.
> —Sigmund Freud, *The Ego and the Id*

> Claudius: But you must know your father lost a father,
> That father lost, lost his, and the survivor bound
> In filial obligation for some term
> To do obsequious sorrow: But to persevere
> In obstinate condolement is a course
> Of impious stubbornness.
> —William Shakespeare, *Hamlet* (Act I: Scene 2)

### *The Ghost of the Dead Author*

The name "Shakespeare" occupies a secure position in the field of modern culture, indeed more so now than during the playwright's own lifetime. Like the spectral presence of the Ghost in *Hamlet*, Shakespeare has cast an inescapable shadow over numerous fields in the arts and popular culture, influencing every aspect of the development of modern subjectivity. Harold Bloom notes that the force exerted by Shakespeare is constitutive of our modern self or psychology inasmuch as his literary representation "compel[s] 'reality' (be it Platonic or Humean, Hegelian or Freudian) to reveal aspects of itself we previously could not discern."[1] The unusual expansion of influence and authority that accompanies this name may be attributed to several factors: most agree on Shakespeare's genius as a dramatist and poet; some laud his penetrating satire, while others praise his hidden philosophical depth or psychoanalytical insight. A vast corpus of Shakespearean scholarship has accumulated in pursuit of more robust support for his perennial authority. Most of these "archaeological" inquiries, in their attempts to discover Shakespeare's hidden values, express little doubt that this eminent influence originates from the very contents of Shakespeare's texts. In other words, such studies seek to lend a tangible materiality to Shakespeare's ghostly presence.

However, a different approach supports the notion that the Bard's incontestable status may result from the particular—even peculiar—psychic response elicited by his texts in individual readers and audiences: that is, our experiences of Shakespearean dramas have been predetermined for us even before we recognize the value and virtue of Shakespeare's texts. Put differently, what is significant in our relation to such a cultural legacy is not the message that the texts deliver across the intervening centuries but rather our expected response to messages from a ghost. The apparently spontaneous respect paid to a certain cultural legacy is predetermined by a set of psychological codes that regulate the reaction to a historical heritage.

In this light, we may argue that the structure of the play *Hamlet*, which opens with the awe-struck watchmen and Horatio, illustrates that the pivotal element for understanding the play is not the Ghost's message but rather how individual characters and, above all, the prince Hamlet respond to the apparition of the dead king. Herein, our analytic focus can be shifted from the textual level to the psychological dimension of human subjects in confrontation with the influence of past generations, which is experienced as the return of a ghost that should be buried deep and remain silent. This shift reveals more secrets about the present and ourselves than about the past and the ghost—that is, about the fundamental dimension of the speaking subject, who is necessarily the haunted subject "as being watched by the dead other and appearing

---

1. Harold Bloom, "Introduction," in *Modern Critical Interpretations: William Shakespeare's Hamlet*, ed. Harold Bloom (New York, New Haven, CT, and Philadelphia, PA: Chelsea House Publishers, 1986), 6–7.

before him as if before the law," if borrowing Collin Davis's words.[2] To examine the cultural transformation that is effected in the process of film adaptation, the shift also facilitates an investigation of screen adaptation from a perspective that contrasts sharply with the traditional approach, which seeks to account for the prolonged and unimpeachable authority of canonical texts over film adaptations. In this chapter, I suggest that the same rule or law that determines our relationship to what emerges from the past may also pave the way for appreciating the adaptation of canonical texts such as Shakespeare's *Hamlet*.

Governed by this "law" of the dead, modern popular culture has constantly explored how we might renew and perpetuate the authority of Shakespeare, who has been dead for four hundred years. Through his undeniable authority, this dead author survives and influences individuals' lives across time and space. It is thus unsurprising that cinema's forefathers explored the potential of their new medium as a vehicle for Shakespeare's dramas as early as 1899—that is, only three years after the Lumière brothers' first film.[3] Moreover, it is not difficult to imagine that, for those wishing to follow in Shakespeare's footsteps by creating a *vision* of his texts through the new medium, the dead author's words functioned as an irresistible command, one which they did not dare to defy. Consequently, the very words that were delivered by actors on the Elizabethan stage continue to be uttered by a rebellious gun-toting teen Romeo in a dystopian desert (Baz Luhrmann's *Romeo + Juliet*, 1996) or an amateur filmmaking Hamlet in a contemporary urban landscape (Michael Almereyda's *Hamlet*, 2000).

Most filmmakers appear unwilling to modernize the words penned by this literary ancestor, carefully limiting themselves to updating the audiovisual aesthetic that is implied and effected by his words. Of course, it is not to deny that there has been the critical and commercial movement to democratize Shakespeare against elitism in alignment with the drive to frame Shakespeare as an entrepreneur. Nevertheless, the cultural authority and paternal influence that Shakespeare's words

---

2. Colin Davis, *Haunted Subjects: Deconstruction, Psychoanalysis and the Return of the Dead* (New York: Palgrave Macmillan, 2007), 143.

3. In 1899, William Kennedy-Laurie Dickson, who was an associate of Thomas Edison, shot a scene from Shakespeare's play *King John* in London. See Kenneth Rothwell's *A History of Shakespeare on Screen*, 2nd edition (Cambridge: Cambridge University Press, 2004) and Samuel Crowl's *Shakespeare and Film: A Norton Guide* (New York and London: W. W. Norton & Company, 2008).

exert over film adaptations of his plays have not been diminished and appear to have become even more resilient. Indeed, as we move ever farther from Shakespeare's time, although the material reality—that is, the authentic look—of his plays may fade, his words become more compelling. This is encapsulated in the clinging farewell that resonates long after the ghost of Hamlet's father has disappeared from the stage: "Adieu, adieu, adieu. Remember me."[4]

## Super-ego versus Super Ego

Even if we accept that some screen adaptations of Shakespeare's plays deliberately resist the influence of the original texts, the process of adapting Shakespeare's dramas for the screen is—of all adaptations—the most subject to the author's spectral presence and the irresistible nature of his authority. Beginning with the undiminished influence exerted by the name of this dead author, this chapter attempts to identify the characteristic psychological traits that are common to film adaptations of canonical literary originals.

To construct a theoretical framework for investigating those characteristics, the following discussion will employ psychoanalytic concepts such as the super-ego and the ego, which are the two major agencies coexisting and contesting with each other in the individual psyche. The application of the psychoanalytic perspective, which regards human subjectivity as a site of the continuous conflict between the super-ego and the ego, will lend a psychological dimension to the pervasive cultural practice of film adaptation at a fundamental level. As quoted above, Freud observed the persistent and even haunting quality of the parental influence of the previous generation on the subject, defining it as a psychic agency called the super-ego and theorizing the super-ego as intimately related to the ego of the human subject. He investigated how this supervisory and controlling force from past generations operates not only in the individual psyche but also within the cultural sphere. In recognizing the same traits as those that characterize the relationship between originals and their

---

4. William Shakespeare, *Hamlet* (I. 5. 91), ed. T.J.B. Spencer (London: Penguin Books, 1980), 92.

screen adaptations, we may plausibly suggest that film adaptations of canonical literary texts such as Shakespeare's plays are, to varying degrees, a cultural manifestation of the interrelation between the super-ego and the ego.

Among the various canonical originals that have been adapted as films, Shakespeare's *Hamlet* offers a particularly illustrative example for the investigation of the super-egotistical authority that original texts exert over their screen adaptations. The play centers on the problematic relationship between Hamlet and the ghost of his dead father. The fundamental drama at the play's core, Hamlet's heated internal conflict, results from his encounter with the authority of the ghost who wishes him to revenge. As noted by several literary and psychoanalytic commentators including Freud, Jones, and Lacan, the play's psychological orientation compels the reader or spectator to confront the space between the past and the present and between the dead and the living. In this sense, Shakespeare's *Hamlet* provides us with a proper locus for a discussion of the psychic dynamics between the super-ego and the ego in the course of the human subject's development. However, before investigating the relation between *Hamlet* and its screen adaptations as an exemplary site representing such a psychological organization of the subject, it is appropriate to examine the Freudian conception of the super-ego and the ego in depth.

Freud, from as early on as his completion of *The Interpretation of Dreams* (1900), recognized that dreams exert a "mental agency which thus remains awake the censor to whom we have had to attribute such a powerful restricting influence" upon the works of the ego seeking pleasure through wish-fulfillment in dreams.[5] After this initial acknowledgment of the psyche's intrinsic self-censoring agency, Freud abandoned his search for the genesis of the ego's segmented structure and proceeded instead to conceptualize the unconscious and establish the core of psychoanalysis around the concept of the unconscious as

---

5. Sigmund Freud, *The Interpretation of Dreams* (1900), trans. James Strachey (London: George Allen & Unwin, 1953), 504.

a descriptive, topological, and functional term.⁶ Thus, without much critical attention, the ego, including a self-regarding component within it, is often regarded as oppositional to the unconscious and as a barrier—even an encumbrance—to accessing the unknown territory of the unconscious.

Yet the significance and the complexity of the ego gradually occupy a central place in Freud's writings from *On Narcissism: An Introduction* (1914). He resumes the theoretical elaboration of the concept of the ego and positions it at the center of his theory on narcissism: "The libido that has been withdrawn from the external world has been directed to the ego and thus gives rise to an attitude which may be called narcissism."⁷ Hereby an ideal ego is formed as a part of the ego, whose aim is to return some part of the libido back to the ego. However, the constant interruption of external forces—the first and most fundamental of which Freud designates as the Oedipus complex—makes it hard for the ego to maintain the narcissistic enclosure centered on an ideal ego that has become the ego's ultimate counterpart.

Consequently, another idealized position emerges within the ego as "the substitute for the lost narcissism of his childhood in which he was his own ideal."⁸ This is *the ego ideal* that, for a certain period,

---

6. The major works in this period—such as "On Dreams" (1901; *S.E., V*), "The Psychopathology of Everyday Life"(1904; *S.E., VI*), "Three Essays on the Theory of Sexuality" (1905; *S.E., VI*), "On the Sexual Theories of Children" (1908; *S.E., IX*), "Analysis of Phobia in a Five-Year-Old Boy" (1909; *S.E., X*), "Notes upon a Case of Obsessional Neurosis" (1909; *S.E., X*)—elaborate the relationship of the unconscious to pathological symptoms as well as everyday experiences from a perspective that particularly emphasizes the libidinal (i.e., sexual) force at work "underneath." "Five Lectures on Psycho-Analysis" (1910; *S.E., XI*) provides a concise summary of these works.

7. Sigmund Freud, "On Narcissism: An Introduction," in *The Standard Edition of the Complete Psychological Works of Sigmund Freud: Volume XIV*, trans. James Strachey (London: The Hogarth Press and the Institute of Psycho-Analysis, 1957), 75.

8. Ibid., 94. Freud uses the two terms—an ego ideal and the super-ego—indiscriminately in several subsequent works. For instance, in *The Ego and the Id*, Freud parenthesizes "Ego Ideal" and puts it next to "the Super-ego," as though the ego ideal were synonymous with the super-ego, in the title of the third section of the book.

## 2. Oedipus Complex in Film Adaptations of Hamlet 43

Freud synonymously uses with *the super-ego*. The remarkable discovery in relation to this psychic agency is that the ego suffers as a result of the (co-)existence of the super-ego because it feels like there is an invisible eye that "constantly watches the actual ego and measures it by that ideal."[9] We are reminded that, along with the vigilant nature of the super-ego, the super-ego, despite its overpowering force, cannot be perceived as a separate or independent entity: it can only be recognized in the ego's illusionary sense of being watched and supervised. Freud's remark on this sensation that one is being watched not only explains the psychological origin of the constant sensation that one is being judged and criticized, which the directors of *Hamlet* films confess to experiencing. An aesthetic challenge should also be considered in association with the very task of adapting *Hamlet* to screen: this challenge is to actualize and materialize on screen the ghost of the dead father, the super-ego, whose menacing gaze is omnipresent throughout the entire play, despite its limited on-stage presence.

Another analytic link may be traced between the Freudian theory of the super-ego and the study of *Hamlet* films: Freud conceptualizes the emergence of the super-ego in terms of the resolution of the Oedipus complex, which has provided many of the play's critical reviewers with a key to understanding Hamlet's (in)famous indecision. In *The Ego and the Id* (1923), Freud focuses on his second topological structure, consisting of the ego (*Ich*), the id (*Es*), and the super-ego (*Über-Ich*), following—and, to a certain degree, replacing—his previous topology of the unconscious, the preconscious, and the conscious. Here, he suggests that the link between the Oedipus complex and the formation of the super-ego elucidates the parental nature of the super-ego as it relates to the ego. As the fear and anxiety aroused by the Oedipus complex are intensified, the ego recognizes the need to repress its own illegitimate Oedipal wishes and imports a restrictive, monitoring character from the parental figures. Such a process results in the libidinal energy being channeled into two kinds of identification—identification with the father (the positive complex) and identification with the mother (the negative/inverted complex). Freud expounds the outcome of the Oedipus complex and its resolution through identification as follows:

> The broad general outcome ... may, therefore, be taken to be the forming of a precipitate in the ego, consisting of these two

9. Ibid., 95.

identifications in some way united with each other. This modification of the ego retains its special position; it confronts the other contents of the ego as an ego ideal or super-ego.[10]

In forming the supervisory agency within itself, the feeble infantile ego internalizes the paternal authority that is borrowed from the figure of the father. This process of introjection represents the ego's self-sacrificing efforts to repress its own forbidden wishes, even at the cost of incorporating the discomfiting figure within itself. Freud assumes that the subject is more likely to introject the figure of the father, whom the child's ego perceives as a major obstacle to the satisfaction of their Oedipal wishes. Consequently, "the super-ego retains the character of the father," and this internalized paternal authority functions as a deeply internal call for repression, inhibition, and conscience in the subject's life.[11] We should remember, however, that Freud does not resolve but rather leaves open the discussion about the ambivalent positioning of the super-ego as a paternal authority, simply by leaving unexamined the maternal trace ascribed to the super-ego in its constitution as the outcome of identification with both paternal and maternal figures. In his discussion of *Hamlet*, Lacan attempts to address this ambivalence by weaving a traditional interrogation of the play—a quintessentially Freudian interpretation of *Hamlet* as an Oedipal drama—with Freud's originality in reading both paternal and maternal aspects in the character of the super-ego. In this sense, *Hamlet* once again functions as a locus for the encounter between the past and the present in the form of the adaptation of psychoanalytic theory itself.

Despite the super-ego's dominant position in its relationship with the ego, the super-ego cannot exist or function without the ego, which must precede it. Regarding the formation of the ego as the nexus of our sense of self, Freud defines the ego as "the part of the id which has been modified by the direct influence of the external world through the medium of the Pcpt.–Cs. (the perceptual system of the conscious)."[12] Contrary to the ego, which is formed as an outcome of the constant transaction between internal and external reality, the super-ego is the introjected form of the parental influence, an inner voice that regulates

10. Sigmund Freud, "The Ego and the Id," in *The Standard Edition of the Complete Psychological Works of Sigmund Freud: Volume XIX*, trans. James Strachey (London: The Hogarth Press and the Institute of Psycho-Analysis, 1963), 34.

11. Ibid.

12. Ibid., 36.

the ego's relationship with the external world. Hence, we may understand why Freud describes the relationship between the ego and the super-ego as an ongoing battle rather than a transitional conflict—the continuous confrontation is what Freud describes as "the conflict between what is real and what is psychic."[13] For Freud, the ego, as the representative of perceived external reality in the present ("what is real"), confronts the super-ego as the representative of internal command inherited from the parental authority of the past ("what is psychic"). In other words, the intersection between the ego and the super-ego occurs at the very site at which the subject endlessly renegotiates the boundary between the surrounding world and their internal impulses as well as between the present and the past.

Moreover, Freud's theory of the super-ego expands its scope by recognizing the same agency at work when culture based on that of a previous generation vigorously seeks to leave its mark on the psyche of future generations. In his later work *Civilization and Its Discontents* (1930), Freud articulates a more discursive dimension of the super-ego, arguing that through internalization of the parental authority and influence on domestic and social senses alike, the super-ego "leads to the survival of what is past … [and] makes itself felt in the fact that fundamentally things remain as they were at the beginning."[14] Freudian theory suggests, therefore, that we should recognize a hidden meaning in the media practice under discussion here: the adaptation of literary texts from the past into present-day film texts refers not only to the recycling or commodification of cultural legacy; rather, the locus of screen adaptation is an exemplary cultural site at which the incessant confrontation and negotiation between the super-ego and the ego in the construction of the human subject can be captured in its most visible form.

As summarized above, Freud conceptualized the constitution of the super-ego as a supervisory agency "over and above" the ego. In this light, it is possible to conceive that a canonical text such as Shakespeare's *Hamlet* might position itself as a super-egotistical *demand* that dominates the adaptation process and the film text as well as the audience's reception of it. However, equal recognition should be afforded to the fundamental role played by cinematic descendants—more precisely the egos of

13. Ibid.

14. Sigmund Freud, "Civilization and Its Discontent," in *The Standard Edition of the Complete Psychological Works of Sigmund Freud: Volume XXI*, trans. James Strachey (London: The Hogarth Press and the Institute of Psycho-Analysis, 1961), 125.

future generations—in initiating the process by which original texts are transformed. Although the present or the ego is under the spell of the past or the super-ego, the ultimate motivation for this cultural practice is none other than the *desire* of filmmakers and audiences to actualize images that are only vaguely evoked by written texts.

In exploring this other aspect of film adaptation, Lacan's mirror stage theory may lead us to comprehend the narcissistic vigor reinstated by and in film adaptations. Lacan's influential theory on the formation and function of the ego in the constitution of the subject is germinated in his article "The Mirror Stage as Formative of the *I* Function as Revealed in Psychoanalytic Experience" and is developed further in his first two seminar series conducted from 1953 to 1955.[15] In these works, Lacan describes "the imaginary origin of the ego's function" as part of his attempt to establish the boundary of the ego through articulating its functional limit in constituting and controlling the subject of the unconscious. His aim is to reduce the ego's supremacy as a major site of psychoanalytic treatment in opposition to the ego psychology, which places the emphasis on the ego's ability to mediate internal forces and external demands.[16] Lacan describes the process whereby the infant "recognizes his own image as such in a mirror," identifies with this "imago" that is exterior to its own body, and misconceives itself to be

---

15. The paper to which I refer is the revised 1949 version of Lacan's paper of the same title first delivered in 1936 as it is printed in *Écrits: The First Complete Edition in English*, trans. Bruce Flink (New York and London: W. W. Norton & Company, 2006), 75–81. The seminar series referred to here is *The Seminar of Jacques Lacan: Book I Freud's Papers on Techniques 1953-1954*, ed. Jacques-Alain Miller and trans. John Forrester (New York and London: W. W. Norton & Company, 1991) and *The Seminar of Jacques Lacan: Book II The Ego in Freud's Theory and in the Technique of Psychoanalysis 1954-1955*, ed. Jacques-Alain Miller and trans. Sylvana Tomaselli (New York and London: W. W. Norton & Company, 1991).

16. Jacques Lacan, "On Narcissism," in *The Seminar of Jacques Lacan: Book I Freud's Papers on Techniques 1953-1954*, ed. Jacques-Alain Miller and trans. John Forrester (New York and London: W. W. Norton & Company, 1988), 115. The term "ego-psychology" refers to the trend of psychoanalysis that is primarily based on Freud's structure of ego, id, and super-ego. Ego-psychology places considerable emphasis on the function of the ego that mediates between the internal impulses (id), moralistic command (super-ego), and external reality. The term itself appeared and was established and consolidated in Anna Freud's *The Ego and the Mechanisms of Defence* (1936) and Heinz Hartmann's *Ego Psychology and the Problem of Adaptation* (1939).

this specular image.[17] Contrary to the presupposition that the ego exists from the human being's inception, Lacan's notion of the ego must be developed through this illusionary identification. Thus, Lacan carefully maps out the development of the ego whereas Freud placed greater focus on that of the super-ego.

Most interestingly, the ego's genesis is facilitated by auto-erotic instincts, which "are there right from the start."[18] The mirror image invested with primordial auto-erotic instincts appears desirable to the ego, and this image is *the ideal ego*—that is, the counterpart to the narcissistic ego. The ideal image anticipated by the ego accompanies the ego from its genesis until the end and "will also be the rootstock of secondary identifications."[19] The bond between the ego and its ideal image, Lacan suggests, is one of the most powerful ties in the human psyche, and this primordial link will permanently affect the ego's ability to incorporate external reality into "*I*." Therefore, the desire to materialize presymbolic images provoked in the course of reading is associated with the most primordial unconscious search for an image, a search that is driven by the ego's need for identification. These images are the ever-unsatisfactory substitutes for their original form, which is an idealized image of the ego itself. Therefore, the essence of Lacan's theoretical elaboration is to explain the ego's function in close relationship to a specular image or the other (*autre*) that now stands in place of the original narcissistic image.[20]

Lacan indicates that there is a highly consistent dimension to the ego's relationship to every image offered in support of this imaginary identification: "this form [imago or the ideal ego] situates the agency known as the ego ... in a fictional direction that will forever remain irreducible for any single individual or, that will only asymptomatically approach the subject's becoming."[21] Hence, the ego's incessant demand for images for identification indicates that the subject cannot escape the retrospective drive but continues to return to the site of the loss

---

17. Jacques Lacan, "The Mirror Stage as Formative of the I Function as Revealed in psychoanalytic Experience," in *Écrits: The First Complete Edition in English*, trans. Bruce Flink (New York and London: W. W. Norton & Company, 2006), 76.

18. Lacan, "On Narcissism," 115.

19. Lacan, "The Mirror Stage," 76.

20. See Jacques Lacan, *The Seminar of Jacques Lacan: Book II The Ego in Freud's Theory and in the Technique of Psychoanalysis 1954–1955* (1988), 243–5.

21. Lacan, "The Mirror Stage," 76.

of the primal oneness between the subject and the world before the symbolic interruption of the Name-of-the-Father. In other words, the primal dimension of the ego's pre-Oedipal identification with the image keeps reminding the subject, which is captured in the symbolic domain, of its imaginary origin. Indeed, this imaginary identification forever returns the subject to "the joint between the Imaginary and the Symbolic."[22] Therefore, Lacan's theory that the ego is formulated and fixed in the structure of the imaginary identification casts a different light on screen adaptation from that cast by Freud's theory of the super-ego: it contributes to understanding how film adaptations provide the canvas for the modern ego to become *enlarged* through imaginary identification with the larger-than-life on-screen images while the commanding words of literary "fathers," such as Shakespeare, function as the super-ego in regulating and inhibiting the excessive expansion of the ego, which seeks a screen on which to project its magnified imago.

Interestingly, the theoretical development and discovery enabled by the acknowledgment of the mirror stage constructs a nexus with other concepts in the first period of Lacan's return to Freud. Lacan's mirror stage theory opens up his detailed discussion of the ego's formation as elementary and constitutive of the subject. Indeed, in understanding the link between Freud and Lacan, the mirror stage theory may be regarded as Lacan's elaboration of Freud's theory of the ego, which ultimately leads Lacan to the concept of the imaginary. As the development of his first two seminar series reveals, the Lacanian structure of the imaginary, the symbolic, and the real was gradually formulated from the conceptualization of the imaginary as the field of the ego into a more extended study of the super-ego as the basis for the Lacanian symbolic. Therein, the psychic contest between the ego and the super-ego functions as a conceptual bridge that connects the Freudian topology of the ego and the super-ego with the Lacanian structure of the imaginary and the symbolic.

The ultimate intersecting point of these two theories is, of course, the Oedipus complex, in its close relationship to the conflict between the ego and the super-ego, as detailed above. Hence, the Oedipus complex emerges as a central framework within which to trace the adaptation of Freud's reading of *Hamlet* to that of Lacan. In other words, the significance of the Oedipus complex lies not in its significance as Freud's answer to the riddle of Hamlet but from the fact that the Oedipus

---

22. Jacques Lacan, *The Seminar of Jacques Lacan: Book I Freud's Papers on Techniques 1953–1954* (1988), 137.

complex itself is the site of a fundamental enigma entailing an endless series of new answers, solutions, or interpretations. Indeed, the Oedipus complex itself is the ghost that constantly returns through numerous artistic creations, such as Shakespeare's *Hamlet*, to sustain a mysterious and mythological domain of the human subject at the juncture between the ego and the super-ego or, in Lacan, between the imaginary and the symbolic. Likewise, every theoretical movement in or strand of psychoanalysis returns to this mythical locus, where the infant born in an almost-animalistic state mysteriously becomes a human subject who is structured through the net of the Law and civilization.

Above all, the unremittingly conflicting agencies of subjectivity—that is, the super-ego versus the enlarged, empowered super ego—reveal the traumatic reality that the subject is never settled within the boundary of the Law even after having undergone Oedipalization. Just like the young prince himself, the subject is doomed to be perpetually haunted by the ghost who is constantly seeking an opportunity to return and to place the subject once again at the traumatic site of Oedipalization. Similarly, the ghost of the dead author haunts adapters, film directors, and audiences in the auditorium, who seek the ego's pleasure through its enlargement via on-screen images for identification.

## *Reading* Hamlet *through the Oedipus Complex*

To measure the influence of the Oedipus complex on the play's treatment in screen adaptations, it is necessary to understand the link between Oedipus and Hamlet as they appear in both psychoanalytical discourse and literary criticism.[23] Above all, Hamlet is not an original character

---

23. Here and later on, I refer to Ernest Jones's paper "The Oedipus Complex as an Explanation of Hamlet's Mystery: A Study of Motive," which was published in the *American Journal of Psychology* in 1910 and is an original version of his much-elaborated and edited work in book form *Hamlet and Oedipus* (1949). The reason for this adherence to the original version is that, aside from the fact that the 1910 paper offers an original form of Jones's idea freshly influenced by Freud's theorization of the Oedipus complex appeared in *The Interpretation of the Dreams* (1900), this article is the text in the scholastic interrelation with Freud's further elaboration of the Oedipus complex: immediately after its publication, Freud himself read this article and referred to it on various occasions in works revised or written after Jones's article. For instance, the 1911 edition of *The Interpretation of Dreams* includes a footnote on Jones's article: "The views on the problem of Hamlet contained in the above passage have since been confirmed and supported with fresh arguments in an extensive study by Dr. Ernest Jones of Toronto (1910)."

created by the author; rather, his origin is as mythological as that of Oedipus in Sophocles' *Oedipus Rex*. This ultimate Shakespearean hero, who is often believed to represent the birth of modern subjectivity, was ironically adapted from a long line of Roman and other European legends of a noble young man intent on exacting vengeance for his father's death. However, it was Shakespeare who transformed the legend's adventurous modality into a tragedy with psychological depth. This insightful transformation elucidated the complexity of the human mind and, three centuries later, attracted the interest of Freud, whose theory of psychoanalysis was then in its infancy. Initially, Freud intuitively rather than analytically linked this story of the Danish prince with the recently developed theory of infant sexuality, a radical view of humanity that also originates from his reading of the Greek tragedy *Oedipus Rex*. *Hamlet*, for Freud, exemplifies and epitomizes the universality and function of the Oedipus complex, which, as he observed in many pathological cases, manifests in various neurotic symptoms.

In return, the psychoanalytic theory of the Oedipus complex offers many literary critics a more plausible explanation of Hamlet's inaction. Critical readings from both fields of study have centered on the fundamental question of why the young prince interminably procrastinates the slaughter of his father's murderer. Hamlet has sufficient reason and means to kill his criminal uncle Claudius, who has violated his mother, the Queen, and usurped the crown of Denmark from his own head. Nevertheless, Hamlet appears to stumble at every opportunity quite deliberately. According to Ernest Jones, "The central mystery in it, namely the cause of Hamlet's hesitancy in seeking to obtain revenge for the murder of his father, has well been called the Sphinx of modern literature."[24] Freud's first reading of the play and its hero along with his analysis of the author can be found in *The Interpretation of Dreams* (1900). Therein, Freud opens up a new perspective on both the character Hamlet and Shakespeare in the light of the Oedipus complex:

> Another of the great creations of tragic poetry, Shakespeare's *Hamlet*, has its roots in the same soil as *Oedipus Rex*. But the changed treatment of the same material reveals the whole difference in the mental life of these two widely separated epochs of civilization: the

---

24. Ernest Jones, "The Oedipus Complex as an Explanation of Hamlet's Mystery: A Study of Motive," *American Journal of Psychology* 21 (1910): 74.

secular advance of repression in the emotional life of mankind. In the *Oedipus* the child's wishful phantasy that underlies it is brought into the open and realized as it would be in a dream. In *Hamlet* it remains repressed; and—just as in the case of a neurosis—we only learn of its existence from its inhibiting consequences. Strangely enough, the overwhelming effect produced by the more modern tragedy has turned out to be compatible with the fact that people have remained completely in the dark as to the hero's character. The play is built up on Hamlet's hesitations over fulfilling the task of revenge that is assigned to him; but the text offers no reasons or motives for these hesitations and an immense variety of attempts at interpreting them have failed to produce a result.[25]

Here and in several other places, Freud advances two main points: one is that Hamlet and Oedipus are the same in terms of the content of their veiled wishes; the other is that they differ with respect to the weight or intensity of repression that rests on their forbidden unconscious impulses. Hamlet has the same unconscious wishes that Oedipus has—that is, the desire for the mother's love and for the father's death. However, the repression that inhibits these incestuous and murderous wishes is relatively flimsy in Oedipus' case: although Oedipus was unaware of his actions in committing patricide and taking his own mother as his wife, the truth of his deeds or crimes eventually becomes clear to both him and the play's other characters as well as to the audience. In *Hamlet*, by contrast, that which is repressed in the deepest layers of the hero's psyche remains unknown and unconscious not only to the young prince himself but also to the author who created the character and to the audience. Freud appears to have alighted on the unconscious motive for Hamlet's hesitation in the latent and invisible Oedipus complex. Freud's discovery of Hamlet's Oedipus complex allows him as well as other readers of *Hamlet* to find a plausible solution to the mystery of Hamlet's vacillation.

According to this psychoanalytical account, Hamlet unconsciously encounters his own repressed childhood wishes realized in Claudius' crimes—to kill his father and marry his mother. Freud explains, "Thus the loathing which should drive him on to revenge is replaced in him by *self-reproaches*, by *scruples of conscience*, which remind him that he

---

25. Freud, *The Interpretation of Dreams*, 264–5.

himself is literally no better than the sinner whom he is to punish."²⁶ Therefore, the reason that Hamlet cannot exact vengeance in the manner commanded by the Ghost, is that what he ought to revenge is what he himself most desires. However, this desire, as realized by criminal Claudius, cannot surface to the level of consciousness. According to Freud, the psychological complexity underlying Hamlet's hesitancy manifests itself as none other than the accumulated weight of mental repression on the more civilized individuals who wrote, acted, watched, and read the play, whereas the childhood wishes of "the same soil" can be acted out by the mythical figure and become conscious in the ancient drama *Oedipus Rex*. It is interesting that the villain's crime, driven by Oedipal impulses, is judged and abhorred by both Hamlets Sr. and Jr. in the play. The indifference that other characters of the play exhibit toward the matter of Claudius' murderous deed and hasty marriage to the King's widow indicates that the play hinges more on an internal and psychological complex and less on external and moral conflicts among society's members.

Jones's 1910 essay, "The Oedipus Complex as an Explanation of Hamlet's Mystery: A Study of Motive," begins with and expands on Freud's insight that the play's hero manifests the repressed Oedipus complex, and Jones emphasizes that the play is an artistic creation betraying Shakespeare's unconscious. Jones, in detail, discusses how "The artist … gives expression to the creative impulse in a form which satisfies his internal need, but in terms which he cannot translate into easily comprehensible language."²⁷ Thus, the play's multifariously disguised expression of the unconscious impulses in Shakespeare himself cannot but appear obscure and distorted at the conscious level of the text. Nonetheless, it seems obvious that the latent level of the play strikes at "problems of vital interest to the human heart"; otherwise, *Hamlet* would not have enjoyed such consistent and unwavering appeal to its various audiences.²⁸

Jones elaborately refutes pervasive critical views of the play's hero, among which Goethe's claim is predominant: to Goethe, Hamlet is "the type of an intellect over-developed at the expense of the will."²⁹ This assumption is based in particular on Hamlet's famous soliloquy "To

---

26. Ibid., 265. (My emphasis.)
27. Ernest Jones (1910), 73.
28. Ibid., 82.
29. Ibid., 76.

be, or not to be," during which his self-reproach provides a seemingly definite clue: Hamlet broods over his lack of will to act and says, "the native hue of resolution/ Is sicklied o'er with the pale cast of thought."[30] However, Jones disagrees with Goethe, finding counter-examples to prove Hamlet's capacity for swift and bold action, such as his slaughter of Polonius in the Queen's closet or sending his schoolfellows to their death by manipulating Claudius' letter. From a completely different perspective, Jones suggests that an important key to Hamlet's secret is *hidden* from the rhetorical surface of soliloquy or dialogue, and one must employ a psychoanalytical lens to investigate the real motivation for his hesitancy.

Jones demonstrates in detail how Hamlet's repressed childhood wishes for the mother's love and the father's death are "re-awakened" by the act of Claudius, whom he is bound to revenge. According to Jones, this particular "*combination* of crimes" committed by "an exceedingly near relative" reminds Hamlet of something that has been repressed from his conscious mind while the repressed wishes insist on remaining impenetrable to his conscious speculation.[31] More significantly, Jones argues, Hamlet's state echoes Shakespeare's own Oedipus complex and further resonates with every reader/audience member who, without significant exception, has been obliged to regulate the same forbidden wishes. The other point that Jones articulates at the end of his essay is the importance of understanding that the process through which cultural heritage is adapted and appropriated runs parallel to the psychological process of repression in the individual psyche.

To support these points—the latter in particular—Jones suggests a broader approach to the play than a mere text-based character analysis. He historicizes the genesis of Shakespeare's *Hamlet* by highlighting the possibility that this literary masterpiece is the *heir*—if borrowing Derrida's use of the term in "The Tower of Babel"—to many cultural forms of the same legend, such as the saga recorded by Saxo Grammaticus in the thirteenth century, the publication by Belleforest in 1564, or the play of the same title allegedly written by Thomas Kyd a dozen years before Shakespeare wrote *Hamlet*.[32] To demonstrate the universality of the Oedipus complex in the process of artistic creation,

---

30. William Shakespeare, *Hamlet* (III. 1. 84–85), ed. T. J. B. Spencer (London: Penguin Books, 1980), 125.

31. Ernest Jones (1910), 91. (Original emphasis.)

32. Ibid., 103–4.

Jones maps out the process of "adapting" the Hamlet legend into "the tragedy of the prince of Denmark" on the basis of the Freudian theory of dream-work (*Traumarbeit*). Jones argues that Shakespeare's *Hamlet* is an extraordinary example that manifests the creative elaboration—or distortion—of the Oedipal wishes shared by most human subjects, who have consequently created cultural products characterized by precisely the same libidinal impulse.

According to Jones, the play, on one level, presents a more civilized approach to representing the primal desire inherent in Shakespeare's own unconscious. More significantly, however, *Hamlet* should be understood as an illustration of how civilization has developed while projecting the most private conflict between one's unconscious Oedipal wish and super-egotistical repression onto discordance within intersubjective relationships. In particular, when seen as part of a genealogy of adaptations of the Hamlet legend, the Shakespearean tragedy demonstrates the course by which the Oedipal conflicts within the individual unconscious are redirected and refined into an antagonism between the new generation and the heritage of the past generation. The psychoanalytic reading of the play teaches us how these two dimensions are merged in an artistic creation. Therein, the ambivalent nature of Hamlet's dilemma may be more clearly understood if one considers that the enigma and complexity of the hero's psychology lead us to "the deepest problem and the intensest conflict that has occupied the mind of man since the beginning of time, the revolt of youth and of the impulse to love against the restraints imposed by the jealous eld."[33]

Although his conclusion sounds slightly at odds with Freud's reading, Jones's insight appears almost prophetic. This is because he, perhaps without much conscious intention, confuses and overlaps the psychic tension of an individual's struggle against forbidden wishes ("the deepest problem and the intensest conflict") with the conflict between the self and what comes to it as a parental command or law ("the revolt of the youth ... against the restraints imposed by the jealous eld"). Considering that the first published version of Jones's article was immediately read and commented on by Freud, it is plausible that Jones's shift in focus foreshadowed Freud's theory of the super-ego,

---

33. Ibid., 113.

which, as outlined above, elaborates the internalization of the law of the threatening father in offering the resolution to the Oedipus complex.

Overall, Freudian analysis of Hamlet as a character suffering from severe Oedipal conflict, I suggest, represents psychoanalysis' attempt to broaden the scope of its discourse beyond the level of the individual psyche. Indeed, this attempt successfully attracted the attention of readers as well as audiences and critics toward the veiled face of humanity. One can easily imagine that the Freudian reading of Shakespeare's drama constituted not only a ground-breaking interpretation of this masterpiece of Western literature but also a radically destabilizing view of modern subjectivity. However, nothing can stay forever new; the power of what was once innovative afforded the Freudian interpretation of Hamlet canonical status, transforming it into another ghost that continually overpowers the perception of the drama, whether on the page, stage, or screen. Consequently, Freud's reading of *Hamlet* in the light of *Oedipus Rex* now haunts every film adaptation of the play.

### *The Man Who Has Lost the Way of His Desire*

As mentioned above, Lacan shifts the grounds on which we comprehend the psychic dynamics between the super-ego and the ego—that is, the relationship between the two psychic agencies can be conceived on the basis of the formation and function of the ego rather than that of the super-ego. This change in perspective relates to a shift in the analytical position from which we seek to comprehend this immense power of the parental demand on the young prince. In his reading of Hamlet as "the man who has lost the way of his desire," Lacan leads us to concentrate more on the location in which this parental imperative operates: the field of Hamlet's desire.[34] According to Lacan's seminars on *Hamlet*, the function of the super-

---

34. Jacques Lacan, Jacques-Alain Miller, and James Hulbert, "Desire and the Interpretation of Desire in *Hamlet*," in *Yale French Studies*, no. 55/56 (1977): 12. This article is based on Lacan's 1958–9 seminar series "Desire and Its Interpretation," which has not been officially published. It is an edited manuscript for publication from three sessions held on April 15, 22, and 29, 1959.

ego manifests not in Hamlet's rather inadvertent ultimate revenge but in his continual failure to cope with the Ghost's command and his inability to desire what he *is asked to* desire—retribution, the crown, and Ophelia as a proper object replacing the forbidden one. In his sixth seminar series from 1958 to 1959, Lacan constructed a new perspective on the concept of desire in clinical treatment and emphasized the centrality of desire as "the determination of symptoms" in the neurotic subject.[35] For Lacan, desire indicates that the subject is wholly dependent on the signifier after the introduction and introjection of the Name-of-the-Father. With the advent of the subject's reliance on the signifier, the libido is no longer "pleasure-seeking" but becomes "object-seeking."[36] His view of *Hamlet* points out that Hamlet is somehow returning to and being captured at the point of intersection, where the subject, in part, renounces its pleasure in the imaginary identification of the ego with its specular image and organizes its field of desire according to a tertiary relation based on its *symbolic* identification with the signifier. In articulating this juncture between the imaginary and the symbolic, Lacan particularly highlights the significant role of the phallus, which *knots* the two domains in a mysterious way. Hence, it is crucial that any study of *Hamlet* begin with the phallus to understand not only Hamlet's dilemma but also the dilemma of *Hamlet* films at the juncture between the imaginary and the symbolic, in which the ghost of the dead author functions ambivalently as the phallus with two faces—the *objet petit a* and the master signifier.

Lacan's excessively elusive account presents the phallus as a nostalgic residue that reminds the subject of the irreversible loss of the reciprocal relationship with the Mother as the Other (*Autre*). It is simultaneously, however, a mark that signifies the void or fundamental lack around which the subject's symbolic structure of desire is constructed. Lacan's conception of the phallus gradually moves from the distinction between the phallus and its primitive status as a real organ—the penis—to the theorization of the phallus' function in initiating the

---

35. Jacques Lacan, *Seminar VI: Desire and Its Interpretation 1958–59*, trans. Cormac Gallagher, 2. (Retrieved from www.lacaninireland.com.)

36. Ibid., 3.

signifying mechanism of desire as a whole.[37] First and foremost, the phallus is recognized as a thing that is anticipated and demanded by this primal authority captured in the term, the Mother, within the dyadic relationship between the mother and the child. Regarding this genesis of the phallus, Lacan clarifies the meaning and function of the imaginary phallus in the mother–child relationship in his seminars on psychoses: in the infantile psyche, the Mother requires an imaginary phallus and uses her child as a support for this demand, and the child happily identifies with the "thing" the Mother demands *over* itself. Here, the phallus functions as a mediator of the symmetrical relationship between the two, yet this "common illusion of reciprocal phallicization" is based on "the imaginary lack of the phallus" on both sides.[38]

Therein, the child assumes the place of a thing, not yet an object, representing the Mother's lack in the original demand. The father, replacing the demanding Mother in the advanced stage of the Oedipus complex, interrupts this reciprocity between the Mother and the child and introduces himself as a carrier, vehicle, and holder of the phallus; he thus functions as a threat, prohibiting the child's pleasure in "being" the imaginary phallus that is to satisfy the Mother's demand. On the dissolution of the Oedipus complex, the phallus attains its symbolic function as the signifier that represents not an anchoring signified but rather its lack. This essence of the significatory function of the imaginary phallus—that is, the veiled lack at the center of the meaning effect of the phallus—organizes the entire system of desire wherein the child's

---

37. Lacan briefly but emphatically mentions the dissimilarity between penis and phallus in *Seminar II* (1955) and suggests that the phallus emerges when the symbolic value is imposed on the real organ "penis" in the imaginary identification of the female subject with "the imaginary man in the place of her own image, her narcissistic image or her ego" (see *Seminar II*, 272); in the 1956 seminar series on psychoses, he applies the symbolic value of the phallus to the relationship between the mother and the phallus with which the child identifies to be the object of her desire (see *Seminar III*, 319); in his 1958 paper "The Signification of the Phallus," Lacan's discussion is fully engaged with the transition or ambivalence of the status of the phallus between the Imaginary and the Symbolic and its symbolic function "to designate meaning effects as a whole."(See *Écrits*, 579.)

38. Jacques Lacan, *The Seminar of Jacques Lacan, Book III: The Psychoses 1955-1956*, ed. Jacques-Alain Miller and trans. Russell Grigg (New York and London: W. W. Norton & Company, 1993), 319.

renunciation of the pleasure of being the imaginary phallus circulates. This signals the birth of the subject, which precipitates the symbolic system of desire to pursue an object to substitute this *lack*. However, the imaginary dimension of the phallus—that is, the image or form of the phallus that the child imagines and identifies with and that links the child to the omnipotent Mother—does not completely dissipate; rather, it is reduced to the *objet petit a* in the domain of the imaginary, which operates in the chain of desire as "a kind of compensation for the missing phallus which, as missing, does not function in the open as an object of desire but makes its presence felt in an unconscious fantasy" as the object *in* desire.[39]

Lacan's teaching on *Hamlet* resumes from the point at which the ego is bound up with the reciprocal relation with the Mother. He explains:

> Our first step ... was to express the extent to which the play is dominated by the Mother as Other [*Autre*]—i.e., the primordial subject of the demand [*la demande*]. The omnipotence of which we are always speaking in psychoanalysis is first of all the omnipotence of the subject as subject of the first demand, and this omnipotence must be related back to the Mother.[40]

According to Lacan's previous explanation of the phallus' role in the Oedipus complex, Hamlet, in his childhood, conceived himself as the object of the Mother's desire through his primary identification with the imaginary phallus, which Lacan designates as narcissistic in its structure and function. Subsequently, in the advent of the Oedipus complex, he saw that it was his father, and not him, who possessed the phallus and he thus renounced his phallic status in place of the father, owing to the fear of castration that the father (or the super-ego in the figure of the father) invokes. His decision to leave the arena of the father's authority and to study in Wittenberg, in a way, indirectly reveals the context of this character: the power of the castration complex could neither be diminished nor resolved for the young Hamlet, and the older Hamlet's reputation as a warrior-king further supports this assumption.

At the beginning of the play, this overwhelming father is suddenly dead. His death opens up the gap that results from the fatal loss of the

---

39. John P. Muller, "Psychosis and Mourning in Lacan's Hamlet," *New Literary History* 12, no. 1 (Autumn 1980): 152.

40. Lacan et al, "Desire and Its Interpretation in *Hamlet*", 12.

## 2. Oedipus Complex in Film Adaptations of Hamlet 59

imaginary phallus during Hamlet's childhood and brings him back to the point at which he lost it—that is, at the very juncture of the imaginary and the symbolic, according to Lacan. Hamlet inarguably requires time to "mourn" this reawakened loss with the help of sufficient communal rituals so that he might *symbolically incorporate* the lost object into himself once again. In doing so, he would be able to transform the fundamental lack signified by the phallus into "the ultimate object *in* desire," which functions as the master signifier of desire in the domain of the symbolic and as the *objet petit a* in the domain of the imaginary. The mourning process is necessary for this system of desire—structured around the lack of the phallus—to regain its power to allow him to live on as the subject of desire.

However, the psychologically complex drama of *Hamlet* illustrates how the Queen's "o'erhasty marriage" to his uncle Claudius confines Hamlet to the reemerged status of pre-Oedipal vulnerability in relation to the omnipotence of the Mother's desire.[41] As a result of this marriage, Claudius assumes the place of the imaginary phallus and turns into the very real embodiment of the phallus in psychological, familial, and political senses: he claims the place of the object of the Mother's desire, the father of Hamlet, and the king of Denmark. The sudden emergence of the real, not symbolic, object in the place of the recently lost phallus deprives Hamlet of the opportunity to properly mourn its loss. Therefore, the tragedy of Hamlet is that even after the death of his father, "the phallus is still here" and "the phallus is located here in a position that is entirely out of place."[42] In Hamlet's own words, the phallus is now in "[a] king of shreds and patches."[43] Upon this paradoxical deprivation of the loss of the phallus, the reason for Hamlet's inability to strike Claudius, Lacan says, is the "narcissistic connection" between him and Claudius, who now occupies the place of the imaginary phallus with which Hamlet still identifies at the unconscious level.[44] Therefore, his famous soliloquy "To be or not to be" reveals that the prince has regressed to the stage of Oedipalization at which the question of to be or not to be the phallus should have evolved into the question of to have or not to have the phallus.

---

41. William Shakespeare, *Hamlet* (II. 2. 57), 104.
42. Lacan et al., "Desire and Its Interpretation in *Hamlet*," 50.
43. William Shakespeare, *Hamlet* (III. 4. 103), 149.
44. Lacan et al., "Desire and Its Interpretation in *Hamlet*," 50.

In Lacan's account of Hamlet's uncanny confrontation with the ambivalent status of the phallus, one may discern a parallel between the phallus' apparition to Hamlet at the juncture of the imaginary and the symbolic and the spectral presence of Shakespeare's play in the process of adaptation. The predominating and preoccupying literary masterpiece functions as the phallus at this intersection, which can be wholly captured neither with the register of the symbolic nor that of the imaginary. On one hand, Shakespeare's written words serve as the commanding master signifier in the domain of the symbolic—that is, the absolute written law that adapters must obey and constantly take into consideration while making film adaptations of the play. However, the words of this literary masterpiece can never be reduced to a single definitive meaning; they are, rather, marked by the lack of a definitive signified, as the diverse and contradictory interpretations of the play confirm. In relation to its adaptations, Shakespeare's *Hamlet* functions as a signifier that refers not to a signified but to the inevitable and necessary void that connects the original text to its film adaptations in the same way as the phallus—or, more precisely, the absence of the phallus—facilitates the illusion of reciprocity between the child and the mother. Indeed, the phallic status of the original text indicates that it operates as the *objet petit a* that initiates the constantly present desire for a screen adaptation in the domain of modern culture. Insofar as this lack of a signified is glimpsed behind the overwhelming fullness of the literary canon, the metonymic chain of desire for a film adaptation, which would offer an imaginary fixation point or anchor for a floating or absent meaning, is perpetually in motion.

As a great number of *Hamlet* films confirms, our desire to produce or watch another *Hamlet* is unwavering. Shakespeare's *Hamlet* itself becomes a ghost that returns repeatedly to the sphere of modern culture to haunt the subject of next generations. What is significant is not the message of the original text, presumably intended by the dead author but its spectral presence in close proximity to the domain of the living as well as its readiness to drag the living toward premature death by interfering with the subject's field of desire. If borrowing Lacan's expressions, the ghost of the original text *Hamlet* is ready to transport cinematic adapters back to the site of the Oedipus complex, which would cause them to momentarily experience, along with the young prince, what it is to have lost the way of one's desire.

## Desire in Film Adaptations of Hamlet

Hitherto, the discussion explained that reading the play's hero through the Oedipus complex is tantamount to understanding a mythological moment in the development of a human subject. Therein, the subject is constituted by the course of repressing or regulating its wishes: the desire for the forbidden object, the mother, and the desire for the removal of the obstacle, the father. Similarly, most screen adaptations reveal their interest in how Hamlet's incestuous desire for his mother might be made visible on screen. All three film adaptations under discussion here—Laurence Olivier's *Hamlet* (1948), Franco Zeffirelli's *Hamlet* (1990), and Kenneth Branagh's *Shakespeare's Hamlet* (1996)[45]— as well as numerous other cinematic productions strive to elaborate the direct and even exclusive connection between Gertrude and her enormous bed formerly shared with Old Hamlet and now with Claudius. In the process of adapting the text on the pages into images for the screen, the erotic desire, mingled with the ego's narcissistic hunger for an image to identify with, enhances the sexual fantasy on display. Without exception, the three films analyzed herein make the cinematic treatment of the mother's bed a central motif in their projection of the original play onto the screen. Exploration of the films' eroticized views of Hamlet's Oedipal conflicts should thus allow us to identify the hidden, fundamental desire in adapting *Hamlet* for the screen.

Another point that warrants closer examination is the films' respective approaches to materializing the ghost of the father on screen. In a psychoanalytic reading, the hero's psychological relationship to the paternal figure is characterized by the sense of guilt evoked in the unconscious by his incestuous and murderous desire. From this perspective, Shakespeare's representation of the dead father as the apparition of the son's guilt appears to epitomize the Freudian conception of the super-ego, which is a self-regarding psychic agent. However, according to Freud's and Lacan's explanations of the representational mode of the super-ego, this paternal authority remains invisible, while its affect is omnipresent at both the individual and sociocultural levels.

---

45. Deborah Cartmell's chapter "The Shakespeare on Screen Industry," in *Adaptations: From Text to Screen, Screen to Text*, ed. Deborah Cartmell and Imelda Whelehan (London and New York: Routledge, 1999), 29–37 offers a succinct comparative reading of the three films. The chapter's reading of the three *Hamlet* films was inspired by Cartmell's analysis.

For film directors working with the visual medium, it is not easy to strike a balance between invisibility and omnipresence. In the on-screen version of *Hamlet*, the dead father, embodying the prohibitive psychic force of the symbolic, must be represented through the photographic image of the figure on screen. This materialization often reduces the Ghost's inextricable authority in the original drama to the illusion or hallucination of Hamlet. Furthermore, because the screen appearance of the Ghost is limited to the two brief encounters in the entire story, the omnipresence of the Ghost may easily be overpowered by the constant on-screen presence of Hamlet, who is often played by renown celebrities such as Laurence Olivier and, thus, demands more attention for film audiences. In this sense, it is possible to infer that adaptation of the play for film manifests the ego's narcissistic desire to shift the super-ego's ontological ground from the enigmatic juncture between the symbolic and the imaginary to the domain of the imaginary. This represents an attempt to overcome the anxiety arising from confrontation with what Freud ascribes as the coercive and persistent nature of the super-ego, which may indicate its origin coming from the id—or, for Lacan, the real. Overall, the eroticization of the Oedipus complex and materialization of the super-ego on screen constitute the two nodal points in a psychoanalytic approach to *Hamlet* films.

It is also remarkable that in the long history of *Hamlet* scholarship, most accounts of the mystery of the original text, whether dealing with the mystery from a perspective of psychoanalysis or other disciplines, appear to be preoccupied with the Ghost's demand. Interpretations of the play largely deal with Hamlet's duty of revenge as a determined narrative goal from the moment of the Ghost's arrival, as though his words cause not only Hamlet but also the reader (or theatrical audience) to freeze, ordering them to listen to and obey the dead father. Once the reader's position is established by the urgent injunction to avenge, it is natural for us to experience difficulties in understanding the hero, in spite of his predominant presence on stage and the extended volume of soliloquies imparting his innermost thoughts. In this light, Hamlet's hesitation remains a mystery. We neither accept nor approve his delay, even more so when we discover that the delay causes several "unnecessary" deaths—those of Polonius, Rosencrantz and Guildenstern, Ophelia, Gertrude, Laertes, and Hamlet himself.[46]

---

46. A.C. Bradley, *Shakespearean Tragedy: Lectures on Hamlet, Othello, King Lear, Macbeth* (New York: Palgrave Macmillan, 2007), 99.

Therefore, we retrospectively affirm that he ought to have obeyed his father and exacted revenge without deliberation.

Put differently, the power of *Hamlet* lies in this super-egotistical authority of the dead father, who exercises power *within* and *outside* of the story. In response to the compelling force of the Ghost's command emanating from Shakespeare's text, the emphatic visibility of the Oedipus complex in cinematic adaptations of *Hamlet* may function as an answer to Hamlet's request with his last breath to "Report me and my cause aright/ To the unsatisfied."[47] Hamlet himself becomes another ghost haunting future generations, as his plea to "report me and my cause aright" emerges like a command from his own specter, compelling us—especially adapters—to make sense of his notorious vacillation— something that never satisfied his father's ghost. Harold Bloom, in examining Hamlet's complex "desires, his ideals or aspirations," asserts that "the prince transcends his play."[48] This Oedipal relationship between father and son in a continuous circuit curiously and interestingly interweaves the interior and exterior of screen adaptations of this literary masterpiece. Hamlet's desire as such stands as a veiled Sphinx, whose riddle the present chapter seeks to unravel.

What follows is the analysis of three representative film adaptations of *Hamlet* through which the chapter attempts to clarify the psychoanalytic points raised above. From over a century worth of screen adaptations of *Hamlet* from all over the world, I have selected these three films because they satisfy several conditions: the films use the original text in English, so that Shakespeare's original sustains a more direct and dominating influence over the films; they are directed by filmmakers whose filmographies include Shakespeare adaptations other than *Hamlet* to indicate these directors' psychic attachment to Shakespeare as an ideal; they are also commercial feature films aimed at general mass audiences, irrespective of whether they have read or seen the original play. The films' clear commercial purpose reveals the broadly shared response to the original text rather than films aimed at small arthouse groups or those produced for pedagogical purposes to educate students and guide them in their reading of the original.

---

47. William Shakespeare, *Hamlet* (V. 2. 333–4), 201.

48. Harold Bloom, *Shakespeare: The Invention of the Human* (New York: Riverhead Books, 1998), 385.

## Laurence Olivier's Hamlet: *The Oedipal Drama of Shadows*

Laurence Olivier desired that his adaptation of *Hamlet* would be recognized as "an 'Essay in *Hamlet*,' and not as a film version of a necessarily abridged classic."[49] Indeed, his "essay," which interprets the hero in the light of the Oedipus complex, has offered an inescapable point of reference for understanding the drama's hero and established the model for later screen adaptations of *Hamlet*. Interestingly, the film's psychoanalytic prism is under the direct influence of Ernest Jones's article, discussed above. In 1936, as a young and rising star of both stage and screen, Olivier was seeking an approach to playing Hamlet that differed from the standard performances of John Gielgud and many other classical actors, who rendered the prince of Denmark as a personification of "the delicate-souled dreamers and thinkers of nineteenth-century tradition."[50] This romanticized view of Hamlet emerged under the profound influence of Goethe's reading of the play. The producer Tyrone Guthrie persuaded Olivier to leave a season at the fashionable West End and venture into the Old Vic, which allowed ambitious young artists and actors to stage their experimental productions. With this suggestion, the producer brought Jones's essay into the discussion. While preparing for the leading role in the 1937 season at the Old Vic under the influence of Jones's "professional point of view," Olivier had the opportunity to meet with Ernest Jones in person and consult him on how Hamlet should be performed.[51] Olivier, in his autobiography *Confessions of an Actor*, recalls the meeting as a crucial and determining moment in his understanding of *Hamlet*: "I have never ceased to think of Hamlet at odd moments, and ever since that meeting I have believed that Hamlet was a prime sufferer from the Oedipus complex—quite unconsciously, of course, as the professor (Ernest Jones) was anxious to stress."[52]

---

49. Kenneth S. Rothwell, *A History of Shakespeare on Screen: A Century of Film and Television* (Cambridge: Cambridge University Press, 1999), 57. (The original quotation is from Laurence Olivier, "An Essay in Hamlet," in *The Film "Hamlet": A Record of Its Production*, ed. Brenda Cross (New York: Saturn Press, 1948), 12.)

50. Peter Donaldson, "Olivier, Hamlet, and Freud," *Cinema Journal* 26, no. 4 (Summer 1987): 24.

51. Ibid., 23. (The original quotation is from Laurence Olivier, *Confessions of an Actor* (London: Weidenfeld and Nicholson, 1982), 101–2.)

52. Ibid.

More than ten years later, after the unexpected success of his first Shakespearean film adaptation, *Henry V* (1944), the freedom of artistic control and a generous budget of £475,000 enabled him to produce *Hamlet* on screen. In the 1948 film, therefore, his Freudian understanding of the play is rendered more visible when compared with what he had been able to achieve in his performance in Guthrie's production at the Old Vic eleven years earlier. Here, it is helpful to focus on two pivotal points: the first is the process by which Hamlet's Oedipal wishes are envisioned—in particular, how the erotic aspect of the unconscious wishes might be insinuated. The other is the materialization of the super-egotistical authority of the overpowering dead author, particularly in accordance with the influential Freudian reading that ties this to the Oedipal relationship between Hamlet and the ghost of his father.

Through the deferential attitude of the director-actor, Laurence Olivier, whose background lay in Shakespearean theatre, it is possible to infer that every film director is haunted by the ghost of the dead author to a certain degree and consequently puts himself or herself in the position of the young prince in the course of adapting *Hamlet* for the screen. Olivier's exemplary account recalls how he took a director's artistic liberty but was limited by the boundary determined for him by the author of the original text:

> Well, I suppose for a craftsman, who is always all the time made conscious that his craft is purely interpretive, who isn't given the opportunity to create, except insofar as the author will allow him to create within the precincts of the character that he has drawn for him. I suppose being a film director is the nearest one gets to feeling like a creator, because the film is entirely the director's medium.[53]

In this insight into Olivier's production of *Hamlet*, we can read his paradoxical wish divided by the two psychic impulses relating to the super-ego and the ego: namely, his remark expresses both his desire to remain faithful toward Shakespeare's play and his ambition to acquire a screen for his own "images" of *Hamlet*. Olivier saw his work as that of the interpreter, obliged to limit his own creative freedom within "the precincts of the character" that Shakespeare had drawn for him.

53. Kenneth Tynan, "The Actor: Tynan Interview Olivier," *The Tulane Drama Review* 11, no. 2 (Winter 1966): 98.

Moreover, his interpretation of *Hamlet* was deeply influenced and fixed by another authoritative figure—Professor Ernest Jones, whose psychoanalytic reading of the play in the light of the Oedipus complex had influenced Olivier's interpretation long before the production of the film began. Therefore, Olivier's position as an adapter, as he describes it, represents the place of the present generation revisited by a multitude of spectral presences from past generations that maintain parental influence over their descendants.

Paradoxically, however, this directorial position is entailed by the adapter's concealed ambition to "feel like a creator." This ambition finds its own echo in the young prince Hamlet, who inherits his name from his father, a great king, and attempts to fill his dead father's shoes and ultimately replace Old Hamlet. Hence, Olivier, at first, appears to modestly assume the role of a son under the authority of super-egotistical fathers, such as Shakespeare and Freud/Jones, in his effort to adapt the play for the screen in the light of the Oedipus complex. However, Olivier's assumption of this role also embodies the desire of the film director, who believed that the silver screen would provide a screen onto which to project his own artistic autonomy. The semiotic shift from theatre to cinema provides the platform—however illusionary or narcissistic—on which he might feel *like* the creator—in other words, a chance to identify with the ghost.

In spite of Olivier's anticipation of exercising creative freedom as a director, the film itself opens with an image of his own death—the young Hamlet played by Olivier. After the opening credits superimposed on the image of a castle, isolated at sea, surrounded and troubled by surging waves, the camera dives from the foggy night sky into Elsinore castle, effecting a bird's-eye view. Olivier's voice-over then reads part of the dialogue from Act 1, Scene 4, with the text also presented on the screen:

> So, oft it chances in particular men
> That through some vicious mole of nature in them,
> By the o'ergrowth of some complexion
> Oft breaking down the pales and forts of reason,
> Or by some habit grown too much; that these men—
> Carrying, I say, the stamp of one defect,
> Their virtues else—be they as pure as grace,
> Shall in the general censure take corruption
> From that particular fault.[54]

---

54. William Shakespeare, *Hamlet* (I. 4. 24–36), 86.

When the narration is over, the camera descends from the highest turret of the castle through thick clouds and fog to eventually find the hero who is *already* dead and being carried by the four captains with Horatio standing alongside. The retrospective narrative structure of the film implies that it is interested only in investigating why and how young Hamlet suffered from his psychological dilemma rather than tantalizing the audience with the mystery of the king's murder or surprising them with the multiple tragic deaths in the final scene, as in the original play.

Coarse though it may sound to many literary critics, Olivier adds his own invented prologue to the voice-over narration reading a part from the original play. This addition introduces the hero in the adapter's own words—"This is the tragedy of a man who could not make up his own mind"—as the camera moves closer to Hamlet's corpse.[55] To Olivier, therefore, Hamlet's vacillation lies at the center of the entire drama, and from this "stamp of one defect," the otherwise virtuous young prince is corrupted and driven to a tragic death. Hence, the main attention of the drama on screen is on the veiled unconscious reasons for the only "mole of nature" in him.[56] The film's retrospective narrative reveals and emphasizes the original play's excessively introspective nature, which was picked up by Freud and several other psychoanalytical commentators. This also safeguards the validity of the psychoanalytical approach, because the play is coded as a psychological drama in which the subject is trapped in the Oedipal conflict between the ego and the super-ego. At the beginning of the film, Hamlet played by Olivier, who has already become a ghost, embarks on a journey into his own psyche in search of the unconscious motive behind the indecision that ultimately leads to his death.

A more compelling aspect of Olivier's film may be found in the psychological complexity realized by camera's gaze, which complicates the drama on the level of the audience's psychological reactions to the narrative and its characters. From the film's opening, an inexplicable unease is present, preventing the audience from comfortably identifying with the camera's gaze. In the bird's-eye view of the castle, the dynamic and self-revealing camera movement appears to invite the audience

---

55. *Hamlet*, directed by Laurence Olivier (1948; Two Cities Film Ltd.).
56. William Shakespeare, *Hamlet* (I. 4. 24), 86.

to join the camera in its inquisitive gaze. While diving into the film's mystical setting, Elsinore, the camera appears to adopt a detached, third-person perspective, guiding the audience to observe Hamlet from a distance as they search for the source of the fault in Hamlet's nature, which is tragically unknown to the prince himself. However, as soon as Olivier's voice-over summarizes Hamlet's tragedy as "the tragedy of a man who could not make up his own mind," the audience's identification with the camera is disrupted and confused: it is at this moment that we realize the *impossibility* of the camera's third-person perspective on Hamlet's corpse coinciding with the voice-over of this dead prince himself. In other words, the camera's gaze embodies a strangely detached scopic position from which Hamlet can see himself dead and, more mysteriously, the audience are made to notice that he is seeing himself dead—a dimension that is absent from or, at least unlikely to be represented in—the original stage play.

On the one hand, the impossible position of the gaze implies the fundamental split of the ego, which Freud highlights when he articulates the position of the super-ego (Over-I or *Über-Ich*) within the ego: "the ego divided, fallen into two pieces, one of which rages against the second ... We have called it the ego ideal (or super-ego), and by way of functions we have ascribed to it *self-observation,* the moral conscience, the censorship of dreams, and the chief influence in repression."[57] The camera's self-regarding gaze thus appears to establish Olivier's super-egotistical position as a director who sees and measures himself as an actor in the role of Hamlet or, in other words, as an "image" of Hamlet.

On the other hand, this meta-narrative position embodies the psychic locus from which the knowing audience, as the director assumes, may cast their doubtful eyes on the rest of the drama to judge how adequately he adapted Shakespeare for the screen. On a more fundamental level, however, I wish to suggest that this particular gaze that comes from nowhere and remains detached from any living body is the very locus from which Shakespeare's *Hamlet*, as it is inscribed in the super-egos of subsequent generations, watches over its film adaptation. In other words, this unusual cinematic apparatus, Hamlet's gazing on his

---

57. Sigmund Freud, "Group Psychology and the Analysis of the Ego," in *The Standard Edition of the Complete Psychological Works of Sigmund Freud: Volume XVIII,* trans. James Strachey (London: The Hogarth Press and the Institute of Psycho-Analysis, 1955), 110. (My emphasis.)

own corpse allows the representation of the original text's gaze, as it is experienced by the adapter's split ego. It embodies the unconscious force of the past, whose power remains and bears down by being introjected as and transformed into the super-ego of the adapter. Characteristically, the omnipresence of this self-critical agency casts its vigilant eye over the ego, while the ego enjoys the pleasure of imaginary and narcissistic identification with the on-screen images. Thus, Shakespeare's original text becomes an unforgiving yardstick to measure how the egoistic and narcissistic young medium—cinema—envisions that which is both written and hidden in the pages of Shakespeare's *Hamlet*. Indeed, Olivier's recollection of the experiences in making and releasing his film adaptation exemplifies the spectral presence of the super-ego in relation to the ego, which feels as though it is being watched or criticized. He confesses:

> It was—as may well be imagined—with feelings of some trepidation, a kind of fearful awe that I approached the idea of a Hamlet film. Indeed, it will be noticed, and doubtless commented upon, that I took the precaution of being in Australia when the film opened in London![58]

On one level, the use of the camera's gaze to represent the psychological force of the super-ego reinforces the Freudian reading of Shakespeare's text as an Oedipal drama. That is, under the camera's super-egotistical gaze, the hero appears to be no better than his criminal uncle, whom he is to punish. In particular, the accusatory character of the camera's gaze is implied by oppressive camera angles and movement, which occasionally frame Hamlet not as a hero of action but as a criminal or prisoner caught in his reawakened incestuous wish, hovering around his parents' bed. Interestingly, the power afforded to the camera's gaze is signaled even before the drama of Hamlet's Oedipus complex begins. In the scene that follows the opening scene discussed above, the film resumes the story of the original text, beginning with the night watch and the Ghost's first appearance to Horatio, Marcellus, and Barnardo. After the Ghost disappears at the break of dawn, the conversation between the three characters concludes with Marcellus saying, "Something is rotten in the state of Denmark."

---

58. Laurence Olivier, forward to *Hamlet: The Film and the Play*, ed. Alan Dent (London: World Film Publications, 1948), 1.

Leaving the characters still atop the battlement, the camera then embarks on a quest to discover why the dead King cannot sleep in his tomb. Unanchored to any characters, the camera spins down to the Great Hall, which is empty except for a table, chairs, and shadows. Empathetically, the camera zooms in on Hamlet's empty chair, in which we will see the young prince seated in subsequent scenes. From the hero's chair, the camera moves toward the window frame, through which the Queen's bed is visible. As the camera zooms in and contemplatively pauses at the bed, which has now been called "a couch for luxury and damned incest," we comprehend the cause of the corruption that has awakened the dead King from his grave. At the same time, the cinematographic connection between Hamlet's chair and the bed confirms Olivier's interpretation of *Hamlet* as the tragedy of the son who suffers from an Oedipal conflict stirred by his mother with his uncle in "the royal bed of Denmark" that turns into "A couch for luxury and damned incest."[59] Herein, the authority of the camera's gaze in the film's narrative, which is structured as a retrospective investigation, is clearly portrayed as something that looks down from *above and over* the hero's conscious mind.

Later, this particular use of the camera's gaze, which is unregistered and unattached to any human character, functions as a visual tactic for embodying the meta-narrative position that represents the authority of the Ghost, whose demand for vengeance binds Hamlet and the audience to its spectral omnipresence throughout the film. At the end of the film's first sequence, the camera clearly indicates that the Ghost's return relates to the young prince's forbidden wish, which is connected to his parents' bed. In this sense, the camera's gaze materializes the reproachful gaze of the Ghost, who secretly accuses his son of Oedipal wishes that are as incestuous and murderous as the crimes of Claudius. Confirming this reading, in both scenes in which Hamlet encounters the Ghost—first on the castle's turret and later in the Queen's closet— the camera's merciless gaze, in oppressive high-angle shots, consistently captures the young prince, who throws himself on the floor and begs for his dead father's mercy. It may be that here, the compelling force of the gaze of the dead author, Shakespeare, overlaps with and is given substance by the overseeing meta-narrative scopic position of the Ghost, before whom Olivier throws himself to the ground. The gaze that signals the presence of the super-egotistical forces—both the Ghost

---

59. William Shakespeare, *Hamlet* (I. 5. 82–3), 92.

and Shakespeare—functions as the cinematic projection of what causes both Hamlet and Olivier to feel as though they are being watched and judged for their forbidden wish to replace the father. This gaze more generally expresses what Freud theorizes as the internalized paternal command of the super-ego in the shape of what often manifests as the father in one's psychic dramatization of the Oedipus complex.

Paradoxically, however, the film's focus on Hamlet's Oedipus complex may function as a therapeutic screen onto which the barely representable psychic conflict between the super-ego and the ego is to be projected. If we regard the Ghost as a representative of all manner of ghosts who haunt and torment the egos of the hero, the adapter, audience and reader alike, then the materialization of this accusatory gaze on screen seriously undercuts the command of the specters who, otherwise, wield their power within an ungraspable and unrepresentable dimension. In the film, the super-ego appears to be momentarily captured within the net of filmic codes, and this visual representation serves to provide a kind of a psychic theatre for the collective and ritual sharing of guilt stemming from illegitimate Oedipal desires. This also explains the desire and pleasure embedded in the cinematic generation's incessant attempts at adapting this canonical text.

Another noteworthy point beyond the film's characteristic portrayal of the Ghost is that the scopic register of cinema articulates the gap or void that resides between the ego and the super-ego—or the imaginary and the symbolic in Lacanian terms—more successfully than the original medium does. As discussed above, the Ghost's alignment with the camera's gaze manifests a level of subjectivity whereby the subject sees itself as an object. This psychic dimension is also envisioned with the help of the spectral figure of the Ghost, which has two black holes in place of eyes and a voice that does not appear to emanate directly from its mouth but rather resonates throughout the whole of the frame. The characterization of the Ghost as such, unlike the other two films, which portray the figure of the Ghost as a humanized character, appears to enable Olivier's film to capture on screen the fundamental gap in the human subject, which otherwise must remain unrecognized. Olivier, as an adapter, makes the most of the uniquely cinematic apparatus— that is, the camera—to actualize on screen the gaze of the super-ego detached from any human "eye." Perceived in a Lacanian sense, the peculiar representation of the Ghost in the film makes the uncanny gaze of the super-ego per se visible as it emerges in the imaginary field of the ego.

Herein, the capability of the new medium may direct our attention toward Lacan's claim that "The *objet a* in the field of the visible is the gaze."[60] Lacan's designation of the gaze as the *objet a*—the object-cause of desire appearing in the domain of the imaginary—indubitably recalls for us the signification of the imaginary phallus, or, more fundamentally, its lack—as the *objet petit a*, as was explained above in relation to Lacan's theory on the phallus. In other words, the visual apparition of the gaze of the super-ego is parallel to the symbolic appropriation of the lack of the imaginary phallus between the child and the mother into the object *in* desire. Therefore, as the *objet petit a*, both the gaze without the eye and the empty space for the imaginary phallus function as a transitional space as well as a permanent knot linking the imaginary domain of the ego and the symbolic domain of the super-ego. This is the locus of the subject that, in the resolution of the Oedipus complex, is constituted on the basis of the lack or void initiating the metonymic chain of desire at the juncture between the imaginary and the symbolic. In this sense, Olivier's adaptation of *Hamlet* suggests that screen adaptation is precisely the cultural site capable of representing this ambivalent locus in the human psyche.

If we consider the centrality of the lack of the phallus in understanding the Oedipus complex in Lacan's reading of *Hamlet*, it is also important to acknowledge the mise-en-scène of the empty bed, chairs, and tables occupied only by shadows as an important visual metaphor. The much-emphasized "emptiness" in the ghostly setting of Elsinore signals that Hamlet, afflicted by the worst luck in confronting his father's "most foul, strange and unnatural" murder and his mother's second marriage at "most wicked speed," is returned once more to the transitional point—the void between the imaginary and the symbolic where the acute manifestation of the Oedipus complex should already be dissolved.[61] From a psychoanalytic view, the film's visual tactics of foregrounding emptiness aptly envision that Hamlet is positioned at the psychic border between a neurosis formatted by the symbolic phallus and a psychosis still overwhelmed by the imaginary phallus; hence, the ambivalence of Hamlet's madness prompts multifarious interpretations of the play.

In response to the trouble posed by Hamlet in this liminal void, Olivier, throughout the film, emphasizes the empty place that the dead

---

60. Lacan, *Seminar XI*, 105.
61. William Shakespeare, *Hamlet* (I. 5. 28) and (I. 2. 156), 90 and 75.

father should occupy until such time as Hamlet gains sufficient power and authority to claim the place for himself through the appropriate mourning process. Throughout the course of his delayed revenge, the empty throne is occupied by Claudius, who symbolizes both Hamlet's illegitimate Oedipal wishes and the shadow of the dead father, whose return from the grave provokes Hamlet's guilt about his Oedipal wishes. With a hint of a narrative arc for coming-of-age story, the film, driven by both artistic and entrepreneurial ambitions, reaches a conclusion that can safely return Hamlet to the hero's rightful place—that is, the film's Act 5 Scene 2 where Hamlet is clearly shown to take back the throne and where his desire becomes central in the progress of the narrative. Ultimately, Olivier's adaptation restores the hero's status as the lawful heir and secures for him the throne of Denmark, unlike the original play's conclusion with Hamlet's dying breath as he lies lifelessly on the floor, having managed to do nothing but bequeath his right to the young Norwegian prince Fortinbras. Cinematographically, in the dying moment Olivier's Hamlet is represented as both the imaginary and symbolic *phallus*; in a low-angle shot, he physically occupies the throne and stands above the courtiers, who kneel around him and mark the dying king's final words. On the surface level, the film indicates that, after overcoming his Oedipal conflicts, Hamlet can erect himself as a king who stands in for the dead King, the older Hamlet.

However, the film's ending, on another level, still refuses to close the irreducible gap that has been opened between the prince and the king, the ego and the super-ego, the eye and the gaze, and the imaginary and the symbolic. The scene that follows that of Hamlet's heroic and kingly death once again interrogates Hamlet's complete identification with the king and renders it doubtful: the film's coda sees the return of the camera's super-egotistical gaze, bracketing the film with a floating camera movement that corresponds with that of the film's opening. The camera rather haphazardly follows the four captains bearing Hamlet's body while freely lingering and pausing on the same objects shown in the opening sequence—the prince's empty chair, the Queen's bed, and back to the dead body of Hamlet. Perhaps the gap is inerasable. The camera's gaze, silently cruising and overseeing the dead prince in the finale of Olivier's *Hamlet*, reinforcing the sense of being watched, measured, and judged, serves to remind us that the film, or any *Hamlet* film, must leave something of the original *Hamlet* unsaid, unseen, and unsatisfied under the scrutinizing gaze of Shakespeare the author, master, and father.

## Franco Zeffirelli's Hamlet: *A Close-Up on the Oedipus Complex*

Contrary to the retrospective narrative of Olivier's *Hamlet* and its meta-narrative contours sustained by the super-egotistical gaze of the camera, Franco Zeffirelli gives his version of *Hamlet* a linear plot. "[W]ith uncanny speed," the film's narrative drives toward a climax in which the libidinal energy of Hamlet's repressed desire for the mother erupts, revealing the psychosexual undercurrent of Shakespeare's drama, viewed from a psychoanalytic angle.[62] This 1990 film adaptation opens with the scene of Old Hamlet's funeral to envision events that precede the first act of Shakespeare's play. The invented funeral scene, absent from both the original play and Olivier's film, establishes the triangular relationship between Hamlet, Claudius, and Gertrude, aligning with the Freudian reading of the play as an Oedipal drama, even before the Ghost's return to confront Hamlet. In this respect, it is possible to read Zeffirelli's film as an extension of Olivier's *Hamlet*—"an essay" on the play informed by the psychoanalytic understanding of the hero suffering from the Oedipus complex. Zeffirelli's well-known admiration for Olivier confirms that the director sought to reinstate Olivier's rather metaphorical use of the Oedipus complex as the play's backbone, though Zeffirelli approaches it in a more direct and visible manner.

The opening scene of Zeffirelli's film affirms its close connection to Olivier's adaptation through various cinematic details. Significantly, the film opens with an extreme long shot of the battlements of Elsinore castle, standing alone above the sea. The subsequent shots rapidly approach the royal castle as though the film were attempting to echo Olivier's bird's-eye-view, swooping down on the maze-like castle complex. The opening scene thus establishes the characterization that the director, following Olivier's interpretation, assigns to Elsinore: the castle is not only the physical location in which the drama will unfold but also a psychological space where the hero's innermost voice will be revealed. In addition, it is not difficult to recognize the similarities between the two films in terms of mise-en-scène, featuring endless staircases and panoptical interiors. The intention behind this analogous construction of Elsinore is to portray the royal castle of Denmark as a claustrophobic background for the traumatic (re-)encounter with the Ghost. Both

---

62. Deborah Cartmell, "Franco Zeffirelli and Shakespeare," in *The Cambridge Companion to Shakespeare on Film*, ed. Russell Jackson (Cambridge: Cambridge University Press, 2000), 219.

films cast the drama's location as a nonhuman character that embodies the omnipresence of the Ghost, oppressing and imprisoning the hero. Overall, Zeffirelli's film, under the heavy influence of Olivier's psychoanalytic lens to *Hamlet*, introduces Elsinore as both sinister stage and psychic architecture for the Oedipal drama.

However, the opening also indicates Zeffirelli's unique way to envision the innate Oedipal theme. As discussed above, Olivier's opening sequence emphasizes the self-exposing camera diving into the castle and capturing the dead Hamlet in an extreme high-angle shot, as though its intention were to express the menacing power of the gaze over the whole scene, including the dead prince. Unlike the self-exposing super-egotistical gaze of Olivier's camera, however, Zeffirelli's camerawork remains naturalistic and essentially invisible throughout the film. For instance, the opening credit sequence, despite its resemblance to Olivier's cinematography engulfing Elsinore with shadows, introduces Elsinore in a few static eye-level shots that are pieced together to guide audience into the castle's interior. Zeffirelli's editing suggests that his film is adopting the classical Hollywood's storytelling in creating a screen for the Oedipus complex. In other words, the repressed and entangled incestuous relationship between the characters is to be unpacked through the less obtrusive cinematography and the seamless continuity editing of conventional costume dramas.

The inserted funeral scene, indeed, foregrounds the incest theme by confirming that the screen offered by Zeffirelli's *Hamlet* is intended for nothing but the most primal fantasy—the origin of all sexual fantasies—revolving around the Oedipal triangle of son, mother, and father on the subject's psychic stage. In the castle's forecourt, the camera slowly moves toward the underground crypt, where the funeral of old Hamlet is taking place. Inside, the mise-en-scène resembles a proscenium, at the center of which lies the coffin, lit in spotlight, around which the family members gather. The theatrical set highlighting the locus of the Oedipal conflicts manifests the centrality of the incest theme to the plot of the film. On this *stage* prepared for the royal family of Denmark, incestuous desire constitutes two different triangular relationships among the characters: on the one hand, the order and size of the shots that show Gertrude (played by Glenn Close), Old Hamlet (played by Paul Scofield), and Claudius (played by Alan Bates) express the Oedipal triangle of the older generation; on the other hand, the editing with elaborate eye-line matches reveals another triangle composed of Claudius, young Hamlet (played by Mel Gibson), and Gertrude.

The editing, which juxtaposes Gertrude, the dead King, and Claudius, reveals the preexisting erotic rivalry between Old Hamlet and Claudius over Gertrude: the reciprocity between the medium shot of the dead King and that of Gertrude who sobs at her husband's death is brutally interrupted by a close-up of Claudius, whose beaming eyes expose his desire for her and his intense jealousy of the dead brother whose death she mourns bitterly. The scene then moves toward the other triad comprising young Hamlet, Claudius, and Gertrude. As Claudius declares that the prince is "the most immediate to our throne" over the body of his murdered brother, Hamlet is shown in close-up, darkened by the heavy cloak covering his head.[63] Gertrude and Claudius then exchange a covert and significant look, followed immediately by another close-up of Hamlet, who appears to have caught the discreet glance shared between his mother and his uncle. The juxtaposition of Hamlet's close-up with the two shots connecting Gertrude and Claudius makes visible the fact that Hamlet's frustration is caused by his alienation from the erotic triangle as well as his disgust at his uncle's sexual desire for his mother. Emphatically, the invented scene of the funeral in Zeffirelli's adaptation reveals the editorial frame through which this film reworks Shakespeare's *Hamlet*. That is, the film proffers the pictorial locus on which the forbidden sexual fantasy imagined by the young prince may be actualized—in other words, on which the Oedipal impulse is given a chance to be enacted and projected on screen, as in *Oedipus Rex,* in a most literal and visible way.

One particularly salient adaptation strategy enables Zeffirelli's film to weave a comprehensible cinematic fantasy out of Shakespeare's extremely evasive *Hamlet*: the film's tactic of setting up Old Hamlet, the Ghost, as an ideal ego rather than an ego ideal or super-ego. From the outset, this figure is deprived of his original authority and is reduced to being only one of the participants in the romantic triangles in the inserted funeral. The film offers a realistic image of the corpse of Old Hamlet, which is carefully hidden and suppressed in most *Hamlet* texts. From this moment, the demystified image of Old Hamlet lying dead in the first scene appears to defy the role of the devouring dead father whose invisible yet omnipresent gaze and threatening voice persist in the psyche of his trembling son.

The later dialogue between young Hamlet and the Ghost confirms this suggestion: in the first confrontation with the Ghost, the normalized

---

63. William Shakespeare, *Hamlet* (I. 2. 109), 74.

conversation between the dead father and the son is presented in a shot-reverse-shot sequence alternating close-ups of the two figures on relatively equal terms. Moreover, the scene begins by framing the dead father within a rather diminishing high-angle shot from the perspective of Hamlet, who is still standing. The Ghost in his first appearance on screen is seen deprived of his "warlike form"—"Armèd at point exactly, cap-a-pe (from head to toe)," as the original play describes.[64] In addition, while the crime of Claudius is unraveled by him, the film refuses to use a flashback that might confirm the truth of what the Ghost imparts and, consequently, the authority of his command to avenge. In a very clear sense, the film employs a visualizing strategy to diminish the Ghost's authority, which differentiates Zeffirelli's film from other film adaptations, whose foci lie on the dead father's super-egotistical power in his ghostly omnipresence. This calm, gentle, and sad figure of the Ghost is represented with no mystifying props and camera techniques, such as a threatening metallic costume, low-angle shots, shadows, or foggy mise-en-scène. In a psychoanalytic sense, the reduced figure of the Ghost in Zeffirelli's adaptation prepares the film's explicitly erotic rendition of the play's climactic confrontation between Hamlet and Gertrude in the closet scene, and allows the scene to bring the repressed Oedipal fantasy to the surface. Overall, the cinematic representation of the Ghost with diminished super-egotistical authority allows the film to actualize the incestuous coitus on screen as literally as the son might have wished it to be in the unconscious.

As mentioned above, Zeffirelli's film clarifies its intention to visualize the Freudian interpretation of the play with the same weight that it affords to Shakespeare's original text. Consequently, the film quite bluntly employs the Freudian interpretation as a central plot device, in contrast to Olivier's more subtle and less eroticized Oedipal lens. The closet scene displays the erotic nature of Hamlet's suppressed incestuous desire, which is concealed in the confrontation between judgmental Hamlet and quickly surrendering Gertrude in Olivier's adaptation. While charging his mother with having an adulterous relationship with Claudius, Hamlet, played by Mel Gibson, clearly mimics sexual intercourse with Gertrude, played by Glenn Close, whose facial expression and scream at her shouting son can be interpreted as sexual ecstasy. Numerous critics have made no attempt to conceal their discontent and resistance in commenting that the film "extends the

---

64. William Shakespeare, *Hamlet* (I. 1. 47) and (I. 2. 200), 65 and 77.

oedipal impulse to an almost obscene limit."[65] What is most remarkable in the film's closet scene is that the explicit representation of the incestuous relationship between a son and his mother bears the mark of an unusual level of challenge to Freud's theory of the super-ego. In other words, the incestuous gesture performed on screen, free from the repression, indicates the film's weakening of the super-egotistical force that Freud himself clearly describes as the persistent agent of repression and regulation, which is necessary for the ego to construct its sexual fantasy. Ironically, then, Zeffirelli's adaptation dismantles itself as either a Shakespearean text or a Freudian text by attempting to cast itself as a Freudian interpretation of Shakespeare's play in an overly literal sense.

If we accept Zeffirelli's refusal to follow the footsteps of its authoritative precursors, how might we understand the adapter's attempt to portray an overtly sexualized rendition of Oedipal desire on screen? Zeffirelli, in his multi-million-dollar endeavor to bring the melancholic prince of the Elizabethan stage to the late twentieth-century screen, intends to create a version that is more accessible to contemporary young audiences, assisted by the star personae borne by the actors who portray the major characters. In particular, Mel Gibson as Hamlet and Glenn Close as Gertrude saturate *Hamlet* with the heavy shadows of their previous roles in commercially successful films: Mel Gibson as a macho action hero with manic depression in *Mad Max* and *Lethal Weapon* and Glenn Close as a femme fatale with sexual power that poses a threat to the hero in both *Fatal Attraction* and *Dangerous Liaisons*.[66] The unabashed use of star casting serves Zeffirelli's intention to "[bring] Shakespeare to the mass," as well as his desire to create "a new kind of Hamlet"—a man of action rather than introspection, whose nature and character are conveyed through by dynamic cinematic visuals rather than Shakespeare's soliloquies on the page.[67]

From a psychoanalytical perspective, the casting in Zeffirelli's adaptation offers film audience a more comfortable and familiar screen for narcissistic identification with Shakespeare's characters whose psychological motivation is notoriously ambivalent in the original.

---

65. Douglas Brode, *Shakespeare in the Movies: From the Silent Era to Today* (New York: Berkeley Boulevard Books, 2001), 137.

66. Ibid.

67. Ace G. Pilkington, "Zeffirelli's Shakespeare," in *Shakespeare and the Moving Image: The Plays on Film and Television*, ed. Anthony Davies and Stanley Wells (Cambridge: Cambridge University Press, 1994), 168 and 174.

Although many critics accuse the film's casting decisions of having flattened the multi-layered original text, we can read here one of the most powerful desires at play in the process of film adaptation—that is, the desire for a less interrupted and more complete imaginary identification. However, this wish for undisrupted identification with the image is complicated in the process of actualizing and enlarging the familiar literary characters on screen. The imaginary identification in this case is constantly interrupted by the symbolic dimension of the original text, which escapes the grasp of the imaginary register of on-screen images.

The paradoxical coexistence of the intense desire for imaginary identification without interruption and the predetermined symbolic interference of an original text in film adaptations, however, touches on the core of the paradox of human desire, according to Lacan. He contends that, after Oedipalization, it is the very impossibility of "the being's identification with its pure and simple image" that allows the subject to proceed along the metonymic chain of desire that has no end but death.[68] Therefore, screen adaptation is intended to adapt literary characters into screen personas for imaginary identification against the intervention of the symbolic signifiers of the originals. This manifests the fundamental loss of the pure narcissistic reciprocity between self and image in the course of the Oedipus complex and the ego's perpetual attempt to find a substitute for this lost original image. As such, the process of adapting literary works on screen reveals the fundamental structure of human desire, I would suggest, more closely than any other artistic expressions.

In this sense, Zeffirelli's adaptation seeks to visualize the forbidden scene repressed in the unconscious of the Oedipalized son, using unambiguous characters shaped through classical continuity editing and the star personas of Hollywood—a "dream factory" that manufactures fantasies for mass consumption. The film's single-mindedness leads us to speculate how, from a psychoanalytic view, the construction of fantasy unfolding on screen is related to the Oedipus complex and, in particular, the repression of Oedipal desire. The connection is first recognized by Freud, who defines the fantasy as a scene "which stages an unconscious desire," the most fundamental of which is the Oedipal

---

68. Lacan, *The Seminar of Jacques Lacan, Book II*, 238.

wish for the love of the mother and the death of the father.⁶⁹ Freud also emphasizes the importance of the visual realm in constructing fantasy, while Lacan, following Freud, "compares the fantasy scene to a frozen image on a cinema screen."⁷⁰

Furthering the idea, Lacan's later teaching focuses on the link between the imaginary structure of fantasy and the trauma of castration at the resolution of the Oedipus complex. In *Seminar XI* on four fundamental concepts of psychoanalysis, Lacan suggests that "the phantasy is never anything more than the screen that conceals something quite primary" and thus traumatic—that is, castration.⁷¹ In this sense, it is possible to interpret Zeffirelli's adaptation, which renders the compound and polysemic original text as a simplistic sexual fantasy, as a *reactionary* text that resists the conscious recognition of the traumatic inaccessibility to meaning that readers and adapters routinely believe Shakespeare's *Hamlet* embraces. Indeed, as many literary critics have complained, the play is a "hermeneutic trap" for any reader.⁷² The memory of castration, triggered by the uncertainty of what Shakespeare truly meant, provokes resistance to the unsettling void experienced when reading *Hamlet*. This resistance spurs the desire for the specular image, a desire that seeks to rivet meaning onto the screen for a direct and immediate identification—one that, rather than the traumatic frustration of our inability to understand, provides us with narcissistic pleasure. This screen is, as Freud and Lacan describe, is what we call fantasy.

We must not forget that it is not only Franco Zeffirelli, as an adapter, who responds to the inaccessibility of concrete meaning in the original text by casting fantasy onto the screen and shaping it into a comprehensible narrative with a seemingly clear-cut causal relation between linguistic signified and cinematic signifier. The appeal for fantasy as a resistance to the anxiety about the void in our symbolic

---

69. Sigmund Freud, "A Child Is Being Beaten," in *The Standard Edition of the Complete Psychological Works of Sigmund Freud: Volume XVII*, trans. James Strachey (London: The Hogarth Press and the Institute of Psycho-Analysis, 1955), 177.

70. Evans, *An Introductory Dictionary of Lacanian Psychoanalysis*, 60.

71. Lacan, *Seminar XI*, 60.

72. Cora L. Diaz de Chumaceiro, "Hamlet in Freud's Thoughts: Reinterpretations in the Psychoanalytic Literature," *Journal of Poetry Therapy* 11, no. 3 (1998): 148.

system is, to varying degrees, involved in every film adaptation of a literary work: that is, every filmmaker's desire to adapt literary texts to the screen is none other than the expression of the subject's resistance to the sheer impossibility of finding one true, unchangeable, and unchallengeable meaning in a text. Moreover, the function of fantasy in this respect is also shared by every reader who is destined to repeat the process of transferring the symbolic register of a written text to the imaginary signifier of images in confrontation with the lack of a confirmed meaning in a linguistic signifier.

More interestingly, the act of resistance through the construction of fantasy is a characteristic psychological reaction on the part of Shakespeare's hero Hamlet. In his father's death, Hamlet encounters the world's meaninglessness. The young prince desperately needs to overcome this inertia, which means death to the subject of desire. His ego appears to bestow the function of the super-ego upon the ghost of the dead father, who chides him for his inability to live on by desiring revenge, crown, and Ophelia, all of which will ultimately enable Hamlet to replace his dead father. From this perspective, the Ghost is a dramatic or psychic voice which is to articulate Hamlet's own turbulent jealousy at his mother's remarriage and it is not incorrect to consider the Ghost as "the very coinage of [the prince's] brain."[73]

To confirm the above point, the dialogue with the Ghost, in the very place of Hamlet's unconscious, appears to dwell obsessively and exclusively on the imagined *sexual scene* between the "most seeming-virtuous Queen" and "that incestuous, that adulterate beast."[74] Oddly enough, the ghost of the dead king, whether in the original play or in most cinematic adaptations, never expresses any concern about Denmark's war-like state in the hands of Claudius, a deceptive political animal. On the unconscious level, from a Lacanian perspective, this sexual fantasy—constructed by Hamlet and voiced through the Ghost—serves as an attempt to mask the traumatic void left by the absence of concrete meaning in Hamlet's life. Similarly, the on-screen portrayal of incestuous gestures functions as a defense against the castration experienced by readers, adapters, and audiences alike, who confront the elusive meaning of Shakespeare's original play. Therefore, Zeffirelli's "obscene" disclosure of what should be kept hidden provides a *close-up* of the mother's "enseaméd bed" designed to keep at arm's length the

73. William Shakespeare, *Hamlet* (III. 4. 137), 151.
74. William Shakespeare, *Hamlet* (I. 5. 46 and 42), 91.

trauma of castration, which would otherwise come too close—both to Hamlet and to the adapter of the play.[75]

### Kenneth Branagh's Hamlet: *The Dream of a Complete* Hamlet

Kenneth Branagh's *William Shakespeare's Hamlet* (1996) is, as Samuel Crowl claims, an extravagant commercial epic that "stretches and challenges our assumptions about what is possible in a Shakespeare film."[76] Along with his screen adaptations of other canonical literary materials, such as Mary Shelley's *Frankenstein,* Branagh has the longest catalogue of Shakespeare films directed and acted by a single film adapter to his name. In particular, his populist approach to Shakespeare has sought to capture mass audiences by aiming to create a "Shakespeare set free from the taint of elitism and 'restored' to his proper status as a commercially viable, accessible playwright for the masses."[77] However, his complete screen adaptation of the four-hour play *Hamlet,* which is the longest of Shakespeare's plays, is not merely an outcome of commercial calculation but is a personal dream with psychological complexity and depth. As Branagh confesses, "This film is simply the passionate expression of a dream. A dream that has preoccupied me for so many years."[78]

Although the adapter's intense psychological investment is not uncommon in films based on Shakespeare's work—in particular, screen adaptations of *Hamlet*—one noteworthy aspect of Branagh's lifelong dream of making an unabridged *Hamlet* for the screen stands out: his self-described "obsession" with creating a "*Hamlet* uncut," despite his experience and knowledge cautioning the seasoned filmmaker as to how

---

75. William Shakespeare, *Hamlet* (III. 4. 93), 149.

76. Samuel Crowl, "Flamboyant Realist: Kenneth Branagh," in *The Cambridge Companion to Shakespeare on Film*, ed. Russell Jackson (Cambridge: Cambridge University Press, 2000), 227.

77. Douglas Lainer, "'Art thou base, common and popular?': The Cultural Politics of Kenneth Branagh's *Hamlet*," in *Spectacular Shakespeare: Critical Theory and Popular Cinema*, ed. Courtney Lehmann and Lisa S. Starks (Madison, WI and Teaneck, NJ: Fairleigh Dickinson University Press, 2002), 149.

78. Kenneth Branagh, "Introduction," in *Kenneth Branagh, Hamlet by William Shakespeare: Screenplay, Introduction and Film Diary* (London: Chatto & Windus, 1996), viii.

difficult and unrealistic it would be to make a full-length commercial *Hamlet*. The completeness of an adaptation, illusionary though may it be, can be explained in two ways. Consciously, that which the filmmaker strives to achieve in an adaptation is a textual scope that embraces all inconsistencies and fills inextricable gaps in any reader's limited understanding of the original's signification. This process appears to express the respectful awe that the adapter experiences in relation to the unimpeachable law, or words, penned by the author of the original. However, at the unconscious level, the desire to produce a complete adaptation may indicate the ambition to produce a metaphor rather than a metonym—in other words, an adapter's dream of a complete replacement of the original text. Viewed from a slightly different angle, this ambitious wish for a replacement, rather than a representation of the original text, corresponds to the engulfing frustration experienced in the traumatic confrontation with the very impossibility of accessing the one true meaning of the literary original. Branagh humbly lets his ignorance be known, saying "I believe I've come happily to realize that of course I cannot explain *Hamlet*."[79] However, he elevates his own film to the same level of incomprehensibility by imparting his inability to explain his own interpretation of *Hamlet*. Most interestingly, he seems assured of the unique position of this full-length adaptation of *Hamlet* for screen as a substitute for the authority of the original on stage, saying in his introductory commentary on the DVD, "no one's done this before, and no one will do it again."[80]

To produce a "complete" screen version or replacement of Shakespeare's *Hamlet*, Branagh seems to do his utmost to keep his distance from the memory of other filmic interpretations of *Hamlet* prior to his. First, he discards the ghostly, gloomy medieval look of Elsinore, which originated from Olivier's claustrophobic and labyrinthine Gothic castle and was repeated and only modestly transformed in other *Hamlet* films by Kozintsev (1964), Richardson (1969), and Zeffirelli (1990). Branagh radically revises the locus of the Elizabethan drama based on the medieval legend into a Victorian palace with excessive decoration and light. In addition to the dazzlingly lit interior set, his film presents a crisp winter landscape, sparkling with snow that covers the entire estate of Elsinore. In a practical sense, the cheerful use of the full color

---

79. Ibid.
80. Kenneth Branagh, introduction to *William Shakespeare's Hamlet*, directed by Kenneth Branagh (Warner Brothers, 1996), DVD.

palette surely attracts the late twentieth-century audience's attention and sustains their interest during the excessively long screening time. Furthermore, as we learn from the production documentary *To Be on Screen: A History of Hamlet*, the film's Victorian aesthetic forms the backdrop for replanting Shakespeare's words into a historical period, which would allow contemporary audiences to understand the drama more easily. At the same time, however, the Victorian setting provides a landscape of the recent past that maintains the distance, neither too far nor too close, from the present that is necessary to comfortably host Shakespeare's Elizabethan language.

However, the self-differentiating filming strategy of Branagh's adaptation is not the only factor that makes this unabridged on screen *Hamlet* unique. Branagh disagrees with the overwhelming psychoanalytic trend in adapting *Hamlet* to screen and clearly resists it by offering his own approach to Shakespeare. The film deliberately shifts its focus away from Hamlet's incestuous relationship with his mother. Branagh's adaptation removes the entangled psychosexual complexity, including the unconscious guilt tied to Hamlet's repressed Oedipal desires and jealousy over Claudius's possession of the forbidden object of his own desire. In Branagh's interpretation, the young prince displays undisguised contempt for his mother, whose untimely passion disgusts him rather than rekindling any suppressed desire. In Branagh's interpretation, the young prince shows undisguised contempt for his mother, whose untimely passion disgusts him rather than revoking his desire. Hence, the film's closet scene includes no sexual connotations, unlike many other film adaptations featuring visual cues that signal the son's erotic desire for his still young and attractive mother. Instead, Branagh's adaptation pays far greater attention to male–male relationships by bringing into the light the play's political and historical implications, consequently—or perhaps intentionally—driving the drama in a more male-oriented direction. Hamlet in this "complete" version is thus represented as a young prince under the pressure of the public gaze rather than as an Oedipal son trapped between his unconscious sexual desire for his mother and the internalized gaze of his dead father.

Branagh's 70mm film often reveals sweeping panoramic views of the snow-covered palace and estate, offering spectators the immersive cinematic experience of Shakespeare's play as an epic, rather than a confined psychological drama. In an effort to emphasize the drama's epic quality, the ghost of the dead king is envisioned as a larger-than-life metal statue of old Hamlet, fully armored for battle and captured in extreme low-angle shots. This spectacular image at the film's opening can, in one sense, be linked to the adapter's intention to highlight the play's political subtext. Branagh's interpretation aligns with the original play, which begins with Denmark in a volatile state due to its war with Norway, a conflict triggered by the sudden loss of Denmark's heroic warrior-king. The on-screen appearance of the Ghost as a heroic king in an epic sets the film's tone, which is further reinforced by close-ups showing the collapse of the statue of old Hamlet—a symbol of the end of Denmark's monarchy, or the conclusion of the Hamlets' reign.

Moreover, the two scenes of Hamlet's encounter with the Ghost hint at the psychological peculiarity of the film's rendition of the Ghost— that is, the Ghost as an amalgamation of the epic warrior-king, the terrifying monster, and Hamlet's loving father. The film's complex characterization of the Ghost, distinct from most *Hamlet* adaptations, is particularly evident in the scene of Hamlet's encounter with his father's spirit. At first, the film's representation of the Ghost combines a majestic epic hero and a supernatural monster, constructed through the conventions from both epic and horror—that is, low-angle shots enlarging the figure, extreme close-ups, shaky camera movements, and a gaseous explosion accompanied by thundering sounds. However, as soon as Hamlet begins conversing with the Ghost, the formidable and monstrous image is undercut and replaced by a romanticized flashback accompanied by a swell of emotionally charged music. This shift seems intended to emphasize the Ghost's tender intensity as Hamlet's loving father, later reinforced through recurring similar flashbacks. Even the closet scene, in which the Ghost of the original play looms before Hamlet to chide him for his indecision, seeks to highlight the melodrama of the Ghost's love for his son and his wife, whom he has unexpectedly had to leave behind.

From the outset, the epic and spectral appearance of the Ghost appears to simply foreground the following father-son melodrama and the affection of Hamlet's father toward his son through the sheer tonal and generic contrast. The melodramatic formulation, moreover, changes the nature of Hamlet's duty evoked by the Ghost's command. The revenge in question in this film suddenly turns from a political duty of the prince to a moral and emotional responsibility that Hamlet takes up voluntarily, out of his love for the father. The alteration in Hamlet's relationship with the Ghost disrupts and redefines the psychic focus found in other *Hamlet* films centered on the Oedipus complex.

In another sense, the inconsistency in characterizing the Ghost in Branagh's film may indicate the latent complexity of the relationship between Hamlet and the ghost of his father. First, the overtly melodramatic rendition of the dead father, right after the Ghost's threatening return in the manner of the epic and horror genres, suggests the internal conflict that Hamlet must navigate to accept the Ghost as the father he used to love. Hamlet's real psychological difficulty may lie in his acceptance of the Ghost not only as the apparition of his dear father but also as the father who is still able to love and be loved. In other words, through the self-contradictory process of characterization, the film appears to unintentionally disclose how traumatic it is for Branagh's Hamlet to encounter the Ghost as a haunting figure with the emotional capacity to sustain a relationship with his son even after his death. Here, the Ghost does not function merely as a representative of a super-egotistical command or a law prohibiting the son's secret desire for the mother; rather, the Ghost is even more demanding, as an un-dead father who claims ongoing love for his son and asks the son's love in return forever. Consequently, in place of the Oedipal conflicts between Hamlet (the ego) and the Ghost (the super-ego) through the Queen as a mediator, Branagh's film explores the exclusive relationship between father and son.

The deliberate indifference to the previous psychosexual interpretation of the play also affects the characterization of Claudius, who is often understood as a foil for the ideal father and a rival in the Oedipal triangle. The scene that follows the first encounter with the Ghost presents the celebration of the marriage between Claudius and Gertrude. The performance of a happy marriage between Claudius and Gertrude as well as between Claudius and Denmark even more clearly suggests the male orientation of the film's dramatic focus. In the other two films under discussion, Claudius is represented as an incestuous and adulterous villain from the character's very introduction. In Olivier's film, he is first seen gulping wine and ruthlessly throwing the cup toward servants standing next to him; in Zeffirelli's film, his desiring eyes eagerly seek Gertrude as she weeps over the dead body of the brother he has just murdered. By contrast, Branagh's film admirably sets up Claudius as the best answer for Denmark in its war-like state as well as for the Queen, whose status in the royal court is seriously threatened by her husband's sudden death. This politically experienced and capable Claudius speaks eloquently and appealingly of his grief and joy to the public as they gather to greet the new king. This competent king is apparently a better option than the inexperienced student-prince who sulkily alienates himself from the optimistic path toward a prosperous future for Denmark.

In his opening speech, Claudius exhibits dexterity in managing public expectations and receiving the Queen's dignified yet passionate embrace. Here, the lavish mise-en-scène, paired with the majestic brass band score, saturate the scene with vividness and grandeur. Above all, the optimistic mood of Claudius's coronation is bolstered by Derek Jacobi's sincere and confident portrayal of the character. Interestingly, Jacobi is famous for his numerous interpretations of Hamlet across stage, radio, and television. In addition, it was Jacobi's performance at the New Theatre in Oxford that profoundly impacted the fifteen-year-old Branagh's life, ultimately inspiring his path to theatre and *Hamlet*.[81] Branagh's repeated emphasis in the making-of documentary and various other interviews on the autobiographical connection between himself and Jacobi, whom he regards as a father figure who led him to Shakespearean theatre, certainly discloses the adapter's covert wish to render the film's Claudius as another paternal figure rather than a villain and romantic rival competing for the Queen's incestuous love. Jacobi's Claudius shows no sign of mockery or cynicism toward Hamlet, when he talks about his "unmanly grief."[82] Rather, this father figure appears to have true affection for his one-time nephew and now son. Furthermore, "the remarkable physical resemblance of the 'son' to his 'uncle-father'" in this film adaptation intensifies the link between Claudius and the prince: he is related to Hamlet not through Gertrude but more directly as his living father.[83] In return, the film's phallocentric redirection signals its undercurrent of resistance to unconscious involvement with the mother. The seeming patrilineal line is completed by the much visible presence and significant role of Fortinbras throughout the film's politicizing rendition of the crisis of Denmark.

In addition, Branagh's *Hamlet* is full of onstage and on-screen Hamlets from the past and the present, including John Gielgud (as Priam), who is a legendary Shakespearean actor and an archetypal Hamlet on stage; Derek Jacobi (as Claudius), one of the most influential Hamlets; Richard Briers (as Polonius), who once played a passionate and hysterical Hamlet; and Michael Marloony (as Laertes), who is

---

81. Kenneth Branagh, *Kenneth Branagh, Hamlet*, v.
82. William Shakespeare, *Hamlet* (I. 2. 94), 73.
83. Crowl, "Flamboyant Realist," 235.

the Hamlet of contemporary theatre. The casting, with the help of the film's mise-en-scène characteristic of numerous mirrors, may imply the ego-maniacal tendency of Branagh's Hamlet to see himself at every turn, whereby other former "Hamlets" in this adaptation function as nothing but a mirror reflecting diverse fragments of Branagh's complete filmic *Hamlet*. Apart from these former Hamlets, the assortment of authoritative masculine icons from both stage and screen—including Brian Blessed (as the Ghost), Charlton Heston (as Player King), Lord Richard Attenborough (as the English Ambassador), and John Mills (as old Norway, the uncle of the young Fortinbras)—demonstrates the film's excessive interest in returning *Hamlet* to its Elizabethan stage without an actress or, in a metaphorical sense, any women to interfere in the transactions conducted between men. Yet, ironically here we see Hamlet surrounded by too many fathers.

Branagh's adaptation may imply that his on-screen Hamlet, both inside and outside the film's diegesis, has overcome the long-lasting Oedipus complex that has been envisaged and projected onto the screen of many *Hamlet* films: Branagh's portrayal of Hamlet in the film appears to succeed in rendering the incestuous desire for the mother "desexualized and sublimated."[84] Freud designates this desexualization of Oedipal desire as the signal of the dissolution of the Oedipus complex. Julie Christie's performance of the Queen does not show a sign of the character's provocation of the son's repressed Oedipal desire. Rather, Gertrude, to Branagh's Hamlet, is a romantic rival with whom Hamlet competes for the love of the father(s), both living and dead. Such characterization explains Hamlet's unmitigated contempt and hostility toward her, with no undertone of the unspeakable Oedipal desire for his mother. The film reaffirms the unambiguously hateful relationship between the judgmental Hamlet and the hysterical Gertrude in the closet scene: here, Hamlet exhibits nothing but disgust and contempt for his mother, and Gertrude responds to his despicable charge with a nervous shriek. In fact, the mother's diminished and alienated position in Hamlet's psyche is subtly suggested in a flashback where Hamlet and his father share a heartfelt embrace, while Gertrude is left in the background with Claudius, out of focus. Throughout the film,

---

84. Sigmund Freud, "Dissolution of the Oedipus Complex," in *The Standard Edition of the Complete Psychological Works of Sigmund Freud: Volume XIX*, trans. James Strachey (London: The Hogarth Press and the Institute of Psycho-Analysis, 1961), 177.

the mother is never given a chance to express her genuine love for her son, who always stands aloof from and looks down on her. The bond between the mother and the son in this film adaptation is dysfunctional, even to the extent that Claudius appears to be utterly mistaken when he delivers the line, "the Queen his mother/ Lives almost by his looks."[85] Branagh's directing of the climactic closet scene seems specifically intended to ensure the film's deliberate exclusion of the incestuous undertone present in the original text and projected on screen in the other two *Hamlet* films under discussion; the incestuous, or at least libidinal, intensity is replaced by Hamlet's undisguised grudge against his mother's betrayal and debauchery.

Moreover, the directorial efforts to dispel Hamlet's Oedipal entanglement with his mother result in an unprecedented emphasis on the erotic relationship between Hamlet and Ophelia. In the scene where Polonius questions the nature of the relationship between Hamlet and Ophelia (played by Kate Winslet), a flashback unveils their overtly sexual association, which is only faintly implied in Shakespeare's play. The film further demonstrates the young couple's romantic and erotic attachment as an ongoing undercurrent through repeatedly inserted flashbacks. In other words, the film's calculated omission of the hero's Oedipus complex from the narrative's surface allows him to engage in a proper sexual relationship with an object of his desire. From Lacan's perspective, this Hamlet is not to be lost in the course of his desire and is capable of desiring a particular object in the place of the phallus, which properly functions as "the signifier of his alienation in signification" once it is completely removed and lost into the unconscious.[86] In this light, Hamlet's ability to operate within the symbolic system of desire appears to suggest that this Hamlet is capable of pursuing what he ought to desire, such as revenge, the crown, and Ophelia.

Most of all, Hamlet appears to make his thoughts and state of mind clearly understood through his unabridged soliloquies, dialogues, and speeches, as the verbal cues are often accompanied by the film's expansive flashbacks, supported by the explanatory use of diegetic and non-diegetic sound and music. In this sense, the film's envisioning of sexual engagement between Hamlet and Ophelia can be aligned with the adapter's efforts to render Hamlet more normal than pathological. Indeed, every effort is made to confirm that, for this Hamlet, the phallus

85. William Shakespeare, *Hamlet* (IV. 7. 11–12), 172.
86. Lacan et al. (1977), 28.

is kept in the right place—within the idealized father figures who pass it to their beloved son—and his Oedipal desire is well repressed and appropriately channeled into something other than the forbidden object, the mother. From a historicizing view, the "long deferred" consummation of sexual contact between Ophelia and Hamlet may be intended to signal the dissolution of the Oedipus complex that has dominated the film adaptations of Shakespeare's enigmatic masterwork. Consequently, Branagh's Hamlet shows no sign of bitter frustration, or draining indecision, or painful alienation in signification. Instead, he is the character most actively engaged on screen, making sense of everything and explaining it to the audience.

The director's dream of a complete *Hamlet* may explain the motive behind the adapter's conscious efforts to portray Hamlet as a hero who is not troubled by his own desire or lack thereof. Often, the dilemma in reading Shakespeare's *Hamlet* stems from the play's first act where the trauma is already inflicted by the phallus being suddenly out of place yet present, leaving the prince, as well as readers or audiences, unable to make sense of anything. Hamlet's inextricable ordeals mirror the difficulty many adapters face in pinning down the meaning of the text, which, like the Ghost, returns as something incomprehensible, unrepresentable, and irresistible. While other on-screen Hamlets reflect the deeply troubled ego of the cinematic son in confrontation with the super-ego embodied in Shakespeare's masterpiece, Branagh's heroic and masculine Hamlet represents the director's dream of a complete substitution of the original *Hamlet*.

## *The Play's the Thing*

This chapter has examined film adaptations of *Hamlet* in light of the Oedipus complex. In doing so, the argument has engaged in theoretical speculation on relevant analytic concepts, such as the super-ego, the ego, and the phallus, in order to comprehend the critical adaptation of this fundamental "law" (i.e., the Oedipus complex) from various angles. Within the outlined psychoanalytic framework, I have analyzed different responses to the authority of the original text as found in three cinematic *Hamlet*s—Olivier's, Zeffirelli's, and Branagh's. The close reading of the three adapters and their films has sought to uncover or, at least, cohere around an alternate correlation among the seemingly contradictory interpretations each film presents. Yet, I find myself struggling to identify an appropriate term for the unrepresentable and unknowable center shared by all cinematic adaptations of the play. Therefore, in concluding this chapter, I would like to speculate on this "thing" between *Hamlet* and its adaptations—that which resists being named and hence remains as "the thing."

At the end of Act 2, Hamlet once again succumbs to deep remorse over his hesitation to avenge his father's death and his inability to act on his passion, particularly after watching the player king recite the tragic end of Priam, with "all his visage waned,/ Tears in his eyes, distraction in's aspéct,/ A broken voice, and his whole function suiting/ With forms to his conceit."[87] Using the power of fiction to tap into the depths of the human psyche, Hamlet devises a plan to expose the murderous heart of his uncle: "The play's the thing/ Wherein I'll catch the conscience of the king."[88] Like many puzzles in *Hamlet*, the use of the indefinite noun *thing* here is obscure and enigmatic. On a textual level, Hamlet is referring to the play "The Murder of Gonzago," which is staged within *Hamlet* and reenacts the murder scene before the murderer himself. As Claudius watches, he recognizes himself in the character of Lucianus, who kills his uncle, the king Gonzago, in the same manner as he himself has murdered his brother.

However, if we focus more on the function of the play that Hamlet believes will expose something that is hidden in the human mind, "the play" Hamlet mentions cannot be reduced simply to "The Murder of Gonzago." In other words, the play as "the thing" is not a specific, closed structure of a text. Rather, the term signifies the universality of theater, where something at the core of the human subject—though typically inaccessible—suddenly and momentarily becomes presentable and perceivable as an external *thing* that nonetheless defies nomenclature. From this perspective, a remarkable similarity emerges between Hamlet's comments on the play as "the thing" and Lacan's elaboration of the Freudian term *das Ding*, or the Thing. Much like Hamlet's belief that the play provides access to hidden truth, Lacan posits that "what one finds in *das Ding* is the true secret"—that is, "the beyond-of-the-signified."[89] This is the primal nucleus of the subject, which is repeatedly drawn back to the point of castration through the circular trajectory of the drive. As Lacan explains, "it is around *das Ding* that the whole

---

87. William Shakespeare, *Hamlet* (II. 2. 552–4), 120.
88. William Shakespeare, *Hamlet* (II. 2. 602–3), 121. (My emphasis.)
89. Lacan, *Seminar VII*, 46 and 54.

adaptive development revolves, a development that is so specific to man insofar as the symbolic process reveals itself to be inextricably woven into it."[90]

Likewise, in the unceasing desire to adapt Shakespeare's *Hamlet* for the screen, *Hamlet* is not an object of desire but the object *in* desire, due to the play's status as "the Sphinx of modern Literature" or "hermeneutic trap" that it is believed to embody. The unnamable within this masterful literary signifier bears countless names and evokes a wealth of meanings. The multitude of names and meanings surrounding this Thing in *Hamlet* manifests the existence of the beyond-of-the-signified, which eludes the castration of the Father and the Law. Nevertheless, I do not suggest that Shakespeare's original play ought to occupy a central, dominant position in our attempts to understand film adaptations of canonical literary works. Rather, film adaptation serves as an exemplary field that reveals the human subject's desire for—and even pathological pleasure in—the Thing that both conceals and signifies the abyss of castration, particularly under the menacing gaze of the super-ego. In the course of repeated attempts to adapt Shakespeare's *Hamlet* for the screen, the original play takes on the position of the Thing or the Ghost that perpetually haunts us, while each film adaptation, in casting the ungraspable Ghost onto the screen of modern mass media, functions as a thing—a tangible reminder of the elusive Thing. Like the play-within-a-play in *Hamlet*, these film adaptations epitomize the psychic drama of the Oedipus complex, through which each of us organizes our own Oedipalized—and thus civilized—self.

90. Ibid., 57.

# 3

# THE RESISTANCE TO THE ORIGINALS IN HITCHCOCK'S ADAPTATIONS

A huge crocodile in whose jaws you are—that's the mother. One never knows what might suddenly come over her and make her shut her trap. That's what the mother's desire is.

—Jacques Lacan, *Seminar XVI*

## *Texts of Doubt: Uncanny, Unpleasure, Anxiety, and the Mother*

This chapter aims to pose a counterthesis to the previous chapter, in which I argued that for adapters, precursor texts function as authoritative commands, akin to the Oedipal father, which must be obeyed and followed. In her 2001 book *Speaking the Unspeakable: Religion, Misogyny, and the Uncanny Mother in Freud's Cultural Texts*, Diane Jonte-Pace uses the term "counterthesis" to refer to that which undercuts Freud's "oedipal master-thesis" built on the child's murderous wish toward the father and incestuous desire for the mother.[1] Jonte-Pace's reading of Freudian texts as counterthesis frequently associates death with the figure of the mother, rather than the threat posed by the Oedipal father. In particular, the book's second chapter, "Death, Mothers, and the Afterlife: At Home in the Uncanny," highlights *The Uncanny* and *Beyond the Pleasure Principle* as key sites for this counterthesis within Freud's work, suggesting that these texts adhere to the Oedipal framework while subtly subverting its core premise. Similarly, my use of "counterthesis" here reflects the relationship between the previous chapter and this one, marking the shift from the Oedipal father to the deadly Mother. Based on close scrutiny of Freud's counterthesis texts and Lacan's elaboration, I will explore the idea that, in adapting works

---

1. Diane Jonte-Pace, *Speaking the Unspeakable: Religion, Misogyny, and the Uncanny Mother in Freud's Cultural Texts* (Berkeley, Los Angeles and London: University of California Press, 2001).

of literature for the screen, the influence of the original is not always welcome.

Contrary to the respectful and awe-struck attitude toward the gravitas of classic authors, the super-egotistical authority of original texts is often radically diminished and even rejected outright when filmmakers adapt relatively contemporary texts produced by less illustrious writers. Alfred Hitchcock's works epitomize this tendency. Throughout six decades of producing, writing, and directing films, Hitchcock self-consciously selected originals for his adaptations that would allow him egoistical freedom, making his films based on less influential originals to be consumed and then forgotten. Widely known as a voracious reader, literature appears to have been Hitchcock's major source of inspiration. Forty-four films out of the fifty-three that constitute Hitchcock's filmography are, in varying degrees, adaptations of literary sources, including novels, short stories, plays, and libretti.[2] Such statistics surely indicate that, for Hitchcock, adaptation is symptomatic rather than a practical choice based on commercial or aesthetic calculation. Nevertheless, none of these originals survives the director-adapter's notoriously irreverent approach to adaptation. Consequently, few of the original texts on which his films are based linger in the audience's memory or garner significant attention from film scholars. Hitchcock's famous interview with François Truffaut reveals his imperious demeanor toward the original texts he adapted for the screen:

> What I do is to read a story only once, and if I like the basic idea, **I just forget all about the book and start to create cinema.** Today I would be unable to tell you the story of Daphne du Maurier's *The Birds*. I read it only once, and very quickly at that.[3]

---

2. The statistics here draw on information from Patrick McGilligan's, *Alfred Hitchcock: A Life in Darkness and Light* (New York: Regan Books, 2003), Leonard J. Leff's *Hitchcock and Selznick: The Rich and Strange Collaboration of Alfred Hitchcock and David O. Selznick in Hollywood* (Berkeley and Los Angeles, CA: University of California Press, 1999) and François Truffaut's *Hitchcock: The Definitive Study of Alfred Hitchcock* (New York: Simon & Schuster Paperbacks, 1983).

3. See Truffaut, *Hitchcock*, 71. (My emphasis.)

Such a dismissive attitude might provoke curiosity, then, as what drove the director to repeatedly adapt literary works while vigilantly erasing traces of the original texts. Indeed, the above comment discloses not only Hitchcock's conscious rejection of the literary text's interference with his cinematic vision but also the unconscious resistance to the influence of the original source in the course of adaptation. In other words, the interview reveals the ironic coexistence of Hitchcock's obsession with literary texts as a source of inspiration for his films and his anxiety over their potential to infiltrate his creations. In interrogating the counterthesis or the *other* side of film adaptation, this chapter will examine the paradoxically incompatible relationship between a literary original and its film adaptation, as epitomized by Hitchcock's case.

In particular, a close analysis of *Rebecca* (1940) and *The Birds* (1963)—both original texts written by the female author Daphne du Maurier—will elucidate the operation of the hidden *drive* that this chapter seeks to investigate.[4] Indeed, the fact that Hitchcock adapted three of Daphne du Maurier's works—*Jamaica Inn*, *Rebecca*, and *The Birds*—indicates a highly unusual level of engagement between the two storytellers. Among these three adaptations of du Maurier's stories, *Rebecca* and *The Birds* form an interesting antithesis. *Rebecca* is remarkably faithful to the original novel when compared with Hitchcock's other adaptations. This extraordinary fidelity may, of course, be attributed to the pressure and influences that the director likely faced in a completely new environment at the time of the film's production: *Rebecca* was Hitchcock's first Hollywood film, made soon after his arrival at the center of the world's film industry. By contrast, *The Birds* stands out as one of Hitchcock's most subversive adaptations, radically altering the setting, narrative structure, characters, and even thematic focus—specifically, the psychic dynamics between humans and birds. More significantly, the latter film appears to revisit *Rebecca* by interrogating psychological elements that Hitchcock had not yet discovered or fully engaged with when making

4. Hitchcock's *Rebecca* (1940) is based on du Maurier's best-seller of the same title, which was published in 1936 and met with immediate and phenomenal popularity in the UK and US markets. *The Birds* (1963) is loosely based on her short story "The Birds," which was first published in 1952. Several years prior to adapting the story, Hitchcock optioned it for the television series he produced and included the story in an anthology entitled *My Favorites in Suspense* (New York: Alfred Hitchcock Presents, 1959).

his first American film. In the interview quoted above, Truffaut suggests that du Maurier's influence permeated many of Hitchcock's later films, which Hitchcock readily concedes:

> **F.T** Making that picture [*Rebecca*], I imagine, was something of a challenge … The experience, I think, had repercussions on the films that came later. Didn't it inspire you to enrich many of them with the psychological ingredients you initially discovered in the Daphne du Maurier novel?
> **A.H** That's true.[5]

However, the work of detecting what the director had deliberately attempted to defy and reject in the process of adaptation requires an approach that goes beyond simply analyzing what is visible and audible in film adaptations. This chapter thus aims to interrogate the operations of the negative psychic tendency that cannot be captured on the textual surface of a film adaptation.

The presence of such a negative tendency is confirmed, paradoxically, by the vigorous denial that attempts to negate the genesis of a film as an adaptation. Working with the negative, moreover, is precisely what the discourse of psychoanalysis has sought to do as a means of accessing that which is denied and thus invisible to consciousness. Nevertheless—or, owing to the very genesis of psychoanalysis as such—in the course of constructing and formulating the discipline of psychoanalysis as a route toward the negative, Freud came to realize that his discourse was invariably haunted by an insistent gap or hole at its heart that resisted any theorizing speculation. The founder of psychoanalysis sought to capture this *something* of pure negativity by endowing it with a multitude of names, including the unconscious, the uncanny, the drive, anxiety, death, and woman. In a number of his works, Freud attempted—almost in vain—to integrate this impasse into the discourse of psychoanalysis, acknowledging that it persistently remained outside his meticulous case studies and comprehensive theorization. Of these texts, I wish to focus on three—*The Uncanny* (1919), *Beyond the Pleasure Principle* (1920), and *Inhibitions, Symptoms and Anxiety* (1926)—as a starting point for examining the insistent drive behind the process of film adaptation that often finds expression in negative forms.

5. Truffaut, *Hitchcock*, 129.

The high degree of ambiguity in these three works requires a more cautious and tactful approach than the straightforward application of psychoanalytic concepts to Hitchcock's film adaptations as a case study. To effectively employ these Freudian concepts in the search for the other side of film adaptation, it is useful to engage with Lacan's return to Freud, which offers a subversive and revelatory re-reading of Freud's works. Lacan's relevance in this chapter lies in his ability to navigate the Freudian field by framing it through a double negation, allowing him to approach the deadlock embedded in Freud's negative concepts. The concepts of the *lack of lack* and anxiety that "is not without an object" exemplify and even epitomize the core characteristics of Lacan's reading of Freud.[6] This chapter will closely examine the radically redefined notion of anxiety in relation to Lacan's subversive speculations about the Mother. The reformulated concept of the Mother opens a gateway to the elusive, self-negating, and uncanny dimension of screen adaptation—a dimension shaped by a different set of psychic dynamics than the Oedipal relationship explored in the previous chapter. Ultimately, through the investigation of the *other* side of screen adaptation, this chapter aims to correlate the drive behind this particular form of media transformation with the uncanny aspect of a speaking subject "that ought to have remained … secret and hidden but has come to light."[7]

## The Uncanny at Home

In his 1919 essay *The Uncanny*, Freud addresses a psychic paradox in his search for the origin of uncanny feelings, a paradox that may provide a key to understanding Hitchcock's ambivalent attitude toward his literary sources. Freud begins with a philological approach to the psychological ambivalence of the uncanny, wherein "feelings of a positive nature," associated with what is "beautiful, attractive and sublime," are intertwined "with the opposite feelings of repulsion and distress."[8] After a lengthy quotation from a German dictionary, Freud

---

6. Jacques Lacan, *Seminar X: Anxiety 1962–1963*, trans. Cormac Gallagher, 58. (Retrieved from www.lacaninireland.com.)

7. Sigmund Freud, "The Uncanny," in *The Standard Edition of the Complete Psychological Works of Sigmund Freud: Volume XVII*, trans. James Strachey (London: The Hogarth Press and the Institute of Psycho-Analysis, 1955), 224.

8. Ibid., 219.

concludes his speculation by highlighting a circular trajectory that links the two opposite terms: *heimlich*, meaning homely, familiar, and intimate, and *unheimlich*, meaning eerie, frightening, and unsettling. He writes, "Thus, *heimlich* is a word the meaning of which develops in the direction of ambivalence, until it finally coincides with its opposite, *unheimlich*. *Unheimlich* is in some way or other a sub-species of *heimlich*."[9]

In a similar vein, the concept of the uncanny sheds light on the existential paradox of film adaptation, manifested in the psychic urge that drives the adapter away from their own starting point. Put differently, an adapter like Hitchcock seems anxious to differentiate the realm of their visual creation from its source of inspiration, as though the written text that sparked their vision contained something unbearable. To avoid the unwanted interference of original texts, Hitchcock's strategy is to restrict himself to reading a literary source very quickly. If possible, he seems to suggest that one should read it only once, in order to wash away the traces of those words on the page and then begin creating purely cinematic images—free from the haunting emotions, impressions, and imagery stirred by the literary text that initially provoked the desire for adaptation. In this sense, Freud's association of the *Heim* with a tinge of the *unheimlich* appears to illuminate the hidden psychological dynamic of Hitchcock's self-contradictory relationship to literary originals. These texts on the page serve as a "home" of creation, yet contain something ominous and repellent that must be spit out—something, in Freud's account, *unheimlich*.

Interestingly, Freud's attempt to articulate and explain the uncanny as a concept resonates with a note of inherent impossibility. He steers his way through his conceptualization of the uncanny with the intention of anchoring it to his master structure based on the Oedipus complex, even though the uncanny, by his own account, is something that resists repression by any signifier. In the second section of the essay, Freud analyzes E. T. A. Hoffmann's story *The Sandman* along with other mythical narratives to highlight how these texts contain elucidatory examples of the nature and the origin of uncanny experiences. His underlying aim of the discussion is, of course, to subsume the concept of the uncanny under his "Oedipal masterplot" by demonstrating that all these cases perceived as uncanny indicate the occasional return of

---

9. Ibid., 226.

the repressed castration complex.[10] However, contrary to his intention to strengthen his masterplot, Freud's essay on the ghostly concept of the uncanny cannot proceed further than to link the uncanny to the subject's encounter with the return of something that has been and should remain repressed.[11] Furthermore, toward the end of the essay, Freud eventually reveals his own doubt as regards a psychoanalytic investigation of the uncanny: he confesses that an extensive enquiry "would be to open the door to *doubts* about what exactly is the value of our general contention that the uncanny proceeds from something familiar which has been repressed."[12] Through his attempt to conceptualize the uncanny, Freud involuntarily demonstrates the impossibility to achieve a solid understanding of the term that would reaffirm his Oedipal masterplot.

A similar impossibility of eliciting an analytical concept from the purely affective realm of the uncanny, I suggest, appears to echo throughout Hitchcock's film career, in which he did his utmost to engender something that is "anti-literary and purely cinematic," paradoxically on the basis of the literary sources that he himself would reject and repress during the adaptation process.[13] Moreover, the impasse of the two masters—Hitchcock and Freud—in confrontation with that which forever frustrates the desire for symbolic mastery is none other than a reflection of the impasse that the speaking subject suffers when confronted with a text with an uncanny note which continually eludes the subject's comprehension. If this is the case, then the repeated psychic drive toward adaptation may reflect the subject's constant search for complete command of a text and its destined failure.

It is thus more fruitful to focus on that which *The Uncanny* touches on only tangentially than to produce the coherent formulation of the uncanny that the text appears to promise. In this light, several salient points emerge relevant to a further analysis of Hitchcock's case and the two adaptations under discussion. The first is that, although Freud fails

10. Jonte-Pace, *Speaking the Unspeakable*, 1.

11. The second half of "The Uncanny" remains obscure and indecisive in terms of the content of the repression, and Freud refers to that which is repressed and, hence, uncannily returns as "something." This rhetorical characteristic will be examined further in the second part of the chapter, in which I shall explore the unrepresentable locus of fear and horror in Hitchcock's two adaptations under discussion.

12. Freud, "The Uncanny," 247. (My emphasis.)

13. Truffaut, *Hitchcock*, 319.

to attribute uncanny feelings to the return of the repressed castration complex, his hypothesis marks a speculative path from the domain of the uncanny to a point that is crucial in discussing Hitchcock's film adaptations—that is, the ambivalent notion of anxiety. Freud once designated the castration complex as the cause of anxiety; however, in his *Inhibitions, Symptoms and Anxiety*, he suddenly dismissed this causal relationship in which he had long believed. By probing *Inhibitions* we shall discover another example of the master's doubt, negation, and anxiety.

The second point of interest in *The Uncanny* is that which Freud calls "a beautiful confirmation of [his] theory of the uncanny," in which he suggests that the "mother's genitals or her body" is the ultimate locus of the uncanny.[14] This is not an anticipated conclusion for an essay in which Freud attempts to reaffirm his theory of the threatening and unquenchable power of patriarchal command in forming the subject of the unconscious. Nonetheless, his insight penetrates the affective, sensuous, and primordial nature of the uncanny and links it to the mother's genitals. In addition, it is noteworthy that, as he points out, the uncanny is often manifested in the form of "repetition of the same thing": it is "the double being" that, Freud believes, "is responsible for the impression of uncanniness."[15] Together, Freud's association of the uncanny with the maternal body and with the notion of the double provides a clue as to the association between Hitchcock's symptomatic practice of adaptation and his films' frequent representation of the sinister mother with two faces. Indeed, the director deftly arouses a sense of disorientation and insecurity in his audience by disclosing the double-sidedness of maternity and revealing the other side of the loving and nurturing mother at home through "those domineering mothers he excels at portraying."[16]

The seminal points in *The Uncanny* offer a foundation for a psychoanalytic hypothesis that explores Hitchcock's ambivalence as an adapter, particularly his tendency to undermine literary "Home" as a source of inspiration. This hypothesis, developed in relation to his biographies and interviews, will advance the chapter's discussion of the resistance and anxiety present in the film adaptation process. According

---

14. Freud, "The Uncanny," 245.
15. Ibid., 236.
16. Truffaut, *Hitchcock*, 16.

to a detailed biography written by Patrick McGilligan, Hitchcock's first and major formal education took place at a disciplinary Catholic school, St. Ignatius College. The school boasted an ambitious curriculum that included "Longfellow, Defoe, Dante, Dickens, and Shakespeare" taught by many fathers.[17] Thus, it is not difficult to imagine that for Hitchcock, as the previous chapter discussed, the world of literature must have been inscribed in the realm of the Father's command, establishing an overdetermined Oedipal complex that he may have addressed throughout his six-decade-long career in *writing with the camera*.

However, before he was introduced to these overpowering and fearful fathers of literature, someone had already aroused his lifelong fascination with storytelling: it was the intimate figure of the mother, who wove together the threads of the child's imagination by telling him bedtime stories. In an interview, he explained his central drive to be a cinematic storyteller through the use of a noteworthy metaphor: he said, "I put myself in the place of a child whose mother is telling him a story … When there's a pause in the narration, the child always says, What comes next, Mummy?"[18] This anecdote, improvised in the interview, indicates that his drive for storytelling, which he strove to convert into his passion for filmmaking, originated from a maternal locus in which he became an inquisitive child eagerly listening to his mother telling stories. For Hitchcock, therefore, the film director's status as heir to the storytelling art may be psychologically ambiguous in that it is ruled superficially by the symbolic father whose influence the director appears to have successfully overcome, yet it is permeated at a more profound level by the persistent presence of the mother. As a screen adapter, the question remains as to whether Hitchcock adopted the position of a legitimate heir to the Father's literary world or was unconsciously caught by the mother who constantly demanded that he return to the psychic site of the pre-Oedipal and exclusively reciprocal relationship between mother and child, precursor and adapter. This speculation leads us to Lacan's account of the omnipresence of the Mother as the Other (*Autre*), who is "on [the subject's] back" all the time

---

17. McGilligan, *Alfred Hitchcock*, 19.
18. Ibid., 9.

and, therefore, is surely more intimidating as the object of the child's incestuous desire forbidden by the threatening father.[19]

Hence, we may link Freud's explanation of the uncanny to that which returns in the course of Hitchcock's repeated practice of literary adaptation and through his multiple portraits of domineering mothers. This repressed material is aligned not with the cultural castration complex under the force of the super-egotistical father from the world of literature but with the province of the uncanny contaminated by the ambivalent figure of the loving yet feared mother. Hitchcock's filmic treatment of the maternal figure suggests that he conceives of the mother as not merely an angelic figure of nurture and care but also as that which is closer to "the Mother as Other [*Autre*]—i.e., the primordial subject of the demand [*la demande*]," in Lacanian terms.[20] The persistent nature of literary adaptation as a principal form of Hitchcock's filmmaking, then, finds its connection to a subject's anxiety that cannot be wholly integrated into the Oedipal masterplot. According to Lacan, this patriarchal plot should articulate how the subject suffers the oppression of the paternal command, and yet it simultaneously bespeaks how the castration complex offers the subject a means of escape from the engulfing Mother who defies the division between subject and object, internal and external.[21]

If I may draw out this speculation a little further, the incomprehensible drive for adaptation, while defying the influence of original texts, may be related to the subject's anxiety regarding something more primordial and prior to the advent of the Name-of-the-Father. In other words, the adapter's anxiety, as detected in the heterogeneous mixture of fascination, obsession, and resistance in a case like Hitchcock's, is perhaps involved with "the desirable and terrifying, nourishing and murderous, fascinating and abject" Mother,

---

19. Lacan describes the entrapping power of the mother as the subject of the demand whose omnipresence is the ultimate cause of anxiety. See Lacan, *Seminar X*, 36.

20. Lacan, Miller, and Hulbert, "Desire and the Interpretation of Desire in *Hamlet*," 12.

21. Jacques Lacan, *The Seminar of Jacques Lacan, Book XVII: The Other Side of Psychoanalysis*, ed. Jacques-Alain Miller and trans. Russell Grigg (New York: W. W. Norton & Company, 2007), 112–13.

to use Julia Kristeva's description.[22] In this sense, Hitchcock's anxiety around being overpowered by original sources finds its unintended and unconscious expression in his beloved motif of the ambiguous mother, a figure who appears repeatedly in many of his films, culminating in his masterpiece *Psycho* (1960).

At the end of *Psycho*, a lengthy pedantic explanation provided by a male psychologist's phallogocentric discourse is retrospectively paralyzed by the undead Mrs. Bates's face superimposed onto Norman's face, which looms large on the screen. The close-up gradually dissolves to reveal Marion's car being pulled out of the swamp; the headlights—reminiscent of the empty gaze of Marion's lifeless eyes after being stabbed to death in the shower—direct a sinister gaze toward the viewer. Indeed, like Freud, who discovered the *unheimlich* at the heart of the *Heim*, Hitchcock, as a director, repeatedly discovered something uncanny at the mother's bosom in the course of his obsessive practice of adaptation, while vehemently defying the inevitable return of the original texts.

Hitherto, the chapter has scrutinized how *The Uncanny* manifests Freud's counterthesis to his previous theoretical elaboration in an attempt to probe beyond Hitchcock's imperious screen adaptation practice. Now, I wish to contemplate the concept of anxiety to better understand Hitchcock's complicated relationship with precursor texts and their potential influence. Before speculating on the Freudian definition of anxiety, it will be useful to outline how the notion of anxiety was first brought into the cultural domain of aesthetic creation, interrelation, and adaptation by Harold Bloom. His book entitled *The Anxiety of Influence*, not without controversy, constituted the first investigation of anxiety as a pivotal notion in meditating on the complex relationship of an author to precursor texts and their influence. In particular, Bloom elaborates on anxiety as a universal impasse that all poets must experience owing to "the immense anxieties of indebtedness" to precursors.[23] In one sense, Bloom's concern is with a handful of Romantic poets who struggled against the overpowering influence of their precursors' poetry, which once had fostered their poetic skills and nurtured their passion. However, as Paul de Man suggests in his review of the book, the value

---

22. Julia Kristeva, *Powers of Horror: An Essay on Abjection*, trans. Leon S. Roudiez (New York: Columbia University Press, 1982), 54.

23. Harold Bloom, *The Anxiety of Influence: A Theory of Poetry* (Oxford: Oxford University Press, 1973), 3.

of Bloom's study lies in the fact that "Bloom's essay has much to say on the encounter between latecomer and precursor as a displaced version of the paradigmatic encounter between reader and text."[24] In other words, the book offers a more fundamental insight into the affective state called anxiety as a universal experience of the speaking subject positioned as a reader in his or her encounter with a text.

Citing Oscar Wilde, Bloom establishes the concept of influence as the object of anxiety before proceeding to offer a detailed account of "[t]he six revisionary movements" in the poetic attempt to deviate from precursors—or, in our broader view, the speaking subject's attempt to adapt a text in his or her own terms.[25] Oscar Wilde himself, according to Bloom, suffered from the anxiety of influence severely enough to regard himself as a failed poet. However, Bloom points out that in his novel *The Picture of Dorian Gray*, Wilde, with remarkable psychoanalytic insight, elucidates the notion of influence as a threat of invasion and a deprivation of one's subjectivity. Through the voice of Lord Henry Wotton, Wilde argues:

> All influence is immoral ... Because to influence a person is to give him one's own soul. He does not think his natural thoughts, or burn with his natural passions. His virtues are not real to him. His sins, if there are such things as sins, are borrowed. He becomes an echo of someone else's music, an actor of a part that has not been written for him.[26]

Here, it is possible to read the essence of what Bloom regards as the cause of anxiety in psychoanalytic terms—that is, the influence of a prior text which presents itself to the subject as a threat, potentially negating one's own subjectivity. This anxiety stems from the fear that the powerful presence of earlier works might overshadow and diminish one's own originality, challenging the subject's sense of individuality and creative expression. If narrowing it to understanding the adaptation process by which precursor texts are adapted into one's own work, we can assume that the anxiety of influence becomes even more intense,

---

24. Paul de Man, "Review of *The Anxiety of Influence* by Harold Bloom," *Comparative Literature* 26, no. 3 (Summer 1974): 273.

25. Bloom, *The Anxiety of Influence*, 10.

26. Oscar Wilde, *The Picture of Dorian Gray* (Ware: Wordsworth Editions, 1992), 18.

secretive, and uncanny in cases like Hitchcock's. This intensification corresponds to his conscious efforts to erase the influence of the literary tradition from his creation of purely cinematic art. Put differently, as a master of cinematic language, Hitchcock positioned his work as the antithesis of literary tradition. Yet, paradoxically, the influence of the written word lingered in his adaptations as an inherent threat—an ever-present risk of annihilating or negating his newly bred artistry.

## Unpleasure and Anxiety

Freud wrote the short essay *The Uncanny* (1919) as a precursor to his ground-breaking *Beyond the Pleasure Principle* (1920), in which he provocatively argued that "The aim of all life is death."[27] The semantic paradox in the above statement is merely a metapsychological variant of the syntactic paradox that threads the canny and uncanny into a single circle. The titles of both texts are similarly permeated with a tone of disruption and disorientation, which negates the rational ground of previous understandings of human experience and the very existence of the human subject. Just as *The Uncanny* constitutes Freud's claim that the prefix "un-" functions as "the token of repression," *Beyond the Pleasure Principle* represents his attempt to confront and release intellectual repression in a manner that ultimately challenges and undermines his own theory of the pleasure principle.[28] He thereby opens up the discourse of psychoanalysis to the deadly force that drives living beings in a direction that is phenomenologically opposite yet ontologically the same as that of the life instinct.[29]

If we acknowledge that the term "adaptation," when used to describe a transformation from a precursor to a posterior text, carries a Darwinian undertone, then the desire for adaptation—particularly

---

27. Sigmund Freud, "Beyond the Pleasure Principle," in *The Standard Edition of the Complete Psychological Works of Sigmund Freud, Volume XVIII*, trans. James Strachey (London: The Hogarth Press and the Institute of Psycho-Analysis, 1955), 38.

28. Freud, "The Uncanny," 245.

29. Here, it is important to note that the German term "*Trieb*" is controversially translated as "instinct" in the Standard Edition. However, many Freudian scholars, including Lacan, argue that the term's meaning and use correspond more to the term "drive."

in response to the Oedipus complex—could be interpreted as a life force governed by the pleasure principle. However, based on Freud's inadvertent discovery in *Beyond the Pleasure Principle*, the repeated efforts to adapt a written text for the screen cannot simply be viewed as culture's evolutionary movement toward the future or as a dialectical progression toward a higher and newer synthesis.[30] On the contrary, the very persistence or compulsiveness, as exemplified in Hitchcock's case, points to the existence of "something that seems more primitive, more elementary, more instinctual than the pleasure principle which it overrides," as Freud describes.[31] Therefore, I would argue that the relentless drive behind screen adaptation surpasses the pleasure-seeking desire to stage the screen as a site for Oedipal fantasies. This deeper, hidden layer of adaptation seems to intersect with the dimension of the "beyond" that Freud sought to understand in *Beyond the Pleasure Principle*, even at the expense of his own "twenty-five years of intense work" aimed at solidifying the Oedipal masterplot as central to human psych.[32]

Since *The Interpretation of Dreams*, the backbone of Freud's theory about the pleasure principle as a fundamental psychic tendency is based on his economic or quantitative model of cathexis. This model regards the increased excitation in the mind as unpleasure (*unlust*) and its diminution as pleasure. As a natural mental reaction to such an unpleasant excess of psychic excitation, Freud explains, "the work of the mental apparatus is directed toward keeping the quantity of excitation low."[33] In short, stability or homeostasis is the aim of the pleasure principle. From *Formulations on the Two Principles of Mental Functioning* (1911), he began to elaborate the dual system of the pleasure principle and the reality principle. The latter contains his attempt to explain the uncontrollable forces from the external world, known as reality. In its response, the ego must deliberately make a "detour," as

---

30. In mentioning Freud's discovery of the death instinct as it appears in *Beyond the Pleasure Principle*, Lacan emphatically uses a passive form to manifest the way in which a speaking subject confronts it in the advancement of knowledge: Lacan explains, "what, as his subsequent discourse shows, was forced upon him (Freud)? Namely, the death drive." In Jacques Lacan, *The Seminar of Jacques Lacan, Book XVII: The Other Side of Psychoanalysis*, 16.
31. Freud, "Beyond the Pleasure Principle," 23.
32. Ibid., 18.
33. Ibid., 11.

reality prevents the ego from immediately achieving the homeostatic reduction of excitation in its more advanced stages of development.

Nonetheless, the reality principle, which forces the subject to endure a certain degree of unpleasure, is not a complete replacement of the pleasure principle. Rather, it is a supplementary regulation that comes into play as the subject gains greater understanding and experience of external reality. As such, the reality principle is a necessary adaptation of the pleasure principle, which continues to strive toward homeostasis. The reality principle, it should be remembered, remains subordinate to the ever-persisting pleasure principle, as it "does not abandon the intention of ultimately obtaining pleasure."[34] Overall, within the broader scheme of the pleasure principle, the reality principle enables the ego to facilitate "the temporary toleration of unpleasure as a step on the long indirect road to pleasure."[35] In theorizing the pleasure principle and its adaptation to the environment, Freud underscores the human subject's capacity to prolong its existence by protecting itself from fatally excessive excitation. This adaptation allows the subject to navigate external demands while still working toward the ultimate goal of achieving pleasure and maintaining psychic equilibrium.

The complication of the duality that pairs the pleasure and reality principles emerges on the surface of his theorization when Freud stumbles over the difficulties of clarifying the nature of the unpleasure that the ego endeavors to avoid or maintain at a minimal level. To simplify the lengthy speculative account that Freud offers in the essay, unpleasure—that is, excessive mental excitations—is present in two states in the human psyche: one is in a bound state, regulated by the pleasure principle; the other is the excitation that is received without the protective shield in effect and, hence, forever remains in an unbound state. This freely mobile form of unpleasant excitation is "incapable of obeying *the secondary process*," a term Freud uses to describe the pleasure principle inclusive of the reality principle.[36]

The unbound unpleasure, never governed by the pleasure principle, remains instinctual in nature (*triebhaft*). Based on this hypothesis, Freud identifies "the track of a universal attribute of instincts and perhaps of organic life in general," an urge inherent in living organisms to return to

---

34. Ibid., 10.
35. Ibid.
36. Ibid., 36.

an earlier state—one prior to birth or existence.³⁷ This instinctual drive toward annihilation is traced from the ego's masochistic tendencies. Positioned "beyond the pleasure principle," this drive predates the incursion of the pleasure principle as a life force, which functions to prolong and preserve life. In other words, it is a primitive and primordial psychic force that moves toward the restoration of the initial inorganic status of organic beings. Characteristically, this force is manifested, Freud argues, in the form of compulsive repetition, defying any interpretive effort on the part of the analyst. Interestingly, Freud admits that his speculative reflection, which began in the fields of biology and psychology, ultimately leads into a philosophical meditation on death as the purpose of life. Thus, this provocative text, *Beyond the Pleasure Principle*, encounters the notion of the death drive, whose haunting existence is uncanny and beyond the systematic functions of the pleasure principle. Or, that is how the death drive was forced on Freud.

Threading the death drive together with anxiety as a response to the threat of one's negation, I now turn to the anxiety that arose in the mind of the master of psychoanalysis himself. This anxiety is perhaps most evident in his counterthesis text *Inhibitions, Symptoms and Anxiety*, where it relates to the concept of the engulfing Mother—an idea Freud had only briefly considered in his speculation on the uncanny. In *Inhibition*, Freud abandons his "earlier view that the cathectic energy of the repressed impulse is automatically turned into anxiety."³⁸ He begins to develop a new perspective, rethinking the origins and dynamics of anxiety:

> Anxiety is not newly created in repression; it is reproduced as an affective state in accordance with an already existing *mnemic image*. If we go further and enquire into the origin of that anxiety—and of affects in general—we shall be leaving the realm of pure psychology and entering the borderland of physiology. Affective states have become incorporated in the mind as precipitates of primaeval traumatic experiences, and when a similar situation occurs they are revived like *mnemic symbols*. … In man and the higher animals it

---

37. Ibid. (My emphasis.)

38. Sigmund Freud, "Inhibitions, Symptoms and Anxiety," in *The Standard Edition of the Complete Psychological Works of Sigmund Freud, Volume XX*, trans. James Strachey (London: The Hogarth Press and the Institute of Psycho-Analysis, 1961), 93.

would seem that the act of birth, as the individual's first experience of anxiety, has given the affect of anxiety certain characteristic forms of expression.[39]

Therefore, we can relate Freud's new insight regarding anxiety as "an affective state in accordance with an already existing mnemic image" to the unpleasure in an unbound state that lies beyond the pleasure principle.[40] Later, he also confirms the temporal priority of "primaeval traumatic experiences" by saying that "the earliest outbreaks of anxiety, which are of a very intense kind, occur before the super-ego has become differentiated."[41] In other words, anxiety has nothing to do with the loss of the mother as the first object of one's erotic desire because, in this "primaeval" stage before the super-ego arrives, the mother is not an object but the Other (*Autre*) itself. This primitive *Autre* operates not on the level of the threat of separation and castration but on the level of the fear of negation or the "fear of being devoured."[42]

Freud exposes a sign of his own anxiety in reaching beyond his theory of anxiety. As he did in *The Uncanny* and *Beyond the Pleasure Principle*, Freud attempts to support and maintain his Oedipal masterplot by incorporating this discovery into the concept of the castration complex. In the fourth part of *Inhibitions, Symptoms and Anxiety*, Freud explains that the anxiety is aroused by "the fear of impending castration," which cannot be transformed into a symptom by repression because anxiety precedes and produces repression not vice versa.[43] The great irony of this statement is that Freud tries to reconcile two incompatible ideas here: one is that anxiety is an affective precipitate of traumatic experience prior to the paternal function of the Oedipus complex, and the other is that the anxiety is a reaction to the untransformed threat of castration evoked by a "real" father figure. Consequently, in agony and anxiety, Freud was obliged to punctuate this part of the essay with "*Non liquet*," which means "it is not clear."[44]

However, I would like to focus on his use of the term *real-* or *realistic fear*, which, in the German original, is expressed as *Realangst*: he refers

39. Ibid. (My emphasis.)
40. Ibid., 93.
41. Ibid., 93–4.
42. Ibid., 104.
43. Ibid., 108.
44. Ibid., 110.

to anxiety as "a realistic fear [*realangst*], a fear of a danger which was actually impending or was judged to be a real one."[45] This term is often mistakenly used to support the idea that the threat of castration as an origin of anxiety belongs to the threat aroused by a *real* father in the familial triangle. It is because Freud's insight on anxiety, of which first experience is linked back to "the act of birth," is often disregarded. If turning to Lacan's sophisticated theorization of the Other, this *realangst* is related to none other than the subject of the original demand that existed before the advent of the paternal super-ego: that is, the mother as the Other. Consequently, castration does not merely denote the deprivation of the penis: it is also a more primordial attack on the human subject, implying the annihilation or negation of oneself. At the point that the subject experiences the anxiety of this existential castration, it uncannily encounters the precondition of human existence as a manifestation of the death drive. Anxiety as a signal of the *real* danger as such "has a very marked character of unpleasure," which tends to return the subject to the same traumatic locus repeatedly.[46]

While I have been attempting to read Freud against his desire to establish the Oedipal masterplot of the human psyche, my approach is not entirely oppositional; rather, it involves a slight temporal dislocation. In the later part of *Inhibitions*, Freud explains that the ego deals with the real danger of castration by redirecting the castration anxiety "to a different object and expressed in a distorted form, so that the patient is afraid, not of being castrated by his father, but of being bitten by a horse or devoured by a wolf."[47] Whereas Freud begins "this substitutive formation" of the real father with another object, such as a horse or a wolf, I propose that prior to such a substitutive formation of the castrating father there existed a more primordial object, concealed even from Freud's awareness due to his own anxiety: the initial substitution of the mother as the Other—the Mother in Lacan's terminology— which evokes *realangst*. However, this first substitution in the chain remains outside the course of Oedipalization and, thus, leaves a gap in the symbolic constitution of the speaking subject. This gap accrues a fundamental gravity around which the subject perpetually circles. Whenever the subject approaches this gap too closely, anxiety emerges

45. Ibid., 108.
46. Ibid., 132.
47. Ibid., 125.

as a signal, indicating the proximity to an unresolved, primordial absence that underpins the subject's psychic structure.

It is possible to discern traces of this same gap in Hitchcock's narrativization of his castration anxiety. Hitchcock frequently remarked in interviews that, despite his reputation for creating fear in others, he was actually the most frightened person of all. His primordial experience of fear occurred when his stern father arranged for the five-year-old Hitchcock to be briefly locked in a jail cell at a local police station as punishment for misbehavior. This anecdote is steeped in the Freudian Oedipal masterplot, where a boy's relationship with the world is shaped by severe paternal rules and authority. The fear of paternal authority remained deeply ingrained in Hitchcock's psyche, manifesting in his films, where the police repeatedly appear as ultimate figures of oppressive control. This persistent depiction of authority reflects the unresolved anxiety at the core of Hitchcock's personal and cinematic narrative. However, an even more intriguing disclosure may be found in a television interview where Hitchcock identified fear as the most primitive emotion experienced by human beings, saying, "I think my mother scared me when I was three months old. You see, she said BOO. It gave me the hiccups. And she apparently was very satisfied. All mothers do it, you know. That is how fear is stuffed in everyone."[48] This anecdote offers a fascinating glimpse into Hitchcock's understanding of fear as something instilled from the earliest stages of life, originating not from paternal authority but from the maternal figure. This aligns with a deeper, more primordial source of anxiety that precedes the Oedipal framework, suggesting that Hitchcock's cinematic portrayal of fear may be rooted in this early, maternal encounter with anxiety, complicating the narrative of his fear of paternal authority.

First, Hitchcock's attempts to recount traumatic events from his childhood in two different and contradictory ways are illustrative of the subject's effort to incorporate what Freud terms "precipitates of primaeval traumatic experiences" into one's conscious memory. The subject strives to transform the inaccessible, anxiety-laden moment into a narrative that is constructed under the phallic or symbolic order, but this effort toward complete replacement remains futile.[49] Given that the subject has already undergone Oedipalization, the symbolic

---

48. *The Dick Cavett Show: Hollywood Greats*, DVD (originally aired in 1972 on ABC; Sony Music, 2006).

49. Freud, "Inhibitions, Symptoms and Anxiety," 93.

register tends to merge the anxiety-inducing trace of the engulfing Mother with the fear of the castrating father. In Hitchcock's Oedipal anecdote, the director substitutes the police for the threatening father, organizing a narrative that seemingly pinpoints his ultimate source of anxiety. However, this narrative leaves a gap—the first substitutive formation, linked to the maternal figure, remains unincorporated into this personal myth.

This recalls the hypothesis that Hitchcock's obsessive approach to screen adaptation as his prime method of filmmaking reflects the persistent residue of the maternal storyteller within him—an influence he sought to replace. In his adaptations, Hitchcock appeared to defy and overcome the literary fathers, but beneath this effort lay a deeper struggle with the maternal figure, whose role as the original storyteller continued to linger. The point I will leave open for now, before returning to it later, is the intriguing fact that Hitchcock also fixates on the deeply sadistic pleasure the mother derives from frightening her infant child, a dynamic that complicates the maternal influence and adds another layer to his exploration of fear and control. This scary mother, fleetingly emerging in the anecdote, recalls his recurring portrayal of the mother as the hidden origin of the protagonist's anxiety in many films. The sadistic character of the Mother is often transmitted to the paternal super-ego, which Hitchcock represents as masculine authority figures, such as police, Nazis, and fathers/husbands who "become harsh, cruel and inexorable."[50]

This attribution also reinforces the earlier assumption that the threatening and devouring figure of the primordial Mother lingers in the background of Hitchcock's consciousness, while the sadistic phallic Other is brought to the forefront of his film adaptations. Hitchcock's portrayal of female characters, often criticized as misogynistic, can thus be understood in relation to the anxiety this devouring Mother evokes during the process of adaptation. The unsettling presence of the maternal figure, repressed yet ever-present, seems to inform his depiction of women, channeling his deeper fears and anxieties into the narrative, where the phallic authority takes center stage as a more visible source of control and oppression. I shall return to this in the following

---

50. Sigmund Freud, "The Economic Problem of Masochism," in *The Standard Edition of the Complete Psychological Works of Sigmund Freud, Volume XIX*, trans. James Strachey (London: The Hogarth Press and the Institute of Psycho-Analysis, 1961), 166.

section, focusing on the relationship between the gaze and the Mother. In doing so, I will attempt to disentangle the anxiety-provoking and menacing gaze of the Mother from the command of the Oedipal father, much like the Ghost in *Hamlet* films.

With reference to Freud's counterthesis texts, I have suggested that anxiety signals the pre-Oedipal and thus pre-symbolic dimension of the Other, which is captured in the flip side of the mother as the origin of life. In this sense, Joan Copjec, in her article entitled "Vampires, Breast-Feeding, and Anxiety," duly points out that anxiety is an extraordinary and affective signal "because it works without the use of any signifiers."[51] In other words, what anxiety signals is the unrepresentable realm of the death drive, which defies all attempts to encapsulate it with the net of signifiers. For Freud as well as Copjec, anxiety signals the approach of the gap—like a black hole—that threatens the subject with the annihilation of its own symbolic ground.

In a similar vein, what Bloom highlights in his concept of influence as a source of anxiety can, at a deeper level, be seen as an encounter with the gap glimpsed in the process of engaging with others' texts and distinguishing one's own work from theirs. This anxiety becomes even more intense in the case of screen adaptation, where the adapter grapples with the challenge of bridging the semiotic gap between linguistic signifiers and cinematic signifiers. Applying Freud's logic of repetition in the uncanny and the resurgence of anxiety, the fundamental gap in the human psyche tends to reemerge within this divide between the language of literature and that of cinema. In other words, for the interest of this chapter, the adapter's struggle to overcome the gap between the two different symbolic systems reflects a more primordial level of human subjectivity in which the speaking subject ardently seeks a signifier to keep the abyss at the center of its subjectivity at bay and in sleep.

## *The Mother and the Gaze*

In examining Hitchcock's films in relation to the Mother and the gaze, it is worth beginning with Laura Mulvey's highly influential 1975 essay "Visual Pleasure and Narrative Cinema." Mulvey reveals, on the basis

---

51. Joan Copjec, "Vampires, Breast-Feeding, and Anxiety," *Rendering the Real* 58 (Autumn 1991): 26.

of Freud's account of scopophilic pleasure and Lacan's mirror stage, an ideological mode of visual pleasure embedded in narrative cinema. The essay focuses on Hollywood films' "skilled and satisfying manipulation of the visual pleasure" by means of the sadistic impact of the masculine gaze on the female object of the erotic desire.[52] Mulvey argues that the camera's gaze objectifies the female character on screen in the service of voyeuristic pleasure of male characters and audiences alike. In support of her argument, Mulvey analyzes Hitchcock's films, including *Vertigo*, *Marnie*, and *Rear Window*, as salient examples of the male gaze in search of voyeuristic pleasure through the mastery of female objects to be looked at.

Although Mulvey's seminal article initiated the discussion surrounding the filmic gaze from a psychoanalytical perspective, Mulvey's association of scopic mastery with masculine power and pleasure attracted various criticisms. Among these, Kaja Silverman's reconsideration attempts to draw out the paradoxical relation between pleasure and unpleasure *beyond* the logic of Mulvey's reading of Hitchcock. Silverman directs our attention toward three diagrams that appear in Lacan's *Seminar XI: Four Fundamental Concepts of Psychoanalysis*, in which Lacan complicates "the relation of the subject with the domain of vision" to emphasize the complexity of our scopic drive and its object.[53] What Silverman encapsulates from Lacan's elaboration in *Seminar XI* is, above all, that the scopic pleasure promised by the objectifying and voyeuristic masculine gaze is illusionary, because at a more primordial level, the viewing subject is looked at by the gaze that emanates from the sides of the objects they see. In deciphering Lacan's three diagrams from *Seminar XI*, Silverman claims "the impossibility of anyone ever owning that visual agency [the gaze], or of him or herself escaping specularity," as Lacan's teaching there confirms that the gaze is on the opposite side of the subject.[54] Furthermore, Lacan notes that the power and mastery that the gaze entails must be differentiated from the eye's agency and power, which constitutes the subject's identity through misrecognition.

52. Laura Mulvey, "Visual Pleasure and Narrative Cinema (1975)," in *Literary Theory: Anthology*, ed. Julie Rivkin and Michael Ryan (Malden, MA: Blackwell, 1998), 586.
53. Lacan, *Seminar XI*, 97.
54. Kaja Silverman, *Male Subjectivity at the Margins* (New York: Routledge, 1992), 152.

Indeed, the gaze in Lacan's theory differs fundamentally from what Mulvey refers to as the male gaze, which is aligned with patriarchal power over the female object. Mulvey's eroticizing *look*, as Silverman terms it, operates within the imaginary domain of the ego, where the subject identifies with and dominates the objects it sees. In contrast, Lacan's gaze belongs to the realm of the real, not the imaginary, and is represented by the *objet petit a*. Though it appears in the scopic field, this gaze functions beyond mere visual identification. In Lacan's topology, the drive manifests through a repetitive, circular movement around this small object, *objet petit a*, which signifies the lack at the heart of the symbolic order—the core of the speaking subject's being. The threat posed by the gaze stems from its capacity to confront the subject with the traumatic collapse of "scopic Cartesianism"—the belief that "seeing constitutes being" and is a source of power.[55] This belief underpins Mulvey's argument, but Lacan's gaze disrupts it by revealing a deeper level of lack and disorientation within the subject's experience of vision. Another crucial point is Lacan's understanding of the screen, which functions as "the locus of mediation" between the subject and the gaze.[56] According to Lacan, the human subject stands on one side of the screen, while the gaze—an intimidating force—remains behind it. Unlike animals, humans "isolate the function of the screen and play with it," indicating an unconscious awareness of the gaze hidden behind the screen, even though the gaze itself remains invisible.[57]

From a Mulveyan perspective, images of women on screen may indicate the director's mastery over the objects that Hitchcock transferred from page to screen, as Mulvey identifies the male gaze with that of the director's camera. Similarly, Hitchcock's incessant practice of adaptation may be construed as a continuous pursuit of satisfying a voyeuristic, pleasure-seeking desire, which aligns with the gaze of his male protagonists. The male gaze, as Mulvey argues, objectifies women, positioning them as passive subjects for visual consumption, and Hitchcock's adaptations could be viewed as a way to assert control and dominance over both the narrative and the female figures within it. However, Lacan shifts the focus to "the gaze that is outside," which is split from the eye and beyond the subject's control.[58] Hitchcock,

55. Ibid., 146.
56. Lacan, *Seminar XI*, 107.
57. Ibid.
58. Ibid., 106.

perhaps inadvertently, realizes this Lacanian gaze in his films by portraying the most threatening gaze as one that looks at characters from the side of objects. This gaze, disconnected from any character's perspective, arouses anxious reactions in both the characters and the audience, especially in moments when the characters attempt to satisfy their voyeuristic desires.

For instance, *Rebecca* features a scene in which a timid young protagonist, the second Mrs. de Winter (played by Joan Fontaine), is compelled toward the closed doors of the room once owned by the deceased first Mrs. de Winter, Rebecca. Hitchcock's cinematographic signature—the camera zooming in while tracking away from an object—captures the uncanny moment when the heroine is watched by the closed doors as she approaches the room with curiosity and desire to peep inside the forbidden realm. The heroine's point-of-view shot in this scene insinuates that the pair of doors decorated with a symmetrical array of panels and knobs somehow return a sinister and unpleasant gaze back toward "us." In *The Birds*, a young and cheeky socialite Melanie (played by Tippi Hedren) follows a handsome lawyer Mitch Brenner (played by Rod Taylor) to his family home. The scene in which she sneaks into the Brenners' house also stages a similar interplay between the protagonist's look and the unsettling gaze that seems to emanate from the objects' side. In this instance, the gaze, detached from human eyes, creates a tension between the seemingly lighthearted, comically romantic moment and the looming sense of impending catastrophe—the birds' attack.

If we assume a link between Hitchcock's repetitive use of this cinematographic tactic to present the anxiety-provoking gaze and the director's own reaction to the intimidating world of things, it is possible to conceive that those heroines' encounters with this gaze represent a reworking of what Hitchcock himself sensed and sought to resist during the adaptation process. The gaze, in this light, would function as the *objet petit a*, which returns the director to the same encircling trajectory around adaptation. In other words, Hitchcock's persistent practice of adaptation may well be the manifestation of the indestructible drive circling around the gaze that is detached from his seeing eyes as well as from the camera. In this sense, the purely cinematic images that Hitchcock believed he could extract from the literary originals should be conceived as the vehicle for the intimidating gaze that looks at him from behind the things he read and imagined from the originals. Nevertheless, as an astute master of cinema, Hitchcock knew how to play with the screen by transferring the uncanny gaze onto this surface and making it felt by his audience. Indeed, Hitchcock's obsessive pursuit of the looked-at-ness of his female leads, as Mulvey detected, can be read as a mere foil for the gaze itself, which returns the voyeuristic look of the male characters, camera, and audience, transforms the human subject into an object, and ultimately highlights its own insubstantiality. Interestingly, if we recall Mulvey's inadvertent comment about the image of woman whose "look, pleasurable in form, can be threatening in content," this gaze is re-presented in the figure of the threatening Mother whose uncanny and unpleasant *other* side penetrates the Hitchcockian screen to reveal our place in the picture as observed from all sides.[59]

## The Function of the Negative

As discussed above, Hitchcock's defiant attitude toward the influence of the literary texts he adapted for the screen may disclose his anxiety in confronting the gap in adaptation rather than reaffirming his mastery over the literary materials he used. In reading his anxiety, I have applied a psychoanalytical method whose function Freud explains in his short essay "Negation" (*Die Verneinung*). Freud begins his essay by claiming,

> The manner in which our patients bring forward their associations during the work of analysis gives us an opportunity for making some interesting observations. "Now you'll think I mean to say something insulting, but really I've no such intention." We realize that this is a repudiation, by projection, of an idea that has just come up. Or: "You ask who this person in the dream can be. It's not my mother." We emend this to: "So it is his mother." In our interpretation, we take the liberty of disregarding the negation and of picking out the subject-matter alone of the association. It is as though the patient had said: "It's true that my mother came into my mind as I thought of this person, but I don't feel inclined to let the association count."[60]

---

59. Mulvey, "Visual Pleasure," 593.

60. Sigmund Freud, "Negation," in *The Standard Edition of the Complete Psychological Works of Sigmund Freud, Volume XIII*, trans. James Strachey (London: The Hogarth Press and the Institute of Psycho-Analysis, 1955), 234.

Similarly, I take the liberty of interpreting Hitchcock's statement "No, I read the original story only once and I cannot remember it" as actually implying "Yes, I read it many times and can remember it well down to its minor details." Freud continues to explain the function of negation in the transaction between the unconscious and the subject's conscious mind: "With the help of the symbol of negation, thinking frees itself from the restrictions of repression and enriches itself with material that is indispensable for its proper function."[61] With this logic of negation as a guide, I wish to analyze Hitchcock's two films that adapt the stories by Daphne du Maurier—*Rebecca* and *The Birds*—with the aim of understanding how original stories may be re-presented while negating their influence. Before proceeding to a reading of the two films, however, it will be useful to embed the logic and function of negation in the philosophical conceptualization of anxiety as a platform from which to closely examine Hitchcock's manifestation of anxiety as a negative phenomenon through the uncanny figure of the Mother at the center of both films.

Among philosophical investigations of anxiety as a concept, Kierkegaard's *The Concept of Anxiety* occupies a unique position. Lacan regards Kierkegaard as the first and seminal reference in intellectual efforts to "come to terms with anxiety."[62] Written under one of Kierkegaard's multiple pseudonyms—Vigilius Haufniensi—*The Concept of Anxiety: A Simple Psychologically Orienting Deliberation on the Dogmatic Issue of Hereditary Sin* addresses anxiety as an existential human experience: "That anxiety makes its appearance is the pivot upon which everything turns."[63] Above all, Kierkegaard argues that anxiety is not the result of hereditary sin—that is, the Fall of Adam—but its presupposition. This subversive and daring account of anxiety as primordial rather than reactionary or symptomatic—in direct opposition to what the Bible teaches—resonates precisely with Freud's second account of anxiety as prior to repression and a signal of the impending danger. Lacan's elaboration of the concept essentially follows this argument. Moreover, Kierkegaard notably relates anxiety to "nothingness" as its object: throughout the book, he repeatedly

---

61. Ibid., 235.
62. Lacan, *Seminar X*, 4.
63. Søren Kierkegaard, *The Concept of Anxiety: A Simple Psychologically Orienting Deliberation on the Dogmatic Issue of Hereditary Sin*, trans. Reidar Thomte (Princeton, NJ: Princeton University Press, 1980), 43.

## 3. Resistance to the Originals in Hitchcock's Adaptations 119

maintains that "it remains true that the object of anxiety is *a nothing*."[64] The philosopher further presents a highly intriguing metaphor for this nothing or nothingness in which we confront an uncanny rendezvous with the gap at the center of the subject's constitution, as mentioned above. What makes the gap, or Kierkegaard's *nothing*, a real threat—or what Freud refers to as *realangst*—is its ability to bring to the edge of our consciousness something that is never bounded: unboundedness itself. In Lacan's terms, this is the "lack of lack," a condition where the symbolic that usually defines limits or absence dissolves, leaving the subject exposed to an overwhelming and unsettling openness that defies containment or resolution. Kierkegaard insightfully describes anxiety as a "dizziness" that one experiences when their eye "happens to look down into the yawning abyss."[65]

Here, the task of capturing the concept of anxiety in relation to nothingness as its object leads the present discussion to the domain of existentialism and to Jean Paul Sartre, who follows Kierkegaard's account of anxiety as a confrontation with the abyss at the center of human existence. Although Kierkegaard and Sartre regard this abyss as the limitless potential of human existence and positivistically call it *freedom*, Sartre's redefinition of Kierkegaard's concept of nothingness as the object of anxiety illuminates the philosophical basis for Lacan's elaboration of anxiety. If setting aside Sartre's violent objection to psychoanalysis and limiting the discussion of Sartre's *Being and Nothingness* to the first part, in which he conceptualizes nothingness in the pursuit of being, Sartre's speculation regarding the notion of nothingness may be construed as an attempt to meditate another possibility of conceptualizing nothingness beyond Hegelian dialectics. Put differently, Sartre attempts to break the oppositional relationship between being and nothingness and to frame nothingness not as an antithesis of being with a distinguishable ontological locus but as that which is concurrent with being. Being imposes a boundary around its locus so that nothingness "exists only on the surface of being" and is, consequently, "surrounding being on every side," haunting it.[66]

64. Ibid., 77. (My emphasis.)
65. Ibid., 61.
66. Jean Paul Sartre, *Being and Nothingness: An Essay on Phenomenological Ontology* (1943), trans. Hazel E. Barnes (London: Methuen, 1957), 11, 16 and 18.

Given that, to Sartre, nothingness is a purely negative notion that lacks any bounded locus, it is possible to take his concept of nothingness as the logical grounding for Lacan's concept of the lack of lack, which evokes anxiety—or, "anguish" in Hazel Barnes's more immediate translation of Sartre's *l'angoisse*. It also elucidates the philosophical foundation on which Lacan invented the *objet petit a* as a non-object whose function as an object is based on its lack. Moreover, Sartre suggests that the only way to encounter nothingness as the negation of being is through anguish or anxiety. Sartre writes, "there is even a permanent possibility of finding oneself 'face to face' with nothingness and discovering it as a phenomenon: this possibility is anguish."[67] It is thus possible to conclude that anxiety serves as a signal through which we experience nothingness as a phenomenon, irrespective of whether we would define this affective experience as an existential encounter, like Kierkegaard and Sartre, or as a psychic one, as Freud and Lacan argue.

In probing plausible ways of conceiving nothingness in relation to Hitchcock's resistance and anxiety in the locus of adaptation, the problematic influence of the original texts that Hitchcock strives to resist in his imperious approach to adaptation does not constitute evidence that the cinematic auteur dismisses the influence of what he has encountered in literary sources. Rather, Hitchcock's resistance ironically becomes linked to his anxiety when confronted with the gap or "nothing" at the center of his subjectivity as an adapter. This anxiety may have been especially pronounced for Hitchcock as an émigré filmmaker, reliant on populist literary originals that were often imposed upon him by Hollywood studio executives.

The shadowy presence of du Maurier's originals in Hitchcock's films, however, differs from the super-egotistical dominance that we saw at work in adaptations of classic authors whose reputations are overpowering. Instead, I would describe this presence as a sort of nothingness that shines on the textual surface of these screen adaptations just as the glittering sardine can that Lacan saw floating on the surface of the waves appeared to gaze back at him, as described

---

67. Ibid., 29.

in *Seminar XI*.⁶⁸ Similar to the gaze that the subject does not notice but which suddenly reveals itself, the glittering sardine can capture the subject's uncanny feeling that they are being looked at from all sides. This gaze that disturbs the certitude of the subject's being suggests another element beyond the super-egotistical in Hitchcock's obsessive circling around the practice of adaptation. In this sense, the thematic centrality of a lack or non-being in the two films—for instance, the complete absence of Rebecca in *Rebecca* or the absence of any cause for the birds' attacks against people in *The Birds*—can be read as *a little nothing* masking the lack of lack for the purpose of keeping "this double, perpetual nihilation" at bay, if borrowing Sartre's words.⁶⁹

## Hitchcock's Rebecca *without Rebecca*

Having worked in the British film industry for nearly two decades, Alfred Hitchcock was seeking to further his career outside the crumbling British market in the late 1930s and his ambition pointed him straight toward Hollywood. His most recent British films—*The Man Who Knew Too Much* and *The Thirty-Nine Steps*—had aroused some attention among the American press and critics, which encouraged the Hitchcocks to pay their first visit to America in 1937 with the inflated expectation that immediate offers from major Hollywood studios would ensue. Despite the welcome extended by the US publicity machine, Hitchcock's first transatlantic trip proved to be a disheartening failure, and he returned with neither a contract nor a satisfiable offer. From 1937, David O. Selznick, one of the major Hollywood producers, kept Hitchcock in unbearable suspense by tantalizing the English director with a prospective film project on "the *Titanic*" yet never sending him a contract to sign. Eventually, Selznick made a relatively benign offer in 1938 and gave him a screen adaptation of Daphne du Maurier's *Rebecca* as his first assignment. Anxious not to disappoint his new employer

68. In his eleventh seminar, Lacan relates his own encounter with the gaze as the *objet petit a* in the scopic field through an anecdote of a sardine can on the sea. He says, "It was looking at me at the level of the point of light, the point at which everything that looks at me is situated—and I am not speaking metaphorically." Lacan, *Seminar XI*, 95.

69. Sartre, *Being and Nothingness*, 18.

or American audiences, the young (yet already established) English director was obliged to confront the experience of not being the center of gravity and power.

In Hollywood, he found that directors under contract with major studios were mere cogs in the studio system's Fordist production line. Even worse, he was forced to work under the panoptical control of the notoriously dictatory producer Selznick. Moreover, Hitchcock felt particularly uneasy about the fact that, once he had finished shooting, his Hollywood debut would leave his hands and be subjected to a re-edit, according to the contract that remarkably limited the director's aesthetic control over the postproduction process. To compound his agony, Hitchcock was struck with the news of the outbreak of the Second World War at home five days before he commenced shooting *Rebecca*. From California, he frantically called his dear mother in London, and when he at last got her on the telephone line, Emma Hitchcock proudly responded with a flat refusal to her youngest son's attempt to bring her to America. With a picture of his mother trapped at the center of the war in his mind's eye, Hitchcock commenced filming on *Rebecca* in September 1939.[70]

As written by du Maurier, *Rebecca* is the story of an orphaned girl who enters a new world represented by a great English mansion, Manderley, after marrying its owner—the middle-aged aristocrat and widower Maxim de Winter—by a stroke of luck. The title of both the original novel and Hitchcock's film adaptation, however, is not the name of this young heroine but rather the given name of Maxim's deceased first wife, while the protagonist herself remains literally nameless to the end of both texts. She begins her life as the new mistress of Manderley only to find that this Gothic mansion, as well as its inhabitants, including her husband, is haunted by the late Mrs. de Winter—the fabulously beautiful Rebecca, adored by everyone even after her mysterious death. Du Maurier's novel, related in the first person, delineates the anxiety of the second Mrs. de Winter, who feels threatened by the invisible yet suffocating presence of Rebecca—the "undead" lady of the grandiose

---

70. A detailed account of the relationship between Hitchcock and David O. Selznick in their first collaboration and the contexts of production of *Rebecca* appears in Leff's *Hitchcock and Selznick*. In its biographical account of Hitchcock's earliest years in Hollywood, the chapter refers to John Russell Taylor's *Hitch: The Life and Times of Alfred Hitchcock* (New York: Da Capo Press, 1996) and McGilligan's *Alfred Hitchcock*.

English estate. Drawing on the conventions of the Victorian female *Bildungsroman* as developed in *Jane Eyre*, du Maurier's *Rebecca* traces the heroine's journey of self-discovery, capturing her struggles to claim the title "Mrs. de Winter" from her marginalized position as a nameless protagonist.[71] She anxiously strives to overcome the sense of her being unbearably insignificant and her inability to function as the mistress of Manderley in comparison with her confident and competent precursor Rebecca. She eventually outgrows her complex upon discovering that Maxim had killed his first wife, who was revealed to be an evil woman hidden beneath the facade of a beautiful, perfect lady.[72]

Despite its controversial and subversive elements, du Maurier's novel was a major commercial success in both the UK and the United States. Selznick International Pictures purchased the rights to the novel for screen adaptation in the same year that Hitchcock signed the contract with the company.[73] David O. Selznick, well-known for his commitment to faithfully adapting literary originals, made it very clear that Hitchcock was to remain loyal to the novel in order

71. For the influence of Victorian women's novels and Gothic conventions on du Maurier's works and particularly on her magnum opus *Rebecca*, see Nina Auberbach's *Daphne du Maurier: Haunted Heiress* (Philadelphia: University of Pennsylvania Press, 2000) and *The Daphne du Maurier Companion*, ed. Helen Taylor (London: Virago, 2007).

72. For further discussion of *Rebecca*, stemming in particular from feminist and queer studies, see Tania Modleski's discussion of Hitchcock's *Rebecca* as "a female Oedipal drama" in which she analyzes the heroine's experience and her relationship with the paternal husband and the dead lady in her book *The Women Who Knew Too Much: Hitchcock and Feminist Theory* (New York: Methuen, 1988). Expanding Modleski's argument with an elaboration of discursive psychoanalytic theories, Karen Hollinger focuses on the "heterosexist, patriarchal" forces operating on the process of transition from the original novel to Hitchcock's adaptation in her 1993 article "The Female Oedipal Drama of *Rebecca* from Novel to Film."

73. Despite having been assigned the task of adapting *Rebecca* by Selznick, Hitchcock himself had already read the novel and attempted to secure the copyright before Selznick, but could not afford it at the time. See Leff, *Hitchcock and Selznick* and McGilligan, *Alfred Hitchcock*. Kyle Dawson Edwards also deals with the producer's strategies and desires behind the adaptation of *Rebecca* in "Brand-Name Literature: Film Adaptation and Selznick International Pictures' *Rebecca* (1940), *Cinema Journal* 45, no. 3 (Spring 2006): 32–58.

to avoid disappointing the millions of readers who embraced *Rebecca* ardently. Aside from the immediate pressure exerted by the extensive readership and the over-respectful producer, there was another source of discomfort to the director—the quiet yet firm demands of the author Daphne du Maurier. She openly expressed her dismay on discovering that Hitchcock was to direct a screen adaptation of her best-seller. A year before the production of *Rebecca*, Hitchcock had directed a film adaptation of her novel *Jamaica Inn* as his last English film, and the author had been very unhappy with the outcome. She sent a message to Selznick, telling him that "she was weeping bitter tears over [Hitchcock's treatment of] *Jamaica Inn*."[74] In his soothing reply to this message, Selznick boasted that he just had thrown out Hitchcock's first draft of *Rebecca* and told the director to rewrite it and promised the author that it was his "intention to do the book and not some botched-up semi-original such as was done with *Jamaica Inn*."[75] This context for Hitchcock's adaptation of du Maurier's *Rebecca* suggests that, as a new settler in Hollywood, Hitchcock found himself surrounded by many demanding gazes, which left him susceptible to feeling threatened by the overflow of so many unanticipated influences.

From the outset of the adaptation process, Hitchcock appears to have suffered as a result of the absence of the story's real heroine, Rebecca, because the novel centers on a woman who is dead before the narrative begins. Indeed, despite the absence of any Rebecca to capture on camera and transfer to the screen, the director was pushed by the producer's, author's, and presumably many readers' demands to "try as far as possible to retain the original"—that is, *Rebecca* without Rebecca.[76]

This fatal absence of the central character, positioned as the origin of the novel's captivating attraction, is the epitome of *the little nothing* as delineated in the previous speculation on the philosophical conceptualization of nothingness. In other words, the nonexistent yet omnipresent Rebecca is the central and, more significantly, constitutive void around which the entire narrative is structured. Each major character in the story has their own memories and perceptions of Rebecca, the first Mrs. de Winter. However, when the young heroine,

---

74. Leff, *Hitchcock and Selznick*, 47.

75. Ibid.

76. Hollinger, "The Female Oedipal Drama," 23. (Originally from *Memo from David O. Selznick*, ed. Rudy Behlmer (New York: Avon, 1972), 267.)

the second Mrs. de Winter, tries to uncover what the deceased woman was truly like, she finds herself unable to access the truth through the recollections of others. The nameless heroine feels haunted by her inability to grasp Rebecca as the object of her inquiry: in the novel, she confides through the first-person narration that "I was following a phantom in my mind, whose shadowy form had taken shape at last. Her features were blurred, her coloring indistinct, the setting of her eyes and the texture of her hair were still uncertain, still to be revealed."[77] For the young Mrs. de Winter, as well as the reader, and, most painfully, for Hitchcock, there is always something about Rebecca that "is left unspoken, is not integrated into the symbolic universe" of the story, despite the fact that she is constantly and exhaustively talked about throughout the novel.[78]

The structure of the original text as delineated above severely challenges and disorients the rational ground for the opposition between being and nothing. However, such ambiguity is neither unusual nor specific to this film adaptation. Rather, it is characteristic and even inevitable owing to the innate impasse at the heart of every screen adaptation, which is the gulf between the linguistic signifiers on the page and the imaginary cinematic signifiers. To explain this from a Lacanian perspective, linguistic signifiers on the page belong to the symbolic, which is organized by and functions through the constitutive gap that divides the signifier and signified. On the contrary, imaginary cinematic signifiers belong to the imaginary, which is based on the reciprocal (and thus gap-less) identification between an object and its image. Therefore, the process by which words are transformed into objects (or, more precisely, their images) on screen draws attention precisely to the intersection between the ego formed in the scopic dimension of the imaginary and the subject positioned in the symbolic universe. In this sense, adaptation brings a speaking being as adapter to "the juncture of the symbolic and the imaginary in the constitution of the real" where the speaking subject glimpses the groundlessness of its being.[79] In *Rebecca*, the traumatizing dimension of the adapter as such is intensified by the ambivalent operation of the invisible but

---

77. Daphne du Maurier, *Rebecca* [1938] (New York: Harper, 2006), 44.

78. Slavoj Žižek, *Looking Awry* (Cambridge MA: MIT Press, 1991), 44.

79. Jacques Lacan, *The Seminar of Jacques Lacan Book I: Freud's Papers on Technique*, ed. Jacques-Alain Miller and trans. John Forrester (New York and London: W. W. Norton & Company, 1991), 74.

invincible Rebecca in the course of adaptation. The eponymous woman functions as an unseen object, whose invisibility creates a void on screen, making her an object of desire—a figure that the audience longs to see but cannot. At the same time, Rebecca is merely an empty name, a floating signifier without a tangible referent—the woman who should bear that name no longer exists, leaving only the haunting absence of her presence.

The concept of lack helps clarify the profound ambivalence of an object like Rebecca in *Rebecca*, who paradoxically exists as both present and absent. Lacan's challenge to the oppositional framework of absence (*fort*) and presence (*da*) offers the authentic foundation for understanding the subject and the objects of its desire in Lacanian psychoanalysis. He introduces the idea of a peculiar object, marked by its indecisiveness regarding presence and absence. This object is distinct from a typical object of desire, which appears to possess its objectivity and seems tangible—an illusion emerging from the imaginary realm in Lacan's topology. The differentiation is to highlight how certain objects resist clear categorization, further complicating the subject's engagement with desire. This object of ambivalence functions as the object-cause of desire and not the object of desire. Lacan coined for it the term *objet petit a* and conceptualized it as the object that anxiety is not without in his tenth seminar on anxiety. Interestingly, the *objet petit a* is the concept that Lacan claims as his unique and sole invention, linking this little nothing to the notoriously unknowable object of psychoanalytic knowledge, anxiety, in the same seminar: the path toward analysis of anxiety veers through the concept of the *objet petit a*.

As Freud duly predicted, anxiety functions as a signal and Lacan's creation of the *objet petit a* serves as a response to Freud's idea, giving rise to one of the most subversive concepts in Lacan's adaptation of Freudian theory. Freud, who left a gaping void in his theorization of anxiety, seems to offer room for Lacan to introduce the *objet petit a* as a way to address this void. In the first meeting of his seminar on anxiety, the *adapter* of Freud's work remarked: "In the discourse, thank God, of *Inhibitions, Symptoms and Anxiety*, everything is spoken about except anxiety."[80] Therefore, the passage to anxiety is, for Lacan, that which is simultaneously both in Freud and not in Freud. Consequently, Lacan cannot avoid relating the conceptualization of the *objet petit a* to castration, which is the point at which Freud places a full stop. From

---

80. Lacan, *Seminar X*, 6.

there, Lacan picks up "the little missing piece" to recapitulate his own path toward castration, this time not to finalize the symbolic account of the subject's birth in its relationship to the Other but to leave it open as "a lack for which the symbol does not supply."[81]

Lacan maintains that the *objet petit a* is the remainder or residue that falls away from the subject's constitution in its relationship to the Other. Here, the Other is designated as that which is determined by its negative operation; Lacan symbolizes it as $(-\varphi)$ and reads it as the minus-phi of castration. In the previous chapter, we discussed why the Other is necessarily a negative function in relation to the speaking subject, by hypothesizing the Mother as the missing element at the onset of the substitutive formation of the phallic Other. As such, the Other is not a positive mandate but rather a gap that emerges with the condition of castration that never allows the subject to move beyond this final point. While the Other is that which is placed in a position of impossibility and characterized as lack or absence, Lacan elaborates the little remainder of the Other, the *objet petit a*, as follows:

> [it appears] at a place that is situated *with respect to an image* which is characterised by a lack, by the fact that what is called for there cannot appear there, that there is profoundly orientated and polarised the function of this image itself, that desire is there, not simply veiled, but essentially placed in relation to an absence, to a possibility of appearing determined by a presence which is elsewhere and determines it more closely, but, where it is, ungraspable by the subject, ... in the function that it fulfils in the phantasy at the place that something can appear.[82]

In short, the *objet petit a* is characterized by its "status [as that which] escapes from the status of the object derived from the specular image ... [and] is at stake everywhere Freud speaks about object when anxiety is involved."[83] Anxiety responds to the impasse that the castrated subject experiences: the subject is incapable of capturing this object, which is deprived of an imaginary dimension, in any way other than "the specular register."[84] Of course, this incapability could not be

81. Ibid., 93.
82. Ibid., 30. (My emphasis.)
83. Ibid., 27.
84. Ibid.

more problematic than in the case of the film director Hitchcock, who sought to render the invisible and ungraspable character Rebecca, the object-cause of his desire, whose lack shines on the surface of the on-screen photographic image. In passing, I wish to highlight here that although Hitchcock dismisses the film *Rebecca* on the grounds that "it is not a Hitchcock picture," this pursuit of non-being is far from non-Hitchcockian; indeed, it is eminently Hitchcockian to the extent that it recalls his signature narrative device, known as the MacGuffin. This refers to Hitchcock's characteristic dramaturgical machine that he not only used frequently but also theorized as a means of constituting an object of false significance that most characters seek to know or obtain yet that does not enhance any aspect of the audience's engagement with the narrative. In Hitchcock's own words, the MacGuffin is that which "has been boiled down to its purest expression: nothing at all!"[85]

However, as Lacan insists, this absence in and of itself does not provoke anxiety. On the contrary, Rebecca's absence serves as the guard against anxiety because anxiety is the signal that indicates that something has come into the place of lack and there approaches the lack of lack. Lacan regards anxiety as a signal "appearing there about everything which manifests itself at this place, to confuse us, as I might say, as regards the structuring function of this void."[86] In this sense, du Maurier's *Rebecca* epitomizes Lacan's elaboration of the concept of anxiety by pinpointing the origin of the young heroine's anxiety as follows:

> Rebecca, always Rebecca. Wherever I walked in Manderley, wherever I sat, even in my own thoughts and in my dreams, I met Rebecca. I knew her figure now, the long slim legs, the small and narrow feet. Her shoulders, broader than mine, the capable clever hands. Hands that could steer a boat, could hold a horse. Hands that arranged flowers, made the models of ships, and wrote "Max from Rebecca" on the fly-leaf of a book. I knew her face too, small and oval, the clear white skin, the cloud of dark hair. I knew the scent she wore, I could guess her laughter and her smile. If I heard it, even among

---

85. For Hitchcock's own account of the MacGuffin and its origin, see Truffaut, *Hitchcock*, 137–9.

86. Lacan, *Seminar X*, 38.

## 3. Resistance to the Originals in Hitchcock's Adaptations     129

a thousand others, I should recognize her voice. Rebecca, always Rebecca. I should never be rid of Rebecca.[87]

Indeed, it is this excess of Rebecca that is truly terrifying: the multitude of reminiscences and residues—objects, in short—endlessly flowing into the empty place that Rebecca has left, suffocating the heroine and threatening to engulf the entirety of her reality.

In a literary creation that bears a little slip between signifier and signified—for instance, a gap between the sign "Rebecca" and what it evokes in the reader's mind—it would not be too difficult to present Rebecca's status as the *objet petit a*, a void named Rebecca, as though it were "the little nothing that she holds in reserve."[88] Consequently, in a written text, it is not impossible to orchestrate the threat that objects might intrude into this gap. However, unlike a literary fiction that is innately capable of presenting the little nothing, a film text is based on the immediate identification between an object and its image and often operates on the condition of the concrete perceptibility and even illusory materiality of those on-screen imaginary signifiers as objects— that is, images to be seen and sounds to be heard are perceived as associated with that which *is* present. Moreover, it is far more complex a requirement for a classic Hollywood film whose editing is meant for the seamless, gap-less, surface of its diegetic world to contain such a constitutive gap or rupture epitomized by Rebecca in du Maurier's *Rebecca*.

Despite the difficulties inherent in envisioning the little nothing, particularly at the cost of anxiety's function in signaling the more terrifying lack of lack on the brink, Hitchcock, as an experienced reader and insightful adapter, was sufficiently sensitive to appreciate that the reader's empathetic experience of the heroine's anxiety constitutes the essence of the novel's power. Therefore, he could restrain himself from ignorant attempts to fill the gap by replacing it with any photographic image of her, which would make Rebecca an object of scopic desire rather than the cause of desire. In writing the script, Hitchcock rejected the easy option of creating a flashback representation of Rebecca, and yet he strove to express his own cinematic caliber so as to differentiate the film from the original novel. This internal tension, I suggest,

---

87. du Maurier, *Rebecca* [1938], 239.
88. Lacan, *Seminar X*, 34.

ultimately allowed him to preserve the novel's uncanny presentation of Rebecca qua the *objet petit a*.

The most intriguing rendition of Rebecca as such emerges in the scene in which Maxim confides what happened on the night Rebecca died. In du Maurier's novel, the reader learns that Maxim shot Rebecca, who had deliberately provoked him to do so after discovering that she had terminal cancer. Maxim placed her body in the cabin of her boat, sailed out to sea, and sank the body to conceal the murder. Sometime later, an unidentified female body emerged in a nearby bay and Maxim, although he knew that it was not Rebecca, claimed the body as hers and buried it in the family crypt. However, the film, made under the Hays production code, could not allow Maxim (played by Laurence Olivier) to go unpunished for his crime. Hitchcock and Selznick thus twisted the original story and the murder of the novel became an accident. At the film's climax, as in the novel, the boat is found by a local diver, with Rebecca's body in the cabin. In the boat house, where Maxim has been hiding from all the commotion, he confesses to the heroine that Rebecca fell on a hard edge after Maxim struck her, and so he placed her body into the boat and sank her because he was afraid that no one would believe that her death had been accidental. As Maxim recalls Rebecca's dying moments, the camera literally shoots "the place or lack of Rebecca" and follows this invisible character, first sitting on the divan with the cigarette stubs and then slowly standing to walk toward Maxim, who stands, as he had stood at the time of her death, by the door.

Hitchcock's filmic treatment of Rebecca, through visualization of the lack or her non-being, confirms this invisible yet omnipresent character's function as the *objet petit a*, which sets in motion every action driven by desire in the narrative and simultaneously marks an irreparable void. It is not unreasonable to suggest that the eerie tension of the climactic scene is aroused not by absence, but by the frame that captures Rebecca's non-being, betraying the expectation or desire that her image will eventually appear as her mystery is directly confronted. This lack itself does not provoke anxiety but refers to a truly traumatic possibility. As Lorenzo Chiesa accurately states, the empty screen enclosing the nothingness of Rebecca as the *objet petit a* is like a "window [that] frames an abyss," which signals that one "might easily fall out of the window" into the abyss, the lack of lack that will engulf the whole of one's being as a subject.[89] In a sense, this unique

---

89. Chiesa, *Subjectivity and Otherness*, 164.

vision of the *objet petit a* that emerged in Hitchcock's adaptation of du Maurier's novel may be conceived as touching on the kernel of his lifelong obsession with adaptation: the persistent force behind repetition that he denied yet could not resist is the drive that blindly aims at the *objet petit a* and traces an endless circuit around this false trace of the primordial lost object.

Further, Hitchcock's film insightfully draws attention to the essence of the novel's complex psychic dynamics between Rebecca and the female narrator. Thanks to his sensitivity as a reader and adapter, the film successfully manifests the meticulous play between the two characters under the same name or signifier of "Mrs. de Winter"—one dead and the other living. Like the novel's first-person narrator, the film's young Mrs. de Winter, the nameless young heroine (played by Joan Fontain), is created as a vehicle for the audience's encounter with the other Mrs. de Winter, Rebecca, who functions as a little nothing, pacifying the truly intimidating lack of lack. Similarly, through the second Mrs. de Winter's constant reactive engagement with the dead Mrs. de Winter, Hitchcock conveys the threat posed by Rebecca, whose painful absence on the audiovisual surface of the film's diegetic world serves as a sinister reminder of the marginalized position the young heroine occupies—a subject on the verge of being engulfed by the lack of lack, or death overwritten on her very name. Put differently, Rebecca qua the *objet petit a* signals the death *writ large* on the young heroine's own name and place—"Mrs. de Winter." In this sense, Hitchcock's *Rebecca* stands out in his six decades' practice of adaptation by virtue of its extraordinary fidelity to the original text but more importantly for its lasting psychological impact, regardless of how fiercely he denied and resisted the original's influence.

What is interesting in the comparison between the original novel and Hitchcock's adaptation is their ways of presenting the young Mrs. de Winter's encounter with Rebecca. In the novel, the young heroine first encounters Rebecca through the latter's handwriting. Amid her budding romantic relationship with Maxim, Maxim presents her with a poetry book that he has rather carelessly picked up from his car. Inside the book's cover, the young heroine finds Rebecca's handwritten dedication to Maxim: "Max from Rebecca." From this moment, the novel's heroine is haunted by the name Rebecca:

Max—from Rebecca. May 17th written in a curious, slanting hand. A little blob of ink marred the white page opposite, as though the writer, in impatience, had shaken her pen to make the ink flow freely. And then, as it bubbled through the nib, it came a little thick, so that the name Rebecca stood out black and strong, the tall and sloping *R* dwarfing the other letters.[90]

The novel's heroine never recovers from this first encounter clearly in the domain of the symbolic by means of letters. She repeatedly returns to Rebecca's peculiar handwriting throughout the novel to the extent that she feels as though the letters written by the dead Mrs. de Winter have come to life, bringing Rebecca too close to her. She meditates, "'Max from Rebecca.' She was dead, and one must not have thoughts about the dead. They slept in peace the grass blew over their graves. How alive was her writing of ink. Done yesterday. It was just as if it had been written yesterday."[91] Here, the novel clearly maps out how the *objet petit a* operates precisely on the level of the gap or slip between signifier and signified, in relation to which Lacan elaborates the concept of the *objet petit a* appearing in "a sort of gap, of residue of the signifying function."[92] To put it differently, Du Maurier's *Rebecca* shows how this empty and floating signifier—that is, a signifier without a signified to designate its place in the signifying chain—functions as a perturbing blot, disconcerting the symbolic structure in which a signifier is taken to be the effect of a signified and a signified to be the cause of a signifier. As such, owing to this radically subversive signifier "Rebecca," which has dropped from the chain of signification, the novel's Rebecca serves as the *objet petit a* that causes desire by pointing at the built-in gap in the symbolic.

In Hitchcock's visual characterization, Rebecca appears as a lack in the imaginary in close relationship to the uncanny (*unheimlich*) home, Manderley, which is haunted by the floating signifier "Rebecca." In other words, the film's young heroine confronts Rebecca only through Manderley, the de Winters' estate, which contains and reserves the lack or hole created by Rebecca. Unlike in the novel, the second Mrs. de Winter never sees a trace of Rebecca before she comes to settle in Manderley. For this reason, the romance under the bright sun of Monte Carlo and the newly married couple's extended honeymoon travelling around Europe form a stark contrast with the suffocating

90. du Maurier, *Rebecca* [1938], 33.
91. Ibid., 58.
92. Lacan, *Seminar X*, 195.

containment of their married life at Manderley. The differentiating visual representation contributes to the contrast—the naturalistic light and exterior scenes for the first part of the film and the German expressionistic cinematography for the days in Manderley.

Hitchcock delicately visualizes the uncanniness of the Gothic mansion. Although Maxim believes that Manderley is a mere *Heim* for him, this place, in effect, is more than a house that he merely possesses, controls, and lives in. This grand mansion with its long history is overwhelming rather than welcoming, particularly to its newcomer. There, the young Mrs. de Winter meets, in private, her faceless precursor, whose name is written all over the place. Over a year after her death, Rebecca's monogram, "R de W" or simply "R," is still everywhere in Manderley, and yet—strangely enough—Maxim, who hates to see or hear of any trace of his dead wife, never notices that this initial is inscribed in every corner of his grand manor. The second Mrs. de Winter thus suffers privately from Rebecca's repeated emergence: through a table napkin, the stationery in the morning room, a blanket, and her handkerchief the young Mrs. de Winter is bombarded by the dead woman's name in her peculiar handwriting. Hitchcock never fails to emphasize these private encounters between the two Mrs. de Winters by using a close-up shot of the initial accompanied by a mesmerizing tune. The music helps to construct a self-contained psychic space, where only the heroine, along with the spectators, secretly and painfully confronts the repetitive appearance of "R de W" or "R" to the extent that the recurrence of this visual motif begins to float free of the film's diegetic reality toward the psychic dimension of both the heroine and audiences.

In Hitchcock's adaptation, the conjugation between the floating signifier "R de W" and Manderley reveals another facet of the *objet petit a* as it relates to anxiety. The imaginary dimension of the signifier without its signified leads the subject, which is constructed on the symbolic plane, to confront its own radical strangeness, binding the subject forever to the uncanny home. This *Heim*, Lacan says, is found "in a point situated in the Other beyond the image of which we are made and this place represents the absence where we are."[93] Put differently, the Other in Lacan's account is the Other that is beyond the imaginary dimension of identification; it is the Other that points to the absence at the center of the symbolic domain. In Hitchcock's film, this association

---

93. Ibid., 32.

of the uncanny with the *objet petit a*, as represented by Rebecca, suggests that this Other certainly does not refer to the forbidding father characterized by its own lack. Rather, this Other appears in "the place [that] represents the absence where we are" and signals the proximity of the omnipresent Mother, which lacks the lack and can thus point to—or "re-present" in Lacan's terms—the lack in the phallic Other that is already barred. Owing to this lack of lack, which neither the imaginary nor the symbolic can contain, the Mother presents itself to a speaking subject as the original lost object, which the subject of desire cannot ever reach but around which it circles forever.

Therefore, Hitchcock's adaptation of du Maurier's *Rebecca*, in a sense, epitomizes how one can respond to anxiety in one's compulsive obsession with framing the lack of lack in an attempt to avoid becoming engulfed by the abyss behind the picture frame. Thanks to this frame, we can cover up the little nothing captured in it with our own fantasies. Hitchcock, in successfully resisting the temptation to conceal the little nothing, left his *Rebecca* without a Rebecca. In doing so, he rendered the being of the young heroine with whom the audience is led to identify as a mere nuisance, awkwardly plunging into the space that should be left empty. This allows us to glimpse the subversion of subjectivity in obliging us to realize that we, like the film's young heroine, are the very detestable object that seeks to cover and fill the place of the *objet petit a*. In a way, such discovery leads the subject to glimpse its own traumatic fall from subject to object. This terrifying and anxiety-provoking encounter with one's own fall is projected on the screen (of film adaptation, for this book's interest) behind which there is the constant and menacing gaze of the Mother, may be that which anxiety warns against.

In this sense, Hitchcock's resistance to the influence of original texts, coupled with his paradoxical obsession with adaptation as his primary mode of creation, seems to stem from a certain anxiety. As Bloom and Kierkegaard point out, this anxiety signals the adapter's fall from a creator to that which is already written by the Mother who lacks the lack. Paradoxically, the act of adaptation is both the traumatic discovery of this fall on the brink and the play with the screen that protects the adapter, film director, and Hitchcock in this case, from the fall. Therefore, despite his attempt to spit out the influence of original texts from his career, Hitchcock's adaptation of du Maurier's original novel—that is, *Rebecca* without Rebecca yet full of Rebecca—epitomizes his obsessive organization of his filmmaking career around the anxiety-evoking void, which, in the course of adaptation, he framed into the little nothing so that he could cover it up with his own images.

## Adaptation in Reverse: The Birds

Although Hitchcock often dismissed du Maurier's *Rebecca* as "novelettish" and "old-fashioned," emblematic of "the whole school of feminine literature at the period," his decision to film her novella *The Birds* for his third adaptation of her works convinced critics like François Truffaut and scholars such as Karen Hollinger and Richard Allen that Hitchcock engaged with her writing on a deeper psychological level than he openly acknowledged.[94] This final section will examine *The Birds* (1963) in the chapter's attempt to interrogate the drive behind the obsession with the never-satisfactory practice of adaptation as manifested in Hitchcock's unique connection to the female author and her works.

His third adaptation of du Maurier's work was released shortly after the pinnacle of his creative force, marked by *Psycho* (1960), and before the lukewarm reception of *Marnie* (1964). In a thematic sense, *The Birds* is often regarded as a continuation of the theme of the domineering Mother in the previous film *Psycho*, which features the undead mother whose murderous gaze and menacing voice continues to exert a hold over her son, even after her death. Moreover, *The Birds* was followed by *Marnie*, which thematizes a child's suffering as a result of the mother's agonizing indifference and absence. If *Psycho* problematizes the excessive presence of the mother and *Marnie* interrogates her traumatically thin

---

94. In the above quotation from Truffaut's interview, Truffaut suggests that the experience of adapting du Maurier's *Rebecca* appears to have exerted a permanent influence on Hitchcock's later works. Karen Hollinger's psychoanalytic investigation explores how Hitchcock (along with the encompassing influence of patriarchal forces embedded in the systems in which he worked) tailored du Maurier's female oedipal drama into the heroine's successful initiation into the patriarchal order. Richard Allen also interrogates the influence of Daphne du Maurier's subversive romance on Hitchcock's undermining of conventional romantic narrative. See François Truffaut's *Hitchcock*; Hollinger's "The Female Oedipal Drama of *Rebecca* from Novel to Film," 17–30; Richard Allen's "Daphne du Maurier and Alfred Hitchcock," in *A Companion to Literature and Film*, ed. Robert Stam and Alessandra Raengo (New York: Blackwell, 2004).

and remote presence, then *The Birds*, standing between the two, may be conceived as a film that deals with the subliminal locus between the mother's terrifying omnipresence and the mother's absence. Therefore, the following analysis of Hitchcock's adaptation *The Birds* shall center this theme of the mother as a pivot with reference to Lacan's conceptualization of the drive as it relates to the above discussed *objet petit a*.

Hitchcock optioned du Maurier's story for his television series several years before making the film adaptation, and the story was included in the 1959 anthology of short stories that was published under his name—*Alfred Hitchcock Presents: My Favourites in Suspense*.[95] The story must have had his attention for some time, lingering in his mind, although he claimed that he had embarked casually on the adaptation project, as though it were something he could complete as an in-between project while waiting for his favorite actress Grace Kelly to return for his next film *Marnie* (which never happened).

Despite the director's seeming light-heartedness, the production process was challenging in many respects. Hitchcock had to work under the financial pressure of a $3.3 million budget, the largest budget in his career to date, as well as the unprecedented technological challenges of dealing with nonhuman actors—birds—as prime antagonists. Aside from these difficulties in production, the crew who worked for him on this project observed that the seasoned filmmaker was suffering from a profound sense of uneasiness. At one point during the film's troublesome shoot, one of the staff asked the director, in bewilderment, what they were making, and, to his surprise, Hitchcock answered he did not know.[96] In a later interview with Truffaut, Hitchcock recalled that he was in an unusual state of distress and could not stop meddling with the script, although it had been finalized in collaboration with the script writer Evan Hunter. In a way that was out of character for him, he recalled being tense and upset even after a day's work during the shooting of the film, caught up in "this emotional siege" and a distinct sense of being lost.[97] "Something happened that was altogether new in my experience ... I began to improvise," he told Truffaut.[98]

---

95. Alfred Hitchcock, *Alfred Hitchcock Presents: My Favourites in Suspense* (New York: Random House, 1959).
96. McGilligan, *Alfred Hitchcock*, 623.
97. Truffaut, *Hitchcock*, 290.
98. Ibid.

The film's characteristic ambivalence as for the motivation of the central action—that is, the birds' attack—is not unrelated to du Maurier's original story, which depicts the inexplicable attacks by birds on a village in Cornwall. The novella's male protagonist, Nat Hocken, is a farm worker who alone foresees the gravity of the attack and strives to protect his wife and two young children by any means. In its apocalyptic mood, du Maurier's novella sustains the inaccessibility to the motivation for the massive deadly attack of birds as a central enigma until its closure: the story concludes with a pessimistic scene in which the Hockens remain confined in their cottage, having discovered that the avian attack is destroying the whole of civilization—or, at least, all of Europe—without knowing what caused these typically tame and benign creatures to behave in this way.

Written after the Second World War and published in 1952, du Maurier's story evokes the traumatic memory of the wars that violated the Mother Nature and her rage against mankind. This thematic concern is revealed through the characterization of Nat, a disabled war veteran who constantly draws on his wartime experience to interpret the apocalyptic events unfolding around him. For instance, after the birds first attack his household, Nat recalls the war: "It was, Nat thought, like air raids in the war. No one down this end of the country knew what the Plymouth folk had seen and suffered."[99] The author provides no definitive explanation for the birds' attack, and the story provokes the reader's anxiety precisely because the attacks symbolize the uncanny malignant force of "death falling from the sky."[100] Mary Ellen Bellanca provides a more specific interpretation, suggesting that the incomprehensible hostility manifested in the seemingly coordinated bird attacks serves as an agent that "places *Homo sapiens* back in the web of predatory nature," viewed through an ecocritical lens.[101] According to Bellanca, du Maurier's story merges "a primal anxiety" about the unfathomable predatory nature behind the birds' attacks with "a very

99. Daphne du Maurier, "The Birds," in *Echoes from the Macabre: Selected Stories* (Larchmont and New York: Queens House, 1952), 285.

100. John Bruns, "'The Proper Geography': Hitchcock's Adaptation of Daphne du Maurier's 'The Birds,'" *Clues* 31, no. 1 (Spring 2013): 57.

101. Mary Ellen Bellanca, "The Monstrosity of Predation in Daphne du Maurier's 'The Birds,'" *Interdisciplinary Studies in Literature and Environment* 18, no. 1 (Winder 2011): 28.

modern anxiety about destruction rained from the sky with powerful human-made weaponry."[102]

From the outset, the birds are considered to be driven by a persistent force of nature: "In spring the birds flew inland, purposeful, intent: they knew where they were bound, the rhythm and ritual of their life brooked no delay."[103] Then, as sinister signs of nature's disorientation emerge in the sudden climate changes, the birds become representative of the "driving urge," compelling them to be restless and destructive. At the end, the far-sighted protagonist contemplates "how many million years of memory were stored in those little brains, behind the stabbing beaks, the piercing eyes, now giving them this instinct to destroy mankind with all the deft precision of machines."[104] Therefore, a central focus in adapting the novella into film lies in developing a cinematic approach to convey the primal force of nature implied by the birds' attack in the original text—a challenge that Hitchcock and his cowriter Hunter seem to have addressed by using the figure of the possessive and jealous mother as the cornerstone of a family romance plot.

The adaptation, initially written by Evan Hunter under Hitchcock's close supervision, appears to differ significantly from the original novella, to the extent that Richard Allen called it an "adaptation in reverse."[105] While du Maurier's text is characterized by its minimal plot and characterization, conveying a prophetic vision of mankind's fate, the film creates a wholly new look for the story: the adaptation script interweaves the narrative of the birds' arrival with a psychologically intricate family romance involving Lydia Brenner, her son Mitch Brenner, and the film's heroine, Melanie Daniels. As Nina Auerbach observes, the plot of the romantic couple troubled by the jealous and possessive mother may be "a comic tweaking of du Maurier's grim earnestness."[106] However, from a psychoanalytical perspective, Hitchcock's incorporation of a familial plot—intertwined with the original story of the birds as a curse from the Mother Nature—paradoxically renders his film adaptation faithful to du Maurier's original, particularly in its evocation of the primal anxiety that looms over both the characters and the audience.

102. Ibid., 27.
103. du Maurier, "The Birds," 277.
104. Ibid., 311.
105. The term "adaptation in reverse" here is quoted from Allen's "Daphne du Maurier and Alfred Hitchcock," 319.
106. Auerbach, *Daphne du Maurier: Haunted Heiress*, 147.

The original text features a male hero, representing patriarchal authority, as he endeavors to keep his simple reality in order and strives to understand this anomalous and chaotic force of nature. Psychoanalytically interpreted, the protagonist's agony and anxiety reflect the inevitable doom of the subject in confrontation with an unfathomable enigma that is thwarting his desire to know. In this light, Nat's ultimate surrender to death descending from the sky in the story's grim ending at home—without understanding its origin or meaning— exemplifies the subject's encounter with "the limited function of desire," as the subject is repeatedly returned to the same place of the unknown.[107] Hitchcock's incorporation of familial complexities in the adaptation enhances, rather than diminishes, the story's ability to evoke the psychic tension and profound sense of crisis felt when confronting the inexplicable and relentless force embodied in the rhythmic, ritualistic attacks of the birds. By transposing the original story from the barren, postwar Cornwall to the vibrant San Francisco of 1960s America, Hitchcock's adaptation creates a strikingly affective parallel between humanity's existential crisis and the intimate, psychic turmoil of a familial triangle. In this triangle, the subject remains unable to fully liberate itself from the counterthesis to the paternal law and the symbolic order—namely, the alluring and inescapable shadow of the Mother, as discussed at the beginning of this chapter.

In his analysis of the film's rendition of birds as a vehicle for the limit of desire, Slavoj Žižek suggests that the film adds psychoanalytic insights to the thematic concerns of the original. In his book *Looking Awry*, Žižek warns against misinterpreting Hitchcock's use of birds as merely a symbol or a signifier: "Although Hitchcock's birds do give body to the agency of the maternal superego, the essential thing is nevertheless not to seize upon the link between the two traits ... as a sign relationships, as a correlative between a 'symbol' and its 'signification.'"[108] This pervasive misreading seems to offer a base for many readings, including Auerbach's, which claims that Hitchcock's film reduces du Maurier's gloomy vision of humanity to a psychosexual drama by framing the birds as a kind of cipher for the possessive and vengeful mother. For Žižek, the film's rendition of the birds is "the objectivization-positivization of a failed symbolization," which refers to the point at which the lack of the signifier suddenly reveals itself in the

---

107. Lacan, *Seminar XI*, 31.
108. Žižek, *Looking Awry*, 104.

signifier of the lack.[109] In other words, this signifier cannot perform its significatory function—because it lacks a signified—but makes obvious the limitation of desire's movement along the chain of signification. The film's true achievement in supplementing the additional diegetic contour of the original drama is to reinforce and make more affective to the audience the *collapse* of the meanings sought by "the psychosexual drama" of desire under the birds' overshadowing and overpowering presence.[110] Therefore, Hitchcock's adaptation underscores that the original "birds" are the pure embodiment of nature's uncanny and annihilating force—like the Mother, both the origin of life and the harbinger of death from the sky—rather than a reductive metaphor for psychosexual conflict within the domestic plot.

A useful point of comparison can be drawn here between the pair of lovebirds that Melanie brings for Mitch's sister's birthday and the birds that launch their attack against people. The contrast becomes evident in the way the lovebirds function as a signifier confined within the chain of signifiers, organizing a reality that can be comprehended, whereas the attacking birds elude every attempt to capture them within the film's network of signifiers. At the beginning of the film, as soon as Mitch recognizes Melanie in a pet shop, he asks for lovebirds while pretending to mistake Melanie for a staff member working in the shop. Mitch's reasons for spelling out the name "lovebirds" are clear, representing that which he is attempting to convey to Melanie. The meaning of the signifier *lovebirds* is communicable among the film's characters, as well as between the film's world and its spectators. In a scene where Melanie briefly converses with Annie, Mitch's ex-girlfriend who chose to settle in his hometown despite relinquishing her hope of marrying him, the term "lovebirds" serves as an equivocal yet intelligible signifier, referring both to the breed of the birds and the budding romantic interest between the two young protagonists: Annie instantly understands what a pair of lovebirds in Melanie's car signifies. When Mitch's mother Lydia meets Melanie for the first time in Tide restaurant, she, too, immediately understands what is going on beneath the exchange of these lovebirds and responds in precisely the same way as Annie, saying "Oh, I see."

By contrast, the attacking birds reside in the realm of the unknown and create a gap in the symbolic reality sustained by the smooth exchange of signifiers such as lovebirds. The cause of their attacks is enigmatic

---

109. Ibid.
110. Auberbach, *Daphne du Maurier: Haunted Heiress*, 147.

and unidentifiable, even to an eloquent ornithologist like Mrs. Bundy, whose dazzling knowledge of birds is no use to understand why these birds suddenly attack people. Unlike the lovebirds locked safely within their cage of signification, the birds out in the open air provoke anxiety owing to the impossibility of locating them in the logic of the symbolic. To meditate on Hitchcock's rendition of the birds as such through the concept of the counterthesis to the Oedipal masterplot, the comparison between the lovebirds and the attacking birds becomes more sharply defined by means of analogy. The Oedipal drama is a theatrical scene in which individual subjects play their parts; the role of the mother is designated therein as the forbidden object of incestuous desire, similar to the way in which the lovebirds' place is fixed by their name. However, the attacking birds point toward something that cannot be forced into this role play in the Oedipus complex, and hence refuses the designated place in the Oedipal drama played out by the human characters. The birds disrupt the psychosexual plot between the film's main characters without revealing the meaning or reason of their interruption. Moreover, the narrative of the family romance, signified by the lovebirds, unfolds under the looming shadow of the attacking birds, which physically and metaphorically oversee the intimate drama of the family complex while resisting any clear significatory function. Positioned outside the drama governed by the rule of desire under the Name-of-the-Father, the attacking birds remain an enigmatic and disruptive force.

As mentioned above, the limited function of desire in the subject's relationship with external reality originates from the fact that everyone is subject to the signifier constituted by the lack in the Other. In the face of such an unfathomable and overpowering urge or force as that presented by the birds' attack, this Other of negative operation, that is ($-\varphi$), fails to secure the certainty for one's objective and positive mode of existence as the subject of desire—that is, the desire for the lack. At this uncanny confrontation with the limited function of desire, the subject is guided toward the radical discovery of the demand of the Other, which—unlike the Other operating on the gap it introduces to the subject—would not allow any gap or distance between its omnipresent gaze and the subject. This Other, which lacks the lack, is none other than the Mother, whose demand Lacan maps onto the organization of the drive. It is possible to suggest that Hitchcock's adaptation of *The Birds* captures and touches the very core of that which is concealed behind the poetic implication of du Maurier's novella—that is, the implied link between the nurturing and caring Mother Nature and the incessant, persistent, and destructive force beyond the known orders of nature. This extraordinary sensitivity of the adapter Hitchcock seems to support the chapter's close reading of the two films by interpreting the director's denial, "I read the story only once and cannot remember anything in it" with the help of the function of negation.

Reading Hitchcock's *Rebecca* and *The Birds* together, it is possible to discern a pattern that characterizes Hitchcock's strategy in adapting du Maurier's works. There is a mother figure whose presence cannot be pinned down on screen in a conventional way with images that might be seen, voices that might be heard, or a rational explanation that might make it understood within the diegetic space. The undead Rebecca, as an overwhelming precursor to the second Mrs. de Winter, and the birds, as the embodiment of nature's undecipherable demand, both remain silent, tantalizing the protagonists and instilling anxiety about their desires. By placing those two presentations of the Mother unseen, unheard, and unexplained, Hitchcock filled the screen ironically with the anxiety provoked by the omnipresence of the malignant Mother. In his seminar on anxiety, Lacan explains the play of presence–absence, drawing on the figure of the mother in a way that is reminiscent of Hitchcock's adaptations of du Maurier's works:

> Do you not know that it is not nostalgia for what is called the maternal womb which engenders anxiety, it is its imminence, it is everything that announces to us something which provokes anxiety? It is not, contrary to what is said, either the rhythm or the alternation of the presence-absence of the mother. And what proves it, is that the infant takes pleasure in repeating this game of presence and absence: this possibility of absence, is what gives presence its security. What is most anxiety-provoking for the child, is that precisely this relation of lack on which he establishes himself, which makes him desire, this relation is all the more disturbed when there is no possibility of lack, what the mother is always on his back … the demand which cannot fail.[111]

What I have attempted to demonstrate in this chapter is that, just as Hitchcock's characters experience anxiety stemming from the absence of a gap between their symbolic reality and the overwhelming presence of the Mother, Hitchcock himself may have been projecting his own

---

111. Lacan, *Seminar X*, 36.

anxieties onto the screen throughout his six-decade career of adapting literary originals into films. In his constant process of adaptation, Hitchcock may have struggled with the persistent presence of elements resistant to cinematic translation and the limitations of his desire to create something purely cinematic. Yet, throughout his filmmaking career, the master of horror and suspense maintained an unwavering belief in the power of cinema, which he once described as "the greatest known mass medium there is in the world and the most powerful."[112] Consequently, Hitchcock continually experimented to maximize his artistry's potential, seizing the audience's anxiety and compelling them to pay even for the unsettling experience of unpleasure.

However, the director's career also reflected his struggle against the encroachment of an anti-cinematic shadow that intruded upon his meticulously crafted world of images, confined within the safety of tiny frames. His persistent urge to fill this darkness became a fortifying act of resistance against the influence of the original texts he adapted for the screen. Despite his vehement resistance, concealed behind his masterful manipulation of the original texts, neither Hitchcock nor anyone else can definitively explain his enduring fascination with the practice of adaptation. However, drawing on psychoanalytic insights from Freud and Lacan, one might suggest that the functions of repetition and resistance subtly point to the enduring force of the drive—a force that appears to tether us to the residue known as the *objet petit a*. This residue could be interpreted as a reminder of our ongoing entanglement with the pre-symbolic influence of the omnipresent Mother. If we are to take Hitchcock's career as an illustrative case uncovering *the other side* of screen adaptation, in opposition to the Oedipal relationship between a fatherly original and its screen descendants, then this chapter may conclude with the observation that cinema's resistance to the discursive domain of literature overlaps with the subject's problematic relationship with the Mother, about which, from the very beginning of civilization, myths have informed us that there is something uncanny and unpleasant in the "home or origin" of our being. In this uncanny domain of "beyond or the other side," the desire to adapt for film may recognize its own annihilation written at the heart of its origin or birthplace, in the same way that, in Hitchcock's representation of the Mother on his screen, one always sees the death writ large.

112. Truffaut, *Hitchcock*, 320.

## 4

# THE THING (*DAS DING*) THAT SPEAKS OF ITSELF IN STANLEY KUBRICK'S *THE SHINING*

> And it is around *das Ding* that the whole adaptive development revolves, a development that is so specific to man insofar as the symbolic process reveals itself to be inextricably woven into it.
> —Jacques Lacan, *Seminar VII*

> Men, listen, I am telling you the secret. I, truth, speak. ... Now that you are already lost, I belie myself, I defy you, I slip away: you say that I am being defensive.
> —Jacques Lacan, "The Freudian Thing"

### *Re-presentation of* das Ding

The purpose of the present chapter, in brief, is to grasp the unnameable "thing" at work in any practice of adaptation. In the two chapters prior to this, I have sought to provide a name to encapsulate the psychological force that drives the subject to constantly engage in adaptation. The previous chapters were structured and ordered according to the historical and theoretical movement of the psychoanalytic conceptualization of human psyche—that is, from Oedipalization in the domain of the symbolic to the more primordial dimension involved in the notion of anxiety. In other words, the thing initially appears to lurk behind the command of the terrifying Father before finding its echo in the call of the devouring Mother.[1] Following this somewhat dialectical path

---

1. The use of gender-specific psychoanalytic terminology here is not intended to be taken literally. Rather, it aligns with feminist interpretations of psychoanalysis, employing these terms to critique and examine the patriarchal foundations of prevailing understandings of the human psyche, rather than to endorse or reinforce them. For a more detailed discussion of the implications of these terms within a feminist psychoanalytic framework, please refer to the introduction.

laid by the previous chapters, this chapter aims to finally confront the elusive nature of the thing that resides and plays between a literary text and its film adaptation(s). That is, the discussion here seeks to move closer with the aim of capturing it as nameless and unrepresentable. To do this, the chapter's first part will draw out the rationale behind the psychoanalytical concept of *das Ding*, whose presence, in Lacan's teaching, reveals itself only through its absence.

For this purpose, the approach to "the thing" concerns the meaning that the adapter seeks to grasp and transfer. On various occasions in his return to Freud, Lacan emphasized the centrality of what Freud really meant in his theorization. Eventually, Lacan named this fundamental object of his search in his 1955 lecture entitled "The Freudian Thing or the Meaning of the Return to Freud in Psychoanalysis." As the title suggests, Lacan here introduces a concept, *das Ding*—or the Thing, with a capital "T" in English—as the nodal point of his attempt to interrogate "the original meaning Freud preserved" in psychoanalytical terms.[2] However, with his usual dose of irony, he warns us that the Thing he seeks cannot be read on the surface of any of Freud's texts: that is, Lacan rules out any possibility of pinning down "the Freudian thing," saying that it is "the enigma of she who slips away as she appears."[3]

If we construe this idiosyncratic logic through which Lacan weaves his theory into the Freudian field as an act of adaptation, it is possible to discern an intriguing similarity between Lacan's adaptation of Freud and director Stanley Kubrick's principle in adapting published literary texts for the screen. Regarding his incessant practice of adaptation, Kubrick explained that his search for "the most truthful" dimension of a literary original drove him to illuminate in his films "*something* [one] can't see in any other way."[4] These two comments of Lacan's and Kubrick's appear to share a rhetorical characteristic that divests

---

2. Jacques Lacan, "The Freudian Thing or the Meaning of the Return to Freud in Psychoanalysis," in *Écrits: The First Complete Edition in English*, trans. Bruce Fink (New York and London: W. W. Norton & Company), 336.

3. Ibid., 340.

4. Thomas Allen Nelson, *Kubrick: Inside a Film Artist's Maze* (Bloomington: Indiana University Press, 1982), 81. (The original quotation is from Joseph Gelmis, *The Film Director as Superstar* [Garden City, NY: Double Day, 1970], 309); Joseph Gelmis, "Interview with Stanley Kubrick," in *Perspectives on Stanley Kubrick*, ed. Mario Falsetto (New York: G. K. Hall, 1996), 32. (My emphasis.)

the nucleus of their adaptive movements of its name. This suggests an unnameable kernel, *das Ding*, as that which initiates the symbolic process yet is paradoxically deprived of its own symbolic coordinates. The meaning or message that the adapter strives to re-present and transmit always remains at the margins of the symbolic process, as evidenced by the fact that Lacan's and Kubrick's lifelong endeavors to articulate it culminated in its being conferred with the most ambiguous name—a thing.

Here, I shall use the hyphenated form "re-present" to more closely associate Lacan's *das Ding* with the present chapter's aim of interrogating screen adaptation as a cultural act in pursuit of *something* not only *from* but more significantly *beyond* a text. What makes *das Ding* significant in a study of the nature of adaptation is that *das Ding* reveals the most elementary dimension of human discourse, which is always saturated with the tone of loss. To clarify, for Lacan, Freud assumes that each representation is subject to the incessant psychic force in the human subject to present *again* that which has been lost on the subject's entrance to the symbolic domain. To borrow Bruce Fink's expression, the subject in and of language re-presents that which "is represented [by signifiers] but never presented."[5]

This assumption of a fundamental loss is none other than the central enigma in the Freudian field to which Lacan repeatedly returns. Lacan's elaboration of *das Ding* seeks to underscore the constitutive role of this fatal loss, which initiates the subject's search for meaning. Furthermore, this primordial sense of loss serves as the foundation for the transcendental leap of sublimation, a psychic dynamic that reveals a new dimension of adaptation. Therefore, the discussion that follows will draw on this aspect of re-presentation as an attempt to retrieve a certain meaning, which is lost and inaccessible yet remains constructive in its absence. Seen in this light, it transpires that re-presentation, as a general practice of signification, is none other than adaptation at its most fundamental level. Thus, the following speculations will focus on how the act of adaptation reaches for the unrepresentable Thing. To this end, Kubrick's adaptation of Stephen King's popular horror novel *The Shining* may serve as an illuminating case study.

5. Fink, "The Real Cause of Repetition," 227.

## The Play of the Thing

Kubrick's filmography reveals that he was an ardent adapter. The majority of his thirteen films are adaptations, with only two early exceptions: *Fear and Desire* (1953) and *Killer's Kiss* (1955).[6] He never shied away from adapting originals of canonical status, such as William Makepeace Thackeray's *The Luck of Barry Lyndon* or highly controversial modern pieces, such as Vladimir Nabokov's *Lolita*. He also chose popular contemporary texts such as Anthony Burgess's *A Clockwork Orange* and Stephen King's *The Shining*. Nevertheless, the poignantly self-expository nature of Kubrick's audiovisual style has marked his films' cinematic aesthetics as the foremost object of consideration for diverse critical reviews and scholarly studies. Moreover, owing to his extreme reluctance to articulate his intentions, ideas, or methodologies, Kubrick is often portrayed as a solitary artist who remained decidedly indifferent to the nature of film as a collaborative, communicative, and—above all—adaptable medium.[7] Perhaps because of his pre-filmic career as a professional photographer, Kubrick has been acknowledged as a perfectionist and a craftsman whose almost-pathological obsession

---

6. Several articles and books have discussed the relationship between Kubrick's films and their literary sources: see, for instance, Greg Jenkins's *Stanley Kubrick and the Art of Adaptation* (Jefferson, NC: McFarland, 1997), Jarrell D. Wright's "Reconsidering Fidelity and Considering Genre in (and with) *The Shining*," which appeared in *Stanley Kubrick: Essays on His Films and Legacy*, ed. Gary D. Rhodes (Jefferson, NC, and London: McFarland, 2008) and Ken Burke, "Novel to Film, Frame to Windows: The Case of Lolita as Text and Image," *Pacific Coast Philology* 38, no. 1 (2003): 16–24. In particular, critical reviews of Kubrick's screen rendition of King's *The Shining* are more readily available in the scholarship focusing on the works of Stephen King, such as Mark Browning's book *Stephen King on the Big Screen* (Bristol: Intellect Books, 2009) and Tony Magistrale's book *Hollywood's Stephen King* (New York: Palgrave Macmillan, 2003). However, in comparison with the accumulated scholarship on Kubrick's stylistic and conceptual diversity and complexity, studies examining Kubrick's oeuvre as screen adaptation remain sparse and scattered.

7. Kubrick's public persona as a least-communicative artist and its relationship to the reception of his works are amply investigated in Robert J. E. Simpson's book chapter "Whose Stanley Kubrick? The Myth, Legacy, and Ownership," in *Stanley Kubrick: Essays on His Films and Legacy*, ed. Gary D, Rhodes (Jefferson, NC, and London: McFarland, 2008), 232–44.

with technical and stylistic flawlessness overtakes and even suffocates any message or meaning implied by the originals—as though his film adaptations were in fact *The Shining*'s maze at the Overlook hotel, engulfing their original texts.

However, despite Kubrick's masterful status as a cinematic auteur and his bold revision of the originals, his attitude and strategy should be distinguished from that of Hitchcock, who deliberately selected "cheap and forgettable" contemporary fictions or short stories to avoid any unnecessary intervention or influence of the literary works on his films. As discussed in the previous chapter, Hitchcock's intentional ignorance of and resistance to his literary sources, based on the psychoanalytic logic of negation, signals the filmmaker's anxiety about the irresistible grip of those letters from the page. Contrary to the reactionary impulse to strictly separate the director's chair from the writer's desk, Kubrick assimilated his work as a film director to the work of the writer. To him, he said, directing a film adaptation was "nothing more or less than a continuation of the writing."[8] Moreover, Kubrick was willing to cooperate with the authors of the literary originals if necessary or possible and, in fact, was willing to share the credit for the screenplay.

For example, during the production of *Lolita* (1962), Kubrick asked Nabokov to write a screenplay for his film and allowed the author to retain screenwriting credit. However, in the 1973 foreword to his published *Lolita* screenplay, Nabokov famously complained that "only logged odds and ends of [his] script had been used" in Kubrick's film.[9] In adapting *Dr. Strangelove, or How I learned to Stop Worrying and Love the Bomb* (1964) and *2001: A Space Odyssey* (1968), Kubrick wrote the screenplay in very close collaboration with the authors of the source texts. Regardless of how successfully Kubrick's intention may be conveyed in actual production, he expounds the process of adaptation as follows:

> [It starts with] the novel which is mainly concerned with the inner life of its characters. It will give the adapter an absolute compass bearing ... on what a character is thinking or feeling at any given moment

---

8. Thomas Leitch, "The Adapter as Auteur: Hitchcock, Kubrick, Disney," in *Books in Motion: Adaptation, Intertextuality, Authorship*, ed. Mireia Aragay (Amsterdam, New York: Rodopi, 2005), 114.

9. Vladimir Nabokov, introduction to *Lolita: A Screenplay* (New York: McGraw-Hill, 1973), xiii.

of the story. And from this he can invent action which will be an objective correlative of the book's psychological content ... without resorting to having the actors deliver literal statements of meaning.[10]

This implies that what concerns Kubrick most is not his wish to depart from the literary texts through his medium of image and sound. Rather, he suggests a desire to give form to something not "acted out" on the page, something that looms, hidden behind the literary signifiers, serving as *a lure*. Interestingly, based on a conversation with Kubrick, Alexander Walker suggests that, for Kubrick, the process of finding a story to adapt on screen was akin to falling in love: as Kubrick told him, "I have always found it to be an accidental process, and never one which can be attacked head-on."[11] In such a contingent encounter with an original that triggered his interest, Kubrick sought to unearth its buried elements and to transmit them to spectators just as Lacan wished to lead his followers to the Freudian Thing, or *das Ding*, that Lacan glimpsed or experienced as a lure within.

However, Lacan's and Kubrick's approaches to the Thing at the center of their own practices of adaptation are not clearly delineated. The two adapters indubitably keep this Thing as an enigma. In Kubrick's case, it remains difficult to pin down the truth of the originals, which Kubrick has attempted to imbue with an image and a voice. The perplexity experienced by critics in search of what Kubrick intended to transfer to screen is disclosed in the lexicon that they employ in describing the message that the director enshrines in his film adaptations. His works are often regarded as variations in tone, ranging across acute sociohistorical critique; acid political satire; sadistic depictions of violence; psychological investigations of human desire; self-reflexive, radical, and—to some—nihilistic comments on modern technoculture.[12] In the end, many critics and viewers fall back on comments that consistently highlight "the sense of distance" created "between

---

10. Nelson, *Kubrick*, 6. (The original quotation is from Stanley Kubrick, "Words and Movies," *Sight and Sound* 61 [Winter 1960]: 14.)

11. Alexander Walker, Sybil Taylor, and Ulrich Ruchti, *Stanley Kubrick, Director* (New York and London: W. W. Norton & Company, 1999), 18.

12. Thomas Allen Nelson's book *Kubrick: Inside a Film Artist's Maze* addresses the challenge of precisely defining the thematic unity in Kubrick's works, presenting a range of diverse interpretations of his "message" in the first chapter.

characters and between character and viewer."[13] The general consensus among critics that Kubrick's films convey a sense of distance—and a resulting emotional "coldness," as Todd McGowan describes it—also underscores the difficulty of establishing any convincing connection between Kubrick's images and his message.[14] Nevertheless, Kubrick's unflinching gaze on the world and humanity remains unapologetically revealing, never attempting to filter human reality through the fantasizing machinery of cinema. One thing that these critical reactions uniformly indicate, however, is Kubrick's attempt to help the audience glimpse beyond any conventional association between images and meanings. More specifically, his goal in adaptation is to cinematically re-present an almost-unrepresentable yet fundamental meaning he encountered, perhaps by chance, in the original text.

The above summary of Kubrick's approach to the practice of adaptation finds its most significant manifestation in his adaptation of Stephen King's supernatural ghost story *The Shining*. First, the film exemplifies how Kubrick's adaptations weave a web around that elusive meaning, aiming to keep it hidden rather than exposing it to the spectators' immediate perception. The central enigma of the story that is assumed to have triggered Kubrick is, as Stephen King himself puts, "What, exactly, is compelling Jack Torrance toward murdering [his family] in the winter-isolated rooms and hallways of the Overlook Hotel?"[15] The author attributes the disorienting quality of his novel to this impasse as well as to the horror that one experiences in the encounter with this insoluble question that lurks within the story. In his introduction to the novel's new edition, King confirms Kubrick's fascination with this enigma: "My single conversation with the late Stanley Kubrick, about six months before he commenced filming on his version of *The Shining*, suggested that it was *this* [genuinely disturbing] *quality* about the story that appealed to him."[16]

Although King and Kubrick share a similar understanding of the story's enigmatic core and its distinct gravity, Kubrick's film seems to approach the riddle from an entirely different angle than King's narrative and characterization. In exploring the central question, King's

---

13. Todd McGowan, *The Real Gaze: Film Theory after Lacan* (Albany, NY: State University of New York Press, 2007), 43.
14. Ibid.
15. Stephen King, introduction to *The Shining* (London: Hodder, 2007), xii.
16. Ibid.

novel exemplifies the typical response expected from a human subject—one who engages in fervent efforts at rationalization to construct an answer. In other words, in its confrontation of the enigma exposed by Jack Torrance's psychotic breakdown, the novel's solution is to fill the void that points to the unrepresentable and uncanny dimension of the human psyche. King's text thus offers illustrative and detailed explanations at every twist and turn. Employing a blend of horror, suspense, and melodrama, Stephen King transforms the enigma into a question or puzzle that the narrative carefully works to resolve. The novel's episodic structure, comprising fifty-eight short chapters, is replete with "meaning-ful" incidents and relatable emotional struggles among the main characters, consistently and explicitly conveyed through first-person narration. Consequently, there is scarcely any room for the Torrances to suffer from ennui during their five months' solitude in the snowbound hotel atop the Rockies.

Kubrick's approach appears to overtly invert King's rationalizing strategy: rather than providing answers, Kubrick's film adaptation systematically deprives the original novel of every plausible explanation. Instead of guiding viewers toward resolution, the film holds them within the labyrinth of the very same unresolved question. No flashback is provided to pinpoint Jack's childhood trauma as a justification for his chronic alcoholism. No family secret of domestic violence foreshadows the story's climax. Kubrick's film entirely omits the numerous colloquial intrusions that permeate the novel, which verbalize the characters' inner states and guide readers' emotional responses to each minute situation. Above all, while he retains the work's original title for his adaptation, Kubrick appears indifferent to the novel's exhaustive elaboration of the central subject matter—a supernatural telepathic power called the "shining"—which ultimately functions as the story's deus ex machina.

Instead, Kubrick invites spectators into a maze. The vast hedge maze, which serves as a locus for the film's uncanny ending, is an expressive materialization of the film's disruptive and disorienting core, functioning as a point of differentiation between Kubrick's *The Shining* and King's novel.[17] Ironically, however, this maze—absent in King's

---

17. The original novel uses the hotel's huge boiler as a time bomb, evoking a sense of threat and suspense throughout its narrative. In the end, the boiler explodes and blows up the Overlook Hotel as well as Jack Torrance (who by then has become a monster possessed by the hotel's evil spirit), whereas the film's ending keeps him frozen in the maze and leaves the hotel unscathed.

novel—connects the film back to the original text or, more precisely, to what in the novel triggered Kubrick. The snow-covered maze in which Jack Torrance (played by Jack Nicholson) meets his death is Kubrick's visual creation, and it presents the "genuinely disturbing" nature at the kernel of King's novel better than any element concocted by the novelist himself.[18] Without any rational explanation, the camera in the film's final moments floats from the image of Jack, frozen to death in the maze, to the sinister return of the smiling Jack captured in the freeze frame of a half-century-old photo.[19] This deliberate lack of resolution disrupts and defies the causality and linearity carefully laid out in the original text. By confining both the hero and our desire for a concrete answer first within the maze and then within the photo frame, the film's ending invalidates the plausible explanations offered in King's novel, while simultaneously inviting any interpretation to fill the enigma or void left behind. I suggest that Kubrick's maze is the epitome of how *das Ding* operates in the course of adaptation. That is, Kubrick's adaptation of *The Shining* indicates that adaptation is neither a means of discovering a way to faithfully envision a message implied by the words of an original text nor an escape from the influence of the words on the page. In its search for *das Ding* as the lost meaning that seeks to be re-presented, an adaptation can reach the level of the *beyond*, where a meaning or signified works itself free from the repression of signifiers. In this sense,

18. Here, it is significant that Kubrick and his cowriter Diane Johnson studied Freud's essay "The Uncanny" while collaborating on the script for *The Shining*. This indicates that his intention was not merely to seek the images implied by the original text but to revive or re-present that which was buried and repressed by signifiers of the original (see Dennis Bingham's "The Displaced Auteur: A Reception History of *The Shining*," in *Perspectives on Stanley Kubrick*, ed. Mario Falsetto (New York: G. K. Hall, 1996), 290).

19. A useful insight into the film's use of still images on various occasions is provided by Brigitte Peucker's article "Kubrick and Kafka: The Corporeal Uncanny," *Modernism/Modernity* 8, no. 4 (November 2001): 663–74. The article explores the film's haunting quality in relation to Freud's text "The Uncanny" and regards the film's emphatic use of photographs as effectively evoking a sense of the uncanny by envisioning a site of "a return of the dead."

Kubrick's field of adaptation points toward the Lacanian locus of *das Ding*, which is "the-beyond-signified."[20]

To invoke the maze in which Lacan places the concept *das Ding*, the chapter opened with Lacan's lecture on the Freudian Thing. The lecture was not simply chosen because it is a gateway to his more elaborate conceptualization of *das Ding* in the 1959–60 seminar on the ethics of psychoanalysis, conducted four years after this 1955 Vienna lecture. The choice was also made so as to return the discussion to this starting point, where Lacan sutures the beginning and the end of his theorization of *das Ding*. Even in the moment of the term's inception, Lacan made it impossible to access the Thing by confessing that the only thing that Truth as *das Ding* says of itself is that "I belie myself, I defy you, I slip away."[21] Through its detour on the way back to where it starts, the chapter seeks to map the maze as the fundamental structure used to configure any attempt at adaptation, as Lacan and Kubrick have sought to disclose it.

## *The* objet petit a *in the Shadow of* das Ding

Lacan's 1955 lecture on the Freudian Thing foreshadows the rhetorical characteristic that will be key to Lacan's conceptualization of *das Ding* in the seminar on the ethics of psychoanalysis in 1959–60. At the beginning of the lecture, he claims that the true meaning of his return to Freud is "situated elsewhere."[22] This statement, which draws our attention to the territory of the *beyond*, is intended not only to criticize the "stupidity" of some analysts who understood the Freudian message too literally but also to reveal the fundamental impasse of the subject caught up in the relationship to things around which the subject's speech circles. In his lecture, Lacan elusively yet repeatedly demonstrates that it is not the subject who speaks about things but rather the Thing that speaks itself through things, with which the subject fantasizes that she or he can capture a meaning. In other words, the speaking being is led to believe

---

20. Jacques Lacan, *The Seminar of Jacques Lacan Book VII: The Ethics of Psychoanalysis*, ed. Jacques-Alain Miller and trans. Dennis Porter (New York: W. W. Norton & Company, 1992), 54.

21. Lacan, "The Freudian Thing or the Meaning of the Return to Freud in Psychoanalysis," 342.

22. Ibid., 334.

that one can possess the Thing by means of one's speech that only circles around things. The fundamental problem is that every human discourse is condemned to a traumatic misfit, which never allows the subject to reach the meaning of its own speech. Lacan explains this as follows:

> While it is to him that you must speak, it is literally about **some-thing** else—that is, about **some-thing** other than what is at stake when he speaks of himself—which is the thing [*das Ding*] that speaks to you. Regardless of what he says, this thing will remain forever inaccessible to him if, being speech addressed to you, it cannot elicit its response in you, and if, having heard its message in this inverted form, you cannot, in re-turning it to him, give him the twofold satisfaction of having recognized it and of making him recognize its truth.[23]

In an attempt to expand the scope of the above meditation on "something," in his seventh seminar entitled *The Ethics of Psychoanalysis* Lacan carefully detached the notion of *das Ding* from that which is recognizable and representable as meaning. *das Ding*, for him, is not a solid meaning that is subject to the symbolic procedure implemented to couple a signifier and a signified. Despite the added density and complexity of the seminar, the way in which Lacan lays his path to the concept remains remarkably consistent with that of the 1955 lecture. At first, his approach appears to rely on the binary logic of symbolic discourse, yet it demonstrates that *das Ding* leads us into the very trap that such logical progress aims to avoid. To do so, he begins his conceptualization by differentiating *das Ding* as an object of representation in comparison with the two most self-evident elements in the field of representation. He says: "The *Sache* is clearly the thing, a product of industry and of human action as governed by language," and "The word [*Wort*] is there in a reciprocal position to the extent that it articulates itself."[24] He continues, "*Sache* and *Wort* are, therefore, closely linked: they form a couple. *das Ding* is found somewhere else."[25] *das Ding* is repeatedly referred to as a paradoxical object that is placed outside the locus of the imaginary and that of the symbolic. For this reason, Lacan's careful elaboration of *das Ding* at first appears to hold a key to investigating the adapter's search for something that is faithful to

23. Ibid., 349. (My emphasis.)
24. Lacan, *Seminar VII*, 45.
25. Ibid.

the literary original, which nonetheless ends up as "something entirely different" from the words on the page.[26]

However, after a painstaking delay in specifying the definition, locus, or function of *das Ding*, Lacan suddenly claims that it is lost at the very moment at which it is supposed to be captured. Lacan makes a dramatic shift by admitting that "being lost" is the fundamental ontological status of *das Ding*: he says, "[i]t is in its nature that the object as such is lost" and frames any attempt to reach it as destined to fail, adding that "it will never be found again."[27] Lacan's lecture appears to enact the frustrating process of searching for the Thing, only to find it already lost before the search even begins. This foreshadows his later conceptualization of the *objet petit a* as a lost object in the 1962–3 seminar on anxiety. Consequently, many readers of Lacan interpret *das Ding* in *Seminar VII* as a concept that was evolving into *objet petit a*. The disappearance of *das Ding* in his later teachings supports this view, as it suggests that his exploration of *das Ding* prefigured the more refined and complex concept of *objet petit a*. Dylan Evans's outline of the concept in *An Introductory Dictionary of Lacanian Psychoanalysis* reinforces this theoretical interpretation of the notion:

> After the seminar of 1959-60, the term *das Ding* disappears almost entirely from Lacan's work. However, the ideas associated with it provide the essential features of the new development in the concept of the *objet petit a* as Lacan develops it from 1963 onwards. For example the *objet petit a* is circled by the drive (S11, 168), and seen as the cause of desire just as *das Ding* is seen as "the cause of the most fundamental human passion" (S7, 97). Also, the fact that the Thing is not the imaginary object but firmly in the register of the real (S7, 112), and yet is "that which in the real suffers from the signifier" (S7, 125), anticipates the transition in Lacan's thought toward locating *objet petit a* increasingly in the register of the real from 1963 on.[28]

Despite the general consensus that the theoretical development of the Thing culminates in the later concept of the *objet petit a*, the significance of *das Ding*, for me, must be considered separately from such a historicizing perspective. Of course, it is not possible to clearly

---

26. Ibid., 52.
27. Ibid.
28. Evans, *An Introductory Dictionary of Lacanian Psychoanalysis*, 205.

distinguish the two terms in view of the fact that the two concepts always appear at the margins of the signifier's articulation. However, it is nonetheless valuable to see that Lacan's intention behind the theoretical movement from *das Ding* to *objet petit a* is not only to elaborate the former and develop the latter; Lacan clearly specifies that the Thing indicates a hole or a primary negativity in the primordial real that is not tackled by repression, whereas the *objet petit a* is a leftover, a residue, and a little reminder of the real. Moreover, Lacan's conceptualization of the Thing should be marked by its connotation of a system, locus, or structure in a highly primitive state; the *objet petit a*, by contrast, is more of an object with respect to its interrelation with the imaginary domain of the ego. In *Seminar VII*, Lacan remarks that the function of *das Ding* is to be "the dumb reality … the reality that commands and regulates."[29] It would thus be too hasty to overlap the features and the functions of the one concept onto the other. To me, Lacan's sophisticated terminology, which separates *das Ding* from the *objet petit a*, confirms his subtle distinction of *das Ding* from his later concept as a reminder of or remainder in his theoretical adaptation of Freud.

Measuring the slight yet significant ill fit between *das Ding* and the *objet petit a* may be useful for illuminating the adaptive movement from King's novel to Kubrick's film, the peculiar character of which is impossible to capture with either the dichotomy of a fidelity test or the dialectic tension between the Father's law and the Mother's entrapment. The transcendental nature of Kubrick's adaptation in comparison with the original novel is coextensive with that of *das Ding* in its relationship to the *objet petit a*. As Lorenzo Chiesa notes in *Subjectivity and Otherness: A Philosophical Reading of Lacan*, "the object *a* is the hole from the standpoint of the symbolic order, it is the hole of the symbolic, whereas the Thing *qua* transcendent hole is somehow independent of the symbolic."[30] If I may add to this explanation, the *objet petit a* is the hole as it is seen from the perspective of the subject whose desire is set in motion owing to this immanent and constitutive lack in the symbolic. However, *das Ding* is the primordial lack even prior to the subject of the unconscious, and its formation is mysterious and inaccessible to the subject and is only comprehensible as that which has been there from the beginning.

29. Lacan, *Seminar VII*, 55.
30. Chiesa, *Subjectivity and Otherness*, 132.

Put differently, one might say that the *objet petit a* stands in for "the pound of flesh" that the subject had to sacrifice on its entrance into the symbolic.[31] Its loss must be subjectified so that it might be constitutive in its relationship to individuals' desire. However, *das Ding* refers to "a pure signifying system" in which the unconscious is written and, hence, the subject emerges as an effect of the signifier.[32] It is experienced as a kind of universe that stands between being and non-being. From there, the constant force or command emerges to bend the linear progress of desire into a circular path of return. Similarly, the transcendental quality of Kubrick's adaptation can be linked to the magnitude of *das Ding*, which may reveal itself in the form of adaptation—that is, adaptation insofar as the adapter recognizes its essence as re-presentation.

Bearing in mind these points of differentiation, I wish to interrogate the movement from King's original to Kubrick's film, whose eeriness—not horror, as most reviews comment that Kubrick's film is not at all scary—appears to come from "somewhere else."[33] The narrative elements in the novel operate within the generic conventions of the horror genre and are strongly connected to the imaginary projection of the psyches of the main characters—that is, the three members of the Torrance family: Jack, Wendy, and their five-year-old son Danny—with whom readers are induced to identify. The original's author expounds the psychological dynamics created by the novel's use of supernatural beings and phenomena in the foreword: "I believe these stories exist because we sometimes need to create unreal monsters and bodies to *stand in for* all the things we fear in our real lives."[34] His intention is made explicit in each incident that the characters confront in the Overlook Hotel, to the extent that King's writing constructs an immediate link between various supernatural or superstitious phenomena and the characters' memories, wishes, and fears. In other words, although the disorienting dimension of King's novel originates explicitly from the things that draw the reader's attention to the irrational, unpredictable, and supernatural aspects of reality, these things—such as the unseasonal appearance of wasps, the enormous topiary animals that chase Danny, the various apparitions haunting the hotel, and the elevator moving by

---

31. Lacan, "The Direction of the Treatment and the Principles of Its Power," in *Écrits*, 526.
32. Lacan, *Seminar VII*, 55.
33. Wright, "Reconsidering Fidelity," 136.
34. King, introduction to *The Shining*, xii and xiii.

itself—nonetheless belong to the territory of *Sache* and *Wort*, in which "the things of the human world are things in a universe structured by words, that language, symbolic processes, dominate and govern all."[35] In short, they function as a psychological screen insofar as they sustain the relationship to *meaning*, which is assumed to be under the symbolic law and, hence, to be representable.

Interestingly, behind the multitude of horrifying objects that populate Stephen King's Overlook Hotel, there emerges an allusive trace of a lack that operates in the same way as the little object, the *objet petit a*, whose obscurity or absence triggers the entire system of the subject's desire. In King's narrative, the central psychological axis that threads the numerous encounters with those objects is brought to the surface by the mysterious old scrapbook that Jack discovers in the hotel's basement. The scrapbook contains old photographs and news clippings chronicling the Overlook's buried history, in which to-be-writer Jack Torrance glimpses a particularly striking story and exclaims: "God, what a story! And they had all been here, right above him, in those empty rooms … There was a story, all right. One hell of a story."[36] The basement subsequently becomes the site of his manic pursuit of the tantalizing lack embodied by this "story," as though it could provide him with the meaning that he has lost in his life as a result of his habitual drinking and sporadic violent explosions. While scavenging through piles of old papers in the basement, Jack is anxious about the possibility that "he might miss exactly the piece of Overlookiana he needed to make the mystic connection that he was sure must be here somewhere."[37] The way the hotel's story—one that neither aspiring writer Jack nor the novelist King ever fully articulates—lurks behind these sinister, monstrous things evokes the origin and operation of the *objet petit a*. Lacan teaches:

> The *objet a* is something from which the subject, in order to constitute itself, has separated itself off as organ. This serves as a symbol of the lack, that is to say, of the phallus, not as such, but in so far as it is

---

35. Lacan, *Seminar VII*, 45.
36. King, *The Shining*, 205.
37. Ibid., 243.

lacking. It must, therefore, be an object that is, firstly, separable and, secondly, that has some relation to the lack.³⁸

Specifically, the story of the Overlook hotel works as the missing piece around which King's novel seems to be constituted. The compelling yet elusive nature of the missing part at the center explains the novel's psychological appeal to the reader, as well as the book's commercial success. In other words, the story that Jack wishes to document stands for the lost object—not only for the main character Jack Torrance but also for readers whose desire to rediscover it is set in motion. It is thus possible that the hidden story may have initiated Kubrick's reading of the story's central void, although the director ultimately traversed its imaginary function as the lost object. King's novel, however, remains at the level of *Sache* (thing) and *Wort* (word) and attempts to conceal this enigma with the promise of meaning, as mentioned above. King's rationalizing tactic, as such, encourages readers to assume the convergence of meanings in that lost object. On the basis of this assumption, the reader is induced to accept the novel's formulaic associations between the supernatural happenings and their seemingly rational meanings. Ironically enhanced by the lack of the story at the novel's heart, the assumed promise of meaning allows words to integrate and domesticate things and, hence, to elicit the predicted and intended responses in the reader under the control of a symbolic causal relation, false and illusionary though it may be.

The film manifests the evocation of a transcendental movement from the *objet petit a* to *das Ding* through the repetitive act of "emptying out" the meanings provided by the original. Put differently, the trajectory of Kubrick's adaptation proceeds in the direction precisely opposite to that in which a subject normally proceeds in making sense of their reality. The movement of the subject's consciousness is a process of materializing that which is unrepresentable to it, resulting in *Sache* (thing). *Wort* (word) is an outcome of signification, which attaches "meaning" to *Sache*, on the basis of which the reciprocal relationship between *Sache* and *Wort* forms a basic unit of representation along the axis of metonymy. However, every *thing* must stumble, and *das Ding* reveals itself at the moment when one begins to query the given

---

38. Jacques Lacan, *The Seminar of Jacques Lacan Book XI: The Four Fundamental Concepts of Psychoanalysis*, ed. Jacques-Alain Miller and trans. Alan Sheridan (New York and London: W. W. Norton & Company, 1981), 103.

meanings of things, wades back to the initial point, and even attempts to traverse the veil of the *objet petit a*, just as Kubrick does in his adaptation practice. In doing so, one encounters a reality beyond the pleasure principle—that is, *das Ding* as an empty point of reference as well as a reality that is dumb yet which commands and regulates. Herein, we can read the significance of the concept *das Ding* in Lacan's adaptation of Freud, because it occupies the nodal point at which Lacan ought to formulate his own means of reconciling the pleasure principle and its beyond—that is, the death drive. Lacan confirms this reading in saying "If I introduce this term [*das Ding*], it is because there are certain ambiguities, certain insufficiencies, in relation to the true meaning in Freud of the opposition between reality principle and pleasure principle."[39] At the film's conclusion, as mentioned above, the maze provides the uncanny locus or—more precisely—the hollow for the impossible encounter between the desire for life, which follows objects as long as they substitute for the *objet petit a*, and the death drive, which is doomed to circle around *das Ding*.

Kubrick's *The Shining* demonstrates how an original text can function as an empty point of reference for the adapter, like Lacan and Kubrick, who reads or glimpses the primordial void beyond the promise of meaning. The film epitomizes the adapter's efforts to pursue to the furthest end the centripetal quest to grasp the Thing, even by betraying the superficial meanings imposed by the original text. At first glance, the final cut of Kubrick's *The Shining* maintains a substantial distance from King's horror story, which encircles the hidden history of the Overlook Hotel as its unobtainable and forbidden center of gravity. It is surprising, however, that during the film's exceptionally extended production schedule, the changes surfaced rather gradually. The making-of documentary, directed by Vivian Kubrick, indicates that Kubrick did not have a completed version of the shooting script; he wrote and revised numerous pieces of the script for a day's shooting on the set, often in collaboration with the film's star Jack Nicholson and other staff. On top of his painstakingly revised script Kubrick rather obsessively insisted on retaking every shot until the actors had become desperate "to reach the last take."[40] Despite the fact that he had spent a prolonged period on the film's postproduction, Kubrick omitted a substantial portion of the film's finished version after its New York premier and US

39. Ibid., 43.
40. Walker, Taylor, and Ruchti, *Stanley Kubrick, Director*, 307.

opening. Among the sections taken out at the eleventh hour was the film's coda, "showing a hospitalized Wendy being congratulated by the Overlook's manager on surviving her horrendous ordeal."[41] The restored ternary relationship between the manager Ullman, Wendy, and Danny in the deleted coda appears to have resembled King's original epilogue substantially. The novel's conclusion documents the restoration of the nuclear family in a rather loose shape, formed by Wendy, Danny, and Dick Hallorann, who assumes a benign paternal role of protecting and encouraging in the physical and mental recovery process after the murderous Jack dies in the hotel's catastrophic, cathartic explosion. The deletion of the filmed final scene is symptomatic of Kubrick's process of adaptation, which is not a way to represent the original but a way to re-present something more closer to the truth of the original than what the original text itself can signify.

Such a slow yet studious process of finding and refinding the Thing demonstrates that what Kubrick sought could not be immediately separated from the things (*Sache*) represented by King's words (*Wort*) in the original text. That is, the movement toward what Kubrick perceives as the Thing looming behind things and words on the surface of the original text follows a path that is labyrinthine rather than straightforward. The journey through such a maze demands excessive amounts of time and resources as well as patience and devotion, all of which Kubrick fortunately possessed to an extraordinary degree. His case clarifies what Lacan designates as the path toward *das Ding*, epitomized by Lacan himself in his incessant quest of the Freudian Thing. Lacan demonstrated that the encounter with *das Ding* may be glimpsed by a speaking subject only through numerous detours in an attempt to transcend the pleasure principle aiming at satisfaction facilitated by the couple of *Sache* and *Wort*.[42] Kubrick's detours certainly transcend the level of objects and words and finally reach the maze. Here the face of the Truth is to be found in the field of adaptation: that is, the maze realizes the most manifest form of adaptation as re-presentation, which points toward *das Ding*.

In approaching the problem of adaptation, as in the case of extraordinary adapters such as Lacan or Kubrick, *das Ding* enables us to question the prevailing structuralist understanding of textual transformation by locating the focus in the concept of representation

41. Ibid., 312.
42. Lacan, *Seminar VII*, 58.

itself. In discussing textual analyses that compare adapted works with their source texts, there is no scope for examining the definition of *Vorstellung* (representation) while employing the term in the exclusive sense of its function. In other words, a philosophical speculation of *Vorstellung* is often disregarded in favor of its operational dimension in textual analyses of adaptation. This treatment of *Vorstellung* as a function limits the scope of adaptation studies by confining adaptation as an outcome rather than a cultural or fundamentally psychic phenomenon. However, Kubrick's work reveals this relatively unexplored dimension of adaptation, directing attention to the abyss between representation and its assumed meaning—where, according to Lacan, *das Ding* resides.

In this pursuit, the site of adaptation becomes a locus of its own dead end, as a film adaptation like Kubrick's *The Shining* seeks to transcend its ontological status as a representational medium. Rather than offering the fantasy of "containing and conveying" the Thing, it uses every cinematic technique to underscore the impossibility of capturing it. More compellingly, this dead end is enigmatically sutured together with the most primordial and initiatory point of reference, that which is empty and lost. The void created by this encircling trajectory of re-discovering and re-presenting *something* that is lost in the course of adaptation is what Lacan found that Freud had understood in his notion of *Vorstellung*. In other words, Lacan found the impossibility of representation in his pursuit of the Freudian knowledge of representation. Lacan elevates Freud's insight beyond that which the history of philosophy might have construed, although he offers little reference to actual Freudian texts in support of his argument. Nevertheless, Lacan emphasizes:

> *Vorstellung* is understood by Freud in a radical sense, in the form in which it appears in a philosophy that is essentially marked by the theory of knowledge. And that is the remarkable thing about it. He assigned to it in an extreme form the character philosophers themselves have been unable to reduce it to, namely, that of an empty body, a ghost, a pale incubus of the relation to the world, an enfeebled jouissance, which through the age-old interrogations of the philosophers makes it the essential feature. And by isolating it in this function, Freud removes it from its tradition.[43]

43. Ibid., 60–1.

Indeed, to push the conceptualization of things or words beyond their operational mode of being *Vorstellung*, as Lacan argues that Freud did, is the only possible means of cornering the concept of *das Ding*, which ultimately tears every representation from its proper meaning and transforms it into a ghost. For me, the abyss glimpsed just beyond the empty body of representation is what Lacan terms *das Ding qua* "the-beyond-of-signified."

The dimension of representation as a ghost is what Kubrick's *The Shining* ultimately seeks to encapsulate by testing the limit of *Vorstellung* in use. For instance, the novel represents the cause of to-be-writer Jack Torrance's struggle and insanity by means of self-evident generic conventions, such as melodrama and horror. However, in adapting Stephen King's novel, Kubrick gradually strips away the meaning of the work and the writing at the center of Jack Torrance's world and invites the film's protagonist—as well as spectators—to look into the abyss between one's speech and its meaning. At first, the film's Jack never labors, although he protests that he puts his job as the Overlook's caretaker before his family. Unlike the novel's handyman Jack, who exhibits both enthusiasm and excellence in coping with the physical aspects of his job, Jack Torrance in Kubrick's film appears to be idle and indifferent to his job as a winter caretaker. Ironically, it is Wendy (played by Shelley Duvall) who busily walks around the hotel performing necessary tasks while her husband Jack oversleeps in bed, idly plays catch against the wall of the central lounge, and taps at a typewriter, engaged in a dubious writing project. Hence, when he explodes at Wendy's proposal that he go down the mountain in search of medical assistance for their son Danny, Jack's furious bark asserting that he has "responsibilities" to stay and look after the hotel echoes as empty and meaningless. In this way, the film subtly hints at an irreparable gap between his symbolic coordinates and what he really is.

At its climax, the film adaptation exposes Jack's insanity by finally revealing what is the "new writing project" with which he has been occupied on screen. The scene of revelation is, like the maze in the hotel's front yard, Kubrick's own creation. Wendy approaches the enormous worktable at the Colorado lounge while he is away and discovers that what he has been writing is the infinite repetition of the same phrase, "All work and no play makes Jack a dull boy." With an eerie soundtrack accompanying the camera's zoom into the stack of yellow paper by the typewriter, we witness precisely that which Lacan means by the nothingness or empty body or ghost of *Vorstellung*. The emphatically lengthy close-up shot lingers on the pile of pages, on which that same sentence is typed in various formats—a play, a poem, a novel, a dialogue, and so on, as Wendy's hand turns over leaf after leaf. The lack of sense in the "work" that Jack has produced not only confirms his irreparably manic mental status, as already hinted at by his hallucinations and eccentric physical and verbal behaviors in the scenes before this discovery. However, the extended close-up of the typed pages also grants the spectators time to recall previous scenes in which Jack has been typing with the sane and grave face of a dedicated writer.

This unique psychoanalytic insight is enacted in the slow course of adaptation of the original in order to unravel a different facet of Jack's insanity besides the original novel's conventional representation of madness. The rendition of Jack's madness as such also goes beyond cinema audience's knowing expectation, based on Jack Nicholson's famous performance of delirium in his previous films such as *Easy Rider* (1969) and *One Flew over the Cuckoo's Nest* (1975). In other words, whereas the on-screen Jack's increasingly unhinged manner and his psychotic breakdown are individualized by familiar means of Nicholson's acting, there remains a tenor of universality that causes greater shock. The shock turns into the genuine fear to retrospectively discover that Jack has lost symbolic mastery over the communicative connections of things and words almost from the beginning of the story, when his sanity has not yet been called into question. Those pages that Jack has been working on are filled with floating signifiers that form a labyrinth rather than a discourse formed of human speech. The most disturbing nature of this labyrinth of words detached from meaning of any kind is that it exposes a vacuum or void—not separate but lying at the very center of the symbolic order shared by every "completely normal individual."[44] Therefore, the fear and horror of the scene echo the most fundamental fear of realizing that the eminently human desire to create representations by connecting objects and words in order to make sense of the world may be none other than the subject's desperate gesture to maintain a distance from the primordial abyss, *das Ding*, that condemns every meaning attempted by human

---

44. Stanley Kubrick's *The Shining* (1980): During the interview, the hotel manager Ullman tells Jack Torrance about Grady, a former caretaker who murdered his family with an axe, and describes Grady as a man who looked like "a completely normal individual" when he was interviewed for the job. This foreshadows the lunacy that has lain dormant in Jack as a writer.

discourse. The horror of the real now comes to the surface of the film's re-presentation of what lurks behind the novel's rendition of Jack's mental breakdown, the cause of which is expectedly rationalized, historicized, and conventionalized as the lure and the possession of the evil embodied in the Overlook's past.

Therefore, despite the chronological progression *from* King's novel *to* Kubrick's film, the terminal point in Kubrick's adaptation deals with a more profound and primordial dimension of the human subject than that which Stephen King's novel encircles. King's novel structures its plot and characters on the basis of the gravitating power of the *objet petit a*—a "little lost object" that domesticates the Thing and keeps it in contact with the subject's desire. By contrast, Kubrick's film seeks to access the dark abyss of *das Ding* by moving beyond the repression of meaning typically involved in an adapter's quest for "the most truthful" adaptation, as discussed in the previous chapter on *Hamlet* films. In this sense, Kubrick's adaptation suggests, in retrospect, that it is within the shadow of *das Ding* that the *objet petit a* maintains its elusive position at the margins of the field of desire. Conversely, it is only by traversing the void marked by loss or lack at the level of desire that one can encounter *das Ding*, which speaks the Truth of the subject through the death of subjectivity.

## *The Maze That Is a Monster*

The previous discussion regarding Lacan's renewal of the notion of representation and its object made three salient points regarding the demarcation of *das Ding* from the *objet petit a*. First, although it cannot be grasped as anything other than an object or thing, *das Ding* is not subordinate to the subject's faculty of desire. Second, the function of this object is concurrent with the subject's inability to re-present it. Most significantly, *das Ding* remains as a locus or structure rather than a remainder of the real, which must be *objectified* to initiate the desire's path. With an eye to these points, Lacan indicates that the discourse of psychoanalysis should adopt a different approach to investigating this intricate concept—that is, the Thing that speaks of itself rather than being spoken about—and how its meaning or message is delivered to the subject.

In this regard, this chapter must pose a different set of questions to understand what Kubrick's adaptation—the object of the chapter's interrogation—says about itself and its rather unrepresentable ways of delivering the message to the spectator. The disoriented relationship between *das Ding* and *Vorstellung* results in the inversion of this peculiar object and the subject "under its spell." Indeed, the Thing—or, more precisely, the void inscribed in the notion of object—is not only alluring but also demanding: in Kubrick's case, he appears to have been driven by the persistent urge to seek the encounter with the Thing through his repetitive and even agonizing process of transcending the obvious and adaptable "meanings" offered by the original texts he adapted. Regarding this inextricable force from *das Ding*, Alenka Zupančič offers a precise question with which to begin: "How is it possible for something that cannot be an object of representation [*Vorstellung*] to determine our will and become the drive behind our actions?"[45]

At first glance, the association between the drive and *das Ding* may appear to contradict the differentiation of *das Ding* from the *objet petit a*, which I sought to draw out in the preceding section. This is because Lacan acknowledges that the drive should be understood in terms of a trajectory toward not *das Ding* but rather toward the *objet petit a*. He clearly designates the *objet petit a* in the place of "the satisfaction of the drive."[46] However, closer speculation regarding this connection will serve as an essential point of departure for answering the question about the driving force of *das Ding* and the subject's response to it. The subject's relationship to *das Ding*, Lacan discovers, invariably entails a certain level of "[p]ressure, urgency," for it is "[s]omething that wishes" rather than something that is wished for by the subject.[47] Lacan emphasizes that this pressure is not merely the command of the Name-of-the-Father and, thus, of language; it is the primal force that "intervenes at the level of the secondary process [such as repression], but in a deeper way than through that corrective activity."[48]

The pressure from *das Ding* thus emerges as a secret that constantly brings the psychoanalytic understanding of human subjectivity "beyond the exercise of the unconscious" in Lacan's words.[49] It pushes the boundary of psychoanalysis to the watershed between humanity and

---

45. Alenka Zupančič, *Ethics of the Real: Kant, Lacan* (London and New York: Verso, 2000), 141.
46. Lacan, *Seminar XI*, 168.
47. Lacan, *Seminar VII*, 46.
48. Ibid.
49. Ibid., 90.

animalism, whose absolute fundamentality renders the notion of the drive merely its reference. Therefore, this mysterious field of *das Ding* functions as both a starting point and a terminal point of psychoanalysis and as the gate that permanently keeps the discourse of psychoanalysis at bay from "something ultimate given, something archaic, primal."[50] As a reference to this completely inaccessible region of *das Ding*, Lacan notes in *Seminar XI* that Freud named the drive the fundamental concept of psychoanalysis and recognized it as the irreducible point around which the discourse of psychoanalysis perpetually circles. Moreover, *das Ding* is "the point where the *Trieb* [the drive] is unmasked."[51] Therefore, the imperative at its purest in the subject's encounter with *das Ding* is neither comprehensible nor representable, whereas the function and trajectory of the *Trieb* are explicable by means of the four terms—namely, thrust, the source, the object, and the aim—with which we can grasp the concept of the drive.

If, however, we carefully strip those terms from the drive, that which is left may tell us something about *das Ding* and its force, regardless of how vague it might be. By its very nature, the pressure in the field of *das Ding* tends to drift because it is not yet localized or fixed to a part of the body. Moreover, the path of this drifting force has not yet been determined, whereas the drive's circuit is structured around the lost object—that is, the *objet petit a*. If we read the first scene of Kubrick's film with the above in mind, it is not difficult to recognize that the camera's movement in the opening shots embodies the free flight of *das Ding*. Cued by the sinister orchestration of Bartok's symphony, the camera mounted on a helicopter rapidly glides across the serene surface of a glacier lake surrounded by snow-covered mountain peaks. In the next shot from the sky, the camera spots and follows a tiny yellow Volkswagen Beetle driving through a vast coniferous forest, as though it were tracking its prey. The sublime landscape of the opening shots introduces the power and autonomy of the free-flying gaze that overwhelms the weak and vulnerable existence of human beings on mountain slopes.

While the camera glides over, swoops down, and sometimes indifferently flies away from Jack Torrance's car in the opening sequence, the editing overlaps the extremely wide and deep-focused shots, which frame the yellow VW at the center or, more precisely, maintain it at

50. Lacan, *Seminar XI*, 162.
51. Lacan, *Seminar VII*, 90.

the frame's vanishing point. The swift and liberated flight of the camera exaggerates the speed of the moving landscape, almost engulfing Jack's car, which appears fixed on a predetermined trajectory, unknown to both the Torrances and the audience. In contrast to the camera's free, almost prescient movement, which often arrives at scenes before the human characters, the film's main characters are confined to structured paths—mountain roads, the Overlook Hotel's winding corridors, and, ultimately, the narrow track between towering hedge walls in the vast maze outside—beyond the reach of the camera's omniscient gaze. This authentic cinematic expression drastically reduces the central focus on the main characters—whose internal voices dominate the original novel—rendering them as faint, peripheral figures, merely pulled toward the overpowering presence of the unknowable.

To return to the matter of the primal and archaic force in the field of *das Ding*, the purely physical and cinematic movement of the gaze in the film's opening scene is experienced as an ineluctable pressure by spectators who are unaware of—or perhaps do not even wonder— whose perspective it might represent. Moreover, the use of cinemascope and extremely wide lens inflates the sense of distance and depth and consequently magnifies the force of the camera's flight. The camerawork in the first scene is visceral and affective rather than efficient or economical in forwarding the narrative and introducing the characters. Kubrick skillfully conveys a potent blend of fear and attraction, relying almost entirely on the continuous, untethered movement of the gaze to underscore how the barely visible yellow VW—echoing Lacan's concept of *Sache* (thing)—seems governed by a more controlled, civilized rule or *Wort* (word) that keeps it firmly "on track." Along the inscribed and localized trajectory, the car turns around mountain corners without any knowledge of what it might confront next. Indeed, with the menacing gaze chasing it up the mountainside, Jack's car almost appears to be pushed and prodded into the territory governed by the unregistered and unregulated power of *das Ding*.

In other words, the car's diminished figure symbolizes the drive's movement as perceived at the level of the subject of the unconscious, whose move is fixated around the alluring *objet petit a*. This unconscious force appears to be secondary to the more compelling magnetic field of the Thing into which these unfortunate characters and spectators are to be thrust. Furthermore, the contrast between the two movements—of the camera and the car, or of the Thing and the subject's drive—signals the inverted roles of subject and object, revealing the primal urge of the Thing that speaks and wishes, that which Lacan recognizes as "a radical structure—in which the subject is not yet placed."[52] It is worth noting that this opening scene serves as a prologue Kubrick created to precede the novel's original beginning, which starts with Jack's job interview in the hotel manager's office. Although the film omits nearly all the supernatural episodes present in the novel, it expands the story beyond the novel's limited focus on the characters' desires and reactions to the supernatural, broadening its psychological scope. As outlined above, the film's opening hints at an uncontrollable psychic force or primal energy that will come into play, allowing Kubrick's adaptation to traverse the fantasy of love and family bonding in which the original text is deeply invested. With help of this foreboding prelude, the film's climax is capable of revealing the most destructive facet of human relationships when the subject's symbolic agency breaks down in the lethal confrontation with *das Ding*.

The most salient feature of the film's visualization of the Overlook Hotel—in reality, an enormous purpose-built set constructed to an unprecedented scale and lavishly detailed—is its endless corridors. Like blood vessels, they link various heterogeneous spaces within the hotel: from a practically decorated lobby to the manager's efficient yet somewhat claustrophobic office, to the majestic Colorado lounge, to the sumptuous Gold Ballroom, to the huge functional kitchen under the harsh fluorescent light, and on to the homely yet shabby apartment in the staff wing. While the original novel dissects this colossal place into numerous small stages for supernatural incidents, the film delivers a sense that one is becoming lost in a somewhat organic structure of its own life. Most of the time, the film's characters are seen in the hotel's tangled passages, walking purposefully or wandering aimlessly or struggling to escape from them. The incessant movement of the Torrance family is chased by the Steadicam, as though it embodies the constant force that makes them restless and transforms every space into a maze for them.

In an example of the film's characteristic use of the compound structure of the set, the sequence entitled "A Month Later" introduces the Torrance family's mundane reality as they settle into the hotel. The sequence starts with Wendy pushing the breakfast trolley through the lobby. While the camera frames and follows Wendy as she walks into the dark passage in the background, the first shot dissolves into

---

52. Lacan, *Seminar XI*, 181–2.

the next shot, in which the camera again follows Danny, who rides his tricycle quickly down a corridor. The direction and position of the two characters and their distance from the camera remain virtually identical in the two shots, and they almost appear as though they are disappearing into the frame's vanishing point. With help from the wide lens and the use of the Steadicam in the relatively narrow space, the cinematography here produces an eerie effect: it appears that it is not the characters but the hotel that moves. Moreover, the editing connects their movement to emphasize the constant push, although Wendy's functional action of bringing breakfast to her husband and the child's aimless joyride appear to have different meanings on the level of narrative.

Eventually, the Torrances are drawn into the real maze outside the hotel that itself is already a maze. As noted earlier, this maze is an addition by Kubrick to King's *The Shining* and serves as one of the film's most elaborate visual and narrative devices. However, on a practical level, one might wonder what purpose the maze actually serves. When showing Jack and Wendy around, the hotel manager, Ullman, casually answers this question on Kubrick's behalf: "It's a lot of fun." In truth, the act of entering the massive hedge maze and allowing oneself to get lost for hours does not align with the economy of the pleasure principle. If there is any pleasure to be found in the maze, it is almost perverse—reflecting how people willingly endure such agonizing and purposeless wandering, only to return to the very point where they began. Lacan offers a more plausible explanation in *Seminar VII*:

> that first demand is the demand of *das Ding*—it seeks whatever is repeated, whatever returns, and guarantees that it will always return, to the same place—and it has driven us to the extreme position in which we find ourselves, a position where we can cast doubt on all places and where nothing in that reality which we have learned to disrupt so admirably responds to that call for the security of a return.[53]

In this light, the maze is a purely geometric structure that draws out the field of the drive, yet paradoxically, it becomes an "extreme position" in which we ultimately begin to suspect "the security of a return" and where, indeed, "the drive is unmasked."[54]

53. Lacan, *Seminar VII*, 75.
54. Ibid., 90.

It is now possible to conclude that Kubrick's invented maze touches the most profound level of King's novel in which the entire troop of the hotel's ghosts continuously chant "Unmask! Unmask!"[55] Despite this purgatory call from the locus of *das Ding*, King's novel makes a return route and resorts to the subject's most common reactionary strategy—that is, the fantasy. Fantasy supports the subject's faculty of desire and, as mentioned above, the novel is led by the fantasy of obtaining the *objet petit a*—for instance, a great story to be written, a happy nuclear family, etc. Kubrick's film appears to penetrate the fantasy by unmaking the superficial values or meanings invested by the fantasy. Above all, the film's "truthful" response to the call of *das Ding* persistently debunks the fundamental level of the subject's fantasy, which is that the subject has agency in its relationship to the desired objects or things.

In Kubrick's adaptation, when Wendy and Danny step into the maze for the first time, she repeatedly asks the boy, "Isn't it beautiful?," as though compelled to impose some value onto this maze—aesthetic or entertaining—as an object. However, through the effects of the claustrophobic mise-en-scène and the ominous music, both her question and Danny's inexpressive response echo as unconvincing and vacant. The more they wander about, the more mechanical their acting becomes. They walk through the maze, resembling a pair of puppets, and Kubrick maximizes the impression in an intriguing manner. The image of Wendy and Danny is intercut with the image of Jack inside the building, where he idles around the hotel alone and finds the miniature of the maze in the lobby. He approaches it and looks down on it with an irrepressible sneer. Jack's perspective uncannily turns into a God's-eye view, and the next shot zooms into the center of the miniature maze. From Jack's perspective, we see Wendy and Danny moving like two dots or tiny toys imprisoned within the model. Cued by their voices, which echo unrealistically loudly in a stark contrast with their almost invisible appearance on screen, the scene again shifts back into the real maze. By means of this uncanny editing enabled by the creative use of special effects, Wendy and Danny at the maze's center now appear more imprisoned and lost, despite Wendy's efforts to keep spirits high with her cheerful exclamation, "Woo, we made it." The only certainty this "fun tour" into the empty space provides for the light-hearted tourists is a return that was always predestined. Yet, the emptiness embodied in the image of the maze's center suggests that, after achieving a certain

---

55. King, *The Shining*, 338.

## 4. The Thing (das Ding) in Kubrick's The Shining

satisfaction upon reaching its vacuous core, a safe return may no longer be possible. The notion of return is merely a fantasy, masked by the mechanical repetition dictated by the imperative command of the Thing—or, in this case, the Maze—in which there is neither progress from beginning to end nor any clear boundary between inside and outside.

I would like to link the maze's lack of direction to the evaporation of moral standards experienced by Jack, which has been foreshadowed by the story of his predecessor Grady, who slaughtered his wife and two daughters with an axe. This will serve to interrogate the eruption of hostility that Jack expresses toward his family from a different light and, ultimately, to question the correlation between the transgression of the moral law and the encounter with *das Ding*. Of course, King's novel carefully elaborates the reasons for and meanings of the conflict between the husband and wife even before they have become involved with the Overlook Hotel. The original text gives its central couple's relational problems psychological depth and complexity, in line with melodramatic conventions. King depicts them as having faced predictable and relatable marital troubles stemming from clashes between individual desires and differing social and familial responsibilities, along with the resulting emotional frustration. The evil residing in the Overlook Hotel merely magnifies the existing problems and eventually enables their disparity to explode. Therefore, there is neither room for the novel's reader to question how this "ordinary" couple has been led to such a violent climax nor an opportunity to penetrate the purest form of hostility that is at play.

On the contrary, Stanley Kubrick deliberately flattens out these main characters and makes them, as discussed above, puppets devoid of any psychological complexity. The conversation sounds functional and dry, and except when they become hysterical, the characters remain generally inexpressive. The couple shows no sign of desire toward one another, and their affection for Danny appears to be somewhat programmed. Their relationship manages to survive as long as they can maintain a certain distance from one another, as in an earlier scene in which Jack calls Wendy from the hotel to inform her that he has gotten a job in a relatively affectionate manner. Throughout the film's entire narrative, the tender moments between the Torrance family in the film happen only when they remain apart or have other people between them.

This point becomes especially clear when examining the scene in which the family drives up to the hotel for the first time. The medium close-up captures all three characters within the same frame, yet this is the only moment in the film where they remain close without anyone else standing between them. The tension from the shot begins even before Wendy suddenly asks Jack about the Donner Party—a party of early settlers known to have become snowbound and resorted to cannibalism for survival. This moment serves as a perfect example of a Freudian slip, signaling the wife's anxiety about the future while also foreshadowing the fate awaiting the family. Kubrick employs a static camera to tightly frame the Torrances within the confined space and extends the scene as a single long take, heightening the discomfort through a series of dissonant eyeline matches among the three characters. In this way, the film invites the viewer to pay greater attention to the potential discomfort and complexity in the proximity between the self and others, highlighting the horror of being held too close—even to one's own family, whom, by moral convention, we are expected to love without facing complex ethical dilemmas.

The theme of cabin fever, which is what Jack Torrance suffers from on the most superficial level, illuminates the moment at which the distance between "I" and the fellow human being—*Nebenmensch* in Lacan's use of Freud's German expression—is disturbed and renders the subject's relationship to other human beings scandalous. Notably, it is in relation to this term *Nebenmensch* that Lacan locates the origin of the concept *das Ding*. At the end of the same chapter of *Seminar VII*, he includes a supplementary comment—indeed, one that is abrupt and enigmatic—on the sudden, exclamatory appearance of one's *Nebenmensch*. He asks, "What does the emission, the articulation, the sudden emergence from out of our voice of that 'You!'(Toi!) mean?"[56] To him, the desperate outcry of "You!" reflects the subject's attempt to tame "the Other with no split," or *das Ding* as the absolute Other, which he describes as "that prehistoric, that unforgettable Other, which suddenly threatens to surprise us and to cast us down from the height of its appearance."[57] When this word of intimate relationship is uttered and, therefore, one is struck by the full stroke of *das Ding* and "Me!"(Moi!) is merely a feeble reaction. In other words, "Me!" is not to announce the presence of "I" but merely serves as a defense of the subject in the encounter with the purest form of threat and hostility coming from the place of "You," when it is spoken by the Thing to "Me." In this sense, the *Nebenmensch*—

---

56. Lacan, *Seminar VII*, 56.
57. Ibid.

fellow human beings and, even more so, one's family in unbearable vicinity—poses the ultimate threat to the subject. Perhaps for that very reason, the command of the Law must tame the antagonism between "You" and "Me" by establishing "You" as the object of desire and love in saying "Thou shalt love thy neighbour as thyself."[58]

Thus, the cabin fever in Kubrick's film serves neither as an intensified symptom of familial conflict nor as a justification for the bloody finale found in King's novel. Rather, the film gradually discloses the fact that cabin fever is one of many names for the subject's fundamental reality in which *das Ding* reigns. Jack's profound hatred and violence against his family confirms his confrontation with the fatal threat of *das Ding* when it unexpectedly surfaces over the figure of fellow human being, neighbor, and family. On this note, the love for your neighbor seems to fade as a secondary command because it was concocted out of the necessity to uphold civilization in the face of *das Ding*—the first demand that precedes the repression of the signifier. Therefore, the film portrays how one can sense the pure hostility in proximity to "You" and how recklessly one might react to it: without hesitation or doubt, the subject transgresses a fundamental moral law, such as the love of one's family. This is at the heart of Kubrick's "most truthful" adaptation of King's conventional horror story.

As mentioned above, the *Nebenmensch* is central to Lacan's adaptation of the Freudian Thing in his seminars on the ethics of psychoanalysis, where it informs his theory of *das Ding*. In fact, it serves as the only link between Freud's brief reference to *das Ding* in his early work *Project for a Scientific Psychology* (Entwurf) (1895) and Lacan's more extended—and sometimes digressive—conceptualization of *das Ding*. Below, I include the quotation from Freud's original text:

> Let us suppose that the object which furnishes the perception resembles the subject—a fellow human-being. If so, the theoretical interest is also explained by the fact that an object like this was simultaneously the [subject's] first satisfying object and further his first hostile object, as well as his sole helping power. For this reason it is in relation to a fellow human-being that a human-being learns to

---

58. In *Seminar VII*, Lacan brings into his discussion of ethics the ambivalent and affective character of the "neighbour or a fellow human being," which Freud briefly mentions in *Entwurf* as the complex of the fellow human being (*der Komplex des Nebenmenschen*).

cognize. Then the perceptual complexes proceeding from this fellow human-being will in part be new and non-comparable—his features, for instance, in the visual sphere; but other visual perceptions—e.g. those of the movements of his hands—will coincide in the subject with memories of quite similar visual impressions of his own, of his own body, which are associated with memories of movements experienced by himself. Other perceptions of the object too—if, for instance, he screams—will awaken the memory of his own screaming and at the same time of his own experiences of pain. Thus the complex of the fellow human-being falls apart into two components, of which one makes an impression by its constant structure and stays together **as a thing**, while the other can be understood by the activity of memory—that is, can be traced back to information from [the subject's] own body. This dissection of a perceptual complex is described as cognizing it; it involves a judgment and when this last aim has been attained it comes to an end.[59]

It is surprising that Freud's concept of the *Nebenmensch*—or a "fellow human-being" in Strachey's translation—is not regarded as an archetype of inter-subjective relationships but rather denotes a controversial amalgam of the subject's relationship with itself and with external reality at its birth. Therefore, the complex of fellow human beings explains that "You" as an object evokes the memory of the first satisfaction and yet at the same time evokes the memory of *the subject's own screaming and pain*. In particular, the one part of this undifferentiated archaic object, in Lacan's re-wording, "remains together as a thing, *als Ding*," the persisting impression or affect which is inscribed in the subject as a structure prior to the subject's own existence.[60] In the above quotation, Freud's conceptualization of the *Nebenmensch* captures the most destitute face of inter-subjective relationships, in which one may "confront that moment when a man or a group of men can act in such a way that the question of existence is posed for the whole of the human species."[61] At such moments, Lacan says, "you will then see

---

59. Sigmund Freud, "Project for a Scientific Psychology," in *The Standard Edition of the Complete Psychological Works of Sigmund Freud: Volume I*, trans. James Strachey (London: The Hogarth Press and the Institute of Psycho-Analysis, 1950), 330. (My emphasis.)

60. Lacan, *Seminar VII*, 51.

61. Ibid., 105.

inside yourself that *das Ding* is next to the subject."[62] Lacan uses the nuclear weapon, a thing, with immeasurable destructive power as an example of the act that enables the Thing to re-emerge on the surface of consciousness by posing a threat to the entire human race. Kubrick's film also flickers the presence of the Thing by describing the real face of the most self-destructive crime of mankind—that is, the slaughter of one's own children. For me, it is Jack Torrance's unforgettably empty yet diabolical gaze as he looks out the window while Wendy and Danny gleefully play in the snow that indicates that he is going through the moment of encounter with *das Ding* next to his being. The lengthy close-up of Jack's pale face with those strangely beaming eyes appears to deliver Lacan's own words in silent voice-over:

> But when the commandment [of "Thou shalt love thy neighbour as thyself"] appeared, the Thing flared up, returned once again, I met my death. And for me, the commandment that was supposed to lead to life turned out to lead to death, for the Thing found a way and thanks to the commandment seduced me; through it I came to desire death.[63]

The point I wish to emphasize with this transference from Freud to Lacan via the mediation of *Nebenmensch* is not merely a new analytical perspective on the hostile relations of the Torrance family; the more significant point is that the discovery of the true face of the *Nebenmensch* clarifies how *das Ding* works in the practice of adaptation.

If one considers an original text to be a neighbor or an "other," that which lures the adapter to it and demands the most agonizing process of re-presenting the "truth" of the original is none other than what we see in the *Nebenmensch* as *das Ding*. The adapter is seduced by the death of his or her own art as representation; behind this death is the Thing or, in Freud's term, the ghost of *Vorstellung*. Indeed, it is a terribly self-destructive acknowledgment to an artist whose identity is determined by their creation of meaning through the practice of representation. For this very reason, however, I suggest that Kubrick's adaptation is an act of creation that aims to be transcendental rather than representational. In other words, Kubrick's adaptation exhibits the potential of an artistic creation in its sublime efforts to re-present the most truthful to an original and bring the presence of *das Ding* to the surface. If we recall

62. Ibid.
63. Ibid., 83.

the overhead shot of the miniature maze from the rather perverse God's-eye view, the maze is seen from Jack's point of view while Jack occupies the position of the unfathomable menace. Certainly, the massive geometric structure of the maze has required immeasurable human labor to grow the hedge into this shape, only to enshrine nothing but a narrow rectangular hollow at its center. The film's visualization of the maze is nothing short of a cinematic metaphor for what Kubrick has done with the original novel in the name of adaptation. The hollow captured by a meticulous elaboration of a craftsman is the essence of all human creation *ex nihilo*: Lacan says, "this Thing will always be represented by emptiness, precisely because it cannot be represented by anything else—or, more exactly, because it can only be represented by something else." He concludes, "All art is characterized by a certain mode of organization around this emptiness."[64]

Like the vase, which is created by the skilled potter to contain nothing, Stanley Kubrick's adaptation or maze encapsulates nothing with extreme care and excessive artistry. The monstrosity of Kubrick's maze is fully revealed at the film's end, when Jack Torrance meets his death, only to be delivered to the realm of eternal life encapsulated in a half-century-old photograph. In this final dissolve—editing Jack's frozen face into the framed photograph—Kubrick's maze disrupts the linear progression from life to death and blurs the ontological boundary between the two. The maze ultimately challenges every attempt on the part of human desire to demarcate the seat of life from that of death. It thus re-presents the mythical point at which the need for life is entirely bound up with the drive to death. In this light, Kubrick's adaptation reimagines a radical form of the Minotaur myth, revealing that no monster lurks in any corner of the maze. The mythical beast of the Cretan labyrinth, once believed to feed on human flesh, is merely a projection of our desire for life—or a detour on the path to death—created so that young Theseus could sustain his desire to slay it. However, the monster cannot deceive everyone: some can confront the Truth, which belies itself and defies us, slipping away. Both erudite adapters, Kubrick and Lacan, who explore the void or non-relation at the heart of a perpetual desire for the maze called adaptation—where the boundaries between original and adaptation, or "You" and "Me," become indistinct—perceive that "there seems to be no other monster than the labyrinth itself."[65]

64. Ibid., 129–30.
65. Jacques Lacan, "The Freudian Thing or the Meaning of the Return to Freud in Psychoanalysis," 338.

# 5

## TRAVERSING THE PHANTASY IN SPIKE JONZE'S *ADAPTATION*

> What the phantasy wears has two names which concern one and the same substance, if you do not mind reducing this term to this function of *surface* ... This surface which I call *bubble* has, properly speaking, two names: *desire* and *reality*.
>
> —Jacques Lacan, *Seminar XIV*

### An Allegory of Adaptation

With a title that explicitly designates the film's generic and ontological status, *Adaptation* (dir. Spike Jonze, 2002) draws our immediate attention to adaptation as a key concept to be probed. Although the term "adaptation" lies at the center of this book, the adaptations discussed in the previous chapters do not self-consciously reflect on the reality and conditions of their *being* on a diegetic level. In other words, the contents of those film adaptations do not embrace the question, which is deeply embedded in the context of their production. In *Adaptation*, this repressed question comes to the surface and asks us, "What is adaptation?" Without openly addressing this question, no analysis of adaptation can justify an attempt to advance beyond the term's limited denotation as a particular mode of textual construction.

This chapter, therefore, seeks to move beyond the conventional analytic framework to interrogate the very definition of the term "adaptation." The intention operates in concomitance with a psychoanalytic perspective that is organized around Freud. Characteristically, his clinical study of individual patients manifests the dimension of *meta*-psychology, whereby the analysis of an individual or a text becomes integrated into more conceptual speculation about the subject of the unconscious. To apply this logic of psychoanalytic discourse to discussion, it is profitable to examine a text like *Adaptation*, which radically complicates an adapter's course of adaptation as textual transformation to interrogate the fundamental definition of adaptation as the subject's mode of being. An analysis of this film will advance the book's discussion by inviting a different set of questions—to those posed by the previous chapters—about the concept of adaptation with reference to the primordial mode of the subject's existence. By interpreting the film as an epitome of the fundamental nature of adaptation, this chapter seeks to explore the subject as an adapter who, as the film illustrates, functions not only as the agent but also as the object of adaptation.

In a unique manner, the film *Adaptation* brings the concept of adaptation to the forefront as both its existential subject matter and the central action driving the protagonist, Charlie Kaufman, who embodies the film's real-life writer on screen. The film's narrative is built around the protagonist's practical task of adaptation, through which this commissioned adapter confronts and gradually uncovers the meaning of his existence in his struggle to complete the work. Interestingly, the ultimate narrative goal is the film's own creation: adaptation is portrayed as an urgent task that must be fulfilled for the film itself to come into being. Herein, spectators are immersed in the role of the adapter who is striving to write the scenario of the film they are watching. The empathetic urgency embedded in the film's psychological configuration draws spectators into the protagonist's task, compelling them to engage as if his desire, agony, and anxiety were enacting their own unconscious impulses, transporting them back to the origins of their subjective construction or the fundamental experience of adapting to the world. In this way, the film seems to elevate the protagonist's personal ordeal to the level of a universal condition, reflecting the experience of every subject faced with the challenge of adaptation as an existential task.

To put differently, the film *Adaptation* functions as an allegory of adaptation, which provides a psychic theatre for what underlies every adaptation. That is, what the film allegorizes is the driving force behind the incessant practice of self-adaptation; the implication is that the task of adaptation is a mode of human existence. In an attempt to engage with the allegory of adaptation encapsulated by the film, the discussion will follow a different path to that pursued in the previous chapters and will be less concerned with the transaction between the original text—Susan Orlean's *The Orchid Thief*—and the film *Adaptation* based on the book. Instead, the chapter will place greater emphasis on how the subject of the unconscious responds to this task of adaptation through various modes of re-presentation, such as transition, transformation, and traversal. This will allow the book's final case study to hark back to the fundamental quest set out at the beginning—namely, the quest to explore "adaptation" as a task that, I suggest, manifests the ontological order to which the human subject is bound.

## The Original Phantasy and Its Adaptations

The film, in brief, illustrates the process of its creation as an adaptation: the content of the film's narrative self-consciously consumes the process of writing the film's script based on Susan Orlean's 1998 bestseller *The Orchid Thief*. The film's actual screenwriter, Charlie Kaufman, creates a screen persona of himself (played by Nicolas Cage) as the film's protagonist, who struggles to complete the intimidating task of adaptation commissioned by a Hollywood studio. Onto this main story line, the film superimposes the context of the original text's composition, whereby the original's author Susan Orlean (played by Meryl Streep) attempts to adapt the true story of a Florida orchid thief, John Laroche (played by Chris Cooper), who narrates his life along a whimsical path of fascination and obsession. Regarding the dazzling effects that result from jumbling several layers of adaptation, Kirk Boyle points out that "[t]he *mise en abyme* effect of textuality leads to a seemingly infinite regress of adaptation—the film is an adaptation of an adaptation of an adaptation, *ad infinitum*."[1] The film explores multiple layers within the concept of adaptation and interweaves them into the narrative structure. Additionally, the idea of adaptation as a textual transition intersects with the question of ontological adaptation, symbolized by the life of a small yet intricate organism, such as an orchid. This multifaceted approach to "adaptation" reflects the film's intent to dismantle, deconstruct, and transcend its purely textual definition. Yet, in doing so, it ultimately reconfigures adaptation as an all-encompassing process that unites all forms of existence, culminating in the notion that adaptation "unites each and every one of us."[2]

In this chapter, I propose that a proper reconsideration of "adaptation" in psychoanalytic terms necessitates positioning the term in close relation to the notion of phantasy. To begin, it is important

---

1. Kirk Boyle, "Reading the Dialectical Ontology of *The Life Aquatic with Steve Zissou* against the Ontological Monism of *Adaptation*," *Film-Philosophy* 11, no. 1 (2007): 3.

2. *Adaptation*, directed by Spike Jonze (2002), DVD.

to acknowledge the striking similarity between the two concepts—"adaptation" and "phantasy"—as both encompass a comparable degree of ambivalence. In psychoanalytical discourse, phantasy denotes both the psychic activity of imagination and its results: in short, the product of phantasy is a phantasy. Laplanche and Pontalis define phantasy as that which designates "imagination, … its content and the creative activity which animates it."[3] The same can be said for the term "adaptation," which encompasses both the process of textual transition and its outcomes; in this sense, the result of adaptation is itself an adaptation. The epistemological ambivalence inherent in the use of both terms highlights the intersection between a textual or psychic process and the outcomes it produces. Furthermore, as long as there is no clear distinction between such transitory processes and their products, it is also impossible to distinguish one phantasy or adaptation from the next, which is processed from the preceding one. For me, this suggests that adaptation and phantasy should be understood as an incessant journey or ongoing action along an axis that has no clean division between any two adjacent points. By linking the two terms in this sense, phantasy will offer a key to understanding the film's representation of adaptation as "a journey we all take."

Freud's conceptualization of phantasy provides a solid foundation for employing this psychoanalytic concept as a tool to interrogate adaptation as a concept. From an early stage in his thinking, Freud associated phantasy with the psychic faculty of modifying, elaborating, and adapting materials from childhood experiences. For instance, in *Screen Memory* (1899), he states that the work of phantasy adapts selected events from childhood to fulfill suppressed wishes, while the processed phantasy, in turn, can transform into unconscious and conscious childhood memories. Indeed, this idea lies at the heart of the Freudian field as a whole, suggesting that psychoanalysis is fundamentally an exploration of the human psyche as a faculty for adaptation in all its forms. In this view, the psyche acts as a mediator or adapter, facilitating transitions between external and internal realms, the representable and the unrepresentable, the conscious and the unconscious, the sociocultural and the sexual, and more. Phantasy, as a psychoanalytic concept, encapsulates these transformative processes occurring within the human psyche. Therefore, the interrogation of adaptation with

---

3. Jean Laplanche, and Jean-Bertrand Pontalis, *The Language of Psycho-Analysis* (New York and London: W. W. Norton & Company, 1973), 314.

reference to phantasy can open up speculation about the transactions between fiction and reality, representation and repression, desire and defense, images and signifiers. Above all, the link between adaptation and phantasy will offer a site for exploring the function and significance of the origin or starting point of this transitional journey. To begin, I shall focus on Freud's discovery of the adaptive nature of the human psyche and how this might be detected through the interpretation of phantasy.

In general, phantasy occupies a central position in the field of psychoanalysis owing to its function as a primary point of access to the unconscious. For instance, the first decade of Freud's theorization of the unconscious relied heavily on the interpretation of his patients' phantasies as a key text. From a clinical perspective, phantasy serves as a vehicle for completing the goal of psychoanalytic treatment, which aims to "unearth the fantasies which lie behind such products of the unconscious as dreams, symptoms, acting out, repetitive behavior, etc."[4] Despite its significance, however, the term "phantasy" is rarely an object of conceptualization in the vast opus of Freud, with the exception of a few occasions. Rather, it remains a secondary notion that facilitates theoretical speculations regarding other concepts, such as dream-work, the pleasure principle, desire, and sexuality. Freud uses the term discursively in his texts in the sense that he acknowledges its ambiguity and flexibility of use. He writes, "I am in the habit of describing the element in the dream-thoughts which I have in mind as a 'phantasy,'" but Freud remains silent about what this "element" in his mind actually is.[5] Consequently, phantasy accrues a wide range of connotations, from the conscious operation of imagination and its contents to the most hidden faculty of imagining in the realm of the unconscious. In particular, Freud hesitates to designate the topological locus of this psychic activity and its outcomes. Sometimes, he treats phantasy as belonging to the realm of the unconscious and thus underlying pathological symptoms. However, he occasionally comments that phantasy is closely linked to conscious activities such as day-dreaming and artistic creation. Ultimately, Freud acknowledges the haunting and forever-adaptive nature of phantasy, saying that "these phantasies ... *find no proper place*

---

4. Ibid., 315.
5. Sigmund Freud, "The Interpretation of Dreams," in *The Standard Edition Volume V*, trans. James Strachey (London: The Hogarth Press and the Institute of Psycho-Analysis, 1955), 490.

in [the subject's psychic] structure."⁶ That is, phantasy is a notion that resists localization in any topological structure that he draws; rather, it offers a dynamic point of contact with the unconscious, which also frustrates any attempt to localize it.

In response to the nature of phantasy as an ongoing process of adaptation, Freud's approach was to seek the starting point that, especially, initiates a chain of pathological phantasies. While interpreting his patients' fantasies as they emerged through free association, Freud carefully traced the origin of this phantasy work, the source from which these phantasmatic scenes were endlessly woven. In this regard, the concept of the primal scene or the original phantasy indicates the direction of Freud's investigation:

> Among the store of unconscious phantasies of all neurotics, and probably of all human beings, *there is one which is seldom absent and which can be disclosed by analysis*: this is the phantasy of watching sexual intercourse between the parents. I call such phantasies ... "primal phantasies".⁷

It should be noted here that the psychoanalytic approach to the process of phantasy reveals traces of the Darwinian concept of adaptation, which assumes the existence of "some one primordial form" from which all organic beings descended.⁸ This innate modernist belief propelled two significant questions that Freud raised in his later work *From the History of an Infantile Neurosis* (1918) and on which the film *Adaptation* sheds a deconstructive light. The first asks whether this initial point of origin belongs to the realm of objective reality and refers back to the patients' lived experiences; the other question concerns the analytic function of the primal scene—that is, whether or not this origin of phantasy named "the primal scene" offers an effective resolution of the

---

6. Freud, "A Child Is Being Beaten," 182. (My emphasis.)

7. Sigmund Freud, "A Case of Paranoia Running Counter to the Psycho-Analytic Theory of the Disease," in *The Standard Edition of the Complete Psychological Works of Sigmund Freud: Volume XIV*, trans. James Strachey (London: The Hogarth Press and the Institute of Psycho-Analysis, 1957), 268. (My emphasis.)

8. Charles Darwin, *The Origin of Species: By Means of Natural Selection or the Preservation of Favoured Races in the Struggle for Life* (London: Penguin Books, 1985), 455.

pathological neurotic symptoms that, in the film, are epitomized by the experience of writer's block.

Freud initially sought to detect an original point that anchors the adaptive movement of phantasy toward the domain of reality, detached from the subject's distorting perception of it. He believed that the existence of such a reference point in reality would enable psychoanalysis, as a clinical practice, to address and undo the underlying causes of various pathological symptoms. However, contrary to his suppositions, which follow in the footsteps of Darwinian discourse, Freud's search for the primal scene unwittingly performed its own deconstruction. Freud's attempt to identify the origin of phantasmatic fabrication in his patients' narratives was never sufficiently successful to detect a specific moment from the patients' lived experiences that might confirm the analyst's interpretation of the patients' dreams and phantasies. Therefore, the validity of his analysis in many cases is left suspended. Instead, the patients' phantasies led Freud to a rather unexpected insight—namely, that no clear demarcation exists between reality and the fictional narratives that patients confide to an analyst. Moreover, the work of phantasy is precisely to link and confound reality and fiction by selectively extracting elements from reality and adapting them into phantasmatic stories or scenes, which the patients, in turn, come to perceive as their lived experiences. In the equivocal conclusion to his case study *From the History of an Infantile Neurosis*, Freud admits that what remains in the final stages of investigation is nothing but the question whose answer is foreclosed to an analyst. He writes:

> I should myself be glad to know whether the primal scene in my present patient's case was a phantasy or a real experience … These scenes of observing parental intercourse, of being seduced in childhood, and of being threatened with castration are unquestionably an inherited endowment, a phylogenetic heritage, but they may just as easily be acquired by personal experience.[9]

Overall, Freud's clinical experiences clearly left him indecisive as to the nature of phantasy—whether it is a reflection of reality or a boundless

---

9. Sigmund Freud, "From the History of an Infantile Neurosis," in *The Standard Edition of the Complete Psychological Works of Sigmund Freud: Volume XVII*, trans. James Strachey (London: The Hogarth Press and the Institute of Psycho-Analysis, 1955), 96.

adaptive construction, one that transcends the limits of lived experience by endlessly weaving fragments of reality into a creative, self-sustaining framework.

With its appreciation of the complexity and ambivalence imposed on the concept of adaptation, the film under the chapter's discussion similarly challenges the distinction between phantasy and reality. First, the conceptual analogy of adaptation and phantasy entails the assumption that the function of an original text in the process of adaptation is comparable to that of the original phantasy in the course of phantasy work. This connection aligns the implied separation between the two terms—adaptation and the original text—with the distinction between phantasy and its origin in reality. On this basis, the film's blurring of the boundary between phantasy and "originary reality" is tied to its underlying aim: to examine the definition of adaptation as a construction, particularly as it relates to the concept of origin, which carries connotations of meaning, truth, and authority. Moreover, the film's complication of the division between phantasy and reality ultimately transgresses the limiting speculation to consider "adaptation" in a reciprocal relationship between the original text and its adaptation. With these aims, the film *Adaptation* directs its meditation about the meaning of adaptation toward the threshold between the two allegedly opposing terms—phantasy and reality.

The original text—*The Orchid Thief*—already contains the potential for such ambivalence and transgression. Susan Orlean's book uses its "sprawling New Yorker style" to interweave its two heterogeneous components: the first is a narrative that renders John Laroche and the writer herself as characters, and the other is an objective account of the history of orchid poaching, Seminole Indians, and Florida. It is difficult, therefore, for the adapter to determine, for instance, the extent to which Laroche should be treated as a "fun character" who is a product of the writer's phantasy and, hence, an object for adaptation. The film's writer, Kaufman, himself is not unfamiliar with the overlap between phantasy and reality and with the act of subverting the distinction between real persons and characters. His film debut, *Being John Malkovich* (1999), is characterized by its peculiar use of a real Hollywood film star, John Malkovich, as a fictional character. In this, it foreshadows *Adaptation*'s polysemous use of a real-life figure as a character to highlight the inseparable permutation between the two realms.

On a broader scale than *Being John Malkovich*, *Adaptation* fuses the characters based on real-life people with a few purely fictional characters.

The film erases the disparity between the film's nonfictional figures, like Carlie Kaufman and Susan Orlean, and the invented characters, such as Donald Kaufman (also played by Nicolas Cage), the twin brother of the on-screen Charlie Kaufman, and Amelia (played by Cara Seymour), who is the on-screen writer's love object. To intensify the sense of disorientation, the opening credits present the name of this fictional twin brother, Donald Kaufman, as the film's screen writer(s) along with the real writer Charlie Kaufman. This shuffle clearly indicates the film's intention to investigate the conceptual division between phantasy and reality as two poles in the adaptation process. The eruption of the fictional character into the context of production also discloses the potential of a phantasmatic creation to overflow into the realm of reality and to adapt itself as a part of the real world.

Interestingly, however, although Freud appears to abandon his search for the original "event" in objective reality and, thus, the demarcation of phantasy from material reality, the opening quotation from his famous case study of the Wolf Man still maintains the dominance of the original phantasy, which is captured in the mold of the primal scene. In other words, while Freud may admit that it is impossible for a psychoanalytic investigation to ensure the authenticity of the patient's bearing witness to the primal scene, he nevertheless considers the original phantasy to hold the key to the unconscious in view of the fact that it occupies the place of the phantasy's origin. In the same text, Freud emphasizes "an uncontradicted premise that a primal scene of this kind ... is indispensable to a comprehensive solution of all the conundrums that are set us by the symptoms of the infantile disorder, that *all the consequences radiate out from it*, just as all the threads of the analysis have led up to it."[10]

From this determining principle, we may detect the strength of the *desire* for a chronological order that would secure the linear and causal relations between the past and the present. Freud's case study of the Wolf Man is characterized by the utmost effort to straighten out the adaptive movement of phantasy-work and to put the primal scene at the beginning of subjectivity. As before, Freud strives to detect a real incident behind the primal phantasy from which the transitory phantasies are endlessly adapted. Having interpreted the Wolf Man's dazzling array of pathological phantasies, Freud terminates his investigation, to our surprise, by *fictionalizing* the patient's witness to

10. Ibid., 54. (My emphasis.)

his parents' "coitus a tergo" at the age of one and a half.[11] Apart from Freud's failure in his search for a degree of truth in the content of the primal scene, this lengthy case study of the Wolf Man is noteworthy in terms of Freud's insistence on developing a linear plot that can thread all phantasies into a straight timeline. To do so, Freud posts numerous time-indicators on the patient's experiences throughout the text. In 1923, Freud added a footnote that minutely documents "the chronology of the events mentioned in this case history" in a detailed timeline from the date of the patient's birth to his outbreaks of obsessional neurosis in his twenties.[12]

In *Adaptation*, we can discover the same desire manifested in the film's repeated use of time-tags in an attempt to establish a coherent chronological progress or adaptation from the chaotic shuffle of scenes from various temporal frames. For instance, the film begins with Kaufman's story when he is commissioned to write an adaptation of Orlean's book. The scene in which Kaufman advocates his view of the book to film executive Valerie (played by Tilda Swinton) cuts directly to a different timeline, in which Susan is writing the book based on a local newspaper story about John Laroche's orchid poaching. The temporal order is determined by the subtitle, which reads "New Yorker Magazine, Three Years Earlier." The image of the female author's tranquil and uninterrupted writing suddenly cuts to a steamy day in Florida, and Laroche's white van loudly skids in front of the camera with another time signal that reads "State Road 29, Florida, Two Years Earlier." In another scene, Kaufman's thoughts drift from a scene of him writing in the present tense to a scene of Charles Darwin's writing, labeled "England, One Hundred Thirty Nine Years Earlier." In addition to these subtitles, which adhere to a chronology, the desire for temporal and causal consistency is also discovered in the protagonist's belief in the power of the origin or the original text to liberate him from all of his neurotic symptoms, which have culminated in severe writer's block. Amid his tangled thoughts and struggle to craft the perfect beginning for his script, Kaufman arrives at the realization that adaptation is a journey of evolution, hoping it will offer a solution to his creative dilemma. The on-screen adapter contemplates the meaning of adaptation, and his voice-over narration confides, "The journey we all take. A journey that

11. Ibid., 38.
12. Ibid., 120 (footnote 1).

unites each and every one of us ... That's it! That's what I need to do. Tie all of history together!"

Nevertheless, adherence to the origin of adaptation fails to provide him with a solution, leaving him deflated and disillusioned in the next scene—much like Freud's pursuit of chronology and his designation of the primal scene as a starting point on the timeline proved unable to resolve the patient's symptoms. This reveals the paradox of the primal scene, which, contradictory to its place and function as hypothesized by Freud, ultimately disturbs the supposedly linear narrative of phantasies. In view of its returning nature and its persistent presence behind every phantasy adapted from the original, the primal scene is an element that resists the analyst's attempts to historicize the adaptive path of the patient's phantasies from the original scene to the present symptoms.

Rather than serving as the origin of subjectivity or the primary cause of the subject's symptoms, the primal scene is revealed to be a dead end in the subject's urgent quest for answers to the questions "Who am I?" or "Where did I come from?" This *fundamental* phantasy recurs in countless variations or adaptations through the continuous work of phantasy.[13] Its persistent reappearance suggests that the primal scene neither resolves the ontological question nor represents the original moment when the question first arises. Instead, it functions as a terminal point in the quest for an answer, signaling the fundamental impossibility of the subject ever arriving at such an answer. Consequently, Freud's case study has a highly unique structure in which, at first, his investigation attempts to dig out this primal scene as the birthplace of phantasmatic reproductions. His search for the origin culminates in his *fictionalizing* the primal scene that marks the dead end of his investigation. The analysis then revisits those secondary phantasies from a different perspective, which now regards each of them as adapted from the omnipresent fundamental phantasy. After inferring—not confirming—the content of the primal scene, Freud writes that "[w]e will first proceed with the study of the relations between this 'primal scene' and the patient's dreams, his symptoms, and the history of his life; and we will trace *separately* the effects that followed from the essential content of the scene and from

---

13. It is important to recognize the shift from the original phantasy to the fundamental phantasy, which places greater emphasis on the force of gravity than a connotation of a temporal origin. I shall return to this point in the next section with reference to Lacan's elaboration of the fundamental phantasy evoking the trajectory of repetition.

one of its visual impression."[14] Herein, the case study follows a circular trajectory, moving toward and then away from the primal scene, which has now become a point of gravity that is characterized by its magnificent centripetal power, like a black hole.

The film insightfully captures the logic of adaptation embedded in the movement of pathological phantasies that Freud identified. Mirroring Freud's approach, the protagonist's journey takes a seemingly retroactive path in an attempt to uncover the original meaning promised by the text he seeks to adapt. From the film's outset, the adapter's pursuit of this original meaning—implicit yet never fully articulated in Orlean's prose—is continually disrupted by a series of phantasies, each an adaptation of the fundamental, repressed phantasy that haunts him as he struggles with writer's block. Paralyzed by his inability to make progress, he spends countless sleepless nights consumed by masturbatory phantasies, all while remaining impotent in his real-life relationship with his love object, Amelia.

However, the web of phantasies ensnaring the sexually and professionally frustrated adapter follows an immanent logic, despite its seemingly haphazard digressions. Significantly, there is a discernible trajectory—or more precisely, a regression—from the existential question, "Who am I, and how did I get here?" posed in the opening scene, to the terminal moment where he becomes a witness to the coitus between John Laroche and Susan Orlean. In other words, the primal scene's significance is captured in the film's climax, where Kaufman, as an adapter unsure of the origins of the meaning he seeks, interrogates the birth of the original story—not on the page but in reality. This interrogation ultimately leads him to witness the most banal of revelations: a drug-fueled, voluptuous love affair between the female author, Orlean, and her interviewee, Laroche. The construction of this climactic scene underscores that the only escape for the adapter lies in fictionalizing the birthplace of the original story—an origin that remains unwritten in Orlean's book. In this highly generic and conventional layer of the film's narrative, which recklessly ventures beyond the written text, the phantasized original meaning of the ghost orchid—embodying Laroche's passion in its purest sense in *The Orchid Thief*—is materialized in *Adaptation* as the source of a psychotropic drug. Consequently, the adapter Kaufman crafts a scene in which the author-character Orlean's search for an experience of infatuation

---

14. Ibid., 38.

culminates in the on-screen Kaufman's disillusioning discovery of her drug-induced passion for Laroche, revealed after her interviews with him for her book.

To magnify the scene's psychic impact on the diegetic Kaufman, framing it as the encounter with the primal scene, the film clearly assigns Laroche and Orlean a parental function as the creators of the original text in the process of completing Kaufman's task of adaptation. The adapter's imagination continues to phantasize, vividly visualizing the encounters between Orlean and Laroche and imagining how her original book emerged from their shared passion for the enigmatic ghost orchid and their mutual understanding of life's embedded meaning in the blind desire for it. Like a child standing before the closed door of his parents' bedroom, Kaufman is consumed by a desperate need to uncover what transpired between the orchid thief and the author. In other words, Laroche and Orlean occupy the place of parents who give birth to the world of *The Orchid Thief*, which is unfathomable to Kaufman yet demands that he make sense of it. Finally, the on-screen adapter, aided by his twin brother Donald, witnesses "the primal scene" of Orlean and Laroche's coitus at the film's climax. This moment serves as a critical turning point, after which he overcomes both his writer's block and his sexual impotence, allowing him to take decisive action. I shall return to this point shortly with reference to what Lacan calls the end of analysis—that is, the traversal of the original phantasy.

The film's presentation of the primal scene is noteworthy as regards the adaptive nature of phantasy. In effect, the film's presentation acknowledges that the primal scene or the original phantasy does not possess the truth value, which might be able to return every piece of the jigsaw puzzle to the right place for good and put an end to every symptom. Rather, it is a re-presentation of the subject's desire, a response to the impossibility of knowing the origin of being; in other words, it reflects a desire provoked by the fundamental impossibility of conceiving adaptation as a linear progression that begins at the very origin of the original, where the subject's identity as an adapter can be positivized. Therefore, the original phantasy itself returns repeatedly to the same place, which I designated previously as an unlocalizable seat of phantasy. Accordingly, the film's narrative does not move linearly toward the final discovery but follows a circular path around the unrepresentable origin of phantasy, which Freud attempted to capture in such terms as "the original phantasy" and "the primal scene."

Clearly, the film's protagonist does not welcome the climax and its obscene materialization of the primal scene on screen, as this act violates the adapter's desire to preserve the original phantasy—a construct that maintains the mysterious, intellectually sophisticated meaning at the inaccessible core of the original text. The climax, therefore, seems to be driven by the necessity of change—an inevitability required both for the completion of his task as an adapter and for the very existence of the film itself. Thus, Donald, the fictional twin brother created for the on-screen adapter Charlie Kaufman, must step in to collaborate on Charlie's assignment, steering the dragging and cyclical storyline and, more importantly, guiding the reluctant protagonist toward the climactic revelation. First, Donald raises a question about the metaphor "Japanese paper balls" from Orlean's book:

> **Donald:** "Sometimes this kind of story turns out to be something more … some glimpse of life that expands like those Japanese paper balls you drop in water and they bloom into flowers, and the flower is so marvelous you can't believe there was a time all you saw in front of you was a paper ball and a glass of water."
> Well, first of all, that's inconsistent. She, she said that she didn't care about flowers.
> **Charlie:** For God's sake, it's just a metaphor.
> **Donald:** But for what? What turned that paper ball into a flower? It's not in the book, Charles.[15]

With Donald's attempt to unveil the secret supposedly encapsulated in the metaphor, the haunting mystery associated with the "original meaning" unravels and collapses.

Donald's investigation gradually propels Charlie Kaufman toward a moment of confrontation, ultimately leading him to discover Orlean's pornographic image on Laroche's website. Despite the undeniable evidence of their erotic relationship, the screen adapter struggles to preserve Orlean's elevated status, as her intentions and desires must remain unknown and unknowable for the "original meaning" to retain its allure and power. Kaufman delays fully confronting the primal scene once again by fabricating a more romanticized adaptation. The moment when Kaufman gazes at Orlean's pornographic image cuts abruptly to a scene of her confession. In this sequence, Orlean's voice-over

---

15. *Adaptation*, directed by Spike Jonze (2002), DVD.

reveals truths she cannot include in her book. However, the inserted flashback—crafted hastily by Kaufman's reactionary imagination—transforms the raw reality into a romanticized narrative between Orlean and Laroche, ironically mirroring the "Hollywood thing" Kaufman had previously condemned in earlier scenes. In response to Kaufman's unbearable discovery of Orlean's indecent image, the film's narrative—a reenactment tool for Kaufman's evolving phantasy work, spurred by the task of adaptation—shifts dramatically into a romance plot. This new direction foregrounds the love affair between Susan Orlean and John Laroche, interwoven with the sinister backstory of "changing the orchids into poppies."

What is most intriguing here is that the subsequent scenes, which dramatize their romantic love-making, seem unmistakably constructed by the diegetic Kaufman himself to satisfy his Oedipal desire for the forbidden object—the mother. The subject, Kaufman, projects his Oedipal desire, which is itself evoked by his fascination with the female author or mother of the original text, onto his phantasy about the romance between Orlean and Laroche. Kaufman completely displaces himself onto Laroche and, through Laroche's voice, Kaufman confesses his seemingly incestuous desire. Over the phone, Laroche confides to the stoned Orlean how isolated he was as a weird child and how long he has been waiting for a woman who would love him just as his mother did: Laroche's voice-over softly echoes, "I had this idea if I waited long enough, someone would come around and just, y'know, understand me. Like my mom, except someone else." To mitigate this Oedipal configuration, the imagery and sound used to depict their coitus inside Laroche's van are deliberately toned down, imbued with a less erotic and more subdued quality compared to the subsequent banal version of the primal scene. In this soft-filtered, romanticized adaptation of the primal scene, Orlean's maternal caressing of Laroche subtly suggests that Laroche serves as a stand-in for Kaufman, who, through this phantasy, navigates his most forbidden desire. Here, we might suggest that this romanticized composition of the primal scene serves as an adaptation that reimagines the love affair between Orlean and Laroche in order to subtly redirect the diegetic adapter's repressed desire into a more socially acceptable narrative framework.

The climax unfolds shortly after the tender, maternal love in Kaufman's phantasy dissipates, replaced by the sight of Orlean rushing into Laroche's van, giggling like a teenage girl. Donald and Charlie Kaufman follow the van to Laroche's house, into which the couple disappears. After a brief moment of contemplation, Charlie decides to confront the need to change and adapt himself by means of action. The decision reminds spectators of the imperative given to the desperate Kaufman by the on-screen Robert McKee (a screen persona of the real-life screenwriting guru, played by Brian Cox) in an earlier scene: McKee commands, "Your characters must change and the change must come from them." This fortitude, encouraged and demanded by the fatherly McKee, leads Kaufman to the dead end of his phantasy, which will offer a turning point in his adaptation journey in both the professional and ontological senses. What he eventually discovers is a more realistic and less phantasmatic scene of sexual intercourse. The rendition of the coitus between Orlean and Laroche now becomes a sexual relationship tainted by drug addiction and lacking in any depth or glamour. The low-key light, deprived of any flattering filter or backlight, casts Susan as a voluptuous femme fatale. *The New Yorker*'s writer delivers indecent lines while shamelessly snorting the drug extracted from the ghost orchid—the very symbol of the mysterious infatuation and passion her book seeks to capture. Meanwhile, Laroche, once surprising both the original author Susan and the screen adapter Kaufman with his words of wisdom, is reduced to a small-time, vulgar, and clumsy criminal.

There is no mythical secret concealing the Truth that Kaufman believes resides within Orlean's original text. Instead, Kaufman witnesses the book—the original meaning he has been striving to adapt onto the screen—deflate into a product of pathetic phantasy born of Orlean's bourgeois desire and Laroche's narcissistic solipsism. Yet, it is crucial to emphasize that it is not the content of the original phantasy that enables the adapter to overcome the pathological neurosis manifested in his writer's block. Rather, this resolution occurs because, at the very end of the original phantasy's adaptive journey, the subject confronts the impossibility, or absolute lack, of an answer—now unmasked. In other words, there is no longer a Truth for the subject to phantasize or endlessly adapt into more sublime and desirable forms, because the Truth has been stripped of its mask, revealing the void beneath. From this perspective, the discovery of the primal scene fails to provide an answer to the adapter's search for the original meaning. Furthermore, the act of bearing witness to this primal scene shatters the spell of the original phantasy, which had kept both Kaufman and his script in a state of suspension. This rupture is driven by the sheer banality of the representation of the supposedly unfathomable original scene. In hindsight, it becomes clear that the centrifugal force of the original scene—the power that draws the subject toward it—is sustained only by its absence of a tangible, conscious-level representation.

To summarize, phantasies can be understood as the by-products woven by the subject in response to the inaccessibility of its own origin. This lack drives the subject into an endless process of adapting the primal scene. At a critical juncture—which I will later connect to the moment of traversing the fundamental phantasy—the subject encounters the primal scene, often by chance. This parallels Kaufman's inadvertent confrontation with the scene of origin: the parental coitus between Laroche, representing the genesis of Orlean's book, and Orlean, the author of the original text for screen adaptation. This encounter illuminates the paradoxical logic of screen adaptation. While the subject aims to progress by crafting new phantasies, this forward motion of adaptation inevitably circles back to the starting point, represented by the gravity of the primal scene—a hidden foundation beneath all phantasies. In the film, Kaufman strives to uncover this origin within the original text he seeks to adapt. Masquerading as the original meaning to be conveyed, the primal scene entices and eludes the adapter, who is ultimately searching for an answer to the ontological question, "How did I come here?" In this sense, the original phantasy stands in for the unknowable origin of being, occupying the position of Truth. The repeated re-presentations of the primal scene serve as an opaque screen, veiling the traumatic "beyond" of castration. The discussion that follows will begin by examining the role of castration in initiating this journey of adaptation.

## *Adaptation* in vitro

Based on the Freudian insight of phantasy's conception in the form of "a scene," Lacan recognizes the importance of the visual quality of phantasy. Lorenzo Chiesa explains the backbone of both the Freudian and Lacanian conceptualizations of phantasy as a scene as follows:

> With fantasy we are in the presence of something that fixes and reduces to the status of a snapshot the course of memory, stopping it at a point called screen memory. Think of a cinematographic movement that takes place rapidly and then suddenly stops at one point, freezing all the characters. This snapshot is distinctive of a reduction of the full scene … to what is immobilized in fantasy

which remains loaded with all the erotic functions included in what [the full scene] expressed and of which [fantasy] is the witness and the support, the last support that remains.[16]

However, as Chiesa observes in *Subjectivity and Otherness* (2007), Lacan emphasizes the predominance of the symbolic order in shaping the meanings and functions of these snapshots. Lacan draws a parallel between phantasy and cinema, both of which rely on a sequence of images governed by a symbolic logic. He frequently likens scenes of phantasy to the frozen images projected on a cinema screen, highlighting their shared mechanisms of representation and mediation.

Nonetheless, this comparison should not be misconstrued as positioning cinema merely as a phantasy that fulfills otherwise unattainable desires through the production and consumption of imagined scenes. The logic underlying phantasmatic images cannot be fully reduced to the pleasure principle, which seeks satisfaction by creating imaginary scenarios onto which the subject projects repressed wishes. Drawing on Freud's observations regarding the beyond of the pleasure principle, Lacan argues that phantasy also functions as a reactionary mental activity, shielding the subject from recurring traumas that resist symbolization. According to Lacan, phantasy acts as a reduction of "the full screen," serving as a defense mechanism that condenses what would otherwise be an overwhelming trauma into a manageable snapshot. This reduction allows the subject to confront the traumatic without being overwhelmed by its unmediated intensity.

At the same time, however, phantasy's mitigating function preserves the unknowability and irrepresentability of what lies barred and excluded beyond its frame. In the framework of Lacan's three psychic registers, the real and its affect are sustained only through the fabrication of phantasy within the imaginary, guided by the binary logic of the symbolic. Moreover, emphasizing the defensive function as a dominant aspect of phantasy work, Lacan highlights the role of the "frozen image" in concealing the enigmatic desire of the Other. This desire, when disrupted, leaves the traumatic but constitutive mark of castration upon the subject. In the context of the earlier discussion on the primal scene, as the terminal point of phantasy work, the various adaptations of the primal scene operate as a kind of patchwork. These adaptations serve to

---

16. Chiesa, *Subjectivity and Otherness*, 149. (The original quotation is from Jacque Lacan's *Le séminire livre IV*, 119–20, translated by Lorenzo Chiesa.)

obscure the irreducible trauma that continuously threatens to resurface, veiling its disruptive force beneath layers of representation.

In parallel with the psychoanalytic concept of phantasy, any film adaptation can be interpreted as a phantasy that masks the traumatic lack perceived in the Other. This Other, in response to whose silent demand the adapter asks, "*Che vuoi* (What do you want)?," often assumes the form of an original text or author that resists conveying the "true meaning" of the original to the screen. The film *Adaptation* analyzes in minute detail how the task of adaptation returns the protagonist—an adapter—to the point of castration and provokes various masturbatory phantasies in his desperate attempt to escape from it. In this allegorical story about the subject's destiny to search for the meaning of his being, Kaufman is confronted by the most primordial and significant function of castration, which is "the cut that constitutes a bar between the signifier and the signified."[17] To Kaufman, there is an intimidating abyss between the original text and its meaning that he is driven to transfer to the screen.

Whenever he closes Susan Orlean's book and returns to his writing desk, the suffocating *unwritten* message of the blank page in the typewriter confronts the adapter in an inverted form, ultimately driving him to cry out, "What do you want from me?" This unanswerable question triggers the faculty of phantasy, functioning as a defense against the trauma of castration, whose revival provokes anxiety and renders the writer both literally and professionally impotent. Phantasy's primary function is to mediate this defensive reaction, translating fragmented images—what Lacan refers to as the still frame—onto the screen to pacify the overwhelming, ungraspable "full screen." More importantly, as Laplanche and Pontalis observe, phantasy serves as "a unique focal point where it is possible to observe the process of transition between the different psychic systems *in vitro*—to observe the mechanism of repression or of the return of the repressed in action."[18] The discussion that follows seeks to explore the relationship between castration and phantasy by examining how phantasy re-presents what is castrated on screen through the act of adaptation. In articulating this relationship, it is essential to consider how castration fixates the subject along the *axis*

    17. Jacques Lacan, "The Subversion of the Subject and the Dialectic of Desire in the Freudian Unconscious," in *Écrits: The First Complete Edition in English*, trans. Bruce Fink (New York and London: W. W. Norton & Company, 2006), 678.
    18. Laplanche and Pontalis, *The Language of Psycho-Analysis*, 316.

of adaptation. This fixation represents the subject's effort to condense the unfathomable "full screen" into a seemingly coherent sequence of snapshots, preventing it from becoming overwhelmed or, as Lacan puts it, lost in "this sea (mer) of variations."[19]

To begin, I wish to briefly revisit Freud's insights into phantasy work in relation to the primal scene and the subject's defensive reactions, which Freud conceptualizes as a veil for the unbearable Truth of being. As Freud moved away from his initial belief in a clear distinction between objective reality and the real of the original scene, as discussed earlier in this chapter, he began to associate the concept of phantasy with castration as a fundamental psychic function. His engagement with patients' narratives of the primal scene may have evoked in him a sense of estrangement and castration from the Truth of the scene itself—a dynamic that resonates with the experience of the adapter Charlie Kaufman, who repeatedly confronts the inaccessible Truth of the original book. In response to this confrontation, Freud's theorization of phantasy appears to reflect an adaptive response to the revived threat of castration, shaping his understanding of the primal scene as both an ontogenetic and phylogenetic construct within psychoanalysis. One might suggest, then, that the primal scene, once foundational to the Freudian field, emerged through a process of adaptation—driven by Freud's need to reconcile the irreducible gaps he had to deal with in his pursuit of a factual ground for the primal scene within his patients' lived experiences. Adaptation, in this sense, becomes a locus of defensive phantasy work, mediating the subject's encounter with the trauma of castration, much like Freud's theoretical evolution in navigating these complexities.

Freud eventually acknowledges that the primal scene may operate as a point of orientation, even though it lacks any basis in the real event of witnessing the parents' coitus or another equivalent experience. The primal scene now puts a stop to the subject's ontological interrogation. Such a conclusion enables him to explore and integrate another field of adaptation into his speculation regarding the psychological adaptation performed by the subject. In various instances, Freud asserts the possibility of "the existence of unconscious schemata transcending individual lived experience and supposedly transmitted by heredity."[20]

---

19. Lacan, *Seminar XIV*, 14.
20. Laplanche and Pontalis, *The Language of Psycho-Analysis*, 315.

Toward the end of the case study of the Wolf Man, he attempts to find a balance between the two seemingly contradictory approaches:

> All that we found in the prehistory of neuroses is that a child catches hold of this phylogenetic experience where his own experience fails him. He fills in the gaps in individual truth with prehistoric truth; he replaces occurrences in his own life by occurrences in the life of his ancestors. I fully agree with Jung in recognizing the existence of this phylogenetic heritage; but I regard it as a methodological error to seize on a phylogenetic explanation before the ontogenetic possibilities have been exhausted. I cannot see any reason for obstinately disputing the importance of infantile prehistory while at the same time freely acknowledging the importance of ancestral prehistory.[21]

Freud's elaboration here introduces a subversive possibility for rethinking the adaptation process, particularly in relation to the construction of the subject. His conceptualization, as outlined above, suggests a correlative—and not contradictory—framework that incorporates both the reality of the external world and the phylogenetic narratives inherited from the past. Consequently, the adaptive process through which phantasies are generated operates on both ontogenetic and phylogenetic levels, reflecting Freud's findings in his exploration of the origins of all phantasy work. The significance of this argument lies in the observation that the father of psychoanalysis, despite his efforts to maintain a scientific foundation for his theory, witnessed his ideas gradually diverging from the strict discourse of science. The construction of the subject of the unconscious relies not only on a factual and biological framework but also on a mythical and allegorical foundation—one that is constructed, sustained, and transmitted through the continually adaptive work of phantasy.

Such a shift in focus is ultimately exemplified in Freud's elaboration of the Oedipus complex, which inextricably intertwines biological and biographical factors with a mythical narrative adapted to individual life. However, this should not be conflated with the Jungian concept of the archetype, as the subject in Freudian and Lacanian theory is not a fixed or static entity, as the notion of the archetype might imply. Instead, to grasp the essence of the subject of the unconscious, the interplay

---

21. Freud, "From the History of an Infantile Neurosis," 96.

between these two constitutive forces—biological and mythical—must remain dynamic. The locus in which the subject is both born and bound is the field of adaptation, where, as Lacan states, "this word 'man' [remains] a transitional term."[22]

The Oedipal myth is none other than a shared psychic drama that phantasizes forbidden desire and its repression. The myth invites Lacan to contemplate the correlation between desire and reality, reflecting on how these two melt into the "most fundamental and truest shape"— namely, phantasy.[23] However, prior to examining Lacan's assertions, I would like to speculate on one more point from Freud's text, in which he describes the perplexity of a child in relation to a certain emergent lack. He writes, "[a] child catches hold of this phylogenetic experience where his own experience fails him. He fills in the gaps in individual truth with prehistoric truth; he replaces occurrences in his own life by occurrences in the life of his ancestors."[24] As Freud describes it, the child makes desperate efforts, grasping at what is not even his own experience in order to fill in the gaps, and becomes sufficiently audacious to relinquish and "replace" a part of his own life experience with that of his ancestors.

My question is what puts the child in this desperate situation. While Freud never articulates what he means by the observation "his own experience fails him," Lacan resumes this very point and identifies what causes the child's experience to fail him and what makes him so desperate to fill in the gaps. It is here that Lacan discovers the arrival of desire. The first stroke of castration exposes a child to the question of who "*I*" am, and desire emerges at the moment when the child's own experience fails to find an answer to it. In Lacan's words, this fundamental dimension of desire seeks an answer to the question of "how *I* comes on the scene."[25] The answer is unavailable because the birth of *I* comes only as a result of castration. The paradox whereby the constitution of the subject is based on its own renunciation is captured in Lacan's dictum, "*I* can [*peut*] come into being by disappearing from my statement [*dit*]."[26] Insofar as the subject comes to be by giving up the answer, being cut off yet

22. Lacan, *Seminar XIV*, 7.
23. Freud, "The Interpretation of Dreams," 620.
24. Freud, "From the History of an Infantile Neurosis," 96.
25. Lacan, "The Subversion of the Subject and the Dialectic of Desire in the Freudian Unconscious," 679.
26. Ibid., 678.

remaining tantalizing, the primal scene is a response to the fatal dead end encountered in the very moment of the birth of subjectivity. The primal scene as the original phantasy thus does not provide a palpable answer; rather, it embraces the origin of phantasy in the sense that, as Laplanche and Pontalis remark, "the origin of the fantasy is integrated in the very structure of the original fantasy."[27] Most importantly, this origin of phantasy at the core of the original phantasy is unfolded in the drama of castration, which marks the impossibility of satisfying the desire to know "the origin of the subject itself."[28]

In Lacan's seminar on the logic of phantasy, he rephrased the above point, which is repeated variously in both the Freudian and Lacanian fields as follows: "At the origin, one does not know where it comes from. It is nothing … but this stroke which is also a cut, starting from which the truth can be born."[29] He goes on to assert that the role of phantasy can be explained as "a first symbolisation" that is required to define "the possible" out of the primordial impossible into which the subject is born. In other words, the fundamental impossibility imposed by castration necessitates "multiple objectifications of the same thing."[30] Here, the subject enters the metonymic chain, leading the speaking being to engage with life by anchoring their desire to an endless sequence of objects as signifiers. From this perspective, the primal scene emerges as the product of this initial act of symbolization—a process that simultaneously mediates the subject's relationship to the void and preserves the void behind it.

Therefore, the endless adaptation of the primal scene offers the speaking subject a means of maintaining its being to protect itself from non-being as the "other" side of the subject's split existence. In fact, adaptation to a subject is more than the transformation of signifiers in one's hands. This process comes to the subject as a manifestation of fate, which demands that the subject adapt itself incessantly and transmit the "original and full" meaning of its being as that which is *given*. This task is neither easy nor satiable in that the original meaning is paradoxically

---

27. Jean Laplanche and Jean-Bertrand Pontalis, "Fantasy and the Origins of Sexuality," in *Formation of Fantasy*, ed. Victor Burgin, James Donald and Cora Kaplan (London and New York: Methuen, 1986), 19.

28. Ibid., 18.

29. Lacan, *Seminar XIV*, 128.

30. Lacan, "The Subversion of the Subject and the Dialectic of Desire in the Freudian Unconscious," 682.

created as a flipside of the absolute lack of such meaning. To address this arduous task, the subject must transform their experiential memory—and ultimately themselves—into a signifier. The writer Charlie Kaufman, who inserts himself as the protagonist in his own film *Adaptation*, exemplifies this process in the most vivid and tangible way.

As the film opens, spectators encounter the same question, which Lacan designates as the mark of the emergence of the subject of the unconscious—that is, "Who is speaking?"[31] If Freud's methodology takes phantasy "as the privileged point where one may catch in the raw the process of transition from one system to another," it is surely an appropriate choice for a film about adaptation to begin with a speaking voice seeking to place the *I* at the launch of a journey of its adaptation.[32] More to the point, the film captures the subversive nature of the Lacanian subject in its construction. Contrary to the developmental framework proposed by ego psychology, the film's opening demonstrates that there is no image or *imago* of the subject prior to the intrusion of the signifier. Even the plethora of images surrounding an infant, without a cue from the symbolic, is an abyss undifferentiated from the complete darkness with which the film chooses to open. While the voice never identifies—or, more precisely, cannot identify—"who is speaking," the opening voice-over draws the audience into a paradoxical experience. In the darkness of the auditorium, where spectacle is denied, spectators are confronted with the perplexing encounter of an *I* that abruptly begins speaking to itself. The spectators, therefore, anxiously anticipate the onset of "[t]his imaginary process … [which] goes from the specular image to the constitution of the ego," seeking to anchor and stabilize the elusive and problematic *I*.[33]

Indeed, the film's opening narration delays the initiation of the imaginary process fundamental to cinema as phantasy. By extending the nascent moment of the *I* to an extreme, the first scene amplifies the subject's urgent need for the metonymic chain of signification—a structure that connects any object or image, as a signifier, to the speaking *I*. In this suspended state, the anticipated image—whether in the mirror or on the screen—becomes a desired anchor for the *I*, even before its emergence within the field of vision. The film comes

31. Ibid., 677.
32. Laplanche and Pontalis, "Fantasy and the Origins of Sexuality," 15.
33. Lacan, "The Subversion of the Subject and the Dialectic of Desire in the Freudian Unconscious," 685. (My emphasis.)

into existence when a male voice suddenly breaks through the darkness, asking, "Do I have an original thought in my head? My bald head?" Notably, even before a name or image emerges to anchor the meaning of this *I*, the word "bald" already infuses the unseen image with a host of subjectified implications. Only with the introduction of this signifier does the image (in this case, of a bald man) become both anticipated and phantasized. The phantasized image takes shape as an object of desire (to see) within the register of the imaginary. Furthermore, this image, even before it appears on screen, begins to serve as "the outlet for [the subject's] most intimate aggressiveness," a dynamic made explicit in the case of the film's self-loathing protagonist.[34] The final line of the opening voice-over underscores the narcissistic constitution of this *I* within the realm of the ego and reveals how the imaginary locus of the *I* is overdetermined by its signification through the signifier "bald and fat." Kaufman's narration concludes with the self-defeating admission: "But I'll still be ugly, though. Nothing's gonna change that."

If we consider adaptation as "the process of transition from one system to another," the demand for such adaptation emerges as a call for images to fill the gap created by the question, "Who is speaking?" This demand arises from within—a search for a means to move from the absence of the signified toward the presence of an image. Importantly, this demand is not limited to the spectators, who expect on-screen images to shield them from directly confronting the lack. More crucially, the demand for adaptation originates within the unseen subject itself, whose voice seeks a semblance to anchor the *I* as "bald and fat," responding to the phantasy already spun by the signifier around this void.

Lacan explains that the overpowering and almost mindless demand of "*I want to see*" lies at the root of the logic of phantasy. As he observes, this fundamental desire underscores that the demand for adaptation— from the inarticulate space of the *I* to the realm of the imaginary—"takes on its dominant function leaving it open to know from where and why I am looked at."[35] Lacan teaches us that this demand manifests itself as a void or black hole and makes the subject designate, therein, the place of the Other, about which nothing can be said "except what we in fact hear, namely, the subject in his *complaint*."[36] Driven by the force of the demand *I want to see*, the subject adapts itself to the world of images

34. Ibid.
35. Lacan, *Seminar XIV*, 63.
36. Ibid.

and objects. Behind this adaptation, the logic of phantasy works to obscure the void toward which the un-localizable speaking *I* inevitably points. The process of adapting a literary text into a screen adaptation, as allegorized in this film, mirrors and re-presents the subject's initial transitional moment. It serves as a reminder that the arrival of the signifier is always accompanied by the urgent and irreducible demand: *I want to see*.

The urgency of such a demand is almost unbearable for the subject, necessitating its displacement from the position of a subject to that of an object—a dynamic Freud identifies in the childhood phantasy of being beaten. Like in a dream, the subject often finds itself thrown into a scene of its own phantasy, compelled to occupy the position of an object rather than proactively asserting itself as an agent or beholder. The film under discussion captures this moment of displacement with striking precision in the mock-documentary scene that follows the opening credits. Transitioning from the jittery voice-over of the unidentifiable *I* over a black screen, the film shifts to mock-documentary footage of the studio set during the filming of Kaufman and Jonze's previous work, *Being John Malkovich*. This scene introduces the protagonist in a highly unconventional manner, emphasizing the lack of agency that defines him and underlining the insignificance of his presence on screen—underscoring the disjunction between the speaking *I* and its visual representation as a displaced object.

After the medium close-ups—accompanied by subtitles identifying the authoritative figures on the set, from Malkovich to the first assistant director to the cinematographer—the camera lingers on Charlie Kaufman, who appears visibly overwhelmed and out of place. The moment the camera's gaze lands on him, a crew member shouts for him to get out of the frame, seemingly unaware that he is the *creator* of the very film they are shooting. This interaction encapsulates a deeper dynamic: despite his role as the *I*, Kaufman is reduced to an object by the camera's merciless gaze, which ejects him from the scene as something obstructive. Surprised and unsettled, the on-screen Charlie Kaufman finds himself positioned as an object, captured by the Other's gaze—a gaze whose commanding force is ironically generated by the subject's own demand, *I want to see*.

With this insightful cue, the film *Adaptation* repositions the writer Kaufman not as the originator or creator of cinematic phantasy but rather as an extraneous element in the mise-en-scène of any phantasy, or a blot in a snapshot, as Lacan might describe it. Lacan famously observed that writer's block vividly reveals the subject's psychic state of displacement, stating: "Ask someone with writer's block about the anxiety he experiences and he will tell you who the turd *is* in his fantasy."³⁷ This displacement is crucial for understanding the function of phantasy, which anchors the subject's relation to *the objet petit a*, as represented in Lacan's matheme: $ ◊ a. In this framework, phantasy bridges demand with the residual trace of the lost primal object, *the objet petit a*, thereby creating a pathway for desire. Desire seeks a substitute object, now signified, to fill the void left by the original loss. For phantasy to align with desire and propel the subject ($) forward in the trajectory of adaptation, the un-localized speaking *I*—the residual agent responsible for the creation of the initial scopic demand—must eventually be expelled, or "spit out." As Lacan suggests, this speaking *I* serves as a persistent reminder of the traumatic lack or impossibility embedded in the demand, *I want to see*. The neurotic symptoms that Kaufman experiences throughout the film—including impotence, inaction, and self-doubt—stem from this profound sense of displacement.

Hitherto, I have speculated as to how the invasion of the speaking *I* entails the constitution of the subject *on top of* the lack or gap. From that moment, this gap—behind the screen of the subject's phantasy—functions as an enigmatic central force of desire for the lost object which is a remainder following castration. In this context, the film's opening succeeds in re-enacting the emergence of the subject in relation to lack. Specifically, the opening illustrates, almost *in vitro,* how this lack is initiated and sustained: that is, the abrupt advance of the speaking *I* generates the demand *I want to see*, and the object of this urgent demand is none other than the *I* itself. A morsel of *I*—or "a pound of flesh," as Lacan expresses it—must be spit out and sacrificed to initiate the chain of objects "properly desired" by the subject of the unconscious. This split inscribed in the subject as a result of castration brings about the compulsory repetition because this object, which is lost as the price for the symbolic or linguistic orientation of a speaking subject, remains irreplaceable and cannot be fully substituted by any other.

Hence, repetition is neither a symptom nor an effect of the signifier but rather operates at the base of the constitution of the subject, whose unconscious is structured like language. Consequently, every object of desire is brought to function as a signifier tied to a lack or gap on the

---

37. Lacan, "The Subversion of the Subject and the Dialectic of Desire in the Freudian Unconscious," 693.

side of the subject, underscoring that every signifier is fated to fail. This failure fuels the cycle of repetition, each attempt seeking to hook what has already been lost. Therefore, adaptation is the journey in search of this lost origin of the *I*, mediated through phantasies that bind the subject to the inevitability of the compulsory repetition. By its very nature, this journey is a detour, forever returning the subject to the point at which the original loss is simultaneously marked and masked by the primal scene. Over the course of the narrative, the film's protagonist gradually confronts this truth of adaptation, revealed through the irresistible force of repetition that reaches its culmination at the film's conclusion. Crucially, it is the fake script written by Kaufman's twin brother—who himself is a repetition of the writer—that enables this encounter.

In a scene where Charlie Kaufman's twin brother, Donald—a novice scriptwriter—pitches his first script, *The Three*, to the established writer Charlie, the dynamic between the two becomes strikingly apparent. Charlie, the on-screen adapter struggling with writer's block, attempts to critique the implausibility of Donald's thriller. He challenges the premise that the three main characters in Donald's script are actually facets of a single individual suffering from a multi-personality disorder:

> **Charlie:** The other thing is, there's no way to write this. Did you consider that? I mean, how could you have somebody held prisoner in a basement and working in a police station at the same time?
> **Donald:** Trick photography?
> **Charlie:** Okay, that's not what I'm asking. Listen closely. What I'm asking is, in the reality of this movie, where there's only one character, right? Okay? How could you … What, what exactly would …

*(Charlie gives up)*

Charlie finds himself unable to fully articulate the flaw he perceives in his brother's circular, self-referential script, where a single character is refracted into every other. Yet, within the confines of this formulaic thriller, Charlie begins to recognize a reflection of his own reality. The task of adaptation has ensnared him in a repetitive, circular trajectory of phantasies—constructed around himself under the lingering spell of castration. Put differently, Charlie's script, in its deferred and repeated birth, becomes nothing more than a reflection of his solipsistic world—a closed loop in which every message sent out inevitably returns to himself. Each character in the narrative of Kaufman's *Adaptation* of *The Orchid Thief* serves as another image or signifier, reiterating the unrepresentable lack that the adapter persistently seeks to avoid. Now, Charlie Kaufman understands that his phantasy "always avoids—if only to find itself [this inextricable 'I'] again later in everything—the same thing."[38] In other words, insomuch as the agonizing writer's block returns Kaufman to the same place—that is, to the very beginning of writing—the film's narrative arc successfully simulates the fatality of repetition *in vitro*.

Moreover, repetition is not solely a source of painful obligation; it also contains a dimension of satisfaction, which Lacan terms "the satisfaction of repetition."[39] This concealed satisfaction fuels the work of phantasy, further fixating the subject within the relentless cyclical motion of adaptation. Eventually, Charlie Kaufman breaks free from his symptomatic attachment to writer's block and confronts the truth that his masturbatory phantasies have been concealing. With newfound fortitude, he declares, "I'm Ouroboros." This is a significant step toward the traversal of the fundamental phantasy, whose repetition exerts a centripetal power and binds the subject in a loop. The recognition of this repetitive pattern of phantasy eventually liberates the on-screen adapter Kaufman from the pathological pleasure that had tethered him to writer's block.

To grasp the role of repetition in the process of adapting the fundamental phantasy, it is essential to recognize that phantasy does not aim at attaining an object. Instead, its function lies in crafting the setting or mise-en-scène for desire. However, because human desire is inherently insatiable, the subject's relationship to phantasy is marked by ambivalence. On the one hand, the subject must believe in their active role in constructing these imaginative settings to sustain the illusion of fulfilling desire. This imaginary position, which grants the subject a sense of autonomy in relation to phantasy, serves as a defense against the unsettling truth that desire is fundamentally a passive mechanism, forever denied ultimate satisfaction. Paradoxically, however, the subject's imagined mastery within phantasy is continually undermined by the recurrence of the primal scene. Despite the subject's efforts to evolve and move forward, the gravity of this primal scene reasserts itself, exposing the persistent grip of repetition.

38. Lacan, *The Seminar of Jacques Lacan, Book XI*, 49.
39. Lacan, *Seminar XIV*, 73.

From the repetition that underpins every phantasy, staging the same unattainable desire, we can infer that the subject of desire is constrained by the task of adaptation. In this sense, adaptation is a retroactive, and at times even regressive, act. This stands in stark contrast to the common belief that views adaptation—whether biological, psychological, theoretical, or textual—as a forward-moving, creative effort to thrive in the world. This is not to suggest that adaptation constitutes a narcissistic regression. Rather, it should be understood as a desperate attempt to grasp the subject's lost origin, prior to the irrevocable division or castration. In this way, adaptation seeks to reaffirm the subject's position within the enigmatic and unfathomable reality into which it is born. This internal struggle predestined for a subject is epitomized by Charlie Kaufman's conflicting position as a creator and an adapter. The protagonist repeatedly circles around the fundamental gap embedded in his position as a subject. In Kaufman's case, this gap manifests as the tension between his role as a writer, who must take "a journey into the unknown," and his role as an adapter, who must "remain true" to someone else's creation—phrases borrowed from the on-screen Kaufman himself. However, I do not regard this as a pessimistic or deterministic view of the fate assigned to one's journey of adaptation. Instead, I suggest that the concept of adaptation should be approached with ambivalence, oscillating between pessimism and optimism, and held within a state of paradox, accounting for a hopeful possibility of traversing the innate and compulsory repetition by means of adaptation. I shall return to this point in this chapter's concluding section.

The essence of any work of adaptation emerges in the uncanny encounter where the subject confronts the lost *I* in a "de-subjectivized form" within their own creation of phantasy.[40] The film embodies this logic by demonstrating how the writer Kaufman confronts the on-screen Kaufman as a de-subjectivized form of *I*. This form, having erupted into existence only to be hastily expelled, persistently reappears within the realm of phantasy. Emerging from the subject's split and unstable condition, the only constant is satisfaction—or more precisely, the recollection of an original satisfaction that occupies a privileged position within the realm of the real. By its very nature, the real is the locus where distinctions such as active and passive, presence and absence, subject and object remain undifferentiated.

40. Laplanche and Pontalis, "Fantasy and the Origins of Sexuality," 27.

As such, the real serves as the locus that safeguards the reminiscence of an unscathed satisfaction. In this context, Lacan connects the theorization of the real to the concept of phantasy, emphasizing the pivotal role of repetition in this dynamic. He describes the relation between the real, phantasy, and repetition as follows: the real occupies a place "which stretches from the trauma to the phantasy—insofar as the phantasy is never anything more than the screen that conceals something quite primary, something determinant in the function of repetition."[41] To sum up, the trauma of lack or impossibility instills an insatiable yearning for satisfaction, a longing that phantasy sustains by propelling the subject into a search for what has been lost. The subject emerges in this attempt to recover the lost object, crafting phantasy after phantasy—or, put differently, adaptation after adaptation. This relentless drive to rediscover the lost lies at the core of the mechanism of repetition, which is intrinsic to every phantasy and adaptation. Consequently, the subject, situated at the intersection of reality and phantasy, becomes fixated on the axis of adaptation. This axis is not linear but instead resembles a Mobius strip—an endless surface without a clear interior or exterior, beginning or end.

In which mode, then, does repetition arrive in the realm of representation and in a text like *Adaptation*? Lacan remarks that the fundamental logic of the phantasy is expressed through "the insistence of the signifier."[42] The identification of this persistent signifier that resurfaces from within is the purpose of psychoanalysis because it will lead the subject to re-encounter—and hopefully traverse—the primal scene, which, as noted earlier, operates as the gravity at the center of phantasy's adaptive loop. In the case of the film *Adaptation*, one can identify a recurring signifier that sustains Kaufman's various phantasies throughout the narrative. Similarly, I propose that every screen adaptation, driven by the imperative to transition from text to media, is shaped by this signifier, whose unconscious operation the film reveals both figuratively and metaphorically on screen. The insistent signifier at play here, I suggest, is *writing*. At first glance, the film's narrative appears to consciously position the "orchid" as a central metaphor on screen. However, the orchid operates as a signified rather than a signifier. Around this signified "orchid," the desires and passions of Laroche, Orlean, and Kaufman intersect and overlap. Within this

41. Lacan, *Seminar XI*, 60.
42. Evans, *An Introductory Dictionary of Lacanian Psychoanalysis*, 164.

framework, writing emerges as the key signifier, charged with the task of capturing the elusive "ghost orchid." Writing, in turn, becomes the nexus connecting Laroche's verbal narration, Orlean's prose, and Kaufman's screenplay. By its very nature, the ghost orchid evokes the absence at the ultimate point of reference or meaning—a lack that both haunts and binds the signifier of *writing* to the endless circular chain of signifiers. Behind this movement of signifiers, shaped like Ouroboros, there lies no definitive meaning—only the persistent, insistent pulse of *writing*.

The film establishes writing as a recurring signifier, crucial for making sense of its seemingly chaotic narrative arc, which intertwines a variety of heterogeneous writings. The three main characters—Charlie Kaufman, Susan Orlean, and Donald Kaufman—are all writers driven by the shared imperative to complete their respective projects. Interspersed images of Charles Darwin writing *The Origin of Species* further reinforce the centrality of writing, which operates as both a thematic anchor and an insistent force within the film. These on-screen writers ultimately serve as avatars of the real writer, Charlie Kaufman, whose omnipresence is reflected through the multiplication of characters at writing tables. The recurring signifier of writing highlights the impossibility of a seamless link between the signifier and the signified, presenting writing instead as an urgent and inescapable command. For the film's protagonist, standing in for the writer Kaufman, this imperative becomes a source of trauma. His fixation on the act of writing drives him to repeatedly return to his writing seat, while he compulsively re-reads the original text in a desperate attempt to escape the suffocating demand of this signifier. Ultimately, it is under the pressure of this insistent mandate that Kaufman is compelled to confront the primal scene lurking behind his pathological symptoms, a confrontation that drives the narrative to its conclusion.

To emphasize the fundamental nature of this signifier, let us revisit the most basic premise of writing. Writing is, at its core, the discursive structure of signifiers that are presented to the subject. Lacan encapsulates the subject's entanglement with this structure in his dictum, "the unconscious is structured like language." Yet, writing also imposes a demand for creativity, as the subject seeks pleasure in producing something new. The locus of adaptation, where the film's protagonist remains stuck, both epitomizes and amplifies the inherent incompatibility embedded within the formidable signifier of writing. This tension underscores the dual nature of writing: as both an imposed structure and a creative imperative. As an adapter, Kaufman feels the heavy obligation to "remain true to someone else's writing," as the original text symbolizes that which is already written—or, in Lacan's terms, what is inscribed and given to the subject as the unconscious. Yet, through the force of writing, the subject becomes bound to the metonymic *progression* of signifiers, driven by a desire for the relentless pursuit of the new and the unknown. Caught between these two opposing imperatives embedded in the signifier of writing, Charlie Kaufman finds no escape. Instead, he descends into a rabbit hole where everything seems to return to the same place—embodied, for him, by the intimidating blank page that stares back from the typewriter.

However, the repetition, which is manifested through the insistence of the signifier *writing*, is not only an inescapable curse for the subject. By the paradoxical logic of phantasy, which resembles the Mobius strip, repetition coincides with subversive resistance to it. These two seemingly contradictory forces, Lacan expounds, "share the same DNA"—that is, it is repetition that requires a variation. As Lacan teaches us in his seminar *Four Fundamental Concepts of Psychoanalysis*:

> Repetition demands the new. It is turned toward the ludic, which finds its dimension in this new ... Whatever, in repetition, is varied, modulated is merely alienation of its meaning. The adult, and even the more advanced child, demands something new in his activities, in his games. But this "sliding-away" (*glissement*) conceals what is the true secret of the ludic, namely, the most radical diversity constituted by repetition in itself.[43]

Lacan observes that the playfulness inherent in phantasy-work enables the traumatic inevitability of repetition to be redirected into the pleasure of variation and adaptation. He explains: "[t]his variation makes one forget the aim of the significance [that is, the significance of returning to the same place] by transforming its act into a game, and giving it certain outlets that go some way to satisfying the pleasure principle."[44] From this, it is possible to conclude that the tantalizing effect of the pleasure principle seduces the subject into believing in the "forward" movement of the wishful and playful phantasy of creation. Employing its full power, phantasy works to obscure the void at the heart of

43. Lacan, *Seminar XI*, 61.
44. Ibid., 62.

repetition by saturating it with a multitude of images. In this light, the film *Adaptation* appears to explore the primordial nature of adaptation as a profound process that balances repetition and diversity, navigating the tension between trauma and pleasure. Most notably, the insistent signifier of *writing* unveils the truth of the subject as the embodiment of repetition oscillating between creation and adaptation. In confronting the task of adaptation, the subject emerges as nothing more than an amalgamation of repetition and variation, *in vitro*.

## *The Traversal of the Phantasy*

Through its exploration of the struggles inherent to the signifier of *writing* within the realm of screen adaptation, *Adaptation* presents an allegory of the adaptation process itself—a space where the adapter is compelled to write the unwritable. According to Lacan's idiosyncratic logic, this signifier is repeated because it is attached to the first *Bedeutung* (meaning or referent), which signifies nothing but lack and, hence, cannot be written. He articulates this in a dense but telling passage: the first meaning is "sufficiently indicated to us by the stimulus that logic received, by submitting itself to the simple operation of writing," yet it "still fails to remember that this only reposes on the function of a lack, in the very thing that is written."[45] This is to suggest that the act of writing conceals the fact that it is grounded in absence—a structural void that underlies the function of signification. In other words, Lacan suggests that the act of writing itself rests on a foundational absence or lack, which underscores its operation as a symbolic system. This lack is not an imperfection but a structural feature, emphasizing the impossibility of fully capturing meaning in the written form.

We might ask, then, what does writing mean to Kaufman? What does it signify to a screen adapter who transforms someone's writing into his own, only to ultimately remove what is written—both the original text and his own script—from the locus of writing? There is no palpable answer, as *writing* in this context is not a mere signifier that can be referred back to another signifier. Writing here is "the Signifier" or master signifier, which propels the forward movement of the signifying chain as such by positioning itself as both the origin and the terminal point on the chain. For a film adapter, the signifier *writing* stands in for

---

45. Lacan, *Seminar XIV*, 31.

the fundamental and irreducible phantasy in which his or her raison d'être starts and ends.

This, however, need not be the final destination, as the work of adaptation is never truly complete. Notably, Lacan suggests that the aim of psychoanalytic treatment is to guide the analysand—much like the film's protagonist at the impasse of his phantasy evoked by Susan Orlean's story—to restart and rewrite a new path to the fundamental phantasy. Psychoanalysis seeks to assist the subject in traversing the fundamental phantasy, which has been adapted into and manifests as pathological symptoms.[46] Before drawing a parallel between adaptation as an act of self-transformation and the traversal of the fundamental phantasy, it is helpful to recapitulate the conceptual journey from the original phantasy to the fundamental phantasy of the real. Thus far, this chapter's close reading of the film and its protagonist has highlighted how the command of the signifier *writing* provokes a search for the primal scene or the original phantasy, which the subject associates with the origin of their being, in Freudian terms. Shifting toward a Lacanian perspective, Lacan acknowledges the existence of a fundamental phantasy that marks the endpoint of the subject's search for origin. Generally, this terminal point resides in the realm of the real. However, it can be glimpsed through the repetition of a particular signifier at the moment "when the mask which is that of the phantasy vacillates."[47]

This moment of vacillation contains the potential for traversing the fundamental phantasy despite its fatal inaccessibility. The film *Adaptation* concludes on a positive note, presenting an exit from the excruciating writer's block that dominates much of the narrative. For the film's writer and protagonist, the task of adaptation helps him to realize that his existing relationship to the masterful signifier *writing* is fraught with pain and offers little in the way of genuine pleasure. In particular, his (fictional) twin brother's effortless and playful approach to writing effectively provides a measure of how excessively consuming, unpleasant, and unsatisfactory it is to Charlie Kaufman. Toward the end of the film, Kaufman can no longer deny his writer's block and he decides to ask Donald to help him with the writing project. Psychoanalytically, Kaufman's decision signifies the end of his impotence and marks the beginning of a transformative shift in his relationship to writing. In essence, Kaufman comes to realize that his writer's block was, in fact,

46. Lacan, *Seminar XI*, 273.
47. Lacan, *Seminar XIV*, 7.

his own resistance to translating and adapting Orlean's writing—work that seemed to embark on a sacred journey into the unknown—into a Hollywood film, despite being explicitly commissioned to create one.

With Kaufman's decision to embrace the necessary shift in his approach to the task of adaptation, the film's narrative accelerates toward its climactic revelation, where the primal scene reveals its most prosaic face to the camera. In Lacan's terms, the mask concealing the fundamental phantasy begins to waver, revealing a newfound transparency. Through this, Kaufman reinterprets—or reduces—Orlean's original text as a replaceable signifier, one that mediates her sexual desire and solipsistic phantasy onto the page. By adapting the primal scene into a new, reductive yet liberating depiction of the drug-induced coitus between Orlean and Laroche, *Adaptation* dismantles the unrepresentable Orlean at the heart of Kaufman's writer's block, exposing her instead as "a lonely, old, desperate, pathetic drug addict." Once seen as the Lady embodying the fundamental signifier *writing*, Orlean had symbolized an unattainable ideal, paralyzing Kaufman with the anxiety-provoking question "*Che vuoi*?" (What do you want?). This final resolution, crafted by the adapter Kaufman, allows the on-screen Kaufman to confront and demystify the root of his creative and existential blockage, ultimately liberating him from its hold. In a low-angle shot, Charlie Kaufman looks down on the on-screen author Orlean, who sits sobbing like a child beside Laroche's corpse. This belittling camera angle underscores the culmination of Kaufman's agonizingly trapped process of adaptation and marks the adapter's traversal of the fundamental phantasy that had fixated his imagination on the unknowability of the original meaning.

Just before this moment of punctuation, the shift in perspective—marking the traversal—is explicitly verbalized in a seemingly banal exchange between the twin brothers, where Donald offers advice to Charlie. Hiding from the murderous Orlean and Laroche, who wish to conceal their affair and drug addiction by killing the two witnesses, the twin brothers find a nook behind a huge log in the swamp. In the pitch darkness, the Kaufman brothers, for the first time in the movie, begin conversing on friendly terms and recall their high school days. Donald recalls having been madly in love with a classmate, and Charlie is surprised to learn that his brother already knew that the girl despised him. To Charlie, Donald confesses: "I loved Sarah, Charles. It was mine, that love. I owned it. Even Sarah didn't have the right to take it away. I can love whoever I want … You are what you love, not what loves you." In this seemingly simplistic piece of advice—one that Charlie might openly disdain—Donald exemplifies the subject's capacity to assume the position of the cause of his desire. This new perspective provides Charlie with a pathway out of his writer's block, as it allows his relationship to writing to be rewritten, freeing him from the spell of "Che vuoi?" Both on and off the screen, Kaufman regains agency in his relationship to the suffocating command of the master signifier *writing*. Bruce Fink explains this new configuration of the subject's fundamental phantasy as the traversal of the phantasy in his 1995 book *The Lacanian Subject: Between Language and Jouissance*:

> The traversing of fantasy involves the subject's assumption of a new position with respect to the Other as language and the Other as desire. A move is made to invest or inhabit that which brought him or her into existence as split subject, to become that which caused him or her. There where it—the Other's discourse, ridden with the Other's desire—was, the subject is able to say "I". Not "It happened to me," or "They did this to me," or "Fate had it in store for me," but "I was," "I did," "I saw," "I cried out."[48]

Elsewhere, Fink highlights the role of psychoanalysis in the subject's encounter with and traversal of the fundamental phantasy, emphasizing that "It should be noted that the fundamental fantasy is not so much something that exists per se prior to analysis, as something constructed and reconstructed in the course of analysis."[49] In other words, the fundamental phantasy is not a static or preexisting entity but something that emerges dynamically during the analytical process. This insight introduces a crucial parallel with the task of adaptation. Much like psychoanalytic treatment—which a patient in pain often undertakes reluctantly—the task of adaptation provides a structured space for the screen adapter to confront and rework their fundamental phantasy. In psychoanalysis, this process involves addressing deeply rooted unconscious structures that shape the subject's desires and sense of self. Similarly, for the screen adapter, the process of adaptation enables a reevaluation of their relationship to the formidable master signifier *writing*. By making this powerful signifier tangible and, thus, subjecting

---

48. Fink, *The Lacanian Subject*, 62.
49. Bruce Fink, *A Clinical Introduction to Lacanian Psychoanalysis: Theory and Technique* (Cambridge, MA: Harvard University Press, 1999), 70.

it to transformation, adaptation becomes more than a technical exercise; it becomes an existential process of self-confrontation and creative liberation.

Adaptation, therefore, inherently involves a profound act of self-adaptation. It highlights the deeply personal nature of the process for the subject, while simultaneously emphasizing its universal inevitability and significance. The film *Adaptation* serves as an allegory for this journey, laying bare the intimidating gap—or abyss—that the subject must leap across to achieve true "adaptation" in every sense of the word. This gap represents not only the distance between an original text and its adaptation but also the psychic effort required to reimagine the original phantasy. In Lacanian terms, this reimagination involves a "renewing repetition" of the phantasy, allowing it to be reborn in the present moment. Ultimately, the film affirms that the subject exists only as that which a signifier or text represents to another signifier. This means that every subject, acting as an adapter, must confront and traverse their own fundamental phantasy to engage fully with the creative and transformative demands of adaptation. Only by doing so can the subject transcend their impasse and unlock the potential for new meaning and expression. The film's coda, in this light, aptly depicts Kaufman—having completed the task of adaptation on his own after Donald's death—confessing his love for Amelia and driving out of a shadowy parking lot into the sunlit streets of Los Angeles.

# CONCLUSION: ADAPTATION, THE METAPHOR FOR SUBJECTIVITY

This book has sought to explore how adaptation operates at the very seat of the unconscious. Each chapter has traced the trajectories of philosophers, theorists, writers, and filmmakers as they navigate a deconstructive yet creative dimension of adaptation, one in which the separation of text from subjectivity becomes untenable. In other words, the discussion has aimed to illuminate adaptation as a process that organizes connections between texts while simultaneously responding to the ontological demands of the human subject in its inherently transitional and adaptive mode of being. The exemplary films analyzed throughout the book were approached as case studies of how adaptation communicates, at the textual level, the primordial and universal unconscious functions of a speaking subject in its relation to reality. This "reality," referred to as the unconscious, emerges as the primal text to be read—a matrix written in letters governed by the symbolic and materialized through the images of the imaginary. Screen adaptation proves fascinating precisely because it enacts this essence of the human psyche, re-presenting or adapting the unconscious "reality" of the subject—split between the symbolic and the imaginary—onto the screen of consciousness. Ultimately, reality itself can be understood as the product of an unceasing process of adaptation, one that continually reconfigures the subject's relation to the symbolic and imaginary orders. In turn, adaptation, understood as a function, underpins the uniquely human conception of reality, serving as the site of perpetual negotiation between text and the subject of the unconscious. Screen adaptation, then, becomes not merely an aesthetic or technical exercise but a profound engagement with the very mechanisms that sustain and structure human reality itself.

In the Introduction, I identified adaptation as a cultural symptom, evidenced by the ubiquity and persistence of screen adaptations in contemporary times. In the following chapter, I introduced the concept of the *real* of a text—conceived here as the effect of the discourse of the unconscious—as that which disrupts, subverts, and protrudes beyond the normative logic of screen adaptation. This real offers a counterpoint to the conventional understanding of adaptation as a commercially and aesthetically calculated media practice. Instead, it signals a radical, underlying dimension of adaptation that resists containment within such frameworks. By placing the real of a text at the center of this book's interrogation, I aim to offer a renewed perspective on adaptation—one that allows my psychoanalytic study of screen adaptation to transgress textual boundaries, dissolving the binary distinctions between literary originals and their cinematic adaptations.

From a psychoanalytic perspective, the four case studies examined each screen adaptation as a symptomatic representation of the *real* of a text, drawing on Freudian and Lacanian concepts such as the Oedipus complex, anxiety, *das Ding*, and phantasy. The *real* of a text, in this context, may manifest as that which is perceived as lost in adaptation: the Father's ghost, whose commanding words dominate the screen; the Mother's devouring omnipresence, evoking profound anxiety in cinematic sons; the monstrous maze of *das Ding*, where the subject encounters its own death drive beyond the desire for adaptation; or the fundamental phantasy, which must be confronted and traversed in the process of adaptation. Each case study illuminated how these psychoanalytic constructs operate within the dynamic interplay between the original text and its screen adaptation, offering a deeper understanding of adaptation as an encounter with the unconscious. While both letter and image are inherently limited in their ability to fully capture the *real* of a text, the subject's access to it appears bound by two axes of representation: metonymy and metaphor. On the one hand, a metonymic shift from one text to another reflects the subject's attempt to evade the confrontation with the *real* of a text, experienced as a fundamental lack in meaning. On the other hand, a metaphoric substitution seeks to create meaning by replacing an anterior text—perceived as a placeholder of meaning—with a new one. The process of adaptation unfolds as the subject oscillates between these two representational axes, navigating the interplay between metonymy and metaphor on both textual and psychic levels. In this light, I wish to conclude this book—whose purpose has been to frame adaptation as both a symptom and a task of the subject of the unconscious—by reflecting on adaptation through the lens of the Lacanian concept of *metaphor*.

In Lacan's terms, metaphor and metonymy represent "the two fundamental facets of the play of the unconscious."[1] Drawing on the linguistic concepts developed by Roman Jakobson, Lacan elaborates these terms to describe the adaptive modes through which the unconscious expresses itself. According to Lacan, metonymy describes the path of desire, which is always "the desire for something else."[2] However, it refers not only to a chain of objects that are wished for one after the other but also, and more importantly, to a chain of signifiers that are waiting for "meaning" to come and retrospectively to make sense of their signification. Therefore, metonymy is ultimately a search for meaning, the attainment of which is perpetually deferred. If we recall that the subject is that which a signifier represents for another signifier, then this endless deferral is unbearable to a speaking subject, whose being—or more precisely becoming—is placed on the eternal slippage from one signifier to another and is thus permanently kept in suspense. The metonymic deferral, as such, is threatening and itself becomes the cause of the subject's subscription to the task of adaptation—if we regard adaptation here as the passing of unfathomable meaning from one signifier or text into another. The interplay between the pleasure principle and the death drive is concealed in the desperate act of adaptation: that is, the subject is continuously sliding through the chain of signifiers, aiming for the signified or meaning that might conclude this journey. In other words, the intention of metonymic structure is to convey "the same signified" without the ability to forge a new meaning, while also precluding the subject from writing their "proper name" or contributing their own meaning to the infinite metonymic chain of the symbolic. Bruce Fink describes this tautology of metonymy as telling "the same story" in different words and, if his account is applied to our discussion of adaptation from literature to films, metonymy is comparable to the industrious production of numerous "faithful" film versions of a literary work.[3]

1. Jacques Lacan, "Appendix II: Metaphor of the Subject," in *Écrits: The First Complete Edition in English*, trans. Bruce Fink (New York and London: W. W. Norton & Company), 755.

2. Jacques Lacan, "The Instance of the Letter in the Unconscious or Reason since Freud," in *Écrits: The First Complete Edition in English*, trans. Bruce Fink (New York and London: W. W. Norton & Company, 2006), 412–41.

3. Bruce Fink, *Lacan to the Letter: Reading Écrits Closely* (Minnesota and London: University of Minnesota Press, 2004), 99.

By contrast, *metaphor* highlights the constitutive and creative moment of signification, where the meaning is *created*—not sought after—through a rupture in the metonymic chain of signifiers. This process is illustrated by the algorithm Lacan presented in his 1957 lecture "The Instance of the Letter in the Unconscious."[4]

$$f\left(\frac{S'}{S}\right)S \cong S(+)s$$

This matheme, representing the structure of metaphor, points at the substitution of one signifier ($S$) with another ($S'$). Clearly, this vertical substitution is fundamentally different from the metonymic referral, where a signifier ($S$) is deferred to a signified ($s$), maintaining the bar (—) in the horizontal signifying chain, as expressed in Lacan's matheme for metonymy.[5]

$$f(S...S') \cong S(-)s$$

In the metaphoric structure, "the substitution of signifier for signifier" generates "a signification effect," Lacan describes, that "is poetic or creative, in other words, that brings the signification in question into existence" rather than merely passing it along the chain.[6] Unlike the horizontal relations of metonymy, where meaning is endlessly deferred, metaphor introduces a vertical, penetrative process that crosses the bar between the signifier and the signified. This crossing constitutes a break with the metonymic sequence, producing a moment of signification that is generative and transformative.

Nevertheless, the former ($S$) does not dissolve but instead remains present as indicated by its position before the symbol "≅", suggesting an asymptotic equivalence between the two sides. Lacan elaborates that "the + sign in () manifests here the crossing of the bar,—, and the constitutive value of this crossing for the emergence of signification."[7] Simultaneously, the plus sign also indicates an *additional* layer of meaning, one that is superimposed upon the preexisting relationship between the original signifier ($S$) and its signified ($s$), itself understood

---

4. Ibid., 429.
5. Ibid., 428.
6. Ibid., 429.
7. Ibid.

as the effect of that original signifier. Through a poetic and creative break, the metaphoric signifier ($S'$ in the matheme for the metaphoric structure) replaces the original signifier ($S$) precisely at the point where its position as a signifier, along with its assumed connection to the target signified ($s$), collapses. This occurs "at the precise moment at which meaning is produced in nonmeaning."[8] In this act of substitution, the metaphorical replacement not only introduces a new layer of meaning but also opens up a new trajectory or "rail" for subsequent metonymic signification. Lacan elucidates this transformative process as follows:

> Metaphor's creative spark does not spring forth from the juxtaposition of … two equally actualized signifiers. It flashes between two signifiers, one of which has replaced the other by taking the other's place in the signifying chain, the occulted signifier remaining present by virtue of its (metonymic) connection to the rest of the chain.[9]

It is essential to recall that Lacan never considers the signified to be an anchor of reference. His understanding of the role of the signified diverges fundamentally from conventional notions of "meaning." For Lacan, the signified, positioned under the bar separating it from the signifier, represents the repressed meaning of the signifier. In this framework, the signified ($s$) is not a fixed point but rather an effect of the signifier ($S$), perpetually assuming a meaning that must be pursued. Likewise, the original text to be adapted exists as one signifier among many in the infinite chain of metonymy. The so-called authentic truth of the original often appears as an elusive mirage, presumed by the adapter in awe of the infinitude of "antecedent arts." Adaptation, in this context, places the adapter at a critical juncture: between a metonymic adherence to the order of the Other, as evoked by the allure of the original text, and a metaphoric leap into the *real* of a text—a realm where neither hidden meaning nor meaning itself can be found. This leap marks the moment where the adapter, through the function of metaphor, breaks free from the chain of signifiers and substitutes one signifier for another, only to see it transform into a signified—or what Lacan refers to as "the occulted signifier."

---

8. Lacan, "The Instance of the Letter in the Unconscious or Reason since Freud," in *Écrits*, 423.

9. Ibid., 422.

For the adapter, substitution is not merely a process of displacement but a radical act of transformation that involves both annihilation and rebirth. Through this metaphorical substitution, the adapter replaces the original text with its cinematic counterpart, demonstrating that their distinction lies not in their inherent nature but in the positions that they occupy within the adaptive process. This act of substitution allows the adapter to confront and transcend the limits of metonymy, where meaning is endlessly deferred. Metaphor becomes essential to the adapter's task, as it sustains the progression of adaptation by introducing moments of creative rupture that generate new meaning. Without these metaphorical substitutions, the adaptive process would become paralyzed, leaving the adapter trapped in an infinite pursuit of resolution. This dynamic reflects the adapter's struggle to mediate between the allure of the original text and the demand to produce something new. Stanley Kubrick's *The Shining* offers an extreme depiction of this frustration: Jack Torrance's futile attempts to escape the maze mirror the adapter's potential entrapment in the endless deferral of metonymy. Unlike Jack, however, Kaufman in *Adaptation* exemplifies the adapter who, by rewriting the primal scene and embracing the creative rupture of metaphor, transforms his relationship with the original text and finds a path forward through his creative impasse.

Thus far, I have examined the two axes of adaptation: metonymy, representing the horizontal trajectory of the desire for adaptation, and metaphor, which signifies a deconstructive and creative moment of substitution. I wish to conclude this discussion by expanding it into a more metaphysical reflection on adaptation as a metaphor for the subject as "a being in the process of becoming."[10] For me, the Lacanian concept of metaphor provides a profound lens through which to understand the fundamentality of adaptation, as it unveils the ontology of the human subject. Lacan's framework challenges the notion of man as either an agent of free will or a fixed, immutable object of philosophical inquiry. Instead, it reveals man as a fluid being, engaged in a perpetual process of adaptation. Lacan underscores the centrality of metaphor in comprehending how the subject navigates reality as text, asserting that "the most serious reality, and even the sole serious reality for man, if

---

10. Jacques Lacan, *The Seminar of Jacques Lacan: Book II The Ego in Freud's Theory and in the Technique of Psychoanalysis 1954–1955*, ed. Jacques-Alain Miller and trans. Sylvana Tomaselli (New York and London: W. W. Norton & Company, 1991), 105.

one considers its role in sustaining the metonymy of his desire, can only be retained in metaphor."[11]

If so, it is possible to draw a comparison between the signifier in metaphor and the subject in its indefinite, adaptive mode of being. From the moment the subject emerges as a speaking being, it is inserted into a reality organized as a metonymic chain of signifiers. From that point onward, the subject is cast into the world—an encompassing textual structure—not as an agent but as an object of adaptation. It is crucial to remember that while the metaphoric leap—where the subject transitions from recognizing itself as an object of adaptation to acting as an adapter, an agent of metaphoric transformation—can be profoundly creative, this confrontation with the *real* as such often elicits a depth of anxiety comparable to the experience of death.

Adaptation is no simple task. Transforming a written text into a film, transposing the narrative and characters of the original source while preserving the "meaning"—unrealizable and ultimately unattainable—behind letter and image, demands that the subject confront its ontology as a de-centered object, neither agent nor bearer of meaning. This confrontation cannot be avoided; it is an irresistible necessity rooted in the *real* of a speaking being, compelling the subject to repeatedly return to the position of adapter. In this sense, adaptation becomes a survival function of subjectivity, without which there is no possibility of moving forward or finding a place for the self. To adapt is to take the profound risk of inscribing oneself into both the original text one adapts and the adaptation one creates. This is the risk that Charlie Kaufman takes in Spike Jonze's *Adaptation*, where the adapter's work becomes inseparable from his subjectivity. This risk also carries the possibility that adaptation might act as a furnace, melting the subject and text together into something entirely new. And yet, if one is fortunate, this process allows the subject to emerge once more as an agent—not in a static role but in one that demands the pursuit of new meaning, perpetually reshaping both text and self.

11. Lacan, "Appendix II," 758.

# BIBLIOGRAPHY

Allen, Richard. "Daphne du Maurier and Alfred Hitchcock." In *A Companion to Literature and Film*, edited by Robert Stam and Alessandra Raengo, 298–325. New York: Blackwell, 2004.

Auberbach, Nina. *Daphne du Maurier: Haunted Heiress*. Philadelphia: University of Pennsylvania Press, 2000.

Bellanca, Mary Ellen. "The Monstrosity of Predation in Daphne du Maurier's 'The Birds.'" *Interdisciplinary Studies in Literature and Environment* 18, no. 1 (Winter 2011): 26–46.

Benjamin, Walter. "The Task of the Translator," translated by Harry Zohn. In *Theories of Translation: An Anthology of Essays from Dryden to Derrida*, edited by Rainer Schulte and John Biguenet, 71–82. Chicago, IL, and London: The University of Chicago Press, 1992.

Benjamin, Walter. "The Task of the Translator," translated by Harry Zohn. In *Walter Benjamin: Selected Writings Volume 1*, edited by Marcus Bullock and Michael W. Jennings, 253–63. Cambridge, MA, and London: Harvard University Press, 1996.

Bingham, Dennis. "The Displaced Auteur: A Reception History of *The Shining*." In *Perspectives on Stanley Kubrick*, edited by Mario Falsetto, 284–306. New York: G. K. Hall, 1996.

Bloom, Harold. *The Anxiety of Influence: A Theory of Poetry*. Oxford: Oxford University Press, 1973.

Bloom, Harold. "Introduction." In *Modern Critical Interpretations: William Shakespeare's Hamlet*, edited by Harold Bloom, 1–10. New York, New Haven, CT, and Philadelphia, PA: Chelsea House Publishers, 1986.

Bloom, Harold. *Shakespeare: The Invention of the Human*. New York: Riverhead Books, 1998.

Bluestone, George. *Novels into Film*. Baltimore, MD: Jons Hopkins Press, 1957.

Boyle, Kirk. "Reading the Dialectical Ontology of *The Life Aquatic with Steve Zissou* against the Ontological Monism of *Adaptation*." *Film-Philosophy* 11, no. 1 (2007): 1–32.

Bradley, A.C. *Shakespearean Tragedy: Lectures on Hamlet, Othello, King Lear, Macbeth*. New York: Palgrave Macmillan, 2007.

Branagh, Kenneth. *Hamlet by William Shakespeare: Screenplay, Introduction and Film Diary*. London: Chatto & Windus, 1996.

Brode, Douglas. *Shakespeare in the Movies: From the Silent Era to Today*. New York: Berkeley Boulevard Books, 2001.

Browning, Mark. *Stephen King on the Big Screen*. Bristol: Intellect Books, 2009.

Bruns, John. "'The Proper Geography': Hitchcock's Adaptation of Daphne due Maurier's 'The Birds.'" *Clues* 31, no. 1 (Spring 2013): 57–66.

Burke, Ken. "Novel to Film, Frame to Windows: The Case of Lolita as Text and Image." *Pacific Coast Philology* 38, no. 1 (2003): 60–74.

Carroll, Rachel. "Introduction: Textual Infidelities." In *Adaptation in Contemporary Culture: Textual Infidelities*, edited by Rachel Carroll, 1–10. New York and London: Continuum, 2009.

Cartmell, Deborah. "The Shakespeare on Screen Industry." In *Adaptations: From Text to Screen, Screen to Text*, edited by Deborah Cartmell and Imelda Whelehan, 29–37. London and New York: Routledge, 1999.

Cartmell, Deborah. "Franco Zeffirelli and Shakespeare." In *The Cambridge Companion to Shakespeare on Film*, edited by Russell Jackson, 216–25. Cambridge: Cambridge University Press, 2000.

Cartmell, Deborah, and Imelda Whelehan. *Screen Adaptation: Impure Cinema*. New York: Palgrave Macmillan, 2010.

Cartmell, Deborah, Timothy Corrigan, and Imelda Whelehan. "Introduction to Adaptation." *Adaptation* 1, no. 1 (2008): 1–4.

Chiesa, Lorenzo. *Subjectivity and Otherness: A Philosophical Reading of Lacan*. Cambridge, MA: MIT Press, 2007.

Cohen, Keith. *Film and Fiction: The Dynamics of Exchange*. New Haven, CT, and London: Yale University Press, 1979.

Copjec, Joan. "Vampires, Breast-Feeding, and Anxiety." *Rendering the Real* 58 (Autumn 1991): 24–43.

Corrigan, Timothy. "Literature on Screen, a History: In the Gap." In *The Cambridge Companion to Literature on Screen*, edited by Deborah Cartmell and Imelda Whelehan, 29–44. Cambridge: Cambridge University Press, 2007.

Crowl, Samuel. "Flamboyant Realist: Kenneth Branagh." In *The Cambridge Companion to Shakespeare on Film*, edited by Russell Jackson, 226–42. Cambridge: Cambridge University Press, 2000.

Crowl, Samuel. *Shakespeare and Film: A Norton Guide*. New York and London: W. W. Norton & Company, 2008.

Darwin, Charles. *The Origin of Species: By Means of Natural Selection or the Preservation of Favoured Races in the Struggle for Life*. London: Penguin Books, 1985.

Davis, Colin. *Haunted Subject: Deconstruction, Psychoanalysis and the Return of the Dead*. New York: Palgrave Macmillan, 2007.

De Chumaceiro, Cora L. Diaz. "Hamlet in Freud's Thoughts: Reinterpretations in the Psychoanalytic Literature." *Journal of Poetry Therapy* 11, no. 3 (1998): 139–53.

De Man, Paul. "Review of *The Anxiety of Influence* by Harold Bloom." *Comparative Literature* 26, no. 3 (Summer 1974): 269–75.

De Man, Paul. "Conclusion: Walter Benjamin's 'The Task of the Translator.'" In *The Resistance to Theory*, 73–105. Minneapolis: University of Minnesota Press, 1986.

Derrida, Jacques. "Des Tours de Babel." In *Difference in Translation*, edited and translated by Joseph F. Graham, 165–207. Ithaca, NY, and London: Cornell University Press, 1985.

Derrida, Jacques. *The Ear of the Other: Otobiography, Transference, Translation: Texts and Discussions with Jacques Derrida*, edited by Christie V. McDonald and translated by Peggy Kamuf. Lincoln: University of Nebraska Press, 1985.

Donaldson, Peter. "Olivier, Hamlet, and Freud." *Cinema Journal* 26, no. 4 (Summer 1987): 22–48.

Donaldson-McHugh, Shannon, and Don Moore. "Spectres of Psycho: Freud, Fear, and Film Adaptation." In *From Camera Lens to Critical Lens: A Collection of Best Essays on Film Adaptation*, edited by Rebecca Housel, 98–109. Newcastle: Cambridge Scholars Press, 2006.

du Maurier, Daphne. "The Birds." In *Echoes from the Macabre: Selected Stories*, 275–311. Larchmont and New York: Queens House, 1952.

du Maurier, Daphne. *Rebecca* [1938]. New York: Harper, 2006.

Eco, Umberto. "Languages in Paradise." In *Serendipities: Language & Lunacy*, translated by William Weaver, 23–52. London: Weidenfeld & Nicolson, 1999.

Edwards, Kyle Dawson. "Brand-Name Literature: Film Adaptation and Selznick International Pictures Rebecca (1940)." *Cinema Journal* 45, no. 3 (Spring 2006): 32–58.

Elliott, Kamilla. "Novels, Films, and the Word/Image Wars." In *A Companion to Literature and Film*, edited by Robert Stam and Alessandra Raengo, 1–22. Malden, MA: Blackwell, 2004.

Elliott, Kamilla. "Adaptation Theory and Adaptation Scholarship." In *The Oxford Handbook of Adaptation Studies*, edited by Thomas Leitch, 680–98. Oxford: Oxford University Press, 2017.

Evans, Dylan. *An Introductory Dictionary of Lacanian Psychoanalysis*. London and New York: Routledge, 1996.

Fink, Bruce. *The Lacanian Subject: Between Language and Jouissance*. Princeton, NJ: Princeton University Press, 1995.

Fink, Bruce. "The Real Cause of Repetition." In *Reading Seminar XI: Lacan's Four Fundamental Concepts of Psychoanalysis*, edited by Richard Feldstein, Bruce Fink and Maire Jaanus, 223–32. Albany, NY: State University of New York Press, 1995.

Fink, Bruce. *A Clinical Introduction to Lacanian Psychoanalysis: Theory and Technique*. Cambridge, MA: Harvard University Press, 1999.

Fink, Bruce. *Lacan to the Letter: Reading Écrits Closely*. Minnesota and London: University of Minnesota Press, 2004.

Freud, Sigmund. *The Standard Edition of the Complete Psychological Works of Sigmund Freud: Volume I*. Translated by James Strachey. London: The Hogarth Press and the Institute of Psycho-Analysis, 1950.

Freud, Sigmund. *The Interpretation of Dreams* [1900]. Translated by James Strachey. London: George Allen & Unwin, 1953.

Freud, Sigmund. *The Origins of Psycho-Analysis: Letters to Wilhelm Fliess, Drafts, and Notes, 1887–1902*, edited by Marie Bonaparte, Anna Freud,

Ernst Kris and translated by Eric Mosbacher and James Strachey. London: Imago, 1954.
Freud, Sigmund. *The Standard Edition of the Complete Psychological Works of Sigmund Freud: Volume V*. Translated by James Strachey. London: The Hogarth Press and the Institute of Psycho-Analysis, 1955.
Freud, Sigmund. *The Standard Edition of the Complete Psychological Works of Sigmund Freud, Volume XIII*. Translated by James Strachey. London: The Hogarth Press and the Institute of Psycho-Analysis, 1955.
Freud, Sigmund. *The Standard Edition of the Complete Psychological Works of Sigmund Freud: Volume XVII*. Translated by James Strachey. London: The Hogarth Press and the Institute of Psycho-Analysis, 1955.
Freud, Sigmund. *The Standard Edition of the Complete Psychological Works of Sigmund Freud, Volume XVIII*. Translated by James Strachey. London: The Hogarth Press and the Institute of Psycho-Analysis, 1955.
Freud, Sigmund. *The Standard Edition of the Complete Psychological Works of Sigmund Freud, Volume XI*. Translated by James Strachey. London: The Hogarth Press and the Institute of Psycho-Analysis, 1957.
Freud, Sigmund. *The Standard Edition of the Complete Psychological Works of Sigmund Freud: Volume XIV*. Translated by James Strachey. London: The Hogarth Press and the Institute of Psycho-Analysis, 1957.
Freud, Sigmund. *The Standard Edition of the Complete Psychological Works of Sigmund Freud, Volume XIX*. Translated by James Strachey. London: The Hogarth Press and the Institute of Psycho-Analysis, 1961.
Freud, Sigmund. *The Standard Edition of the Complete Psychological Works of Sigmund Freud, Volume XX*. Translated by James Strachey. London: The Hogarth Press and the Institute of Psycho-Analysis, 1961.
Freud, Sigmund. *The Standard Edition of the Complete Psychological Works of Sigmund Freud, Volume XXI*. Translated by James Strachey. London: The Hogarth Press and the Institute of Psycho-Analysis, 1961.
Freud, Sigmund. *The Standard Edition of the Complete Psychological Works of Sigmund Freud: Volume XV*. Translated by James Strachey. London: The Hogarth Press and the Institute of Psycho-Analysis, 1963.
Gelmis, Joseph. *The Film Director as Superstar*. Garden City, NY: Doubleday, 1970.
Gelmis, Joseph. "Interview with Stanley Kubrick." In *Perspectives on Stanley Kubrick*, edited by Mario Falsetto, 26–37. New York: G. K. Hall, 1996.
Hitchcock, Alfred. *Alfred Hitchcock Presents: My Favourites in Suspense*. New York: Random House, 1959.
Hollinger, Karen. "The Female Oedipal Drama of *Rebecca* from Novel to Film." *Quarterly Review of Film & Video* 14, no. 4 (1993): 17–30.
Hutcheon, Linda. *A Theory of Adaptation*. New York: Routledge, 2006.
Jenkins, Greg. *Stanley Kubrick and the Art of Adaptation*. Jefferson, NC: McFarland, 1997.
Jones, Ernest. "The Oedipus Complex as an Explanation of Hamlet's Mystery: A Study of Motive." *American Journal of Psychology* 21 (1910): 72–113.

Jonte-Pace, Diane. *Speaking the Unspeakable: Religion, Misogyny, and the Uncanny Mother in Freud's Cultural Texts*. Berkeley, Los Angeles and London: University of California Press, 2001.

Kierkegaard, Søren. *The Concept of Anxiety: A Simple Psychologically Orienting Deliberation on the Dogmatic Issue of Hereditary Sin*. Translated by Reidar Thomte. Princeton, NJ: Princeton University Press, 1980.

King, Stephen. *The Shining*. London: Hodder, 2007.

Kranz, David L., and Nancy C. Mellerski. "Introduction." In *In/Fidelity: Essays on Film Adaptation*, edited by David L. Kranz and Nancy C. Mellerski, 1–11. Newcastle: Cambridge Scholars Publishing, 2008.

Kristeva, Julia. *Powers of Horror: An Essay on Abjection*. Translated by Leon S. Roudiez. New York: Columbia University Press, 1982.

Lacan, Jacques. *The Seminar of Jacques Lacan, Book XI: The Four Fundamental Concepts of Psychoanalysis*, edited by Jacques-Alain Miller and translated by Alan Sheridan. New York and London: W. W. Norton & Company, 1981.

Lacan, Jacques. "Introduction to the Names-of-the-Father Seminar." *October* 40 (Spring 1987): 81–95. Translated by Jeffrey Mehlman.

Lacan, Jacques. *The Seminar of Jacques Lacan, Book I: Freud's Papers on Technique, 1953–1954*, edited by Jacques-Alain Miller and translated by John Forrester. New York and London: W. W. Norton & Company, 1991.

Lacan, Jacques. *The Seminar of Jacques Lacan, Book II: The Ego in Freud's Theory and in the Techniques of Psychoanalysis 1954–1955*, edited by Jacques-Alain Miller and translated by Sylvana Tomaselli. New York and London: W. W. Norton & Company, 1991.

Lacan, Jacques. *The Seminar of Jacques Lacan, Book III: The Psychoses 1955–1956*, edited by Jacques-Alain Miller and translated by Russell Grigg. New York and London: W. W. Norton & Company, 1993.

Lacan, Jacques. *Seminar VI: Desire and Its Interpretation 1958–1959*. Translated by Cormac Gallagher. Retrieved from www.lacaninireland.com.

Lacan, Jacques. *The Seminar of Jacques Lacan, Book VII: The Ethics of Psychoanalysis 1959–1960*, edited by Jacques-Alain Miller and translated by Dennis Porter. New York and London: W. W. Norton & Company, 1992.

Lacan, Jacques. *The Seminar of Jacques Lacan, Book XX: On Feminine Sexuality, the Limit of Love and Knowledge, 1972–1973*, edited by Jacques-Alain Miller and translated by Bruce Fink. New York and London: W. W. Norton & Company, 1999.

Lacan, Jacques. *Seminar X: Anxiety 1962–1963*. Translated by Cormac Gallagher. Retrieved from www.lacaninireland.com.

Lacan, Jacques. *Seminar XIV: The Logic of Phantasy*. Translated by Cormac Gallagher. Retrieved from www.lacaninireland.com.

Lacan, Jacques. "Appendix II: Metaphor of the Subject." In *Écrits: The First Complete Edition in English*, translated by Bruce Fink, 755–8. New York and London: W. W. Norton & Company, 2006.

Lacan, Jacques. "The Direction of the Treatment and the Principles of Its Power." In *Écrits: The First Complete Edition in English*, translated by Bruce Fink, 489–542. New York and London: W. W. Norton & Company, 2006.

Lacan, Jacques. "The Function and Field of Speech and Language in Psychoanalysis." In *Écrits: The First Complete Edition in English*, translated by Bruce Fink, 197–268. New York and London: W. W. Norton & Company, 2006.

Lacan, Jacques. "The Freudian Thing or the Meaning of the Return to Freud in Psychoanalysis." In *Écrits: The First Complete Edition in English*, translated by Bruce Fink, 334–63. New York and London: W. W. Norton & Company, 2006.

Lacan, Jacques. "The Instance of the Letter in the Unconscious." In *Écrits: The First Complete Edition in English*, translated by Bruce Fink, 412–41. New York and London: W. W. Norton & Company, 2006.

Lacan, Jacques. "The Mirror Stage as Formative of the I Function as Revealed in Psychoanalytic Experience." In *Écrits: The First Complete Edition in English*, translated by Bruce Fink, 75–81. New York and London: W. W. Norton & Company, 2006.

Lacan, Jacques. "The Signification of the Phallus." In *Écrits: The First Complete Edition in English*, translated by Bruce Fink, 575–84. New York and London: W. W. Norton & Company, 2006.

Lacan, Jacques. "The Subversion of the Subject and the Dialectic of Desire in the Freudian Unconscious." In *Écrits: The First Complete Edition in English*, translated by Bruce Fink, 671–702. New York and London: W. W. Norton & Company, 2006.

Lacan, Jacques. "The Youth of Gide, or the Letter and Desire." In *Écrits: The First Complete Edition in English*, translated by Bruce Fink, 623–44. New York and London: W. W. Norton & Company, 2006.

Lacan, Jacques. *The Seminar of Jacques Lacan, Book XVII: The Other Side of Psychoanalysis*, edited by Jacques-Alain Miller and translated by Russell Grigg. New York and London: W. W. Norton & Company, 2007.

Lacan, Jacques, Jacques-Alain Miller, and James Hulbert. "Desire and the Interpretation of Desire in *Hamlet*." *Yale French Studies*, no. 55/56 (1977): 12.

Lainer, Douglas. "'Art thou base, common and popular?': The Cultural Politics of Kenneth Branagh's Hamlet." In *Spectacular Shakespeare: Critical Theory and Popular Cinema*, edited by Courtney Lehmann and Lisa S. Starks, 149–71. Madison, WI, and Teaneck, NJ: Fairleigh Dickinson University Press, 2002.

Laplanche, Jean, and Jean-Bertrand Pontalis. *The Language of Psycho-Analysis*. New York and London: W. W. Norton & Company, 1973.

Laplanche, Jean, and Jean-Bertrand Pontalis. "Fantasy and the Origins of Sexuality." In *Formation of Fantasy*, edited by Victor Burgin, James Donald and Cora Kaplan, 5–34. London and New York: Methuen, 1986.

Leff, Leonard J. *Hitchcock and Selznick: The Rich and Strange Collaboration of Alfred Hitchcock and David O. Selznick in Hollywood*. Berkeley and Los Angeles: University of California Press, 1999.

Leitch, Thomas. "The Adapter as Auteur: Hitchcock, Kubrick, Disney." In *Books in Motion: Adaptation, Intertextuality, Authorship*, edited by Mireia Aragay, 107–24. Amsterdam, New York: Rodopi, 2005.

Leitch, Thomas. *Film Adaptation and Its Discontents: From Gone with the Wind to the Passion of the Christ*. Baltimore, MD: Johns Hopkins University Press, 2007.

Luepnitz, Deborah. "Beyond the Phallus: Lacan and Feminism." In *The Cambridge Companion to Lacan*, edited by Jean-Michel Rabaté, 221–37. Cambridge: Cambridge University Press, 2003.

Magistrale, Tony. *Hollywood's Stephen King*. New York: Palgrave Macmillan, 2003.

McFarlane, Brian. *Novel to Film: An Introduction to the Theory of Adaptation*. Oxford: Clarendon Press, 1996.

McFarlane, Brian. "Reading Film and Literature." In *The Cambridge Companion to Literature on Screen*, edited by Deborah Cartmell and Imelda Whelehan, 15–28. Cambridge: Cambridge University Press, 2007.

McGilligan, Patrick. *Alfred Hitchcock: A Life in Darkness and Light*. New York: Regan Books, 2003.

McGowan, Todd. *The Real Gaze: Film Theory after Lacan*. Albany, NY: State University of New York Press, 2007.

McGowan, Todd. *Psychoanalytic Film Theory and the Rules of Game*. New York: Bloomsbury, 2015.

Mitchell, Juliet. *Psychoanalysis and Feminism: A Radican Reassessment of Freudian Psychoanalysis*. Middlesex: Penguin Books, 1974.

Modleski, Tania. *The Women Who Knew Too Much: Hitchcock and Feminist Theory*. New York: Methuen, 1988.

Muller, John P. "Psychosis and Mourning in Lacan's *Hamlet*." *New Literary History* 2, no. 1, Psychology and Literature: Some Contemporary Directions (Autumn 1980): 147–65.

Mulvey, Laura. "Visual Pleasure and Narrative Cinema (1975)." In *Literary Theory: Anthology*, edited by Julie Rivkin and Michael Ryan, 585–95. Malden, MA: Blackwell, 1998.

Nabokov, Vladimir. *Lolita: A Screenplay*. New York: McGraw-Hill, 1973.

Naremore, James. "Introduction: Film and the Reign of Adaptation." In *Film Adaptation*, edited by James Naremore, 1–18. New Brunswick, NJ: Rutgers University Press, 2000.

Nelson, Thomas Allen. *Kubrick: Inside a Film Artist's Maze*. Bloomington: Indiana University Press, 1982.

Olivier, Laurence. *The Film "Hamlet": A Record of Its Production*. Edited by Brenda Cross. New York: Saturn Press, 1948.

Olivier, Laurence. *Hamlet: The Film and the Play*. Edited by Alan Dent. London: World Film Publications, 1948.

Olivier, Laurence. *Confessions of an Actor*. London: Weidenfeld and Nicholson, 1982.

Peucker, Brigitte. "Kubrick and Kafka: The Corporeal Uncanny." *Modernism/Modernity* 8, no. 4 (November 2001): 663–74.

Pilkington, Ace G. "Zeffirelli's Shakespeare." In *Shakespeare and the Moving Image: The Plays on Film and Television*, edited by Anthony Davies and Stanley Welles, 163–79. Cambridge: Cambridge University Press, 1994.

Pletsch, Carl. E. "Freud's Case Studies and the Locus of Psychoanalytic Knowledge." *DYNAMIS: Acta Hispanica ad Medicinae Scientiarumque Historiam Illustrandam* 2 (1982): 263–97.

Ray, Robert B. "The Field of Literature and Film." In *Film Adaptation*, edited by James Naremore, 38–53. New Brunswick, NJ: Rutgers University Press, 2000.

Rothwell, Kenneth S. *A History of Shakespeare on Screen: A Century of Film and Television*. Cambridge: Cambridge University Press, 1999.

Sanders, Julie. *Adaptation and Appropriation*. London: Routledge, 2006.

Sartre, Jean Paul. *Being and Nothingness: An Essay on Phenomenological Ontology* (1943). Translated by Hazel E. Barnes. London: Methuen, 1957.

Shakespeare, William. *Hamlet*. Edited by T. J. B. Spencer. London: Penguin Books, 1980.

Silverman, Kaja. *Male Subjectivity at the Margins*. New York: Routledge, 1992.

Simpson, Robert J. E. "Whose Stanley Kubrick? The Myth, Legacy, and Ownership." In *Stanley Kubrick: Essays on His Films and Legacy*, edited by Gary D. Rhodes, 232–44. Jefferson, NC, and London: McFarland, 2008.

Stam, Robert. "Beyond Fidelity: The Dialogics of Adaptation." In *Film Adaptation*, edited by James Naremore, 54–78. New Brunswick, NJ: Rutgers University Press, 2000.

Stam, Robert. "Introduction: The Theory and Practice of Adaptation." In *Literature and Film: A Guide to the Theory and Practice of Film Adaptation*, edited by Robert Stam and Alessandra Raengo, 1–52. Malden, MA: Blackwell, 2005.

Taylor, Helen, ed. *The Daphne du Maurier Companion*. London: Virago, 2007.

Taylor, John Russell. *Hitch: The Life and Times of Alfred Hitchcock*. New York: Da Capo Press, 1978.

Truffaut, François. *Hitchcock: The Definitive Study of Alfred Hitchcock*. New York: Simon & Schuster Paperbacks, 1983.

Tynan, Kenneth. "The Actor: Tynan Interview Olivier." *The Tulane Drama Review* 11, no. 2 (Winter 1966): 71–101.

Walker, Alexander, Sybil Taylor, and Ulrich Ruchti. *Stanley Kubrick, Director*. New York and London: W. W. Norton & Company, 1999.

Whelehan, Imelda. "Adaptations: The Contemporary Dilemmas." In *Adaptations: From Text to Screen, Screen to Text*, edited by Deborah Cartmell and Imelda Whelehan, 3–20. London and New York: Routledge, 1999.

Wilde, Oscar. *The Picture of Dorian Gray*. Ware: Wordsworth Editions, 2008.

Wood, Robin. *Hitchcock's Films Revisited: Revised Edition*. New York: Columbia University Press, 2002.

Wright, Jarrell D. "Reconsidering Fidelity and Considering Genre in (and with) *The Shining*." In *Stanley Kubrick: Essays on His Films and Legacy*, edited by Gary D. Rhodes, 136–48. Jefferson, NC, and London: McFarland, 2008.

Žižek, Slavoj. *Looking Awry*. Cambridge, MA: MIT Press, 1991.

Žižek, Slavoj. *Enjoy Your Symptom!* New York and London: Routledge, 2008.

Žižek, Slavoj. *Everything You Always Wanted to Know about Lacan, but Were Afraid to Ask Hitchcock*. London and New York: Virgo, 1992.

Žižek, Slavoj. *Tarrying with the Negative: Kant, Hegel, and the Critique of Ideology*. Durham, NC: Duke University Press, 1993.

Zupančič, Alenka. *Ethics of the Real: Kant, Lacan*. London and New York: Verso, 2000.

## Films in Use

*Adaptation*. Directed by Spike Jonze. 2002. Columbia, 2002. DVD.

*Hamlet*. Directed by Laurence Olivier. 1948. The Criterion Collection, 2006. DVD.

*Hamlet*. Directed by Franco Zeffirelli. 1990. Warner Brothers, 2004. DVD.

*Rebecca*. Directed by Alfred Hitchcock. 1940. MRA Entertainment, 2003. DVD.

*The Birds*. Directed by Alfred Hitchcock. 1963. Universal Studio, 2001. DVD.

*The Dick Cavett Show: Hollywood Greats*, DVD (originally aired in 1972 on ABC; Sony Music, 2006).

*The Shining*. Directed by Stanley Kubrick. 1980. Warner Brothers, 2007. DVD.

*William Shakespeare's Hamlet*. Directed by Kenneth Branagh. 1996. Warner Brothers, 2007.

# INDEX

abject 102–3
absence 33, 81, 111, 126–8, 133–4, 142, 146–7, 159, 195, 203, 208, 212
act 32, 81, 134, 146–7, 160, 171, 177, 186, 192, 197, 210, 212–13, 216, 219, 222–3
alienation 76, 89–90, 211
allegory 25–6, 179–80, 212, 216
antithesis 95, 105, 119
anxiety 13–14, 43, 62, 80, 93, 100, 102–5, 108–13, 117–20, 126–30, 133–4, 137–9, 141–3, 145, 149, 156, 174, 180, 197, 205, 218, 223
archetype 176, 199
*Aufgabe* (task) 25–7
auteur 120, 149, 153, 224, 229
*autre* 29, 47, 56, 58, 101–2, 109

Babel 8, 19, 23–7, 29–30, 33, 35
bar 197, 220–1
*Bedeutung* (meaning or referent) 212
Belleforest 53
Benjamin, Walter 19–23, 26, 28–9, 33, 35
beyond-of-the-signified 91–2
*The Birds* 94–5, 116, 135–42
Bloom, Harold 37, 63, 103–4, 113, 134
Branagh, Kenneth 82–90

canon 60
   canonical 2, 11, 13, 39–41, 45, 55, 71, 82, 92, 148
Cartmell, Deborah 2–3, 61
castration 58, 80–2, 91–2, 99–100, 102, 109–11, 126–7, 185, 195–8, 200–1, 205–6, 208
cause 34–5, 100, 102, 104, 156, 166, 189, 215, 219
*Che Vuoi* 197, 214–15
consciousness 52, 96, 112, 160, 177, 217
Copjec, Joan 113
Corrigan, Timothy 2, 18
counterthesis 93, 95, 103, 108, 113, 139, 141
cut 197, 201

Dante 23
Darwin, Charles 184, 188, 210
   Darwinian 6–7, 105, 184–5
*das Ding* 14, 91, 145–7, 149–51, 153–77, 218
deconstruction 15, 29, 185
   deconstructive 6, 184, 217, 222
deferral 219–20, 222
demand 24, 27–8, 45, 47, 55, 57–8, 102, 110, 141–2, 171, 175, 203–5, 210
deprivation 14, 19, 23, 59, 104, 110
Derrida, Jacques 7–8, 19–21, 23–9, 33, 35, 53
dream-work 54
drive 91, 95–7, 99, 101–2, 106, 108, 110, 113–16, 131, 135–6, 141, 156, 161, 167–8, 171, 178, 209, 218–19
du Maurier, Daphne 95–6, 122–5, 129, 132, 135, 137–8

Eco, Umbert 23, 33
ego 40–9, 55–8, 65, 67–9, 71–3, 76, 78, 81, 86, 90, 106–7, 110, 115, 125, 157, 202–3, 222, 228
*Entwurf* 175
ethics 154–5, 175
*ex nihilo* 178

fantasies 16, 75, 79, 106, 183–4
fantasy 14–15, 58, 61, 76–81, 163, 170, 172–3, 195–6, 201–2, 205, 208, 215
feminism 12
   feminist 12, 123, 145
fidelity 2–5, 11, 17–18, 20, 30, 95, 131, 148, 157
Fink, Bruce 30, 35, 146–7, 197, 215, 219
Freud, Sigmund 4, 10, 14–15, 33, 37, 40–5, 47–52, 54, 62, 64, 66–8, 71, 78–80, 88, 96–100, 103, 105–13, 117–20, 126–7, 143, 146–7, 154, 157, 161, 163–4, 168, 175–9, 182–5, 187–91, 198–200, 204

gaze 43, 67–76, 84, 103, 113–17, 121, 134–5, 168–9, 177, 204
Goethe 52–3, 64
*Grammaticus, Saxo* 53

*Hamlet* 12–13, 37–41, 43–5, 47–92, 113, 166
Heim 98, 103, 133
  *heimlich* 98
Hitchcock, Alfred 94–6, 98, 100–1, 103, 105, 111–12, 114–16, 120–5, 128–31, 133–6, 138, 142–3, 149
Hollinger, Karen 123–4, 135
homeostasis 106–7
Hutcheon, Linda 1–2

identification 43–4, 47–9, 56–8, 68–9, 73, 78–9, 115, 125, 129, 133, 209
imaginary 6, 14, 28, 31–3, 35, 46–9, 56–60, 62, 69, 71–3, 79, 115, 125–7, 132, 134, 155, 196, 203, 207, 217
incest 70, 75
  incestuous 51, 61, 69–70, 75, 77–8, 81, 84, 86–9, 93, 102, 141, 193
inter-subjective 176
inter-subjectivity 4
inter-textuality 4

*jouissance* 27, 30, 35, 163

Kant 34
Kierkegaard 118–20, 134
Kristeva, Julia 103
Kubrick, Stanley 145–55, 157–8, 160–73, 175, 177–8

labyrinth 152, 165, 178
Lacan, Jacques 5–6, 9, 12–17, 19, 21–2, 27–34, 41, 44, 46–9, 55–9, 62, 72, 79–80, 89, 91, 93, 97, 102, 105–6, 114–15, 118, 120–1, 125–9, 132–3, 139, 141–3, 145–7, 150–1, 154–64, 166–8, 170–1, 174–9, 191, 195–8, 200–5, 207, 209–13, 219–22
lack 13, 15, 17, 19, 23, 32–3, 35, 53, 56–60, 72, 81, 90, 97, 111, 115, 119–21, 124, 126–36, 139–42, 146–7, 153, 157, 159–60, 165–6, 173, 194–5, 197, 200, 202–5, 207–10, 212, 218
Laplanche 182, 197–8, 201
libido 42, 56
  libidinal 5, 42–3, 54, 74, 89
*Lolita* 148–9

*Marnie* 114, 135–6
masterplot 98–9, 102, 106, 109–11, 141
maternal 44, 100–2, 111–12, 139, 142, 193
matheme 205, 220–1
McGowan, Todd 10, 151
meta-narrative 68, 70, 74
metonymy 160, 218–23
Minotaur 178
mirror (stage) 46–8, 114
*mise-en-scène* 72, 74–5, 77, 87–8, 172, 204, 207
Mobius 209, 211
Modleski, Tania 123
Mother 13–14, 43, 56–8, 60–1, 70, 72, 75–8, 80, 84, 86–90, 93, 97, 100–3, 109–13, 117–18, 122, 127, 134–43, 145, 193
Mulvey, Laura 113–15, 117

Nabokov, Vladimir 148–9
Name-of-the-Father 12, 48, 56, 141, 167
narcissism 42
narcissistic 42, 46–7, 57–9, 61–2, 69, 78–80, 194, 203, 208
*Nebenmensch* 174–7
non-being 14, 121, 128, 130, 158, 201
nothingness 15, 118–20, 124, 130, 164

object-cause 72, 126, 128
*objet petit a* 31, 56, 58–60, 72, 115–16, 120–1, 126–7, 129–34, 136, 143, 154, 156–61, 166–9, 172, 205
Oedipus 12–13, 37, 39, 41–3, 45, 47–53, 55, 57–67, 69, 71–5, 77, 79–81, 83, 85, 87–92, 98, 106, 109, 141, 199, 218
  Oedipal 13–14, 43–4, 52, 54–5, 61, 63–5, 67, 69–71, 73–9, 84, 86, 88–90, 93, 97–9, 101–2, 106, 109–13, 123–4, 135, 141, 143, 193, 200
  Oedipalization 49, 59, 79, 110–11, 145
Olivier, Laurence 62, 64–75, 77, 83, 86, 130

ontology 7, 119, 181, 222–3
Ophelia 56, 62, 81, 89–90
Orlean, Susan 180–1, 186–8, 190–5, 197, 209–10, 213–14
Other 7, 13, 15, 25, 27–8, 31, 56, 58, 101–2, 106, 109–10, 112–13, 127, 133–4, 141, 174, 176, 196–7, 203, 215, 221
Ouroboros 207, 210

panoptical 74, 122
phallus 12, 56–60, 72–3, 89–90, 159
phallic 58, 60, 111–12, 127, 134
phallocentric 87
phallogocentric 103
phantasy 51, 80, 127, 179, 181–7, 189–91, 193–205, 207–9, 211–16, 218
phantasmatic 184–5, 187, 189, 194, 196
phantasy-work 187, 211
phylogenetic 185, 198–200
pleasure principle 93, 96, 105–9, 161–2, 171, 183, 196, 211, 219
Pontalis, Jean-Bertrand 182, 197, 201
pre-Oedipal 48, 59, 101, 113
pre-symbolic 113, 143
psychosexual 74, 84, 86, 139–41

real 6, 19, 22–35, 45, 48, 53, 56–7, 59, 62, 115, 125, 156–7, 166, 171–2, 177, 186–7, 196, 198, 208–9, 213, 217–18, 221, 223
*realangst* 109–10
*Rebecca* 95–6, 116, 121–6, 128–32, 134–5, 142

Selznick, David O. 94, 121–4, 130, 226
Shakespeare 37, 39–40, 48, 50, 52–3, 59, 61, 63–8, 70, 72–4, 76–8, 80–2, 84, 87, 89, 91, 101
*The Shining* 145, 147–9, 151–3, 155, 157–9, 161, 163–5, 167, 169, 171–3, 175, 177, 222
Stam, Robert 2–5, 18, 29–30
subject 6–7, 10, 13–14, 16, 19–23, 25–8, 30–3, 35, 38, 40–1, 44–9, 56–61, 67, 71–2, 79, 81, 91, 97, 99–100, 102, 104–7, 110–11, 113–15, 117, 119, 121, 125–7, 130–1, 133–4, 139, 141, 145, 147, 152, 154–5, 157–60, 162, 166–7, 169–70, 172, 174–7, 179–81, 189, 193–213, 215–19, 222–3
subjectivity 11–12, 16, 19, 22, 29–30, 32, 37, 40, 50, 55, 71, 104, 113, 120, 134, 166–7, 187, 189, 201, 217, 223
super-ego 37, 40–9, 54–5, 58, 61–2, 65, 67–9, 71–3, 76, 78, 81, 86, 90, 92, 109–10, 112
symptom 5–10, 12, 16, 27, 33, 42, 50, 56, 96, 100, 108–9, 175, 191, 205, 210, 213, 217–18

task 7–9, 11, 15, 17–27, 29, 33, 35, 43, 51, 119, 123, 180–1, 191–3, 197, 201–2, 206, 208, 210, 212–16, 218–19, 222–3
textuality 16, 181
the-beyond-signified 154
*Thing* (das Ding) 14, 35, 90–2, 145–51, 153–7, 159, 161–3, 165–7, 169–71, 173–5, 177–8
trauma 33, 80, 82, 90, 152, 196–8, 209–10, 212
traversal 180, 191, 207, 212–15
*Trieb* 105, 168
Truffaut, François 94, 96, 128, 135–6

*Über-Ich* 43, 68
uncanny 97–100, 102–3, 105, 108–9, 113, 132–4, 137, 140–1, 143, 152–3, 161
unconscious 5–6, 10–11, 14, 19, 28–9, 31, 34, 41–3, 46, 51–2, 54, 59, 61, 67, 77, 79, 81, 84, 89, 96, 100, 103, 118, 157–8, 167, 169, 179–80, 182–4, 187, 197, 199, 205, 209–11, 217–20
*unheimlich* 98, 103, 132
unpleasure 93, 105–7, 109–10, 114, 143

*Verneinung* (negation) 117
*Vorstellung* (representation) 163–4, 167, 177

Whelehan, Imelda 2–3

Zeffirelli, Franco 74, 78, 80, 83
Zupančič, Alenka 167, 232

**Volumes in the Series**

*Mourning Freud*
by Madelon Sprengnether
*Does the Internet Have an Unconscious?:
Slavoj Žižek and Digital Culture*
by Clint Burnham
*In the Event of Laughter: Psychoanalysis, Literature and Comedy*
by Alfie Bown
*On Dangerous Ground: Freud's Visual Cultures of the Unconscious*
by Diane O'Donoghue
*For Want of Ambiguity: Order and Chaos in Art, Psychoanalysis, and Neuroscience*
by Ludovica Lumer and Lois Oppenheim
*Life Itself Is an Art: The Life and Work of Erich Fromm*
by Rainer Funk
*Born After: Reckoning with the German Past*
by Angelika Bammer
*Critical Theory Between Klein and Lacan: A Dialogue*
by Amy Allen and Mari Ruti
*Transferences: The Aesthetics and Poetics of the Therapeutic Relationship*
by Maren Scheurer
*At the Risk of Thinking: An Intellectual Biography of Julia Kristeva*
by Alice Jardine, edited by Mari Ruti
*The Writing Cure*
by Emma Lieber
*The Analyst's Desire: The Ethical Foundation of Clinical Practice*
by Mitchell Wilson
*Our Two-Track Minds: Rehabilitating Freud on Culture*
by Robert A. Paul
*Norman N. Holland: The Dean of American Psychoanalytic Literary Critics*
by Jeffrey Berman
*Psychological Roots of the Climate Crisis: Neoliberal Exceptionalism and the Culture of Uncare* by Sally Weintrobe

*Circumcision on the Couch: The Cultural, Psychological and Gendered Dimensions of the World's Oldest Surgery*
by Jordan Osserman

*The Racist Fantasy: Unconscious Roots of Hatred*
by Todd McGowan

*Antisemitism and Racism: Ethical Challenges for Psychoanalysis*
by Stephen Frosh

*The Ethics of Immediacy: Dangerous Experience in Freud, Woolf, and Merleau-Ponty*
by Jeffrey McCurry

*Analyzed by Lacan: A Personal Account*
by Betty Milan

*Visual Culture in Freud's Vienna*
by Mary Bergstein

*Genius After Psychoanalysis*
by K. Daniel Cho

*Psychoanalysis and the Patriarchal Tradition: Augustine to Milton*
by Peter L. Rudnytsky

*Film Adaptation and the Real: Subjectivity and Cinematic Mediation*
by Hee-seung Irene Lee